226

28: what about concurrents Type?

47, 48

175: Mobile Archive Sucker

306

231 Imp

292

296

298 expl.

P: 300 302

?: 315

307 g

chk

272 297

215 318

273

232

240

241

242

290

GLASSHOUSE

GLASSHOUSE

Charles Stross

ACE BOOKS, NEW YORK

THE BERKLEY PUBLISHING GROUP
Published by the Penguin Group
Penguin Group (USA) Inc.
375 Hudson Street, New York, New York 10014, USA
Penguin Group (Canada), 90 Eglinton Avenue East, Suite 700, Toronto, Ontario M4P 2Y3,
Canada (a division of Pearson Penguin Canada Inc.)
Penguin Books Ltd., 80 Strand, London WC2R 0RL, England
Penguin Group Ireland, 25 St. Stephen's Green, Dublin 2, Ireland (a division of Penguin Books Ltd.)
Penguin Group (Australia), 250 Camberwell Road, Camberwell, Victoria 3124, Australia
(a division of Pearson Australia Group Pty. Ltd.)
Penguin Books India Pvt. Ltd., 11 Community Centre, Panchsheel Park, New Delhi—110 017, India
Penguin Group (NZ), Cnr. Airborne and Rosedale Roads, Albany, Auckland 1310, New
Zealand (a division of Pearson New Zealand Ltd.)
Penguin Books (South Africa) (Pty.) Ltd., 24 Sturdee Avenue, Rosebank, Johannesburg 2196,
South Africa

Penguin Books Ltd., Registered Offices: 80 Strand, London WC2R 0RL, England

This book is an original publication of The Berkley Publishing Group.

This is a work of fiction. Names, characters, places, and incidents either are the product of the
author's imagination or are used fictitiously, and any resemblance to actural persons, living or
dead, business establishments, events, or locales is entirely coincidental. The publisher does not
have any control over and does not assume any responsibility for author or third-party websites
or their content.

First edition: July 2006

Library of Congress Cataloging-in-Publication Data

Stross, Charles.
    Glasshouse / Charles Stross.— 1st ed.
        p.   cm.
    ISBN 0-441-01403-8
    I.   Title.

PR6119.T79G57   2006
813'.6—dc22

PRINTED IN THE UNITED STATES OF AMERICA   2006004358

10   9   8   7   6   5   4   3   2   1

For Ken MacLeod

Acknowledgments

Thanks due to: James Nicoll, Robert "Nojay" Sneddon, Cory Doctorow, Andrew J. Wilson, Caitlin Blasdell, David Clements, Sean Eric Fagan, Farah Mendlesohn, Ken MacLeod, Juliet McKenna, and all the usual suspects.

"This apparatus," said the Officer, grasping a connecting rod and leaning against it, "is our previous Commandant's invention. . . . Have you heard of our previous Commandant? No? Well, I'm not claiming too much when I say that the organization of the entire penal colony is his work. We, his friends, already knew at the time of his death that the administration of the colony was so self-contained that even if his successor had a thousand new plans in mind he would not be able to alter anything of the old plan, at least not for several years . . . It's a shame that you didn't know the old Commandant!"

—"In the Penal Colony," Frank Kafka

Who still talks nowadays about the Armenians?

—Adolf Hitler, 1939

Note

The polities descended from the Republic of Is do not use days, weeks, or other terrestrial dating systems other than for historical or archaeological purposes; however, the classical second has been retained as the basis of timekeeping.

Here's a quick ready-reckoner:

one second
One second, the time taken for light to travel 299,792,458 meters in vacuum

one kilosecond
Archaic: 16 minutes

one hundred kiloseconds (1 diurn)
Archaic: 27 hours, 1 day and three hours

one megasecond (1 cycle)
Ten diurns. Archaic: eleven days and six hours

thirty megaseconds (1 m-year)
300 diurns. Archaic: 337 Earth days (11 months)

one gigasecond
Archaic: approximately 31 Earth years

one terasecond
Archaic: approximately 31,000 Earth years (half age of human species)

one petasecond
Archaic: approximately 31,000,000 Earth years (half elapsed time since end of Cretaceous era)

Duel

A dark-skinned human with four arms walks toward me across the floor of the club, clad only in a belt strung with human skulls. Her hair forms a smoky wreath around her open and curious face. She's interested in me.

"You're new around here, aren't you?" she asks, pausing in front of my table.

I stare at her. Apart from the neatly articulated extra shoulder joints, the body she's wearing is roughly ortho, following the traditional human body plan. The skulls are subsized, strung together on a necklace threaded with barbed wire and roses. "Yes, I'm a nube," I say. My parole ring makes my left index finger tingle, a little reminder. "I'm required to warn you that I'm undergoing identity reindexing and rehabilitation. I—people in my state—may be prone to violent outbursts. Don't worry, that's just a statutory warning: I won't hurt you. What makes you ask?"

She shrugs. It's an elaborate rippling gesture that ends with a wiggle of her hips. "Because I haven't seen you here before, and I've been coming here most nights for the past twenty or thirty diurns. You can earn extra rehab credit by helping out. Don't worry about the parole ring, most of us here have them. I had to warn people myself a while ago."

I manage to force a smile. A fellow inmate? Further along the program? "Would you like a drink?" I ask, gesturing at the chair next to me. "And what are you called, if you don't mind me asking?"

"I'm Kay." She pulls out the chair and sits, flipping her great mass of dark hair over her shoulder and tucking her skulls under the table with two hands as she glances at the menu. "Hmm, I think I will have an iced double mocha pickup, easy on the coca." She looks at me again, staring at my eyes. "The clinic arranges things so that there's always a volunteer around to greet nubes. It's my turn this swing shift. Do you want to tell me your name? Or where you're from?"

"If you like." My ring tingles, and I remember to smile. "My name's Robin, and you're right, I'm fresh out of the rehab tank. Only been out for a meg, to tell the truth." (A bit over ten planetary days, a million seconds.) "I'm from"—I go into quicktime for a few subseconds, trying to work out what story to give her, ending up with an approximation of the truth—"around these parts, actually. But just out of memory excision. I was getting stale and needed to do something about whatever it was I was getting stale over."

Kay smiles. She's got sharp cheekbones, bright teeth framed between perfect lips; she's got bilateral symmetry, three billion years of evolutionary heuristics and homeobox genes generating a face that's a mirror of itself—*and where did that thought come from?* I ask myself, annoyed. It's tough, not being able to tell the difference between your own thoughts and a postsurgical identity prosthesis.

"I haven't been human for long," she admits. "I just moved here from Zemlya." Pause. "For my surgery," she adds quietly.

I fiddle with the tassels dangling from my sword pommel. There's something not quite right about them, and it's bugging me intensely. "You lived with the ice ghouls?" I ask.

"Not quite—I *was* an ice ghoul."

That gets my attention: I don't think I've ever met a real live alien before, even an ex-alien. "Were you"—what's the word?—"born that way, or did you emigrate for a while?"

"Two questions." She holds up a finger. "Trade?"

"Trade." I remember to nod without prompting, and my ring sends me a flicker of warmth. It's crude conditioning: reward behavior indicative of recovery, punish behavior that reinforces the postsurgical fugue. I don't like it, but they tell me it's an essential part of the process.

"I emigrated to Zemlya right after my previous memory dump." Something about her expression strikes me as evasive. What could she be omitting? A failed business venture, personal enemies? "I wanted to study ghoul society from the inside." Her cocktail emerges from the table, and she takes an experimental sip. "They're so strange." She looks wistful for a moment. "But after a generation I got . . . sad." Another sip. "I was living among them to study them, you see. And when you live among people for gigaseconds on end you can't stop yourself getting involved, not unless you go totally post and upgrade your—well. I made friends and watched them grow old and die until I couldn't take any more. I had to come back and excise the . . . the impact. The pain."

Gigaseconds? Thirty planetary years each. That's a long time to spend among aliens. She's studying me intently. "That must have been very precise surgery," I say slowly. "I don't remember much of my previous life."

"You were human, though," she prods.

"Yes." Emphatically yes. Shards of memory remain: a flash of swords in a twilit alleyway in the remilitarized zone. Blood in the fountains. "I was an academic. A member of the professoriat." An array of firewalled assembler gates, lined up behind the fearsome armor of a customs checkpoint between polities. Pushing screaming, imploring civilians toward a shadowy entrance—"I taught history." That much is—was—true. "It all seems boring and distant now." The brief flash of an energy weapon, then silence. "I was getting stuck in a rut, and I needed to refresh myself. I think."

Which is almost but not quite a complete lie. I didn't volunteer, someone made me an offer I couldn't refuse. I knew too much. Either consent to undergo memory surgery, or my next death would be my last. At least, that's what it said I'd done in the dead-paper letter that was waiting by my bedside when I awakened in the rehab center, fresh from having the water of Lethe delivered straight to my brain by the molecular-sized robots of the hospitaler surgeon-confessors. I grin, sealing the partial truths with an outright lie. "So I had a radical rebuild, and now I can't remember why."

"And you feel like a new human," she says, smiling faintly.

"Yes." I glance at her lower pair of hands. I can't help noticing that she's fidgeting. "Even though I stuck with this conservative body plan." I'm *very* conservatively turned out—a medium-height male, dark eyes, wiry, the stubble of dark hair beginning to appear across my scalp—like an unreconstructed Eurasian from the pre-space era, right down to the leather kilt and hemp sandals. "I have a strong self-image, and I didn't really want to shed it—too many associations tied up in there. Those are nice skulls, by the way."

Kay smiles. "Thank you. And thank you again for not asking, by the way."

"Asking?"

"The usual question: Why do you look like, well . . ."

I pick up my glass for the first time and take a sip of the bitingly cold blue liquid. "You've just spent an entire prehistoric human lifetime as an ice ghoul and people are needling you for having too many arms?" I shake my head. "I just assumed you have a good reason."

She crosses both pairs of arms defensively. "I'd feel like a liar looking like . . ." She glances past me. There are a handful of other people in the bar, a few bushujo and a couple of cyborgs, but most of them are wearing orthohuman bodies. She's glancing at a woman with long blond hair on one side of her head and stubble on the other, wearing a filmy white drape and a sword belt. The woman is braying loudly with laughter at something one of her companions just said—berserkers on the prowl for players. "Her, for example."

"But you were orthohuman once?"

"I still am, inside."

The penny drops: She wears xenohuman drag when she's in public because she's shy. I glance over at the group and accidentally make eye contact with the blond woman. She looks at me, stiffens, then pointedly turns away. "How long has this bar been here?" I ask, my ears burning. *How dare she do that to me?*

"About three megs." Kay nods at the group of orthos across the room. "I really would avoid paying obvious attention to them, they're duelists."

"So am I." I nod at her. "I find it therapeutic."

She grimaces. "I don't play, myself. It's messy. And I don't like pain."

"Well, neither do I," I say slowly. "That's not the point." The point is that we get angry when we can't remember who we are, and we lash out at first; and a structured, formal framework means that nobody else needs to get hurt.

"Where do you live?" she asks.

"I'm in the"—she's transparently changing the subject, I realize— "clinic, still. I mean, everything I had, I"—liquidated and ran—"I travel light. I still haven't decided what to be in this new lifetime, so there doesn't seem much point in having lots of baggage."

"Another drink?" Kay asks. "I'm buying."

"Yes, please." A warning bell rings in my head as I sense Blondie heading toward our table. I pretend not to notice, but I can feel a familiar warmth in my stomach, a tension in my back. Ancient reflexes and not a few modern cheat-codes take over and I surreptitiously loosen my sword in its scabbard. I think I know what Blondie wants, and I'm perfectly happy to give it to her. She's not the only one around here prone to frequent flashes of murderous rage that take a while to cool. The counselor told me to embrace it and give in, among consenting fellows. It should burn itself out in time. Which is why I'm carrying.

But the postexcision rages aren't my only irritant. In addition to memory edits, I opted to have my age reset. Being postadolescent again brings its own dynamic of hormonal torment. It makes me pace my apartment restlessly, drives me to stand in the white cube of the hygiene suite and draw blades down the insides of my arms, curious to see the bright rosy blood welling up. Sex has acquired an obsessive importance I'd almost forgotten. The urges to sex and violence are curiously hard to fight off when you awaken drained and empty and unable to remember who you used to be, but they're a lot less fun, the second or third time through the cycle of rejuvenation.

"Listen, don't look round, but you probably ought to know that someone is about to—"

Before I can finish the sentence, Blondie leans over Kay's shoulder and spits in my face. "I demand satisfaction." She has a voice like a diamond drill.

"Why?" I ask stonily, heart thumping with tension as I wipe my cheek. I can feel the rage building, but I force myself to keep it under control.

"You exist."

There's a certain type of look some postrehab cases get while they're in the psychopathic dissociative stage, still reknitting the raveled threads of their personality and memories into a new identity. The insensate anger at the world, the existential hate—often directed at their previously whole self for putting them into this world, naked and stripped of memories—generates its own dynamic. Wild black-eyed hatred and the perfect musculature of the optimized phenotype combine to lend Blondie an intimidating, almost primal presence. Nevertheless, she's got enough self-control to issue a challenge before she attacks.

Kay, shy and much further advanced in recovery than either of us, cowers in her seat as Blondie glares at me. *That* annoys me—Blondie's got no call to intimidate bystanders. And maybe I'm not as out of control as I feel.

"In that case"—I slowly stand up, not breaking eye contact for a moment—"how about we take this to the remilitarized zone? First death rules?"

"Yes," she hisses.

I glance at Kay. "Nice talking to you. Order me another drink? I'll be right back." I can feel her eyes on my back as I follow Blondie to the gate to the RMZ. Which is right beside the bar.

Blondie pauses on the threshold. "After you," she says.

"Au contraire. Challenger goes first."

She glares at me one more time, clearly furious, then strides into the T-gate and blinks out. I wipe my right palm on my leather kilt, grip the hilt of my sword, draw, and leap through the point-to-point wormhole.

Dueling etiquette calls for the challenger to clear the gate by a good ten paces, but Blondie isn't in a good mood, and it's a very good thing that I'm on the defensive and ready to parry as I go through because she's waiting, ready to shove her sword through my abdomen on the spot.

She's fast and vicious and utterly uninterested in playing by the rules, which is fine by me because my own existential rage now has an outlet and a face. The anger that has been eating me up since my surgery, the hatred of the war criminals who forced me into this, of the person I used to be who surrendered to the large-scale erasure of their memories—I can't even remember what sex I was, or how tall—has a focus, and on the other end of her circling blade, Blondie's face is a glow of concentration and fury to mirror my own.

This part of the remilitarized zone is modeled on a ruined city of old Urth, shattered postnuclear concrete wastelands and strange creeping vegetation shrouding the statues of conquerors and the burned-out wreckage of wheeled cars. We could be alone here, marooned on a planet uninhabited by other sapients. Alone to work out our grief and rage as the postsurgical fugue slowly dissipates.

Blondie tries to rush me, and I fall back carefully, trying to spot some weakness in her attack. She prefers the edge to the point and the right to the left, but she's not leaving me any openings. "Hurry up and die!" she snaps.

"After you." I feint and try to draw her off-balance, circling round her. Next to the gate we came in through there's a ruined stump of a tall building, rubble heaped up above head height. (The gate's beacon flashes red, signifying no egress until one of us is dead.) The rubble gives me an idea, and I feint again, then back off and leave an opening for her.

Blondie takes the opening, and I just barely block her, because she's fast. But she's not sly, and she certainly wasn't expecting the knife in my left hand—taped to my left thigh before—and as she tries to guard against it, I see my chance and run my sword through her belly.

She drops her weapon and falls to her knees. I sit down heavily opposite her, almost collapsing. *Oh dear. How did she manage to get my leg?* Maybe I shouldn't trust my instincts quite so totally.

"Done?" I ask, suddenly feeling faint.

"I—" There's a curious expression on her face as she holds on to the basket of my sword. "Uh." She tries to swallow. "Who?"

"I'm Robin," I say lightly, watching her with interest. I'm not sure I've ever watched somebody dying with a sword through their guts before. There's lots of blood and a really vile smell of ruptured intestines. I'd have thought she'd be writhing and screaming, but maybe she's got an autonomic override. Anyway, I'm busy holding my leg together. Blood keeps welling up between my fingers. *Comradeship in pain.* "You are . . . ?"

"Gwyn." She swallows. The light of hatred is extinguished, leaving something—puzzlement?—behind.

"When did you last back up, Gwyn?"

She squints. "Unh. Hour. Ago."

"Well then. Would you like me to end this?"

It takes a moment for her to meet my eyes. She nods. "When? You?"

I lean over, grimacing, and pick up her blade. "When did *I* last back myself up? Since recovering from memory surgery, you mean?"

She nods, or maybe shudders. I raise the blade and frown, lining it up on her neck: it takes all my energy. "Good question—"

I slice through her throat. Blood sprays everywhere.

"Never."

I stumble to the exit—an A-gate—and tell it to rebuild my leg before returning me to the bar. It switches me off, and a subjective instant later, I wake up in the kiosk in the washroom at the back of the bar, my body remade as new. I stare into the mirror for about a minute, feeling empty but, curiously, at peace with myself. *Maybe I'll be ready for a backup soon?* I flex my right leg. The assembler's done a good job of canonicalizing it, and the edited muscle works just fine. I resolve to avoid Gwyn, at least until she's in a less insensately violent mood, which may take a long time if she keeps picking fights with her betters. Then I return to my table.

Kay is still there, which is odd. I'd expected her to be gone by now.

(A-gates are fast, but it still takes a minimum of about a thousand seconds to tear down and rebuild a human body: that's a lot of bits and atoms to juggle.)

I drop into my seat. She *has* bought me another drink. "I'm sorry about that," I say automatically.

"You get used to it around here." She sounds philosophical. "Feeling better?"

"You know, I—" I stop. Just for a moment I'm back in that dusty concrete-strewn wasteland, a searing pain in my leg, the sheer hatred I feel fueling my throw at Gwyn's head. "It's gone," I say. I stare at the glass, then pick it up and knock back half of it in one go.

"What's gone?" I catch her watching me. "If you don't mind talking about it," she adds hastily.

She's frightened but concerned, I suddenly realize. My parole ring pulses warmth repeatedly. "I don't mind," I say, and smile, probably a trifle tiredly. I put the glass down. "I'm still in the dissociative phase, I guess. Before I came out this evening I was sitting in my room all on my own, and I was drawing pretty lines all over my arms with a scalpel. Thinking about opening my wrists and ending it all. I was angry. Angry at myself. But now I'm not."

"That's very common." Her tone is guarded. "What changed it for you?"

I frown. Knowing it's a common side effect of reintegration doesn't help. "I've been an idiot. I need to take a backup as soon as I go home."

"A backup?" Her eyes widen. "You've been walking around here wearing a sword and a dueling sash all evening, and you don't have a *backup*?" Her voice rises to a squeak. "What are you trying to *do*?"

"Knowing you've got a backup blunts your edge. Anyway, I was angry with myself." I stop frowning as I look at her. "But you can't stay angry forever."

More to the point, I'm suddenly feeling an awful, hollow sense of dread about the idea of rediscovering who I am, or who I used to be. What does it mean, to suddenly begin sensing other people's emotions again only after you run someone through with a sword? Back in the dark ages it would have been a tragedy. Even here, dying isn't something most people take lightly. For a horrible moment I feel the urge to rush out and find Gwyn and apologize to her—but that's absurd, she won't remember, she'll be in the same headspace she was in before. She'd probably challenge me to another duel and, being in the same insensate rage, turn me into hamburger on the spot.

"I think I'm reconnecting," I say slowly. "Do you know somewhere I could go that's safer? I mean, less likely to attract the attentions of berserkers?"

"Hmm." She looks at me critically. "If you lose the sword and the sash, you won't look out of place round the block in one of the phase two recovery piazzas. I know a place that does a really good joesteak—how hungry are you feeling?"

IN the wake of the duel I have become hungry for food just as my appetite for violence has declined. Kay takes me to a charmingly rustic low-gee piazza of spun-diamond foam and bonsai redwoods, where quaint steam-powered robots roast succulent baby hams over charcoal grills. Kay and I chat and it becomes clear that she's mightily intrigued to see me recovering visibly from the emotional aftereffects of memory surgery. I pump her for details of life among the ice ghouls, and she quizzes me about the dueling academies of the Invisible Republic. She has a quirky sense of humor and, toward the end of the meal, suggests that she knows a party where there's fun to be had.

The party turns out to be a fairly laid-back floating orgy in one of the outpatient apartments. There are only about six people there when we arrive, mostly lying on the large circular bed, passing around a water pipe and masturbating each other tenderly. Kay leans me up against the wall just beside the entrance, kisses me, and does something electrifying to my perineum and testicles with three of her hands. Then she vanishes into the hygiene suite to use the assembler, leaving me panting. When she returns I almost don't recognize her—her hair has turned blue, she's lost two arms, and her skin has turned the color of milky coffee. But she walks right up to me and kisses me again and I recognize her by the taste of her mouth. I carry her to the bed and, after our first urgent fuck, we join the circle with the pipe—which is loaded with opium and an easily vaporized phosphodiesterase inhibitor—then explore each other's bodies and those of our neighbors until we're close to falling asleep.

I'm lying next to her, almost face-to-face, when she murmurs, "That was fun."

"Fun," I echo. "I needed—" My vision blurs. "Too long."

"I come here regularly," she offers. "You?"

"I haven't—" I pause.

"What?"

"I can't remember when I last had sex."

She places one hand between my thighs. "Really?" She looks puzzled.

"I can't." I frown. "I must have forgotten it."

"Forgotten? Truly?" She looks surprised. "Could you have had a bad relationship or something? Could that be why you had surgery?"

"No, I—" I stop before anything more slips out. The letter from my older self would have said if that was the case, I'm certain of that much. "It's just gone. I don't think that usually happens, does it?"

"No." She cuddles up against me and strokes my neck. I feel a momentary sense of wonder as I stiffen against her, then I begin to trace the edges of her nipples, and her breath catches. It must be the drugs, I think; I couldn't possibly stay aroused this long without some external input, could I? "You'd be a good subject for Yourdon's experiment."

"Yourdon's what?"

She pushes at my chest and I roll onto my back obligingly to let her mount me. There are toys scattered round the bed, mewing and begging to be used, but she seems to need to do this the traditional way, bareback skin on skin: she probably sees it as a way of reconnecting with what it means to be human or something. My breath hisses as I grab her buttocks and pull her down onto me.

"The experiment. He's looking for serious amnesia cases, offering a referral fee to finders. I'll tell you later."

And then we stop talking, because speech is simply getting in the way of communication, and in the here and now, she's all I need.

AFTERWARD, I walk home through avenues carpeted with soft, living grass, roofed in green marble slabs carved from the lithosphere of a planet hundreds of teraklicks away. I am alone with my thoughts, netlink silenced save for a route map that promises me a five-kilometer walk avoiding all other persons. Though I carry my sword, I don't feel any desire to be challenged. I need time to think, because when I get home my therapist will be waiting for me, and I need to be clear in my own head about who I think I am becoming before I talk to it.

Here I am, awake and alive—whoever I am. *I'm Robin, aren't I?* I have a slew of fuzzy memories, traces left behind by memory washes that blur my earlier lives into an impressionist haze. I had to look up my own age shortly after I woke. Turns out I'm nearly seven billion seconds old, though I have the emotional stability of a postadolescent a tenth that age. Once upon a time people who lived even two gigaseconds were senescent. How can I be so old yet feel so young and inexperienced?

There are huge, mysterious holes in my life. Obviously I must have had sex before, but I don't remember it. Clearly I have dueled—my reflexes and unconscious skills made short work of Gwyn—but I don't remember training, or killing, except in mysterious flashes that could equally well be leftover memories of entertainments. The letter from my earlier self said I was an academic, a military historian specializing in religious manias, sleeper cults, and emergent dark ages. If so, I don't remember any of it at all. Maybe it's buried deep, to re-emerge when I need it—and maybe it's gone for good. Whatever grade of memory excision my earlier self requested must have been perilously close to a total wipe.

So what's left?

There are fractured shards of memory all over the lobby of my Cartesian theatre, waiting for me to slip and cut myself on them. I'm in male orthohuman form right now, orthodox product of natural selection. This shape feels right to me, but I think there was a time when I was something much stranger—for some reason, I have the idea that I might have been a *tank*. (Either that, or I mainlined one too many wartime adventure virtches, and they stuck with me through memory surgery even when more important parts went missing.) The sense of implacable extensibility, coldly controlled violence . . . yes, maybe I *was* a tank. If so, at one time I guarded a critical network gate. Traffic between polities, like traffic within a polity, passes over T-gates, point-to-point wormholes linking distant locations. T-gates have two endpoints, and are unfiltered—anything can pass through one, from one end to the other. While this isn't a problem within a polity, it's a *huge* problem when you're defending a network frontier against attack from other polities. Hence the firewall. My job, as part of the frontier guard, was to make sure that inbound travelers went straight into an A-gate—an assembler array that disassembled, uploaded, and analyzed them for threats, before routing them as serial data to another A-gate on the inside of the DMZ for reassembly. Normally people would only be routed through an A-gate for customs scanning or serialization via a high-traffic wormhole aperture dedicated to data traffic; but at that time there were no exceptions to the security check because we were at war.

War? Yes: it was the tail end of the censorship wars. I must have been infected at some point because I can't remember what it was about, but I was definitely guarding cross-border—longjump—T-gates for one of the successor states that splintered from the Republic of Is when its A-gates were infected by the redactionist worms.

And then I seem to faintly recall . . . *yes!* Once upon a time I was one of the Linebarger Cats. Or I worked for them. But I wasn't a tank, then. I was something else.

I step out of a T-gate at one end of a musty-smelling corridor running through the stony heart of a ruined cathedral. Huge pillars rise toward a black sky on either side of me, ivy crawling across the latticework screens that block off the gaps between them. (The pillars are a necessary illusion, markers for the tunnel field that holds in the atmosphere; the planet beneath this gothic park is icy cold and airless, tidally locked to a brown dwarf primary somewhere in transsolar space within a few hundred trillion kilometers of legendary dead Urth.) I walk across decaying tapestries of crimson-and-turquoise wool, armored and gowned ortho-humans fighting and loving across a gulf of seconds so vast that my own history dims into insignificance.

Here I am, stranded at the far end of time in a rehabilitation center run by the hospitaler surgeon-confessors of the Invisible Republic, pacing the abandoned halls of a picturesque folly on the surface of a brown dwarf planet as I try to piece together my unraveled identity. I can't even remember how I got here. So how am I meant to talk to my therapists?

I follow the blinking cursor of my netlink map into a central atrium, then hang a left into a nave that leads past stone altars topped with the carved skeletons of giants. The nave leads shortly to a rectangular hole in space delineated by another T-gate. Stepping through the wormhole, I feel light-footed: gravity here declines to hold me, and there is a pronounced Coriolis force tugging toward my left. The light is brighter, and the floor is a blue liquid lake with surface tension so high that I can skate along it, my feet dimpling the surface. There are no doors at water level but niches and irregular hollows cut into the walls, and the air carries a tang of iodine. If I had to hazard a guess, I'd say this route was leading through a chamber in one of the enigmatic routers that orbit so many brown dwarfs in this part of the galaxy.

At the end of the corridor I pass several moving human-sized clouds—privacy haze fuzzing out the other travelers so that we do not have to notice each other—and then into another chamber, with a ring of T-gate wormholes and A-gate routers circling the wall. I take the indicated door and find myself in a familiar-looking corridor paneled to either side in living wood, an ornamental fountain occupying the courtyard at the far end. It's peaceful and friendly, lit with the warm glow of a yellow star. This is where I, and a handful of other rehabilitation subjects, have been assigned apartments. This is where we can come to socialize safely with people in the same state of recovery, when it is safe for us to do so. And this is where I come to meet my therapist.

TODAY'S therapist isn't remotely humanoid, not even bushujo or elven; Piccolo-47 is a mesomorphic drone, roughly pear-shaped, with a variety of bizarre-looking extensible robot limbs—some of them not physically connected to Piccolo's body—and nothing that resembles a face. Personally, I think that's rude (humans are hardwired at a low level to use facial expressions to communicate emotional states: Not wearing a face in public is a deliberate snub), but I keep the thought to myself. It's probably doing it on purpose to see how stable I am—if I can't cope with someone who doesn't have a face, how am I going to manage in public? Anyway, picking fights with my counselor is not going to help my emotional wobbles. I'm tired, and I'd like to have a long bath and go to sleep, so I resolve to get this over without any unpleasant incidents.

"You fought a duel today," says Piccolo-47. "Please describe the events leading up to the incident in your own words."

I sit down on the stone steps beneath the fountain, lean back until I can feel the cool splashing of water on the back of my neck, and try to tell myself that I'm talking to a household appliance. That helps. "Sure," I say, and summarize the diurn's events—at least, the public ones.

"Do you feel that Gwyn provoked you unduly?" asks the counselor.

"Hmm." I think about it for a moment. "I think I may have provoked her," I say slowly. "Not intentionally, but she caught me watching her, and I could probably have disengaged. If I'd wanted to." The admission makes me feel slightly dirty—but only slightly. Gwyn is walking around right now with no memory of having been stabbed in the guts. She's lost less than an hour of her lifeline. Whereas my leg is still giving me twinges of memory, and I risked—

"You said you have not taken a backup. Isn't that a little foolhardy?"

"Yes, yes it is." I make up my mind. "And I'm going to take one as soon as we finish this conversation."

"Good." I startle slightly and stare at Piccolo-47, disturbed. Therapists don't normally express opinions, positive or negative, during a session; it's just broken the illusion that it's not there, and I feel my skin crawl slightly as I look at its smooth carapace. "Examination of your public state suggests that you are progressing well. I encourage you to continue exploring the rehabilitative sector and to make use of the patient support groups."

"Um." I stare. "I thought you weren't meant to intervene . . . ?"

"Intervention is contraindicated in early stages of recovery of patients with severe dissociative psychopathology consequential to memory excision. However, in later stages, it may be used where appropriate to provide guidance for a patient who is showing significant progress." Then Piccolo-47 pauses. "I would like to make a request. You are free to disregard it."

"Oh?" I stare at its dorsal manipulator root. It's something like an iridescent cauliflower, flexing and shimmering and breathing, and something like a naked lung, turned inside out and electroplated with titanium. It's fascinatingly abhuman, a macroscopic nanomachine so complex it seems almost alive in its own right.

"You said that Patient Kay mentioned the Yourdon experiment to you. Historian Professor Yourdon is one of my coworkers, and Kay is perfectly correct. Your relatively deep therapy means that you would be an ideal participant for the project. I also believe that your long-term recovery may benefit from participation."

"Hmm." I can tell when I'm being stroked for a hard sell. "You'll have to tell me more about it."

"Certainly. One moment?" I can tell Piccolo-47 is going into quicktime and messaging someone else: its focus of attention wanders—I can see the sensor peripherals unfocusing—and the manipulator root stops shimmering. "I have taken the liberty of transmitting your public case profile to the coordination office, Robin. The experiment I allude to is a cross-disciplinary one being conducted by the departments of archaeology, history, psychology, and social engineering within the Scholastium. Professor Yourdon is its coordinator-general. If you volunteer to participate, a copy of your next backup—or your original, should you choose total immersion—will be instantiated as a separate entity within an experimental community, where it will live alongside roughly a hundred other volunteers for thirty to a hundred megaseconds." Roughly one to three old-style years. "The community is designed as an experiment to probe certain psychological constraints associated with life prior to the censorship wars. An attempt to reconstruct a culture that we have lost track of, in other words."

"An experimental society?"

"Yes. We have limited data about many periods in our history. Dark ages have become all too frequent since the dawn of the age of emotional machines. Sometimes they are unintentional—the worst dark age, at the dawn of the emotional age, was caused by the failure to understand informational economics and the consequent adoption of incompatible data representation formats. Sometimes they're deliberate—the censorship wars, for example. But the cumulative result is that there are large periods of history from which very little information survives that has not been skewed by observational bias. Propaganda, entertainment, and self-image conspire to rob us of accurate depictions, and old age and the need for periodic memory excision rob us of our subjective experiences. So Professor Yourdon's experiment is intended to probe emergent social relationships in an early emotional-age culture that is largely lost to us today."

"I think I see." I shuffle against the stonework and lean back against the fountain. Piccolo-47's voice oozes with reassurance. I'm pretty sure it's emitting a haze of feel-good pheromones, but if my suspicions are correct it won't have thought of the simple somatic discomforts I can inflict on myself to help me stay alert. The pitter-patter of icy droplets on my neck is a steady irritant. "So I'd, what, go live in this community for ten megs? And then what? What would I do?"

"I can't tell you in any great detail," Piccolo-47 admits, its tones conciliatory and calm. "That would undermine the integrity of the experiment. Its goals and functions have to remain uncertain to the subjects if it is to retain any empirical validity, because it is meant to be a living society—a real one. What I can tell you is that you will be free to leave as soon as the experiment reaches an end state that satisfies the acceptance criteria of the gatekeeper, *or* if the ethics committee supervising it approves an early release. Within it, there will be certain restrictions on your freedom of movement, freedom of access to information and medical procedures, and restrictions on the artifacts and services available to you that postdate the period being probed. From time to time the gatekeeper will broadcast certain information to the participants, to guide your understanding of the society. There is a release to be notarized before you can join. But we assure you that all your rights and dignities will be preserved intact."

"What's in it for me?" I ask bluntly.

"You will be paid handsomely for your participation." Piccolo-47 sounds almost bashful. "And there is an extra bonus scheme for subjects who contribute actively to the success of the project."

"Uh-huh." I grin at my therapist. "That's not what I meant." If he thinks I need credit, he's sadly mistaken. I don't know who I was working for before—whether it really was the Linebarger Cats or some other, more obscure (and even more terrifying) Power—but one thing is certain, they didn't leave me destitute when they ordered me to undergo memory excision.

"There is also the therapeutic aspect," says Piccolo-47. "You appear to harbor goal-dysphoria issues. These relate to the almost complete erasure of your delta block reward/motivation centers, along with the associated memories of your former vocation; bluntly, you feel direction-less and idle. Within the simulation community, you will be provided with an occupation and expected to work, and introduced to a community of peers who are all in the same situation as you. Comradeship and a renewed sense of purpose are likely side effects of this experiment. Meanwhile you will have time to cultivate your personal interests and select a direction that fits your new identity, without pressure from former associates or acquaintances. And I repeat, you will be paid hand-somely for your participation." Piccolo-47 pauses for a moment. "You have already met one of your fellow participants," he adds.

A hit.

"I'll think about it," I say noncommittally. "Send me the details and I'll think about it. But I'm not going to say yes or no on the spot." I grin wider, baring my teeth. "I don't like being pressured."

"I understand." Piccolo-47 rises slightly and moves backward a me-ter or so. "Please excuse me. I am very enthusiastic for the experiment to proceed successfully."

"Sure." I wave it off. "Now if you'll excuse me, I really do need some privacy. I still sleep, you know."

"I will see you in approximately one diurn," says Piccolo-47, rising farther and rotating toward a hole that is irising open in the ceiling. "Goodbye." Then it's gone, leaving only a faint smell of lavender behind, and me to the strikingly vivid memory of the taste and feel of Kay's tongue exploring my lips.

2

Experiment

WELCOME to the Invisible Republic.

The Invisible Republic is one of the legacy polities that emerged from the splinters of the Republic of Is, in the wake of the series of censorship wars that raged five to ten gigaseconds ago. During the wars, the internetwork of longjump T-gates that wove the subnets of the hyperpower together was shattered, leaving behind sparsely connected nets, their borders filtered through firewalled assembler gates guarded by ferocious mercenaries. Incomers were subjected to forced disassembly and scanned for subversive attributes before being rebuilt and allowed across the frontiers. Battles raged across the airless cryogenic wastes that housed the longjump nodes carrying traffic between warring polities, while the redactive worms released by the Censor factions lurked in the firmware of every A-gate they could contaminate, their viral payload mercilessly deleting all knowledge of the underlying cause of the conflict from fleeing refugees as they passed through the gates.

Like almost all human polities since the Acceleration, the Republic of Is relied heavily on A-gates for manufacturing, routing, switching, filtering, and the other essentials of any network civilization. The ability of nanoassembler arrays to deconstruct and replicate artifacts and organisms from raw atomic feedstock made them virtually indispensable—not merely for manufacturing and medical purposes, but for virtual transport (it's easier to simultaneously cram a hundred upload templates through a T-gate than a hundred physical bodies) and molecular firewalling. Even when war exposed them to subversion by the worms of censorship, nobody wanted to do without the A-gates—to grow old and decrepit, or succumb to injury, seemed worse than the risk of memory corruption. The paranoid few who refused to pass through the verminous gates dropped away, dying of old age or cumulative accidental damage; meanwhile, those of us who still used them can no longer be certain of whatever it was that the worm payloads were designed to hide in the first place. Or even who the Censors were.

But the stress of the censorship caused people to distrust all gates that they didn't control themselves. You can't censor data or mass flowing through a T-gate, which is simply a wormhole of twisted space-time connecting two distant points. So even short-range traffic switched to T-gates, while new mass assemblies became scarce because of generalized distrust of the Censored A-gates. There was an economic crash, then a splintering of communications, and entire T-gate networks—networks with high degrees of internal connectivity, not necessarily spatial proximity—began to disconnect from the wider net. Is became Was, and what was once a myriad of public malls with open topologies sprouted fearsome armed checkpoints, frontier posts between firewalled virtual republics.

That was then, and this is now. The Invisible Republic was one of the first successor states to form. They built an intranetwork of T-gates and fiercely defended them from the outside until the first generation of fresh A-gates, bootstrapped painfully all the way from hand-lithographed quantum dot arrays, became available. The Invisibles started out as a group of academic institutions that set up a distributed trust system early in the censorship; they still retain their military-academic roots. The Scholastium views knowledge as power and seeks to restore the data lost during successive dark ages—although whether it is really a good idea to uncover the cause of the censorship is a matter of hot debate. Just about everyone lost parts of their lives during the war, and tens of billions more died completely: Re-creating the preconditions for the worst holocaust since the twenty-third century is not uncontroversial.

Ironically, the Invisible Republic is now the place where many people come in order to forget their pasts. We who remain human (while relying on A-gate redaction to save our bodies from senescence) sooner or later need to learn to forget. Time is a corrosive fluid, dissolving motivation, destroying novelty, and leaching the joy from life. But forgetting is a fraught process, one that is prone to transcription errors and personality flaws. Delete the wrong pattern, and you can end up becoming someone else. Memories exhibit dependencies, and their management is one of the highest medical art forms. Hence the high status and vast resources of the surgeon-confessors, into whose hands my earlier self delivered me. The surgeon-confessors learned their skills by forensic analysis of the damage done to the victims of the censorship wars. And thus, yesterday's high crime leads to today's medical treatment.

A few diurns—almost half a tenday—after my little chat with Piccolo-47, I am back in the recovery club, nursing a drink and enjoying the mild hallucinations it brings on in conjunction with the mood music the venue plays for me. It's been voted a hot day, and most of the party animals are out in the courtyard, where they've grown a swimming pool. I've been studying, trying to absorb what I can of the constitution and jurisprudential traditions of the Invisible Republic, but it's hard work, so I decided to come here to unwind. I've left my sword and dueler's sash back home. Instead, I'm wearing black leggings and a loose top festooned with a Menger sponge of empty pockets stitched out of smaller pockets and smaller still, almost down to the limits of visibility—woven in free fall by hordes of tiny otaku spiders, I'm told, their genes programmed by an obsessive-compulsive sartorial topologist. I feel pretty good about myself because my most recent therapist-assignee, Lute-629, says I'm making good progress. Which is probably why I'm not suffi-ciently on guard.

I'm sitting alone at a table minding my own business when, without any kind of warning, two hands clap themselves over my eyes. I startle and try to stand up, tensing in the first instinctive move to throw up a blocking forearm, but another pair of hands is already pressing down on my shoulders. I realize who it is only just in time to avoid punching her in the face. "Hello, stranger," she breathes in my ear, apparently un-aware of how close I came to striking her.

"Hey." In one dizzy moment I smell her skin against the side of my cheek as my heart tries to lurch out of my chest, and I break out in a cold sweat. I reach up carefully to stroke the side of her face. I'm about to suggest she shouldn't sneak up on me, but I can visualize her smiling, and something makes me take a more friendly tone. "I was wondering if I'd see you here."

"Happens." The hands vanish from my eyes as she lets go of me. I twist round to see her impish grin. "I'm not disturbing anything impor-tant, am I?"

"Oh, hardly. I've just had my fill of studying, and it's time to relax." I grin ruefully. *And I would be relaxing if you weren't giving me fight-or-flight attacks!*

"Good." She slides into the booth beside me, leans up against my side, and snaps her fingers at the menu. Moments later a long, tall something or other that varies from gold at the top to blue at the bot-tom arrives in a glass of flash-frozen ice that steams slightly in the hu-mid air. I can see horse-head ripples in the mist, blue steam-trails of self-similarity. "I'm never sure whether it's polite to ask people if they want to socialize—the conventions are too different from what I'm used to."

"Oh, I'm easy." I finish my own drink and let the table reabsorb my glass. "Actually, I was thinking about a meal. Are you by any chance hungry?"

"I could be." She chews her lower lip and looks at me pensively. "You said you were hoping to see me."

"Yes. I was wondering about the, uh, greeter thing. Who runs it, and whether they need any volunteers."

She blinks and looks me up and down. "You think you're sufficiently in control? You want to volunteer to—remarkable!" One of my external triggers twitches, telling me that she's accessing my public metadata, the numinous cloud of medical notes that follow us all around like a swarm of phantom bees, ready to sting us into submission at the first sign of undirected aggression. "You've made really good progress!"

"I don't want to be a patient forever." I probably sound a bit defensive. Maybe she doesn't realize she's rubbed me up the wrong way, but I really don't like being patronized.

"Do you know what you're going to do when your control metrics are within citizenship bounds?" she asks.

"No idea." I glance at the menu. "Hey, I'll have one of whatever she's drinking," I tell the table.

"Why not?" She sounds innocently curious. Maybe that's why I decide to tell her the unembellished truth.

"I don't know much about who I am. I mean, whoever I was before, he put me in for a maximum wash, didn't he? I don't remember what my career was, what I used to do, even what I was interested in. Tabula rasa, that's me."

"Oh my." My drink emerges from the table. She looks as if she doesn't know whether to believe me or not. "Do you have a family? Any friends?"

"I'm not sure," I admit. Which is a white lie. I have some very vague memories of growing up, some of them vivid in a stereotyped way that suggests crude enhancement during a previous memory wash—memories I'd wanted to preserve at all costs, two proud mothers watching my early steps across a black sandy beach . . . and I have a strong but baseless conviction that I've had long-term partners, at least a gigasecond of domesticity. And there are faint memories of coworkers, phantoms of former Cats. But try as I might, I can't put a *face* to any of them, and that's a cruel realization to confront. "I have some fragments, but I've got a feeling that before my memory surgery I was pretty solitary. An organization person, a node in a big machine. Can't remember what kind of machine, though." *Fresh-spilled blood bubbling and fizzing in vacuum.* Liar.

"That's so sad," she says.

"What about you?" I ask. "Before you were an ice ghoul . . . ?"

"Oh yes! I grew up in a troupe, I had lots of brothers and sisters and parents. We were primate fundamentalists, you know? It's kind of embarrassing. But I still hear from some of the cousins now and then—we exchange insights once in a while." She smiles wistfully. "When I was a ghoul, it was one of the few things that reminded me I had an alien side."

"But did you, when you were a ghoul, did you have . . . ?"

Her face freezes over: "No, I didn't." I look away, embarrassed for her. Why did I imagine I was the only liar at the table?

"About that food idea," I say, hastily changing the subject, "I'm still trying out some of the eateries around here. I mean, getting to know what's good and figuring out who hangs out where. I was thinking about going for a meal and maybe seeing if a few acquaintances are around afterward, Linn and Vhora. Do you know them? They're in rehab, too, only they've been out a bit longer than us. Linn's doing craft therapy, ad hoc environmental patching, while Vhora's learning to play the musette."

"Did you have anywhere in particular in mind to go and eat?" She unfreezes fast once we're off the sensitive subject.

"I was thinking a pavement cafe in the Green Maze that hangs off the back of the Reich Wing looked like a possibility. It's run by a couple of human cooks who design historically inauthentic Indonesian tapas in public. It's strictly recreational, a performance thing: They don't actually expect you to eat their prototypes—not unless you want to." I raise a finger. "If that doesn't interest you, there's a fusion shed, also in the Green Maze, that I cached yesterday. They do a decent pan-fried calzone, only they call it something like a dizer or dozer. And there's always sushi."

Kay nods thoughtfully. "Plausible," she agrees. Then she smiles. "I like the sound of your tapas. Shall we go and see how much we can eat? Then let's meet these friends of yours."

They're not friends so much as nodding acquaintances, but I don't tell her that. Instead, I pay up with a wave at the billpoint, and we head for the back door, out onto the beautiful silvery beach that the rehab club backs on to, then over to a rustic-looking door that conceals the gate to the green maze. Along the way, Kay pulls a pair of batik harem pants and a formally cut black-lace jacket out of her waist pouch, which is an artfully concealed gate opening on a personal storage space. Both of us are barefoot, for although there is a breeze and bright sunlight on our skin, we are fundamentally as deep indoors as it is possible for humans to get, cocooned in a network of carefully insulated habitats floating at intervals of light kiloseconds throughout a broad reach of the big black.

The Green Maze is one of those rectilinear manifolds that was all the fashion about four gigasecs ago, right after the postwar fragmentation bottomed out. The framework consists of green corridors, all straight, all intersecting at ninety-degree angles and held together by a bewildering number of T-gates. Actually, it's a sparse network, so you can go through a doorway on one side of the maze and find yourself on the far side, or several levels up, or even two twists, a hop, and a jump behind the back of your own head. Lots of apartment suites hang off it, including the back entrance to my own, along with an even more startling range of cubist-themed public spaces, entertainment nooks, eateries, resteries, entertainment venues, and a few real formal hedge mazes built in a style several tens of teraseconds older.

Needless to say, nobody knows their way around the Green Maze by memory or dead reckoning—some of the gates move from diurn to diurn—but my netlink knows where I'm going and throws up a firefly for me. It takes us about a third of a kilosec to walk there in companionable silence. I'm still trying to work out whether I can trust Kay, but I'm already sure I like her.

The tapas place is open plan, ancient cast-iron chairs and tables on a grassy deck beneath a dome under a pink sky streaked with clouds of carbon monoxide that scud across a cracked basalt wilderness. The sun is very bright and very small, and if the dome vanished, we'd probably freeze to death before the atmosphere poisoned us. Kay glances at the ornamental archway surrounding the T-gate, overgrowth with ivy, and picks a table close to it. "Anything wrong?" I ask.

"It reminds me of home." She looks as if she's bitten a durian fruit while expecting a mango. "Sorry. I'll try to ignore it."

"I didn't mean to—"

"I know you didn't." A small, wry, smile. "Maybe I didn't erase enough."

"I'm worried that I erased too much," I say before I can stop myself. Then Frita, one of the two proprietor/cook/designers wanders over, and we're lost for a while in praise of his latest creations, and of course we have to sample the fruits of the first production run and make an elaborate business of reviewing them while Erci stands by strumming his mandolin and looking proud.

"Erased too much," Kay prods me.

"Yes." I push my plate away. "I don't know for sure. My old self left me a long, somewhat vague letter. Written and serialized, not an experiential; it was encoded in a way he knew I'd remember how to decrypt, he was very careful about that. Anyway, he hinted about all sorts of dark things. He knew too much, rambled on about how he'd worked for a Power and done bad things until his coworkers forced him into excision and rehab. And it was a thorough job of assisted forgetting they did on me. I mean, for all I know I might be a war criminal or something. I've completely lost over a gigasecond, and the stuff before then is full of holes—I don't remember anything about what my vocation was, or what I did during the censorship, or any friends or family, or anything like that."

"That's awful." Kay rests a slim hand atop each of mine and peers at me across the wreckage of a remarkably good aubergine-and-garlic casserole.

"But that's not all." I glance at her wineglass, sitting empty beside the carafe. "Another refill?"

"My pleasure." She refills my glass and raises it to my lips while taking a sip from her own without releasing my hands. I smile as I swallow, and she smiles back. Maybe there's something to be said for her hexa-pedal body plan, although I'd be nervous about doing it to myself—she must have had some pretty extensive spinal modifications to coordinate all those limbs with such unconscious grace. "Go on?"

"There are hints." I swallow. "Pretty blatant ones. He warned me to be on my guard against old enemies—the kind who wouldn't be content with a simple duel to the death."

"What are we talking about?" She looks concerned.

"Identity theft, backup corruption." I shrug. "Or . . . I don't know. I mean, I don't *remember*. Either my old self was totally paranoid, or he was involved in something extremely dirty and opted to take the radi-cal retirement package. If it's the latter, I could be in really deep trouble. I lost so much that I don't know how the sort of people he was involved with behave, or why. I've been doing some reading, history and so on, but that's not the same as *being* there." I swallow again, my mouth dry, because at this point she might very well stand up and walk out on me and suddenly I realize that I've invested quite a lot of self-esteem in her continued good opinion of me. "I mean, I think he may have been a mercenary, working for one of the Powers."

"That would be bad." She lets go of my hands. "Robin?"

"Yes?"

"Is that why you haven't had a backup since rehab? And why you're always hanging out in public places with your back to the most solid walls?"

"Yes." I've admitted it, and now I don't know why I didn't say it be-fore. "I'm afraid of my past. I want it to stay dead."

She stands up, leans across the table to take my hands and hold my face, then kisses me. After a moment I respond hungrily. Somehow we're standing beside the table and hugging each other—that's a *lot* of contact with Kay—and I'm laughing with relief as she rubs my back and holds me tight. "It's all right," she soothes, "it's *all right*." Well, no it isn't—but *she's* all right, and suddenly my horizons feel as if they've doubled in size. I'm not in solitary anymore, there's someone I can talk to without feeling as if I might be facing a hostile interrogation. The sense of release is enormous, and far more significant than simple sex.

"Come on," I say, "let's go see Linn and Vhora."

"Sure," she says, partly letting go. "But Robin, isn't it obvious what you need to do?"

"Huh?"

"About your problem." She taps her toe impatiently. "Or haven't the therapists been giving you the hard sell, too?"

"You mean the experiment?" I lead her back into the Green Maze, cueing my netlink for another firefly. "I was going to say no. It sounds crazy. Why would I want to live in a panopticon society for ten or fifty megs?"

"Think about it," she says. "It's a closed community running in a disconnected T-gate manifold. Nobody gets to go in or comes out after it starts running, not until the whole thing terminates. What's more, it's an experimental protocol. It'll be anonymized and randomized, and the volunteers' records will be protected by the Scholastium's Experimental Ethics Service. So—"

Enlightenment dawns. "If anyone *is* after me, they won't be able to get at me unless they're inside it from the start! And while I'm in it I'll be invisible."

"I knew you'd get it." She squeezes my hand. "Come on, let's find these friends of yours. Do you know if they've been approached, too?"

WE find Linn and Vhora in a forest glade, enjoying an endless summer afternoon. It turns out that they've both been asked if they're willing to participate in the Yourdon study. Linn is wearing an orthohuman female body and is most of the way out of rehab; lately she's been getting interested in the history of fashion—clothing, cosmetics, tattoos, scarification, that sort of thing—and the idea of the study appeals to her. Vhora, in contrast, is wearing something like a kawaii pink-and-baby-blue centaurform mechabody: she's got huge black eyes, eyelashes to match, perfect breasts, and piebald skin covered in Kevlar patches.

"I had a session with Dr. Mavrides," Linn volunteers diffidently. She has long, auburn hair, pale, freckled skin, green eyes, upturned nose, and elven ears: her historical-looking gown covers her from throat to floor. It's a green that matches her eyes. Vhora, in contrast, is naked. Linn leans against Vhora's flank, one arm spread lazily across her back to toy idly with the base of the fluted horn that rises from the center of Vhora's forehead. "It sounds interesting to me."

"Not my cut." Vhora sounds amused, though it's hard to judge. "It's historical. Premorphic, too. Sorry but I don't do ortho anymore, two lifetimes were enough for me."

"Oh, Vhora." Linn sighs, sounding exasperated. She does something with one fingertip near the base of the horn that makes the mecha tense for a moment. "Won't you . . . ?"

"I'm not clear on the historical period in question," I say carefully. To be perfectly truthful, I'd deliberately ignored the detailed pitch Piccolo-47 mailed me until Kay pointed out the advantages of disappearing into a closed polity for a few years, because I was totally uninterested in going to live in a cave and hunt mammoths with a spear, or whatever Yourdon and his coinvestigators have in mind. I don't like being taken for a soft touch, and Piccolo-47's attitude is patronizing at best. Mind you, Piccolo-47 is the sort of self-congratulatory, introspectively obsessed psych professional who'd take any suggestion that their behavior displayed contempt for the clients as projection, rather than treating it as an attempt to work around real social deficiencies. In my experience, the best way to deal with such people is to politely agree with everything they say, then ignore them. Hence my lack of information about the exact nature of the project.

"Well, they're not telling us everything," Linn apologizes. "But I did some digging. Historian Professor Yourdon has a particular interest in a field I know something about, the first postindustrial dark age—that would be from the mid-twentieth to mid-twenty-first centuries, if you're familiar with Urth chronology. He's working with Colonel-Doctor Boateng, who is really a military psychologist specializing in the study of polymorphic societies—caste systems, gender systems, stratification along lines dictated by heredity, astrology, or other characteristics outside the individual's control. He's published a number of reports lately asserting that people in most societies prior to the Interval

Monarchies couldn't act as autonomous agents because of social constraints imposed on them without consent, and I suspect the reason the Scholastium funds his research is because it has diplomatic implications."

I feel Kay shiver slightly through my left arm, which is wrapped around her uppermost shoulders. She leans against me more closely, and I lean against the tree trunk behind me in turn. "Like ice ghoul societies," she murmurs.

"Ice ghouls?" asks Vhora.

"They aren't tech—no, what I mean is that they are still developing technologies. They haven't reached the Acceleration yet. No emotional machines, no virtual or self-replicating toolsets. No Exultants, no gates, no ability to restructure their bodies without ingesting poisonous plant extracts or cutting themselves with metal knives." She shudders slightly. "They're prisoners of their own bodies, they grow old and fall apart, and if one of them loses a limb, they can't replace it." She's very unhappy about something, and for a moment I wonder what the ice ghouls she lived with meant to her, that she has to come here to forget.

"Sounds icky," says Linn. "Anyway, that's what Colonel-Doctor Boateng is interested in. Polities where people have no control over who they are."

"How's the experiment meant to work, then?" I ask, puzzling over it.

"Well, I don't know all the details," Linn temporizes. "But what happens . . . well, if you volunteer, they put you through a battery of tests. You're not supposed to go in if you've got close family attachments and friends, by the way; it's strictly for singletons." Kay's grasp tightens around me for a moment. "Anyway, they back you up and your copy wakes up inside.

"What they've prepared for the experiment is a complete polity—the briefing says there are over a hundred million cubic meters of accommodation space and a complete shortjump network inside. It's not totally uncivilized, like a raw planetary biome or anything. There are a couple of catches, though. There are no free assemblers, you can't simply

$$\left(10^4\right)^2 = 10^8 = \left(10^2\right)^3 \times 100$$

5km × 10km × 2m

request any structure you want. If you need food or clothing or tools or whatever, you're supposed to use these special restricted fabricators that'll only give you what you're entitled to within the experiment. They run a money system and provide work, so you have to work and pay for what you consume; it's intended to emulate a pre-Acceleration scarcity economy. Not too scarce, of course—they don't want people starving. The other catch is, well, they assign you a new orthohuman body and a history to play-act with. During the experiment, you're stuck in your assigned role. No netlink, no backups, no editing—if you hurt yourself, you have to wait for your body to repair itself. I mean, they didn't have A-gates back before the Acceleration, did they? Billions of people lived there, it can't be *that* bad, you just have to be prudent and take care not to mutilate yourself."

"But what's the experiment about?" I repeat. There's something missing; I can't quite put my finger on it . . .

"Well, it's supposed to represent a dark ages society," Linn explains. "We just live in it and follow the rules, and they watch us. Then it ends, and we leave. What more do you need?"

"What are the rules?" asks Kay.

"How should I know?" Linn smiles dreamily as she leans against Vhora, fondling the meso's horn, which is glowing softly pink and pulsing in time to her hand motions. "They're just trying to reinvent a microcosm of the polymorphic society that's ancestral to our own. A lot of our history comes out of the dark ages—it was when the Acceleration took hold—but we know so little about it. Maybe they think trying to understand how dark ages society worked will explain how we got where we are? Or something else. Something to do with the origins of the cognitive dictatorships and the early colonies."

"But the rules—"

"They're discretionary," says Vhora. "To prod the subjects toward behaving in character, they get points for behaving in ways in keeping with what we know about dark ages society, and they lose points for behaving wildly out of character. Points are convertible into extra bonus money when the experiment ends. That's all."

I stare at the meso. "How do you know that?" I ask.

"I read the protocol." Vhora manages an impish smirk. "They want to make people cooperate and behave consistently without being prescriptive. After all, in every society people transgress whatever rules there are, don't they? It's a matter of balancing costs with benefits."

"But it's just a points system," I say.

"Yes. So you can tell if you're doing well or badly, I suppose."

"That's a relief," Kay murmurs. She holds me tight. The afternoon sunlight in the forest glade is soft and yellow, and while there's a buzzing and rasping of insects in the background, the biome leaves us alone. Linn smiles at us again, a remarkably fey expression, and strokes that spot on top of Vhora's head. There's something unselfconsciously erotic about her gesture, but it's not an eroticism I share. "Shall we be going?" Kay asks me.

"Yes, I think so." I help her to her feet, and she in turn helps me up.

"Nice of you to visit," purrs Vhora, shivering visibly as Linn tickles the base of the horn again. "Are you sure you don't want to stay?"

"Thank you for the offer, but no," Kay says carefully, "I have a therapy appointment in a kilosec. Maybe some other time."

"Goodbye then," says Linn. Vhora is working one-handed at the laces on the back of her gown as Kay and I leave.

"Too bad about the therapy session," I say, once we're through the first gate and round the first corner. I hold my hand out, and she takes it. "I was hoping we could spend some time together."

Kay squeezes my hand. "What kind of therapy did you have in mind?"

"You mean you—"

"Hush, silly. Of course I lied! Did you think I was going to share you with ponygirl back there?"

I turn and back her against the wall, and suddenly she's all around me, greedy hands grasping and stroking and squeezing. Her mouth tastes of Kay and lunchtime spices, indescribable and exotic.

• • •

SOMETIME later we surface in a privacy bower in a restery neither of us knows, somewhere in the Green Maze, sweaty and naked and tired and elated. I've had sex with Kay in her private naked orthobody before, but this is different. She can do things with those four cunning hands that make me scream with delightful anticipation, holding me on the razor-fine edge of orgasm for a timeless eternity. I wish I could do something back to her, something similar. Maybe one day I will, if I get it together to go xenomorphic myself. I don't usually regret being tied to my self-image so strongly, but Kay's giving my inhibitions a good stretch.

Afterward, she rolls away from me, and I cradle her in my arms.

"They don't take couples," she says quietly.

"You said I need to go."

"That's true." She sounds tranquil about it. I don't know, I haven't asked—but is this simply an extended fling?

"I don't *have* to go."

"If you're in danger, I'd rather you were safe."

I cup her breast, one-handed. She shivers.

"I'd rather I was safe, too. But with you."

"We'd be in different bodies," she murmurs. "We probably wouldn't even recognize each other."

"Would you be all right like that?" I ask anxiously. "If you're shy—"

"I can pretend it's an extended disguise. I've done it before, remember."

Oh. "We'd have to lie." It slips out without my willing it.

"Why?" she asks. "We aren't actually a couple"—my heart skips a beat—"not yet."

"Are you mono? Or poly?" I ask.

"Both." Her nipple tightens under my fingertips. "It's easier to handle the emotional balance with just one partner, though." I feel her back tense slightly. "Do you get jealous?"

I have to think hard about it. "I don't think so, but I'm not certain. I don't remember enough to be sure. But . . . back there, when Linn invited us. I don't think I felt jealous then. As long as we're friends."

"Good." She begins to roll over toward me, then pushes herself up on all her arms and climbs across me until she's on top, hanging there like the spider goddess of earthly delights. "Then we won't be lying, exactly, if we tell them we aren't in a long-term relationship. Promise you'll look me up when we get inside? Or afterward, if you can't find me? Or if you end up not going inside after all?"

I stare into her eyes from a distance of millimeters, seeing hunger and desire and insecurity mirrored there. "Yes," I say, "I promise."

The spider goddess approves; she descends to reward her mate, holding him spread-eagled with four arms as she goes to work on him with her mouthparts and remaining limbs. While for his part, the male wonders if this is going to be their last time together.

AS I make my solitary way home from our assignation, someone tries to murder me.

I still haven't taken a backup, despite what I told Piccolo-47. It seems a somewhat irrevocable step, signifying my acceptance of my new state. Backing up your identity adds baggage, just as much as memory excision sheds it. In my case, however, it seems that I really *should* take a backup as soon as I get back to my room. It would probably hurt Kay if I were to die now and revert to the state I was in before we became involved, and not causing her pain has become important to me.

Maybe that's why I survive.

After we leave the restery we split up, with a shy wave and a glistening look for each other. Kay has a genuine therapy session to go to, and I am trying to hold myself to a routine of reading and research that demands I put in at least ten more kilosecs this diurn. We take our leave reluctantly, raw with new sensibilities. I'm still not sure how I feel, and the thought of going into the experimental polity worries me (will she recognize me? Will I recognize her? Will we care for each other in our assigned new forms and point-scoring roles?), but still, we're both mature adults. We have independent lives to lead. We can say goodbye if we want to.

I don't want company right now (apart from Kay's), so I tell my netlink to anonymize me as I head home via the graph of T-gates that connect the Green Maze. People reveal themselves to my filtered optic nerves as pillars of fog moving in stately silence, while my own identity is filtered out of their sensory input by their netlinks.

But not recognizing people is not the same as not knowing somebody is there, and you have to be able to dodge passersby even if you can't tell who they are. About halfway home I realize that one of the fogpillars is following me, usually a gate or two behind. *How interesting,* I tell myself as reflexes I didn't know I had kick in. They're clearly aware that I've got anonymity switched on, and it seems to be giving them a false sense of security. I tell my netlink to tag the fogpillar with a bright red stain and keep my positional sense updated with it. You can do this without breaking anonymity—it's one of the oldest tricks in the track and trail book. I carry on, taking pains to give no hint that I've recognized my shadow.

Rather than retracing the route we took through the Green Maze, I head directly toward my apartment's corridor. The fogpillar follows me, and I casually ease my left hand into the big hip pocket on my jacket, feeling my way through the spongy manifold of T-gates inside it until I find the right opening.

I'm walking along the nave of altars in the temple of the skeletal giants when my tail makes its move. There's nobody else about right now, which is probably why they pick this particular moment. They lunge toward me, thinking I can't see them, but the tag my netlink has added to their fogpillar gives them away—I've got a running range countdown in my left eye and as soon as they move, I cut the anonymity filter, spin, and draw.

He's a small, unremarkable-looking male—nut brown skin, black hair, narrow eyes, wiry build—and he's wearing a totally unremarkable-looking kilt and vest; in fact the only remarkable thing about him is his sword. It isn't a dueling sword, it's a power-assisted microfilament wire, capable of slicing through diamond armor as if it isn't there. It's completely invisible except for the red tracking bead that glows at its tip, almost two meters from his right hand.

Too bad. I brace, squeeze the trigger for a fraction of a second, then let go and try to blink away the hideous purple afterimages. There's a tremendously loud thunderclap, a vile stench of ozone and burned meat, and my arms hurt. The sword handle goes skittering across the worn flagstones, and I hastily jump out of the way—I don't want to lose a foot by accident—then I glance about, relying on my peripheral vision to tell me if anyone else is around.

"Scum!" I hiss in the direction of Mr. Crispy. I feel curiously unmoved by what I've just done, although I wish the afterimages would go away faster—you're supposed to use a blaster with flash-suppression goggles, but I didn't have time to grab them. The blaster is a simple weapon, just a small T-gate linked (via another pair of T-gates acting as a valve) to an endpoint orbiting in the photosphere of a supergiant star. It's messy, it's short-range, it'll take out anything short of full battle armor, and because it's basically just a couple of wormholes tied together with superstring, it's impossible to jam. On the minus side my ears are ringing, I can already feel the skin on my face itching with fresh radiation burns, and I think I melted a couple of the crypts. It's considered bad form for duelists to use blasters—or indeed anything that isn't strictly hand-powered—which is probably why he wasn't expecting it.

"Never bring a knife to a gun fight," I tell Mr. Crispy as I turn away from him. His right arm thinks about it for a moment, then falls off.

The rest of my journey home is uneventful, but I'm shaking, and my teeth are chattering with the aftershock by the time I get there. I shut the door and tell it to fuse with the walls, then drop into the single chair that sits in the middle of my room when the bed isn't extended. Did he know I hadn't recorded a backup? Did he realize my older self wouldn't have erased all my defensive reflexes, or that I'd know where to get hold of a blaster in the Invisible Republic? I've no idea. What I *do* know is someone just tried to kill me by stealth and without witnesses or the usual after-duel resurrection, which suggests that they want me offline while they find and tinker with my backups. Which makes it attempted identity theft, a crime against the individual that most polities rate as several degrees worse than murder.

There's no avoiding it now. I'm going to have to take a backup—and then I'm going to have to seek sanctuary inside the Yourdon experiment. As an isolated polity, disconnected from the manifold while the research project runs, it should be about as safe as anywhere can be. Just as long as none of my stalkers are signed up for it . . .

3

Nuclear

TAKING a backup is very easy—it's dealing with the aftereffects that's hard.

You need to find an A-gate with backup capability (which just means that it has a booth big enough to hold a human body and isn't specifically configured for special applications, like a military gate). There's one in every rehab apartment, used for making copies of furnishings and preparing dinner as well as deconstructing folks right down to the atomic level, mapping them, and reassembling them again. To make a backup snapshot you just sit down in the thing and tell your netlink to back you up. It's not instantaneous (it works by brute-force nanoscale disassembly, not wormhole magic), but you won't notice the possibly disturbing sensation of being buried in blue factory goop, eaten, digitized, and put back together again because your netlink will switch you off as soon as it starts to upload your neural state vector into the gate's buffer.

I'm nervous about the time gap. I don't like the idea of being offline for any length of time while an unknown party is trying to hijack my identity. On the other hand, not to make a backup, complete with my current suspicions, would be foolhardy—if they succeed in nailing me, I want my next copy to know exactly what the score is. (And to know about Kay.) There really isn't any way around it, so I take precautions. Before I get into the booth, I use the A-gate to run up some innocuous items that can be combined to make a very nasty booby trap. After installing it, I take a deep breath and stand still for nearly a minute, facing the open door of the booth. Just to steady my nerves, you understand.

I get inside. "Back me up," I say. The booth extrudes a seat, and I sit down, then the door seals and flashes up a WORKING sign. I just have time to see blue milky liquid swirling in through the vents at floor level before everything goes gray and I feel extremely tired.

Now, about those aftereffects. What should happen is that after a blank period you wake up feeling fuzzy-headed and a bit moist. The door opens, and you go and shower off the gel residue left by the gate. You've lost maybe a thousand seconds, during which time a membrane studded with about a thousand trillion robotic disassembly heads the size of large protein molecules has chewed through you one nanometer at a time, stripping you down to molecular feedstock, recording your internal state vector, and putting a fresh copy back together behind it as it scans down the tank. But you don't notice it because you're brain-dead for the duration, and when the door to the A-gate reopens, you can just pick up your life where you left it before the backup. You naturally feel a bit vague when you come up again, but it's still you. Your body is—

Wrong.

I try to stand up too fast, and my knees both give way under me. I slump against the wall of the booth, feeling dizzy, and as I hit the wall I realize *I'm too short.* I'm still at the stage of feeling rather than thinking. The next thing I know I'm sitting down again and the booth is uncomfortably narrow because *my hips are too wide* and I'm too short in the trunk as well. There's something else, too. My arms feel—odd, not wrong, just different. I lift a hand and put it in my lap, and my thighs feel too big, and then there's something else. *Oh,* I realize, sliding my hand between my legs, *I'm not male. No, I'm female.* I raise my other hand, explore my chest. *Female and orthohuman.*

This in itself is no big deal. I've been a female orthohuman before; I'm not sure when or for how long, and it's not my favorite body plan, but I can live with it for the time being. What makes me freak and stand up again, so suddenly I get black spots in my visual field and nearly fall over, is the corollary. *Someone tampered with my backup!* And then the double take: *I am* the backup. Somewhere a different version of me has died.

"Shit," I say aloud, leaning against the frosted door of the cubicle. My voice sounds oddly unfamiliar, an octave higher and warmer. "And more shit."

I can't stay in here forever, but whatever I'm going to find out when I open the door can't be good. Steeling myself against a growing sense of dread, I hit the door latch. It's about then that I realize I'm not wearing anything. That's no surprise—my manifold jacket was made from T-gates, and T-gates are one of the things that an A-gate can't fabricate—but my leggings have gone, too, and they were ordinary fabric. *I've been well and truly hacked,* I realize with a growing sense of dread. The door slides open, admitting a gust of air that feels chilly against my damp skin. I blink and glance around. It looks like my apartment, but there's a blank white tablet on the low desk beside the chair, the booby trap has gone, and the door is back in the wall. When I examine it I see that it's the wrong color, and the chair isn't the one I ran up on the apartment gate.

I look at the tablet. The top surface says, in flashing red letters, READ ME NOW.

"Later." I glance at the door, shudder, then go into the bathroom. Whoever's got me is clearly not in any hurry, so I might as well take my time and get my head together before I confront them.

The bathrooms in the rehab suites are interchangeable, white ceramic eggs with water and air jets and directionless lighting that can track you wherever you go and drainage ducts and foldaway appliances that live in the walls. I dial the shower up to hot and high and stand under it, shivering with fear, until my skin feels raw and clean.

I've been hacked, and there's nothing I can do about it except jump through whatever hoops they've laid out for me and hope they kill me cleanly at the end or let me go. Resistance, as they say, is futile. If they've hacked my backup so deeply that they can force a new body plan on me, then they can do anything they want. Mess with my head, run multiple copies of me, access my private keys, even make a zombie body and use it to do whatever they want it to do while masquerading as me.

If they can wake me up in the A-gate of another rehab apartment, then they've trapped my state vector. I could run away a thousand times, be tortured to death a hundredfold—and I'd still wake up back in that booth, a prisoner once more.

Identity theft is an ugly crime.

Before I leave the bathroom, I take a good look at my new body in the mirror. After all, I haven't seen it before, and I've got a nasty feeling it'll tell me something about the expectations of my captors.

It turns out that I'm orthohuman and female all right, but not obtrusively so. I think I'm probably fifteen centimeters shorter than I was, axisymmetrical, with good skin and hair. It's a pretty good-looking body, but they haven't forced exaggerated sexual characteristics on me—I'm not a doll. I've got wide hips, a narrow waist, breasts that are bigger than I'd have gone for, high cheekbones and full lips, skin that's paler than I like. My new forehead is clear and high, above Western-style blue eyes with no fold—they look oddly round and staring, almost kawaii—and brown hair that's currently plastered across my shoulders. My shoulders? It's *that* long. *Why do I have long hair?* My fingernails and toenails are short. I frown. It's oddly inconsistent. I stretch my arms up over my head and get a nasty shock. I'm *weak*—I've got no upper-body musculature to speak of. I probably couldn't hold a saber at arm's length for half a kilosec without dropping it.

So, in summary, I'm short and weak and unarmed, but cute if your sense of aesthetics centers on old-fashioned body plans. "How reassuring," I snarl at my reflection. Then I go back into the bedroom, sit down, and look at the tablet. READ ME NOW, it says. "Read to me," I tell it, and the words morph into new shapes:

Dear Participant
Thank you for consenting to take part in the Yourdon-Fiore-Hanta experimental polity project. (If you do not recall giving this consent, tap HERE to see the release form you signed after your last backup.) We hope you will enjoy your stay in the polity. We have prepared an orientation lecture for you. The next presentation will be conducted by Dr. Fiore in 1294 seconds. To assist with maintaining the correct

setting, please attend wearing the historically authentic costume supplied (see carton under chair). There will be a cheese and wine reception afterward at which you will be given a chance to meet your fellows in the current intake of participants.

I blink. Then I reread the tablet, frantically searching for alternate meanings. *I didn't sign that! Did I?* Looks like I did—either that or I've been hacked, but my having signed the release is more likely. I tap the link, and it's there in black and white and red, and the sixteen-digit number works when I feed the fingerprint to my netlink. I signed a contract, and it says here I'm committed to living in YFH-Polity under an assumed identity, name of *Reeve,* for the next . . . hundred megaseconds? *Three years?* During which time my civil rights will be limited by prior mutual agreement—not extending to my core sentient rights, they're not allowed to torture or brainwash me—and I can't be discharged from my obligation without the consent of the experimenters.

I find myself hyperventilating, as I oscillate between weak-kneed relief that I'm not a victim of identity theft and apprehension at the magnitude of what I've signed up for. They have the right to unilaterally expel me *(Well, that's all right, then, I just have to piss them off if I decide I want out),* and they have the right to dictate what body I can live in! It's a ghastly picture, and in among the draconian provisions I see that I also agreed to let them monitor my every action. Ubiquitous surveillance. I've just checked into a dark ages panopticon theme hotel! *What can possibly have possessed me to—oh.* Buried in the small print is a rider titled "Compensatory Benefits."

Aha.

Firstly, the Scholastium itself guarantees the experimenters against all indemnities and will back any claims. So if they violate the limited rights they've granted me, I can sue them, and they've got nearly infinitely deep pockets. Secondly, the remuneration is very satisfactory. I do a brief calculation and work out that what they've promised to pay me for three Urth years in the rat run is probably enough to see me in comfort for at least thrice that long once I get out.

I begin to calm down. I haven't been hacked; I did this to myself of my own free will, and there are some good sides to the picture. My other self hasn't completely taken leave of his senses. It occurs to me that it's going to be *very* hard for the bad guys, whoever they are, to get at me inside an experimental polity that's only accessible via a single T-gate guarded by a firewall and the Scholastium's shock troops.

I'm supposed to act in character for the historical period we're pretending to live in, wearing a body that doesn't resemble me, using an alias and a fake background identity, and not discussing the outside world with anyone else in the study. That means any assassin who comes after me is going to start with *huge* handicaps, like not knowing what I look like, not being allowed to ask, and not being able to take any weapons along. If I'm lucky, the me who isn't in here will be able to take care of business within the next hundred megs, and when I come out and we merge our deltas I'll be home free *and* rich. And if he doesn't succeed, well, I can see if they'll let me keep this assumed identity when I leave . . .

I pull the carton of clothes out from under the bed and wrinkle my nose. They don't smell bad or anything, but they're a bit odd—historically accurate, the tablet said. There's a strange black tunic, very plain, that leaves my arms and lower legs bare, and a black jacket to wear over it. For footwear there's a pair of shiny black pumps, implying a strongish grav zone, but with weird, pointed toes and heels that converge to a spike three or four centimeters long. The underwear is simple enough, but I take a while to figure out that the filmy gray hose go on my legs. Which, I notice, are hairless—in fact, I've got no hair except on my head. So my body's ortho, but not undomesticated. I shake my head.

The weirdest thing of all is that the fabric is dumb—too stupid to repel dirt or eat skin bacteria, much less respond to style updates or carry on a conversation. And the costume comes with no pockets, not even an inconspicuous T-gate concealed in the jacket lining. *When did they invent them?* I wonder. *I'll have to find an outfit with more brains later.* I put everything on and check myself out in the bathroom mirror. My hair is going to be a problem—I search the place, but all I can find is an elastic loop to pull it through. It'll have to do until I can cut it back to a sensible length.

Which leaves me with nothing to do now but go see this orientation lecture and "cheese and wine reception." So I pick up my tablet, open the door, and go.

THERE'S a wide but narrow room on the far side of the door. I've just come out of one of twelve doors that open off three of the walls, which are painted flat white. The floor is tiled in black and white squares of marble. The fourth wall, opposite my door, is paneled in what I recognize after a moment as sheets of wood—your actual dead trees, killed and sliced into planks—with two doors at either side that are propped open. I guess that's where the lecture is due to be held, although why they can't do it in netspace is beyond me. I walk over to the nearest open door, annoyed to discover that my shoes make a nasty clacking sound with every step.

There are seven or eight other people already inside a big room, with several rows of uncomfortable-looking chairs drawn up before a podium that stands before a white-painted wall. We—I've got to get used to the idea that I'm a voluntary participant, even if I don't feel like one right now—are a roughly even mix of orthohuman males and females, all in historical costume. The costume seems to follow an intricate set of rules about who's allowed to wear what garments, and everybody is wearing a surprising amount of fabric, given that we're in a controlled hab. Those of us who are female have been given one-piece dresses or skirts that fall to the knee, in combination with tops that cover our upper halves. The men are wearing matching jacket and trouser combinations over shirts with some sort of uncomfortable-looking collar and scarf arrangement at the neck. Most of the clothing is black and white or gray and white, and remarkably drab.

Apart from the archaic costume there are other anomalies—none of the males have long hair, and none of the females have short hair, at least where I can see it. A couple of heads turn as I walk in, but I don't feel out of place, even with my long hair yanked back in a ponytail. I'm just another anonymous figure in historic drag. "Is this the venue for the lecture?" I ask the nearest person, a tall male—probably no taller than I used to be, but I find myself looking up at him from my new low vantage—with black hair and a neatly trimmed facial mane.

"I think so," he says slowly, and shrugs, then looks uncomfortable. Not surprising, as his outfit looks as if it's strangling him slowly. "Did you just come through? I found a READ ME in my room after my last backup—"

"Yeah, me, too," I say. I clutch the tablet under my arm and smile up at him. I can recognize nervous chatter when I hear it and Big Guy looks every bit as uneasy as I feel. "Do you remember signing, or did you do that after your backup, too?"

"I'm not the only one?" He looks relieved. "I was in rehab," he says hastily. "Coming out of the crazy patch you go through. Then I woke up here—"

"Yeah, whatever." I nod, losing interest. "Me too. When is it starting?"

A door I hadn't noticed before opens in the white wall at the back and a plump male ortho walks in. This one is wearing a long white coat held shut with archaic button fasteners up the front, and he waddles as he walks, like a fat, self-satisfied amphibian. His hair is black and falls in lank, greasy-looking locks on either side of his face, longer than that of any of the other males here. He walks to the podium and makes a disgusting throat-clearing noise to get our attention.

"Welcome! I'm glad you agreed to come to our little introductory talk today. I'd like to apologize for requiring you to come in person, but because we're conducting this research project under rigorous conditions of consistency, we felt we should stay within the functional parameters of the society we are simulating. They'd do it this way, with a face-to-face meeting, so . . . if you would all like to take seats?"

We take a while to sort ourselves out. I end up in the front row, sitting between Big Guy and a female with freckled pale skin and coppery red hair, not unlike Linn, but wearing a cream blouse and a dark gray jacket and skirt. It's not a style I can make any sense of—it's vertically unbalanced and, frankly, a bit weird. But it's not that different from what they've given me to wear, so I suppose it must be historically accurate. *Have our aesthetics changed that much?* I wonder.

The person on the podium gets started. "I am Major-Doctor Fiore, and I worked with Colonel-Professor Yourdon on the design of the experimental protocol. I'm here to start by explaining to you what we're trying to achieve, albeit—I hope you'll understand—leaving out anything that might prejudice your behavior within the trial polity." He smiles as if he's just cracked a private joke.

"The first dark ages." He throws out his chest and takes a deep breath when he's about to say something he thinks is significant. "The first dark ages lasted about three gigaseconds, compared to the seven gigaseconds of the censorship wars. But to put things in perspective, the first dark ages neatly spanned the first half of the Acceleration, the so-called late-twentieth and early-twenty-first centuries in the chronology of the time. If we follow the historical record forward from the pretechnological era into the first dark age, we find we're watching humans who lived like technologically assisted monkeys—very smart primates with complex mechanical tools, but basically unchanged since the species first emerged. Then when we look at the people who emerged from the first dark age, we find ourselves watching people not unlike ourselves, as we live in the modern era, the 'age of emotional machines' as one dark age shaman named it. There's a gap in the historical record, which jumps straight from carbon ink on macerated wood pulp to memory diamond accessible via early but recognizable versions of the intentionality protocols. Somewhere in that gap is buried the origin of the posthuman state."

Big Guy mutters something under his breath. It takes me a moment to decode it: *What a pompous oaf.* I stifle a titter of amusement because it's no laughing matter. This pompous oaf holds my future in his hands for the next tenth of a gigasec. I want to catch his next words.

"We know why the dark age happened," Fiore continues. "Our ancestors allowed their storage and processing architectures to proliferate uncontrollably, and they tended to throw away old technologies instead of virtualizing them. For reasons of commercial advantage, some of their largest entities deliberately created incompatible information formats and locked up huge quantities of useful material in them, so that when new architectures replaced old, the data became inaccessible.

"This particularly affected our records of personal and household activities during the latter half of the dark age. Early on, for example, we have a lot of *film* data captured by amateurs and home enthusiasts. They used a thing called a cine camera, which captured images on a photochemical medium. You could actually decode it with your eyeball. But a third of the way into the dark age, they switched to using magnetic storage tape, which degrades rapidly, then to digital storage, which was even worse because for no obvious reason they encrypted everything. The same sort of thing happened to their audio recordings, and to text. Ironically, we know a lot more about their culture around the beginning of the dark age, around old-style year 1950, than about the end of the dark age, around 2040."

Fiore stops. Behind me a couple of quiet conversations have broken out. He seems mildly annoyed, probably because people aren't hanging on his every word. Me, I'm fascinated—but I used to be an historian, too, albeit studying a very different area.

"Will you let me continue?" Fiore asks pointedly, glaring at a female in the row behind me.

"Only if you tell us what this has got to do with us," she says cheekily.

"I'll—" Fiore stops. Again, he takes a deep breath and throws his shoulders back. "You're going to be living in the dark ages, in a simulated Euromerican cultura like those that existed in the period 1950–2040," he snaps. "I'm *trying* to tell you that this is our best reconstruction of the environment from available sources. This is a sociological and psychological immersion experiment, which means we'll be watching how you interact with each other. You get points for staying in character, which means obeying the society's ground rules, and you lose points for breaking role." I sit up. "Your individual score affects the group, which means everyone. Your cohort—all ten of you, one of the twenty groups we're introducing to this section of the polity over the next five megs—will meet once a week, on Sundays, in a parish center called the Church of the Nazarene, where you can discuss whatever you've learned. To make the simulation work better, there are a lot of nonplayer characters, zombies run by the Gamesmaster, and for much of the time you'll be interacting with these rather than with other experimental subjects. Everything's laid out in a collection of hab segments linked by gates so they feel like a single geographical continuum, just like a traditional planetary surface."

He calms down a little. "Questions?"

"What are the society's ground rules?" asks a male with dark skin in a light suit from the back row. He sounds puzzled.

"You'll find out. They're largely imposed through environmental constraints. If you need to be told, we'll tell you via your netlink or one of the zombies." Fiore sounds even more smug.

"What are we meant to do here?" asks the redhead in the seat beside me. She sounds alert if a little vague. "I mean, apart from 'obey the rules.' A hundred megs is a long time, isn't it?"

"Obey the rules." Fiore smiles tightly. "The society you're going to be living in was formal and highly ritualized, with much attention paid to individual relationships and status often determined by random genetic chance. The core element in this society is something called the nuclear family. It's a heteromorphic structure based on a male and a female living in close quarters, usually with one of them engaging in semi-ritualized labor to raise currency and the other preoccupied with social and domestic chores and child rearing. You're expected to fit in, although child rearing is obviously optional. We're interested in studying the stability of such relationships. You'll find your tablets contain copies of several books that survived the dark ages."

"Okay, so we form these, uh, nuclear families," calls a female from the back row. "What else do we need to know?"

Fiore shrugs. "Nothing now. Except"—a thought strikes him—"you'll be living with dark ages medical constraints. Remember that! An accident can kill you. Worse, it can leave you damaged: You won't have access to assemblers during the experiment. You really don't want to try modifying your bodies, either; the medical technology that exists is quite authentically primitive. Nor will you have access to your netlinks from now on." I try to probe mine, but there's nothing there. For a panicky moment I wonder if I've gone deaf, then I realize, *He's telling the truth! There's no network here.* "Your netlinks will communicate social scoring metrics to you, and nothing else. There *is* a primitive conversational internetwork between wired terminals here, but you aren't expected to use it.

"We've laid on a buffet outside this room. I suggest you get to know each other, then each pick a partner and go through that door"—he points to a door at the other side of the white wall—"which will gate you to your primary residence for in-processing. Remember to take your slates so you can read the quickstart guide to dark ages society." He looks around the room briefly. "If there are no more questions, I'll be going."

A hand or two goes up at the back, but before anyone can call out, he turns and dives through the door he came in. I look at Redhead.

"Huh, I guess that's us told," she says. "What now?"

I glance at Big Guy. "What do *you* think?"

He stands up. "I think we ought to do like he said and eat," he says slowly. "And talk. I'm Sam. What are you called?"

"I'm R-Reeve," I say, stumbling over the name the tablet said I should use. "And you," I add glancing at redhead, "are . . . ?"

"You can call me Alice." She stands up. "Come on. Let's see who else is here and get to know them."

OUTSIDE the lecture theatre there are two long tables heaped with plates of cold finger food, fruit and "cheese"—strong-smelling curds fermented from something I can't identify—and glasses of wine. Five of us are male and five of us are female, and we partition into two loose clumps at either table, at opposite sides of the room. Besides Alice the redhead there's Angel (dark skin and frizzy hair), Jen (roundish face, pale blond hair, even curvier than I am), and Cass (straight black hair, coffee-colored skin, serious eyes). We're all looking a little uncomfortable, moving in jerks and tics, twitchy in our new bodies and ugly clothes. The males are Sam (whom I met), Chris (the dark-skinned male from the back row), El, Fer, and Mick. I try to tell them apart by the color of their suits and neckcloths, but it's hard work, and the short hair gives them all a mechanical, almost insectile, similarity. *It must have been a very conformist age,* I think.

"So." Alice looks round at our little group and smiles, then picks a cube of yellowish 'cheese' from her woodpulp plate and chews it thoughtfully. "What are we going to do?"

Angel produces her tablet from a little bag that she hangs over her arm. If I had one, I didn't notice it, and I kick myself mentally for not thinking of improvising something like that. "There's a reading list here," she says, carefully tapping through it. I watch over her shoulder as scrolls dissolve into facsimile pages from ancient manuscripts. "There's that odd word again. What's a 'wife'?"

"I think I know that one," says Cass. "The, uh, family thing. Where there were only two participants, and they were morphologically locked, the female participant was called a 'wife' and the male was called a 'husband.' It implies sexual relations, if it's anything like ice ghoul society."

"We aren't supposed to talk about the outside," Jen says uncomfortably.

"But if we don't, we don't have any points of reference for what we're trying to understand and live in, do we?" I say, fighting the urge to stare at Cass. *Is that you in there, Kay?* It might just be a coincidence, her knowing something about ice ghouls—there was a huge fad for them about two gigasecs ago, when they were first discovered. Then again, the bad guys might have noticed Kay and sent a headhunter after me, armed with whatever they can extract from her skull for bait . . .

"I want to know where they got these books," I say. "Look, all they've got is publication dates and rough sales figures, so we'll know they were popular. But whether they're accurate indicators of the social system in force is another matter."

"Who cares?" Jen says abruptly. She picks up a glass and splashes straw-colored wine into it from a glass jug. "I'm going to pick me a 'husband' and leave the other details for later." She grins and empties her glass down her throat.

"What diurn?" Cass's brow furrows as she grapples with the tablet's primitive interface. It's the nearest thing we've got to a manual, I realize. "Aha," she says. "We're on *day* five of the *week*, called 'Thursday.' Weeks have seven days, and we are supposed to meet on day one, about two-fifty kilo—no, three days—from now."

"So?" Jen refills her glass.

Cass looks thoughtful. "So if we're supposed to mimic a family, we probably ought to start by pairing off and going to whatever dwelling they've assigned us. After a diurn or so of ploughing through these notes and getting to know each other, we'll be better able to work out what we're supposed to be doing. Also, I guess, we can see if the partnering arrangement is workable."

Jen wanders off toward the knot of males at the other side of the room, glass in hand. Angel fidgets with her tablet, turning it over and over in her hands and looking uncertain. Alice eats another lump of cheese. I feel quite ill watching her—the stuff tastes vile. "I'm not used to the idea of living together with someone," I say slowly.

"It's not so bad." Cass nods to herself. "But this is a very abrupt and arbitrary way of starting it."

Alice rests a hand on her arm, reassuring. "The sexual relationship is only implicit," she says. "If you pick a husband and don't get on, I'm sure you can choose another at the Church meeting."

"Perhaps." Cass pulls away and glances nervously at the group of males and one female, who is laughing loudly as two of the males attempt to refill her glass for her. "And perhaps not."

Alice looks dissatisfied. "I'm going to see what the party's about." She turns and stalks over toward the other group. That leaves me with Cass and Angel. Angel is busily scrolling through text on her tablet, looking distracted, and Cass just looks worried.

"Cheer up, it can't be that bad," I say automatically.

She shivers and hugs herself. "Can't it?" she asks.

"I don't think so." I pick my words carefully. "This is a controlled experiment. If you read the waivers, you'll see that we haven't relinquished our basic rights. They have to intervene if things go badly wrong."

"Well, that's a relief," she says. I look at her sharply.

"Look, we need to pick a 'husband' each," Angel points out. "Whoever's last won't get much of a choice, and as it is we'll be stuck with whomever the others have rejected. For whatever reason." She looks between us, her expression guarded. "See you."

I stare at Cass. "What you said earlier, about the ice ghouls—"

"Forget it." She cuts me off with a chopping gesture. "Maybe Jen was right." She sounds downbeat.

"Did you know anyone else who was going into the experiment?" I ask suddenly, then wish I could swallow my own tongue.

Cass frowns at me. "Obviously not, or they wouldn't have admitted me to the study." Then she looks away, slowly and pointedly. I follow the direction of her gaze. There's an unobtrusive black hemisphere hanging from the ceiling in one corner. She sets her shoulders. "We'd better socialize."

"If you're worried about the implications of pair-bonding, I don't see why we couldn't share an apartment for a couple of diurns," I offer, heart pounding and palms sticky. *Are you really Kay, Cass?* I'm almost certain she is, but she won't talk where we might be being monitored. And if I ask and she isn't, I risk giving away my own identity to whoever's hunting me, if any of them have followed me in here.

"I don't think that would be allowed," she says guardedly. She makes a minute nod in my direction, then jerks her chin toward the others, who by now are making quite a buzz of conversation. "Shall we go and see who they've fixed us up with?"

On the other side of the room it turns out that Jen has broken the ice by insisting that all the males compete to demonstrate their merit, by pouring her a drink and presenting it to her elegantly. Needless to say she's stinking drunk but giggly. She seems to have settled on Chris-from-the-back-row as her target—he seems to be a little embarrassed by her antics, I think, but he can't get away because Alice and Angel have zeroed in on three of the others and are leaving him to Jen's clutches. Big Guy, Sam, is standing stiffly with his back to the wall, looking almost as uneasy as Cass. I glance at Cass, who's hanging back, then mentally shrug and approach Sam, bypassing Jen's raucous gaggle.

"Life of the party," I say, tipping my head at Jen.

"Er, yes." He's holding an empty glass and swaying a little. Maybe his feet are sore. It's hard to read his expression—the black mane of fur around his mouth obscures the muscles there—but he doesn't look happy. In fact, if the floor opens up beneath his feet and swallows him, he'll probably smile with relief.

"Listen." I touch his arm. As expected, he tenses. "Just come over here with me for a moment, please?"

He permits me to lead him away from the swarm of orthos trying to vector through the social asteroid belt.

"What do you make of this setup?" I ask quietly.

"It makes me nervous." His eyes glance between my face and the doors. *Figures.*

"Well, it makes me nervous, too. And Cass." I nod at the bunch across the room. "And, I think, even Jen."

"I've read part of the backgrounder." He shakes his head. "It's not what I expected. Neither was this—"

"Well." My lips have gone dry. I take a sip from my glass and look at Sam, calculating. He's bigger than I am. I'm physically weak (and wait until I get my hands on the joker who set *that* parameter up), but unless I'm misreading him badly he's well socialized. "We might as well make the best of things. We're expected to go set up a joint apartment with someone who is a different gender. Then we get settled in, read the briefings, do whatever they tell us to do, and go to the Church on Sunday to see how everyone else is doing. Do you think you can do that if you treat it as a vocational task?"

Sam puts his empty glass down on the table with fastidious precision and pulls out his tablet. "I *could*, but it says here that the 'nuclear family' wasn't just an economic arrangement, there's sex involved, too." He pauses for a moment. "I'm not good at intimacy. Especially with strangers."

Is that why you're so tense? "That's not necessarily a problem." I take another sip of wine. "Listen"—I end up glancing at the camera dome (*thank you, Cass*)—"I'm sure none of these arrangements are going to end up permanent. We'll get a chance to sort out any mistakes at the meeting on First—uh, Sunday? Meanwhile"—I look up at him—"I don't mind your preference. We don't have to have sex unless we both want to. Is that okay by you?"

He looks down at me for a while. "That might work," he says quietly.

I realize I've just picked a husband. I just hope he isn't one of the hunters . . .

What happens next is anticlimactic. Someone's probably been watching the group dynamics through that surveillance lens, because after another few centisecs our tablets tinkle for attention. We're instructed to go through the doorway at the back of the lecture theatre in pairs, at least two seconds apart. We're already in YFH-Polity, in the administration subnet, beyond the longjump T-gate leading back to the Invisible Republic. There's some kind of framework with a bundle of shortjump gates behind the next door, ready to take us to our homes. So I take Sam's hand—it's enormous, but he holds mine limply, and his skin is a bit clammy—and I lead him over to the door. "Ready?" I ask.

He nods, looking unhappy. "Let's get this over with."

Step. "Over with? It's going to take"—*step*—"at least three years before it's over with!" And we're standing in a really small room facing another door, surrounded by the most unimaginable clutter, and he lets go of my hand and turns around, and I say, "Is this *it*?" Ending on a squeak.

4

Shopping

REEVE and Sam Brown—not their, *our*, real names—are a middle-class couple circa 1990–2010, from the middle of the dark ages. They are said to be "married," which means they live together and notionally observe a mono relationship with formal approval from their polity's government and the ideological/religious authorities. It is a publicly respectable role.

For purposes of the research project, the Browns are currently both unemployed but have sufficient savings to live comfortably for a "month" or thereabouts while they put their feet down and seek work. They have just moved into a suburban split-level house with its own garden—apparently a vestigial agricultural installation maintained for aesthetic or traditional reasons—on a road with full-grown trees to either side separating them from other similar-looking houses. A "road" is an open-walled access passage designed to facilitate ground transport by automobile and truck. (I think I have seen automobiles somewhere, once, but what's a "truck"?) At this point the simulation breaks down, because although this environment is meant to mimic the appearance of a planetary surface, the "sky" is actually a display surface about ten meters above our heads, and the "road" vanishes into tunnels which conceal T-gate entrances, two hundred meters in either direction. There are cultivated barriers of vegetation to stop us walking into the walls. It's a pretty good simulation, considering that according to the tablet it's actually contained in a bunch of habitat cylinders (which orbit in the debris belts of three or four brown dwarf stars separated by a hundred trillion kilometers of vacuum), but it's not the real thing.

Our house . . .

I step out of the closet Sam and I materialized in and look around. The closet is in some kind of shed, with a rough ceramic-tiled floor and thin transparent wall panels (called "windows," according to Sam) held in a grid of white plastic strips that curve overhead. There's *stuff* everywhere. Baskets with small colorful plants hanging from the wall, a door—made of strips of wood, cunningly interlocking around a transparent panel—and so on. There's some kind of rough carpetlike mat in front of the door, the purpose of which is unclear. I push the door open, and what I see is even more confusing.

"I thought this was meant to be an apartment?" I say.

"They weren't good at privacy." Sam is looking around as if trying to identify artifacts that mean something to him. "They had no anonymity in public. No T-gates either. So they used to keep all their private space at home, in one structure. It's called a 'house' or a 'building,' and it has lots of rooms. This is just the vestibule."

"If you say so." I feel like an idiot. Inside the house itself I find myself in a passageway. There are doors on three sides. I wander from room to room, gawping in disbelief.

The ancients had carpet. It's thick enough to deaden the annoying *clack-clack* of my shoes. The walls are covered in some sort of fabric print, totally static but not unpleasant to look at. Windows in the front room look out across a hump of land planted with colorful flowers, and at the back across an expanse of close-cropped grass. The rooms are all full of furniture, chunky, heavy stuff, made of carved-up lumps of wood and metal, and a bit of what I assume must be structural diamond. They were big on rectilinear geometry, relegating curves to small objects and the odd obscure piece of dead-looking machinery. There's one room at the back with a lot of metal surfaces and what looks like an open-topped water tank in it, and there are odd machines dotted over the cabinet tops. There's another small room under the staircase with a recognizable but primitive-looking high-gee toilet in it.

I prowl around the upstairs corridor, opening doors and trying to puzzle out the purpose of the rooms to either side. They separate rooms by function, but most of them seem to have multiple uses. One of them might be a bathroom, but it's too large and appears to be jammed—all the hygiene modules are extended and frozen simultaneously, as if it's crashed. A couple of the rooms have sleeping platforms in them, and other stuff, big wooden cabinets. I look in one, but there's nothing but a pole extending from one side to the other with some kind of hooked carrier slung over it.

It's all very puzzling. I sit down on the bed and pull out my tablet just as it dings for attention. *What now?* I ask myself.

The tablet's sprouted a button and an arrow and it says, POINT AT OBJECT TO IDENTIFY.

Okay, so this must be the help system, I think. Relieved, I point it at the boxy cabinet and press the button.

WARDROBE. Storage cabinet for clothes awaiting use. Note: used clothing can be cleaned in the UTILITY ROOM in the basement by means of the WASHING MACHINE. As new arrivals, you have only one set of clothes. Suggested task for tomorrow—go downtown and buy new clothes.

My feet itch. I kick my shoes off impulsively, glad to be rid of those annoying heels. Then I shrug out of the black pocketless jacket and stash it in the wardrobe, using the hook-and-arm affair dangling from the bar. It looks lonely there, and I suddenly feel very odd. *Everything* here is overwhelmingly strange. *How's Sam taking it?* I wonder, feeling concerned; he wasn't doing so well in the reception session, and if this is as weird for him as it is for me . . .

I wait for my head to stop spinning before I go back downstairs. (A thought strikes me on the way. Am I supposed to wear the same outfit inside my 'house' as I do in public? These people have a marked public/private split personality—they probably have different costumes for formal and informal events.) In the end, I leave the jacket but, a trifle regretfully, put the shoes back on.

I find Sam slumped in one corner of a huge sofa in the living room, facing a chunky black box with a curved lens that shows colorful but flat images. It's making a lot of indistinct noise. "What is that?" I ask him, and he almost jumps out of his skin.

"It's called a television," he says. "I am watching football."

"Uh-huh." I walk round the sofa and sit down halfway along it, close enough to reach out and take his hand, but far enough away to maintain separation if both of us want to. I peer at the pictures. Some kind of mecha—no, they're ortho males, right? In armor—are forming groups facing each other. They're color coded. "Why are you watching this?" I ask. One of them throws something alarmingly like an assault mine at the other group of orthos, who try to jump on it. Then they begin running and squabbling for ownership of the mine. After a moment someone blows a whistle and there's a roaring noise that I realize is coming from the crowd watching the—ritual? Competitive-self-execution? Game?—from rows of seats behind them.

"It's supposed to be a popular entertainment." Sam shakes his head. "I thought if I watched it I might understand more—"

"What's the most important thing we can understand?" I ask, leaning toward him. "The experiment, or how to live in it?"

He sighs and picks up a black knobby rectangle, points it at the box, and waits for the picture to fade to black. "The tablet said I ought to try it," he admits.

"*My* tablet said we have to go and buy clothing tomorrow. We've only got what we're wearing, and apparently it gets dirty and smelly really fast. We can't just throw it away and make more, we have to buy it downtown." A thought strikes me. "What do we do when we get hungry?"

"There's a kitchen." He nods at the doorway to the room with the appliances that puzzled me. "But if you don't know how to use it, we can order a meal using the telephone. It's a voice-only network terminal."

"What do you mean, if *you* don't know how?" I ask him, raising an eyebrow.

"I'm just repeating what the tablet says." Sam sounds a little defensive.

"Here, give that to me." He passes it and I rapidly read what he's looking at. Domestic duties: the people of the dark ages, when living together, apparently divided up work depending on gender. Males held paid vocations; females were expected to clean and maintain the household, buy and prepare food, buy clothing, clean the clothing, and operate domestic machinery while their male worked. "This is crap!" I say.

"You think so?" He looks at me oddly.

"Well, yeah. It's straight out of the most primitive nontech anthro cultures. *No* advanced society expects half its workforce to stay home and divides labor on arbitrary lines. I don't know what their source for this rubbish is, but it's not plausible. If I had to guess, I'd say they've mistaken radical prescriptive documentation for descriptive." I tap my finger on his slate. "I'd like to see some serious social conditions surveys before I took this as fact. And in any event, we don't have to live that way, even if it's how they direct the majority of the zombies in the polity. This is just a general guideline; every culture has lots of outliers."

Sam looks thoughtful. "So you think they've got it wrong?"

"Well, I'm not going to say that for certain until I've reviewed their primary sources and tried to isolate any bias, but there's no way I'm doing all the housework." I grin, to take some of the sting out of it. "What were you saying about being able to request food using the 'telephone'?"

DINNER is a circular, baked, bread-type thing called a pizza. There's cheese on it, but also tomato paste and other stuff that makes it more palatable. It's hot and greasy and it comes to us via the shortjump gate in the closet in the conservatory, rather than on a 'truck.' I'm a bit disappointed by this, but I guess the truck can wait until tomorrow.

Sam unwinds after dinner. I take off my shoes and hose and convince him he'll feel better without his jacket and the thing called a necktie—not that he needs much convincing. "I don't know why they wore these," he complains.

"I'll do some research later." We're still on the sofa, with open pizza boxes balanced on our laps, eating the greasy hot slices of food with our fingers. "Sam, why did you volunteer for the experiment?"

"Why?" He looks panicky.

"You're shy, you're not good in social situations. They *told* us up front we'd have to live in a dark ages society for a tenth of a gigasec with no way out. Didn't it strike you as not being a sensible thing to do?"

"That's a very personal question." He crosses his arms.

"Yes, it is." I stop talking and stare at him.

For a moment he looks so sad that I wish I could take the words back. "I had to get away," he mumbles.

"From what?" I put my box down and pad across the carpet to a large wooden chest with drawers and compartments full of bottles of liquor. I take two glasses, open a bottle, sniff the contents—you can never be sure until you try it—and pour. Then I carry them back over to the sofa and pass him one.

"When I came out of rehab." He stares at the television, which is peculiar because the machine is switched off. Under his shoes he's wearing some sort of short, thick hose. His toes twitch uneasily. "Too many people recognized me. I was afraid. It's my fault, I think, but they might have hurt me if I'd stayed."

"Hurt you?" Sam is big and has thick hair and isn't very fast moving, and he seems to be very gentle. I've been thinking that maybe I lucked out with him—there's potential for abuse in this atomic relationship thing, but he's so shy and retiring that I can't see him being a problem.

"I was a bit crazy," he says. "You know the dissociative psychopathic phase some people go through after deep memory redaction? I was *really* bad. I kept forgetting to back up and I kept picking fights and people kept having to kill me in self-defense. I made a real fool of myself. When I came out of it . . ." He shakes his head. "Sometimes you just want to go and hide. Perhaps I hid too well."

I look at him sharply. *I don't believe you*, I decide. "We all make fools of ourselves from time to time," I say, trying to hang a reassuring message on the observation. "Here, try this." I raise my glass. "It says it's vodka."

"To forgetfulness." He raises his glass to me. "And tomorrow."

I wake up alone in a strange room, lying on a sleeping platform under a sack of fiber-stuffed fabric. For a few panicky moments I can't remember where I am. My head's sore, and there's a gritty feeling in my eyes: If this is life in the dark ages, you can keep it. *At least nobody's trying to kill me right now*, I tell myself, trying to come up with something to feel good about. I roll out of bed, stretch, and head for the bathroom.

It's my fault for being so distracted. On my way back to my bedroom to get dressed I walk headfirst into Sam. He's naked and bleary-eyed and looks half-asleep, and I sort of plaster myself across his chest. "Oof," I say, right as he says, "Are you all right?"

"I think so." I push back from him a few centimeters and look up at his face. "I'm sorry. You?"

He looks worried. "We were going to buy clothes and, uh, stuff. Weren't we?"

I realize, momentarily unnerved, that we're both naked, he's taller than I am, and he's hairy all over. "Yes, we were," I say, watching him warily. *All that hair*: He's a lot less gracile than I'd normally go for, and then I realize he's looking at me as if he's never seen me before.

It's a touchy moment, but then he shakes his head, breaking the tension: "Yes." He yawns. "Can I go to the bathroom first?"

"Sure." I step aside and he shambles past me. I turn to watch him. I don't know how I feel about this, about sharing a "house" with a stranger who is stronger and bigger than I am and who has a self-confessed history of impulsive violent episodes. But . . . who am I to criticize? By the time I'd known Kay this long, we'd gone to a wild orgy together and fucked each other raw, and if *that* isn't impulsive behavior, I don't know . . . maybe Sam's right. Sex *is* an unpleasant complication here, especially before we know what the rules are. If there *are* rules. Vague memories are trying to surface: I've got a feeling I was involved with both males and females back before my excision. Possibly poly, possibly bi—I can't quite remember. I shake my head, frustrated, and go back to my room to get into costume.

While I'm getting ready, I pick up my tablet. It tells me to look in the closet in the conservatory. I go downstairs and find the conservatory is chilly—don't these people have proper life support?—and inside the cupboard that held a T-gate yesterday there's now a blank wall and a couple of shelves. One of the shelves holds a couple of small bags made of dumb fabric. They've got lots of pockets, and when I open one I find it's full of rectangles of plastic with names and numbers on them. My tablet tells me that these are "credit cards," and we can use them to obtain "cash" or to pay for goods and services. It seems crude and clumsy, but I pick up the wallets all the same. I'm turning away from the door when my netlink chimes.

"Huh?" I look round. As I glance at the wallets in my hand a bright blue cursor lights up over them, and my netlink says, TWO POINTS. "What the—" I stop dead. My tablet chimes.

Tutorial: social credits are awarded and rescinded for behavior that complies with or violates public norms. This is an example. Your social credits may also rise or fall depending on your cohort's collective score. After termination of the simulation all individuals will receive a payment bonus proportional to their score; the highest-scoring cohort will receive a further bonus of 100% on their final payment.

"Okay." I hurry back inside to give Sam his wallet.

Sam is coming downstairs as I go inside. "Here," I say, holding both the wallets out to him, "this one is yours. Can you put these in a pocket for me until I buy one of those shoulder bags? I've got nowhere to put mine."

"Sure." He takes my stuff. "Did you read the tutorial?"

"I started to—I needed something to help me get to sleep. Let's . . . how do we get downtown?"

"I called a taxi. It'll be here to pick us up in a short while."

"Okay." I look him up and down. He's back in costume again. It still looks awkward. I can't help tapping my toes with impatience. "Clothing, first. For both of us. Where do we go? Do you know how the stuff is sold?"

"There's something called a department store, the tutorial said to start there. We might run into some of the others."

"Hmm." A thought strikes me. "I'm hungry. Think there'll be somewhere to eat?"

"Maybe."

Something large and yellow appears outside the door. "Is that it?" I ask.

"Who knows?" He looks twitchy. "Let's go see."

The yellow thing is a taxi, a kind of automobile you hire by the centisecond. There's a human operator up front, and something like a padded bench seat in the rear. We get in, and Sam leans forward. "Can you take us to the nearest department store?" he asks.

The operator nods. "Macy's. Downtown zone. That will be five dollars." He holds out a hand and I notice that his skin is perfectly smooth and he has no fingernails. *Is he one of the zombies?* I wonder. Sam hands over his "credit card" and the operator swipes it between his fingers, then hands it back. Sam sits back, then there's a lurch, and we're moving. The taxi makes various loud noises, so that I'm afraid it's about to suffer a systems malfunction—there's a loud rumbling from underneath and a persistent whine up front—but we turn into the road and accelerate toward the tunnel. A moment of darkness, then we're somewhere else, driving along a road between two short rows of gray-fronted buildings. The taxi stops and the door next to Sam clicks open. "We have arrived at downtown," says the operator. "Please disembark promptly."

Sam is frowning over his tablet, then straightens up. "This way," he says. Before I can ask why, he heads off toward one of the nearest buildings, which has a row of doors in it. I follow him.

Inside the store, I get lost fast. There's stuff everywhere, piled in heaps and stacked in storage bins, and there are lots of people wandering about. The ones in the odd-looking uniforms are shop operators who're supposed to help you find things and take your money. There are no assemblers and no catalogues, so I suppose they can only sell the stuff they've got on display, which is why it's all over the place. I ask one of the operators where I can find clothes, and she says, "on the third floor, ma'am." There are moving staircases in a central high-ceilinged room, so I head for the third level and look around.

Clothes. Lots of clothes. More clothes than I've ever imagined in one place—and all of them made of dumb fabric with no obvious way of finding what you want and getting it adjusted to the right size! How did they ever figure out what they needed? It's a crazy system, just putting everything in the middle of a big house and letting visitors take their chances. There are some other people walking around and fingering the merchandise, but when I approach them they turn out to be zombies, playing the part of real people. None of the others are here yet. I guess we must be early.

I wander through a forest of racks hung with jackets until I catch a shop operator. "You," I say. "What can I wear?"

She looks like an orthohuman female, wearing a blue skirt and jacket and those shoes with uncomfortable heels, and she smiles at me robotically. "What items do you require?" she asks.

"I need—" I stop. "I need underwear," I say. The stuff doesn't clean itself. "Enough for a week. I need some more pairs of hose"—since I tore the one on my left leg—"and another outfit identical to this one. And another set of shoes." A thought strikes me. "Can I have a pair of pants?"

"Please wait." The shop operator freezes. "Please come this way." She leads me to a lectern near a display of statues wearing flimsy long gowns, and another operator comes out of a door in the wall carrying a bundle of packages. "Here is your order. Pants, item not available in this department. Please identify a template, and we will supply correctly sized garments."

"Oh." I look around. "Can I choose anything here?"

"Yes."

I spend a couple of kiloseconds wandering the shop floor, looking for stuff to wear. They sell very few pants here, and they look damaged—made of a heavy blue fabric, ripped open at the knees. Eventually I end up in another corner of the store where there's a rack of trousers that look all right, plain black ones with no holes in them. "I want one of these in my size," I say to the nearest operator, a male one.

"Item not available in female fitting," he says.

"Oh. Great." I scratch my head. "Can you alter it?"

"Item not available in female fitting," he repeats. My netlink bings. A red icon appears over the rack of pants: SUMPTUARY VIOLATION.

"Hmm." So there are restrictions on what they'll sell to me? This is getting annoying. "Can you provide one in my size fitting? It's for a male exactly the same size as myself."

"Please wait." I wait, fidgeting impatiently. Eventually another male operator appears from an inconspicuous door in the shop wall, carrying a bundle. "Your gift item is here."

"Uh-huh." I take the pants, suppress a grin, and think about these irritating shoes and how . . . "Take me to the shoe department. I want a pair of shoes in my size fitting, for a male—"

When I pay using the "credit card," I score a couple more social points: I've made five so far.

I catch up with Sam down in the furniture department about five kiloseconds later. We're both massively overloaded with bags, but he's bought a portable container called a 'suitcase' and we shove most of our purchases into it. I've bought a shoulder bag and a pair of ankle boots that have soft soles and don't clatter when I walk—I shoved my old shoes into the bag, just in case I need them for some reason—and I'm a lot more comfortable walking around now. "Let's go find somewhere to eat," he suggests.

"Okay." There's an eatery on the other side of the road from Macy's, and it's not unlike a real one, except that the food is delivered by human (no, zombie) attendants, and is supposed to be prepared by other humans in the kitchen. Luckily, this is a simulation, or I'd feel quite ill. For deep combat sweeps they teach you how to synthesize food from biological waste or your dead comrades, but that's different. This is supposed to be civilization, of a kind. We order from a menu printed on a sheet of white film, then sit back to wait for our food. "How did your shopping go?" I ask Sam.

"Not too badly," he says guardedly. "I bought underwear. And some trousers and tops. My tablet says there are a lot of social conventions surrounding clothing. Stuff we can wear, stuff we can't wear, stuff we *must* wear—it's a real mess."

"Tell me about it." I tell him about my difficulty ordering trousers that didn't have holes in them.

"It says—" He pulls his tablet out. "Ah, yes. Sumptuary conventions. It's not legally codified, but trousers weren't allowed for females early in the dark ages, and skirts weren't allowed for males at all." He frowns. "It also says the customs appear to have changed sometime around the middle of the period."

"You're going to stick by the book?" I ask him, as a zombie walks up and deposits a glass of pale yellow liquid called beer next to each of our settings.

"Well, they can always fine us," he says, shrugging. "But I suppose you're right. We don't have to do anything we're not comfortable with."

"Right." I hike my right leg up and put my foot on the table. "Look at this."

"It's a heavy boot."

"A boot from the males-only department. But they sized it for me when I told them it was a gift for a male the same size as me."

"Oh?"

I realize I'm showing the leg with the torn hose and put it back under the table. "We've got some autonomy, however limited. Now we're in here, we can live however we want, can't we?"

Plates of food arrive—synthetic steaks, fake vegetables designed to look as if they'd grown in a muddy corner of a wild biosphere, and cups of brightly colored condiments. For a while I busy myself with my plate. I'm really hungry, and the food is flavorsome, if a bit basic. At least we're not going to starve in here. I fill up quickly.

"I don't know if we can," Sam mumbles around a full mouth. "I mean, the points system—"

"Doesn't stop us doing anything," I interrupt, sliding my plate away. "All we have to do is to agree to ignore it, and we can do whatever we want."

"I suppose so." He forks another piece of steak into his mouth.

"Anyway, we've got no idea what they take to be a violation of the system. I mean, what do I have to do to lose a point? Or to gain points? They haven't actually *told* us anything, they've just said 'obey the rules and collect points.'" I stab my fork in his direction. "We've got these reference texts in our tablets, all this stuff about how it's a genetically determinist society and there are all these silly customs, but I don't see how that can affect us unless we let it. All societies have some degree of flexibility, but these guys have just picked the first narrowly normative interpretation that came to hand. If you ask me, they're just plain lazy."

"What will the others think?" he asks.

"What will they think?" I stare at him. "We're here for a hundred megs. Do you really think they'll put a bonus payment at the end of the experiment ahead of, say, having to wear stupid pointy shoes that make your feet hurt for three years?"

"It depends." Sam puts his knife down. "It all depends on how they balance the relative convenience of making other people uncomfortable against their own future wealth." His expression is pensive. "The protocol is . . . interesting."

"Okay." I stand up. "Let's test it." I shrug out of my jacket and lay it over the back of my chair. A couple of the dining zombies look round. "Hey, look at me!" I yell. I unzip my dress and drop it around my ankles. Sam is startled. I watch his face as I reach behind my back and unlatch my breast halter, drop it, then step up onto my chair and push down my hose and G-string. "Look at me!" Sam looks up, and my face feels hot as I see his expression—

Then there's a red flash that blots out my visual field, and a loud chime from my netlink, like the decompression alert we all learn to fear before we can walk. MINUS TEN POINTS FOR PUBLIC NUDITY, says the link.

When my vision clears, I can see waitrons and the maître d' rushing toward me holding up towels and aprons, ready to do something, anything, to cover the horrible sight. Sam is still looking up at me, and I'm not the only one who's blushing. I climb down off the chair and three or four male zombies, all bigger than me, converge and between them pin my arms and carry me bodily into the back. I bite back a scream of

fright: *I can't move!* But they take me straight to the females-only lava-
tory and simply shove me through the door, on my own. A moment
later, while I'm still trying to catch my breath, the door whips open and
someone throws my discarded clothes at me.

Minus ten points, causing a public nuisance, intones my netlink.
Police have been summoned. Help function advises you to correct your
dress code infraction and leave.

Oh shit, shit . . . I scrabble around for a moment, pulling the dress
over my head and then shrugging into the jacket. Underwear can wait—
I don't know what these "police" are, but they don't sound good. I pull
the door open and glance round the corner but there's nobody about,
nothing but a short corridor with doors back to the restaurant and one
that says FIRE ESCAPE in green letters. I shove it open and find myself
standing in a narrow road with lots of wheeled containers. It stinks of
decaying food. Shaking slightly, I walk to the end, then turn left, and
left again.

Back on the road I walk right into Sam. "*Now* will you take the
protocol seriously?" he hisses in my ear. "They nearly arrested me!"

"Arrested? What's that?"

"The police." He's breathing heavily. "They can take you away,
lock you up. Detention, it's called." He's still flushed in the face and
clearly concerned. "You could have been hurt."

I shiver. "Let's go home."

"I'll call a taxi," he says grumpily. "You've done enough damage
for one day."

SAM has bought a thing called a cell phone—a pocket-sized replacement for the blocky network terminal wired into the wall. He keeps it
in a pocket. He speaks to it for a while, and a few cents later a taxi pulls
up. We go home, and he stomps into the living room, leaving the suitcase in the front hall, and turns on the television. I tiptoe around for a
while before looking in on him to find that he's engrossed in the football, a faintly puzzled expression on his face.

I spend some time in my bedroom, reading from my own tablet. It's got lots of advice about how people lived in the dark ages, none of which makes much sense—most of what they did sounds arbitrary and silly when you strip it of the surrounding social context and the history that explains how their customs developed. The way my experiment in the restaurant backfired still burns me (how can not wearing clothes be so harmful in any rational social context?), but after a while I realize that I didn't get zapped this morning when I went around the house naked. So I take off my new boots, then my dress, which is beginning to get a bit whiffy. I go downstairs and open the suitcase, take out my purchases, and carry them up to my room. I stash them in the wardrobe, but there's enough space for ten times as much stuff, which leaves me puzzled. But I don't feel like trying the new costumes on right now. In fact, I feel like shit. Sam is ignoring me pointedly (a defensive reaction, I think), we're living in a crazy experiment that doesn't make sense, and I won't even get a chance to find out if everyone else thinks it's mad until the day after tomorrow.

I'm reading the tablet's explanation of how vocations—excuse me, "work"—worked in dark ages society, boggling slightly, when a bell rings from the low table next to my bed. I look toward it and my tablet flashes: ANSWER THE PHONE.

Oh. I didn't realize I had one. I fumble around for a while then find the chunky gadget on a cord that you're supposed to hold to your face. "Yes?" I say.

"R-Reeve! Is that you?"

"Cass? Kay?" I ask, blanking on names for a moment.

"Reeve! You've got to help me get out of here! He's crazy. If I stay here, I'm sure he's going to end up hitting me again. I need somewhere to go." I've heard panic before, and this is it. Cass (*Kay?* a little corner of me insists) is desperate. *But why?*

"Where are you?" I ask. "What's happening? Calm down and tell me everything."

"I need to get away from here," she insists again, her voice breaking. "He's crazy! He's read the manuals and he's insisting he's going to get the completion bonus, and if he has to, he's going to force me to do everything by the book. He went out this morning, locking me in and

taking my wallet—he's still got it—and when he got back, he threatened
to beat me up if I didn't prepare a meal for him. He says that for maximum points the female must obey the male, and if I don't do what the
guidelines say, he'll beat me up—shit, he's coming."

Click.

I'm left holding the receiver, staring at the wall behind the bed in
horror. I drop it and rush downstairs to the living room. "Sam! We've
got to do something!"

Sam looks up from his tablet. "Do what?"

"It's K—Cass! She just phoned. She needs help. Her husband is
crazy—he's taken away her wallet, locked her indoors, and is threatening to beat her up if she doesn't obey him. We've got to do something!
There's no way she can defend herself—"

Sam puts his tablet down. "Are you sure of this?" he asks quietly.

"Yes! That's what she told me!" I'm just about jumping up and
down, beside myself with fury. (If I ever catch the joker who leeched all
my upper body strength, I swear I am going to graft their head to a tree
sloth and make them run an endurance race.) "We've got to do something!"

"Like what?" he asks.

I deflate. "I'm not sure. She wants to get out. But—"

"Did you check our cumulative score?"

"My—no, I didn't. What's that got to do with it?"

"Just do it," he says.

"Okay." *What is our cohort's cumulative score?* I ask my netlink.
The result sets me back. "Hey, we're doing well! Even after . . ." I falter.

"Well yes, if you look in the subtotals, you'll see that we get points,
lots of them, for forming 'stable normative relationships.'" His cheek
twitches. "Like Cass and, who is it, Mick."

"But if he's hurting her—"

"Is he really? All right, we take her word for it. But what can we do?
If we break them up, we cost everyone in our cohort a hundred points,
just like that. Reeve, have you noticed the journal log? Infractions are
public. Everyone noticed your little—experiment—at lunchtime. It's all
over their journal, in red digits. Caused quite a stir. If you do something

that costs the cohort a stable relationship, some of them—not me, but the ones who will be obsessing with that termination bonus—will start to hate you. And as you pointed out earlier, we're stuck here for the next hundred megs."

"Shit. Shit!" I stare at him. "What about you?"

He looks up at me from his corner of the sofa, his face impassive. "What about me?"

"Would you hate me?" I ask, quietly.

He thinks for a moment. "No. No, I don't think so." Pause. "I wish you'd be a little more discreet, though. Lie low, think things through before you act, try to at least look as if you're planning on fitting in."

"Okay. So what *should* I be thinking? About Cass, I mean. If that scumbag is taking advantage of his greater physical strength . . ."

"Reeve." He pauses again. "I agree in principle. But first we must know what we need to do. Can she leave him of her own accord, without our help? If so, then she ought to—it's her choice. If not, what can we do to help? We have to live with the consequences of our early mistakes for a very long time. Unless Cass is in immediate danger, it would be best to try and get the entire cohort to take action, not go it alone."

"But right now, we've got to stop him doing anything. Haven't we?"

I don't know what's come over me. I feel helpless, and I hate it. I should be able to go round to the scumsucker's house and kick the door down and give him a taste of cold steel in his guts. Or failing that, I ought to plan a cunning two-pronged assault that whisks the victim to safety while booby-trapping his bathroom and putting itching powder in his bed. But I'm just spinning my wheels, venting and emoting and unloading on Sam. My normal network of resources and capabilities is missing, and I'm letting the environment dictate my responses. The environment is set up to inculcate this weird gender-deterministic role play, so I'm . . . I shake my head.

"We don't want anyone to get the idea that hurting or imprisoning members of our cohort is a good way to earn points," Sam says thoughtfully. "Do you have any ideas about how to do that?"

I think for a moment. "Phone him," I say, before the idea is completely formed in my head. "Phone him and . . . yeah." I look out at the garden. "Tell him we'll see him, and Cass, at Church, the day after to-morrow. There's no need to be nasty," I realize. "It says we're supposed to dress up and look good in Church. It's a custom thing. Tell him we could lose points if she doesn't look good. Collectively." I turn to Sam. "Think he'll get the message?"

"Unless he's very, very stupid." Sam nods, then stands up. "I'll call him right away." He pauses. "Reeve?"

"Yes?"

"You're not . . . you're making me nervous, smiling like that."

"Sorry." I think for a moment. "Sam?"

"Yes?"

I'm silent for a few second while I try to work out how much I can safely tell him. After a while I shrug mentally and just say it. I don't think Sam is likely to be a cold-blooded assassin in the pay of whatever enemies my earlier self made. "I knew Cass. Outside the experiment be-fore we, uh, before we volunteered. If that turd-faced scum hurts her I—well, right now I can't punch his teeth so far down his throat that he has to eat with his ass, but I'll think of something else to do. Something equivalent. And, Sam?"

"Yes?"

"I can be very creative when it's time to get violent."

5

Church

SAM picks up the phone and asks the Gatekeeper to connect him to Mick's household. I linger at the top of the stairs and listen to him, down in the front hall. It sounds like he's trying not to lose his temper. After a couple of cents, he puts the phone down hard and stomps back to the living room. I spend most of the rest of the evening avoiding him, instead worrying myself into a black depression at the possibility that I might have made things worse for Cass by getting Sam involved.

Points. Collective accountability. Stable couples. Peer pressure. My head's spinning. It's not that I'm unused to the idea of daily life having rules—at least, in peacetime—but it somehow seems indecent for them to make it so explicit. Societies cohere through tacit understanding, a nod and a wink and—very occasionally—a lookup in a legal database. I'm used to learning how things work as I go along and this experience, a headfirst collision with a fully formed set of rules to live one's life by, has given me a big shock.

I speculate that I'd be able to handle things better if I weren't trapped in a frankly inadequate body. I'm not normally conscious of my own size or strength, and I'm not interested in mesomorphic tinkering—but then again, I would never consciously choose to make myself small and frail. I'm borderline malnourished, too. When I go to the bathroom and use the mirror, I can almost see my ribs under a layer of subcutaneous fat. I'm not used to being a waif, and when I get my hands on whoever did this to me . . . *Hah, but I won't be able to do anything to them, will I?* "Assholes," I mutter darkly, then head for the kitchen to see if there are any high-protein options on offer.

Later on, I explore the basement. There are a bunch of machines down here that my tablet says are for household maintenance. I puzzle over the clothes washing machine. There's something very crude and mechanical about it, as if its shape is rigidly fixed. It's not like a real machine, warm and protean and accommodating to your needs. It's just a lump of ceramic and metal. It doesn't even answer when I tell it I need to clean my dress—it's really stupid.

Farther back in the basement there's something else, a bench with levers attached, for developing upper body muscle mass the hard way. I'm a bit skeptical, but the tablet says these people had to develop musculature by repeatedly lifting weights and other exercises. I find the manual for the exercise machine and after about a kilosecond I manage to reduce myself to a quivering, sweat-smeared jelly. It's like some kind of psychological torture, a lesson that rams home just how weak I am.

I stumble upstairs, shower, and collapse into an uneasy sleep, troubled by dreams of drowning and visions of Kay reaching toward me with all her arms outstretched, begging for something I don't understand. Not to mention faint echoes of something terrible, immigrants pushing and shoving under the gun, begging and screaming to be allowed through the gates of Hel. I startle awake and lie shivering in the darkness for half an hour. *What's happening to me?*

I'm trapped in another universe. It's true what they say: The past is another polity, but I don't think most people mean it quite like this.

THE next morning, I'm in the kitchen trying to puzzle out the instructions for using the coffeemaker when the phone rings. There's a terminal in the hall, so I go there to pick it up, wondering if something's wrong. "Call for Sam," buzzes a flat voice. "Call for Sam."

I stare at the handset for a moment, then look up the stairs. "It's for you!" I yell.

"I'm coming." Sam takes the staircase two steps at a time. I pass him the handset. "Yes?" He listens for a moment. "What is—I don't understand. Can you repeat that? Oh. Yes, yes, I will." Listening to a conversation on one of these old telephones has an eerie feel. They exist in a strange space, a half-duplex information realm devoid of privacy.

Sam continues to listen, looking puzzled then annoyed as the instructions continue. Finally, he puts the phone down. "Well!" He says emphatically.

"I'm trying to cook the coffee," I tell him. "Come and tell me about it."

"They're sending a taxi. I've got half an 'hour'—that's nearly two kilosecs, isn't it?—to get ready."

"Who are 'they'?" I ask. My stomach clenches with anxiety.

"I've been assigned a temporary job," says Sam. "They're picking me up for induction training. It's to show me how the labor system here works. I may be given a different job later."

"Huh." I turn back to the coffee machine so he won't see me frown. If that's the hydroxide tank, then this must be the venturi nozzle . . . the disassembled metal bits don't make any more sense to me than they did before I took it to pieces. "What am I supposed to do? Are they going to assign me a labor duty, too?"

"I don't think so." He pauses. "You can ask for a job, but they don't expect you to. This one, the manual says it's a starting point." He doesn't look too happy. "We get paid collectively," he adds after a few seconds.

"What? You mean they make you work, and I get half of it?"

"Yes."

I shake my head, then screw the machine back together. After a bit I get to the point where it's making gurgling whining noises and dribbling brown liquid. I stare at it, then wonder, *Isn't it supposed to make a cup first?* Silly me, no assemblers! I hastily rummage through the cupboards until I find a couple of cups and jam one under the nozzle. "Stupid, stupid," I mutter, unsure whether I'm describing myself or the long-dead designers of the machine.

A taxi shows up in due course, and Sam goes off to his work induction training. I wander around the house for a bit, trying to figure out where everything is and what it does. The washing machine apparently has physical switches you have to set to make it work. It runs on water, and you have to add something called detergent to the clothes, a substitute for properly designed fabrics. After I read about fabrics in the manual *Designed for Living*, I feel a bit queasy and resolve to only wear artificial ones. There's something deeply disturbing about wearing clothes made from dead animals. There's stuff called "silk" that's basically bug vomit, and the idea of it makes my skin crawl.

After a couple of hours I get bored. The house is deeply uncommunicative (if this was a real polity, I'd say it was autistic), and the entertainment resources are primitive, to say the least. I try the telephone, thinking I'll call Cass and see how she's doing—at a guess, Mick will be undergoing work induction, too, just like Sam—but the phone just makes that idiotic bleeping for a minute or so (I'm trying to adjust to the strange time units the ancients used). Maybe she's asleep, or shopping. Or could she be dead? For a moment I daydream randomly: After Sam's call, Mick hit her over the head with the handlebars from an exercise machine and chopped her up in the basement. Or he strangled her while she was asleep . . .

Why am I harboring these gruesome fantasies? Something is very wrong with me. I feel trapped, that's a large part of it. I'm isolated here, stuck alone in a suburban house while my husband goes to his assigned job. Which is all wrong because what's *really* going on is that there's an assassin or assassins looking for me because of—*because of what?* Something that happened before my memory surgery—and I'm isolated, stuck here floundering around in my ignorance.

I need to get out of here.

Ten minutes later I'm standing outside the conservatory, wearing my dress-code-violating boots and trousers and with a bag over my shoulder containing my wallet and an extremely sharp knife I found in the kitchen. It's absolutely pathetic, especially given the shape of my arm muscles (which feel as if I've been whacking on them with a hammer), but it's the best I can do right now. With any luck, the assassins will be in the same situation, and I'll have time to prepare myself before they're ready to make their move.

Item number one on the checklist for the well-prepared fugitive: Know your escape routes.

I don't call a taxi. Instead, I walk to the side of the road and look up and down it. The neighborhood is peaceful, if a bit peculiar. Huge deciduous plants grow to either side, and the vegetation gets wild and out of control near the boundaries of the garden associated with our house. Hidden invertebrates make creaking, grating noises like malfunctioning machinery. I try to remember the direction the taxi took us in. *That* way. I turn left and walk along the side of the road, ready to jump out of the way if a taxi appears suddenly.

There are other houses along the road. They're about the same size as mine, clumps of rectangular boxes with glass-fronted openings in frames, sporting oddly tilted upper surfaces. They're painted a variety of colors but look drab and faded, like dead husks shed by enormous land-going arthropods. There's no sign of life in any of them, and I guess they're probably just part of the scenery. I've got no idea where Cass lives, and I wish I did. I could go and visit her: For all I know she's in the next house along from me. But I don't know, and directory services are only one of the netlink-mediated facilities that are missing here, and Sam is right about one thing—the ancients were incredibly territorial. If they can call the public security forces and detain people simply for wearing the wrong clothes in public, what might they do if I went into someone else's house?

A couple of hundred meters along the road, I come to a rise in the ground. The road continues on the level, descending into a deep trench, finally diving into a dark tunnel in the hillside. Looking up the sides I notice that something isn't quite right about the trees. *Gotcha,* I think. This must be the edge of a hab module. I can just barely imagine what's right beneath my feet—complex machinery locked within a skin of structural diamond, a cylinder kilometers long spinning in the void, orbiting in the icy darkness. Emptiness for a few tens of millions of kilometers, then a brown dwarf star little bigger than a gas giant planet, then tens of trillions of kilometers more to the nearest other star system. Scale is the first enemy.

I walk into the tunnel and see a bend ahead, beyond which it gets very dark. This is disturbing—I didn't notice it when I was in the back of the taxi, even though my attention was being grabbed by every weird thing I saw. But if there's a T-gate in here . . . Well, there's only one way to find out. I keep my right hand in contact with the tunnel wall as it curves round into darkness. I keep walking slowly ahead, and after maybe fifty meters it begins to bend the other way. I pass another curve, then there's light from the end of the tunnel, and I'm walking along a road where the buildings to either side are distinctly different in shape and size. There's a sign ahead that reads: WELCOME TO THE VILLAGE. (A village is a small community; a downtown is the commercial area of a village. At least, I think that's how it works.)

I've been doing my reading like a good citizen, and there are several places I need to go shopping, starting with a hardware store. The thing is, it seems to me that because these people couldn't simply order any design patterns they needed out of an assembler, they had to make things themselves from more primitive components. This means "tools," and it's surprisingly easy to convert a good basic toolkit into an arsenal of field-expedient weapons. I'm probably safe in here as long as I don't disclose my identity, but "probably" doesn't get you very far when the alternative is lethal, and I'm already lying awake at night worrying about it.

I spend about half an hour in the hardware store, during which time I discover that the operator zombies aren't programmed to stop females buying axes, crowbars, spools of steel wire, arc-welding rigs, subtractive volume renderers, or just about any other tool I can see. The kit I go for costs quite a bit and is bulky and very heavy, but they say they'll deliver and install them in our "garage," an externally accessible subbuilding that I haven't explored yet. I thank them and add some billets of metal feedstock and some lengths of spring steel to the order.

Walking out of the store with a basic workshop on its way over to my house and an axe hidden in a workman's holster under my coat, I feel a lot better about the outlook for the near-term future. It's a bright, warm morning: small feathery dinosaurs are issuing territorial calls from the deciduous plants between the buildings, and for the first time since I arrived I am beginning to feel as if I'm in control of my own destiny.

Which is when I run into Jen and Angel, walking arm in arm along the sidewalk toward a rustic-looking building with a sign above the door saying, YE OLDE COFFEE SHOPPE.

"Why, hello there!" Jen gushes, spreading her arms to drag me into an embrace, while Angel stands back, smiling faintly. I yield to Jen's hug stiffly, hoping she won't feel the axe—but no such luck. "What's *that* you're wearing? And what have you got under your coat?" she demands.

"I've just been to the hardware store," I explain, forcing myself to smile politely. "I was buying some tools for Sam for the, the garden, and I didn't have room for them in my bag so I'm carrying them in the shoulder pouch he asked me to get." The lies flow easily the more I practice them. "How are *you* doing?

"Oh, we're doing really well!" Jen says expansively, letting go of me.

"We were just about to stop for a coffee," says Angel. "Would you like to join us?"

"Sure," I say. There doesn't seem to be any polite way to say no. Plus, I haven't had any human contact except Sam for the past hundred kilosecs, and I wouldn't mind a chance to pick their brains. So I follow them into Ye Olde Coffee Shoppe, and we sit down at a booth with shiny red vinyl seats and a bright white polymer-topped table while the waitrons attend to our needs.

"So how are you settling in?" asks Angel. "We heard you had some trouble yesterday."

"Yes, darling." Jen smiles brilliantly as she nods. She's wearing a bright yellow dress and some kind of hat that vaguely resembles a ballistic shuttlecraft. She's applied some kind of paint-powder to her face to exaggerate the color of her lips (red) and eyelashes (black), and something she's used on her skin has left her smelling like an explosion in a topiary. "I hope you're not going to make a habit of it?"

"I'm sure she won't," Angel chides her. "It's just a natural settling-in mistake. We can all expect to make a few, can't we?" She glances sideways at the waitron: "A double chocolate iced latte made with fair-trade beans and whipped cream, no sugar," she snaps.

"I'll have the same," I manage to say just as Jen starts rambling about the contents of the price board above the counter, changing her mind three times before she reaches the end of every sentence. I study Angel while I'm about it. Angel is wearing a jacket-and-skirt combination—a "suit," they call it, though it doesn't look like the version permitted to males—and while it's darker and drabber than Jen's outfit, she's got some shiny lumps of metal stuck to her earlobes. I can see it's meant to be jewelry, but it looks painful. "What's that on your ears?" I ask.

"They're called earrings," Angel tells me. "There's a salon up the road that'll pierce your ears, then you can hang different pieces of jewelry from them. Once the hole heals," she adds, with a slight wince. "They're still a little sore."

"Hang on, that's not glued onto your skin or properly installed? They shoved it *through* your ear rather than rebuilding your ear around it? And it's *metal*?"

"Yes," she says, giving me an odd look. I don't know what to say to that, but luckily I don't have to because Jen finishes ordering her cafe americano and turns back to focus on us.

"I'm so pleased we ran into you today, darling!" She leans toward me confidingly. "I've been doing some research, and we're not the only cohort here—in fact, all six will be meeting at Church tomorrow, and we wouldn't want anyone to let the side down."

"I'm sorry?" I ask, taken aback.

"She means, we need to keep up appearances," Angel says, with another of those expressive looks that I can't decode.

"I don't understand."

A faint frown wrinkles the skin between Jen's eyebrows. "It's not just about *yesterday*," she emphasizes. "Everyone's entitled to their little mistakes. But it turns out that in addition to our points being averaged within the cohort, each cohort in the parish gets to talk about what they've achieved in the preceding week, and the other cohorts rate them on their behavior before voting to add or subtract bonus points."

"It's an iterated prisoner's dilemma scenario, with collective liability," Angel cuts in, just as one of the operator zombies twiddles a knob on a polished metal tank behind the bar that makes a noise like a pressure leak. "Very elegant experimental design, if you ask me."

"It's an—" *Oh shit.* I nod, guardedly, unsure how much I can reveal: "I think I see."

"Yes." Angel nods. "We're going to have to defend your behavior yesterday, and the other groups can add points or subtract them depending on whether they think we deserve it and on whether they think we'll hold a grudge when it's their turn in the ring."

"That's really devious!"

"Yes." Angel again.

Jen smiles. "Which is why, darling, you're not going to show up the side by violating the dress code, and you'll be suitably remorseful about whatever the silly incident yesterday was about—no, I don't want to know all the sordid details—and we'll do our bit by backing you up and trying to bury the whole matter as deeply as we can under a pile of every other cohort's sins. Won't we?" She glances at Angel. "We're the new group, we can expect to be picked on. It's going to be bad enough with Cass, as it is."

"What's wrong with Cass?" I ask.

"She's not settling in," says Jen.

Angel looks as if she's about to open her mouth, but Jen waves her hand dismissively. "If you've been getting any silly phone calls from her, just ignore them. She's only doing it to get attention, and she'll stop soon enough."

I stare at Jen. "She told me Mick's threatening to hurt her," I say. The zombie delivers the first of our coffee cups.

"So?" Jen stares right back at me, and there's a cold core of steel behind her expression: "What business of ours is it? What's between a wife and her husband is private, as long as it doesn't threaten to drag our points down or get our whole cohort in trouble. Apart from the other thing, of course."

"What other—"

Angel cuts in. "You get social points for fucking," she says, her voice self-consciously neutral. Again, she gives me that odd look. "I thought you'd have figured it out by now."

"For *sex*?" I must sound faintly scandalized, or shocked or something, because Jen's face relaxes into a mask of amusement.

"Only with your husband, darling." She sips her coffee and looks at me calculatingly. "That's something else we've noticed. I don't want to hurry you or anything, but . . ."

"Who I fuck is none of your business," I say flatly. My coffee arrives, but right now I'm not feeling thirsty. My mouth tastes as dry and acrid as if I've just chewed half a kilogram of raw caffeine. "I'll dress up for the Church meeting and say I'll be good and do whatever else you want me to do in public. And I'll try not to cost you any points. But." I tap the table in front of Jen's coffee cup, insultingly close. "You will not, *ever*, tell me whom I may associate with or what I will do with my chosen associates. Or with whom I have sex." The silence grows icicles. I take an unwisely large gulp of hot coffee and burn the roof of my mouth. "Do I make myself clear?"

"Quite clear, darling." Jen's eyes glitter like splinters of frozen malice.

I make myself smile. "Now, shall we find something civilized to talk about while we drink our coffee and eat our pastries?"

"I think that would be a good idea," says Angel. She looks slightly shaken. "After lunch, how about we buy you something suitable to wear to Church?" She asks me. "Just in case. Meanwhile, I was wondering if you've used your washing machine yet? It has some interesting features . . ." And she's off into an exploration of techniques for gaining points in the women's world, generated by game theory and policed by mutual scorefile surveillance.

BY the end of our lunch, I think I've got a handle on them. Angel means well but is too calculatedly fearful for her own good. She's afraid of stepping out of line, unwilling to jeopardize her score, and worried about what people will think of her. This combination makes her an easy target for Jen, who is flamboyant and aggressively extroverted on the outside, but uses it to conceal an insecure need for approval, which leads her to bully people until they give it to her. She's as ruthless as anyone I can recall meeting since my memory surgery, and I've met some hardcases around the clinic. The surgeon-confessors tend to attract such. (What's even more disturbing is that I have faint ghost-recollections of knowing similar people before, but with no details attached. Who they were or what they meant to me has sunk into the abyss where memories go when their owners no longer need them.)

The two of them, working by unspoken assent, appoint themselves as my personal shopping assistants for the afternoon. They're not crude about it, but they're very persistent and make no real attempt to conceal their desire to modify my behavior along lines compatible with their enhanced scorefiles.

After coffee and cakes (for which Angel pays), they escort me to a series of establishments. In the first of these I am subjected to the attentions of a hairstylist. Angel sits with me and chats interminably about kitchen appliances while Jen goes off somewhere to do something of her own, and the zombie immobilizes me and applies a fearsome array of knives, combs, chemical reagents, and compact machine tools to my head. Once I get out of the chair, I have to admit that my hair's different—it's still long, but it's several shades lighter, and whenever I turn my head it moves like a solid lump of foamed plastic.

"Perhaps we should get you some clothing for tomorrow," Jen says, smiling broadly. It's phrased as a suggestion, but the way she says it makes it an order. They lead me through a series of boutiques, where I am induced to present my credit card. She insists that I try on the costume, and while I'm showing her how it looks, Angel gets the store zombies to parcel up my stuff. I end up looking like one of them, the ladies who lunch. "We're getting there," Jen says, something almost like approval on her face. "You need a makeover, though."

"A what?"

They just laugh at me. Probably just as well; if they told me in advance, I'd try to escape. And, as I keep reminding myself (with an increasing sense of dread), I'll have nearly a hundred tendays—three years—in which to regret any mistakes I make today.

THE lights are turning red and sinking toward the tunnel at the edge of the world when the taxi we're crammed into stops outside my house, and the door opens. "Go on," says Angel, pushing my bag at me, "go

and surprise him. He'll have had a long day and will need cheering up."
I realize she's using the generic *he*—they don't care who *he* is, all they
care about is the fact that he's my husband, and we can earn them points.

"Okay, I'm going, I'm going," I say, harassed. I take the bag, and as
I turn, something bites me on the leg. "Hey!" I look round but the taxi
is already pulling away. "Shit," I mumble. My leg throbs. I reach down
and feel something lumpy stuck in it. I pull it out. It's some sort of
lozenge with a needle coming out of one end. *"Shit."* I stumble up the
path in the new shoes they insisted I buy—the heels are steeper and less
comfortable than the first pair—and in through the door. I dump the
bags and head for the living room, where the TV is on. Sam is lying in
front of it, his eyes closed and his tie loosened, and I feel a stab of com-
passion for him. The injection point on my leg aches, a cold reminder.

"Sam. Wake *up*!" I shake his shoulder. "I need your help!"

"Whu—" He opens his eyes and looks at me. "Reeve?" His pupils
dilate visibly. I probably smell weird—Jen and Angel tried half the contents of a scent bar on me, for no reason I can fathom.

"Help." I sit down next to him and hike up my skirt to show him
the mark on my thigh. "Look." I hold up the ampoule where he can see
it. "They got me. What in seven shades of shit *is* that stuff?" My crotch
is unnaturally sensitive and I feel slightly dizzy, worryingly relaxed and
unstressed in view of what's just happened.

"It's—" He blinks. "I don't know. Who did this to you?"

"Jen and Angel. They dropped me off from a taxi and I think Angel
got me with this thing as I left." I lick my lips. I'm feeling distinctly odd.
"What do you think? Poison?"

"Maybe not," he says, staring at me. Then he picks up his tablet
and pokes at it. "There," he says, holding it for me. "Must be their idea
of fun."

I thrust my hands between my thighs and clamp them together, my
eyes blurring as I read. My crotch is tingling. "It's a—huh!" Fury
washes over me. "The bitches!"

Sam shakes his head. "I've had a really tiring day, but it sounds like
you've had an exciting one. Coming home dressed like a—and your
friends, spiking you for sexual arousal." He raises an eyebrow. "Why

did they do that, do you suppose?" Sam can remain analytical and composed in the most trying situations. I wish I had half his grace under pressure.

"I—" I force myself to move my hands. "Bitches."

"What's going on, Reeve? Is the peer pressure really that compelling?" He sounds concerned, sympathetic.

"Yes." I grit my teeth. He's sitting too close to me, but I don't want to risk moving. The drug is hitting me hard in warm, tingly waves, and I'm afraid of leaving a damp patch on the sofa. "It's the social points. We knew the points were shared with our cohort, but there are extra compulsion mechanisms we didn't know about. Jen and Angel told me about them, but I didn't . . . shit. And then you can score points for . . . other activities."

"What other activities?" he asks gently.

"Use your imagination!" I gasp, and bolt for the bathroom.

SAM knocks on the bathroom door once, tentatively, as I'm lying in the bottom of the shower cubicle in a daze of lust, letting waves of hot water sluice over me like a tropical storm—*Since when do I know what a tropical storm on Urth felt like?*—and trying to feel clean. Part of me wants to invite him in, but I manage to bite my lip and stay silent. I guess I can cross Jen and Angel off my list of possible assassins, but I find myself fantasizing in the shower, fantasizing about getting them alone and the myriad revenges I'll take. I know these are just fantasies—you can't kill somebody more than once in this place, and once you've killed them, they're out of reach—but something in me wants to make them hurt, and not just because they've destroyed any chance of my ever having honest sex with this curiously introverted, thoughtful, bear of a husband I've acquired. So I work my arms to exhaustion on the weight machine down in the basement, then go to bed alone and uneasy.

Sunday dawns bright and hot. I reluctantly put on the dress Jen and Angel made me buy and go to meet Sam downstairs. I have no pockets, don't know if I'm allowed to carry a bag, and I feel very unsafe without even a utility knife. Sam's wearing a black suit, white shirt, black tie.

Very monochrome. He looks solid, but going by his face he feels as unsure of himself as I am. "Ready?" I ask.

He nods. "I'll call the taxi."

The Parish Church is a big stone building some distance away from where we live. There's a tower at one end, as sharp and axisymmetrical as a relativistic impactor (if warships were made of stone and had holes drilled in their dorsal end with huge parabolic chimes hanging inside). The bells are ringing loudly, and the car park is filling with taxis and males and females dressed in period costume as we arrive. I see a few faces I know, Jen's among them. But I find I don't recognize most of the people in the crowd as we wait outside, and I hang on to Sam's arm for fear of losing him.

Internally, the Church contains of a single room, with a platform at one end and rows of benches carved from dead trees facing it. There's an altar on the platform, with a long naked blade lying atop it beside a large gold chalice. We file in and sit down. As soft music plays, a procession walks up the aisle from the rear of the building. There are three males, physically aged but not yet senescent, wearing distinctive robes covered in metallic thread. They climb the platform and take up set positions. Then the one at the front and right begins to speak, and I realize with a start that he's Major-Doctor Fiore.

"Dear congregants, we are gathered here today to remember those who have gone before us. Frozen faces carved in stone, the frozen faces of multitudes." He pauses, and everyone around us repeats his words back to him, a low rumbling echo that seems to go on and on forever.

Fiore continues to recite gibberish in portentous tones at an increasing pace. Every sentence or two he stops, and the congregation repeats his words back to him. I *hope* it's gibberish—some of it is not only baffling but vaguely menacing, references to being judged after our deaths, punishment for sins, rewards for obedience. I glance sideways but quickly realize everybody else is watching him. I mouth the words but feel deeply uneasy about it. Some folks seem to be getting worked up, shouting the responses.

Next, a zombie in an alcove strikes up a turgid melody on some sort of primitive music machine, and Fiore tells us to turn the paper books in front of us to a set page. People begin singing the words there, and clapping in time, and they don't make any sense either. The name "Christian" features in it repeatedly, but not in any context I understand. And the message of the sing-along is distinctly sinister, all about submission and conformity and reward feedback loops. It's as if I've got some sort of deep-rooted reflex that refuses to let me absorb propaganda uncritically: I end up reading the book with a frown on my face.

After half an hour or so, Fiore signals the zombie to stop playing. "Dearly beloved," he says, his tone unctuous and confiding. He leans forward on the lectern, searching our faces. "*Dearly* beloved." I add my own sarcastic mental commentary to the proceedings—*Too dear for you to afford*, I footnote him. "Today I would like you all to extend a warm welcome to our newest members, cohort six. We are a loving Church, and it behooves us"—*He actually used the word "behooves," he actually said that!*—"to gather them to our breast and welcome them fully into our family." He smiles ecstatically and clutches the lectern as if a zombie catamite hidden behind it is sucking his cock. "Please welcome our newest members, Chris, El, Sam, Fer, and Mick, and their wives Jen, Angel, Reeve, Alice, and Cass."

Everyone around me—except Sam, who looks as confused as I feel—suddenly starts smacking their hands together in front of them. It's some kind of welcoming ritual, I guess, and the noise is surprisingly loud. Sam catches my eye and begins to clap, tentatively, but then Fiore holds up a hand and everybody stops.

"My children," he says, gazing down at us fondly, "our new brethren have only been here for three days. In that time, they have had much to learn and see and do, and some of them have made mistakes. To err is human, and to forgive is also human. It is ours to forgive and to pardon. To pardon, for example, Mrs. Alice Sheldon of number six, for her difficulty with plumbing. Or to Mrs. Reeve Brown of number six, for her unfortunate public display of nudity the other day. Or to—"

He's drowned out by laughter. I look round and see that suddenly people are laughing at me and pointing. I feel a rush of embarrassment and anger. How *dare* he do this? But it's intimidating, too. There must be fifty people here, and some of them are staring as if they're trying to figure out what I look like without any clothes on. If I was me, if I was in my own self-selected body, I'd call him out on the spot—but I'm not. In the sick pit of my stomach I realize that they're never going to forget that I've been singled out, and that this makes me a target. After all, that's how peer pressure works, isn't it? That's what this is about. The experimenters can't expect to generate a workable dark ages society in just three years by dumping a bunch of convalescents in orthohuman bodies into the polity and letting them wander around. They need a social mechanism to make us require conformity of one other, and the best way to do that is to provide a mechanism to make us punish our own deviants—

"—Or to forgive Cass, for her tendency to oversleep. Such as today, when she seems to have forgotten to come to Church."

They're not looking at me anymore, but they're muttering, and there's a dark undercurrent of disapproval at work. I catch Sam's eye, and he looks frightened. He reaches out sideways, and I grab his hand and cling to it as if I'm drowning.

"I urge you all to give your sympathies to Mick, her husband, who has to support such a slothful wife, and to help her out when next you see her." And now I can follow everybody's gaze to Mick. He's short and wiry and has a big, sharp nose and dark, brooding eyes. He looks angry and defensive, for good reason. The bruising weight of a five-point infraction has left me feeling weak in the knees and frightened, and now he's getting it as a proxy for his wife's failure to get up in the morning—

Failure to get up in the morning? I feel like yelling at Fiore: *It's an excuse, idiot, an excuse for not being seen in public!*

Fiore moves on to discuss other people, other cohorts, stuff that's meaningless to me right now. My netlink comes up, insisting I vote on whether to add or subtract points to each of the other cohorts, with a list of sins and achievements tallied against each name. I don't vote for any of them. In the end our own cohort gets dumped on unanimously by the voters of the five older ones. We all lose a couple of points, signaled by the tolling of a sullen iron bell hanging in an archway near the back of the Church. Fiore signals the zombie to strike up the organ and leads us in another meaningless song, then it's the end of the service. But I can't run away and hide just yet because the auto-da-fé is followed by a social reception in honor of the new cohort, so we can smile brittle smiles and eat canapés under the magnolia trees while they politely sneer at us.

There are tables laid out in the ornamental garden called a graveyard that backs onto the Church. They're covered with white cloths and stacked with glasses of wine. We're led outside and left to fend for ourselves. Taxis don't run on Sunday during Church services. I find myself standing stiffly with my back as close to the churchyard wall as I can get, clutching a wineglass with one hand and Sam with the other. My shoes are pinching, and my face feels set in a permanent grimace.

"Reeve! And Sam!" It's Jen, dragging along Angel and their husbands, Chris and El, in her undertow. She looks a little less ebullient than she was yesterday, and I can guess why.

"We didn't do so well," El grunts. He spares me a lingering glance that hits me like a punch in the guts. It's really creepy. I know exactly what he's thinking, just not why he's thinking it. Is it because he thinks I cost him his points or because he's trying to imagine me with no clothes on?

"We could have done worse," says Jen, her words clipped and harsh-sounding. She's strangling her handbag in a death grip.

"On the outside." I take a deep breath. "I'd challenge Fiore if he made a crack like that at me in public."

"But you're not on the outside, darling," Jen points out. She smiles at Sam. "Is she like this at home, or only when she's got an audience?"

I am close, *very* close, to throwing the contents of my wineglass in her face and demanding satisfaction just to see if she'll crack, but my butterfly mind sees a distraction sneaking furtively past behind her—it's Mick. So instead of doing something stupid I do something downright foolhardy and march right over to him.

"Hello, Mick," I say brightly.

He jumps and glares at me. He's tense, wound up like a spring, positively fizzing. "Yes? What do *you* want?" he demands.

"Oh, nothing." I smile and inspect his face. "I just wanted to sympathize with you, having a wife who doesn't get up in the morning for Church. That's downright inconvenient. Will I see her here next week?"

"Yes," he grates. He's holding his hands stiffly by his sides, and they're clenched into fists.

"Oh, good! How marvelous. Listen, you don't mind me visiting to see her this afternoon, do you? We've got a lot to talk about, and I thought she'd—"

"No." He glares at me. "You're not seeing the bitch. Not today, or—whenever. Go *away*. Whore."

I'm not sure what the word means, but I get the general picture. "Okay, I'm going," I say tensely. If I'd had a few more days with the bench press and the weights, things might be difficult: But not right now. Not yet.

I turn and walk back over to Sam. He doesn't say anything when I lean against him, which is just as well because I don't trust myself to be tactful, especially not while we're in public, and I can't escape. My heart's pounding, and I feel sick with suppressed anger and shame. Cass is being treated as a virtual prisoner by her husband. I'm being publicly ridiculed and making enemies just for trying to maintain my sense of identity. This whole polity is rigged to try to make us betray our friends . . . but somewhere out there, people are looking for me with murder in mind. And if I don't keep a low profile, sooner or later they'll find me.

6

Sword

AFTER Church we go home. Sam doesn't have to work on Sunday, so he watches television. I go and explore the garage. It's a flimsy structure off to one side of the house, with a big pair of doors in front. There's a workbench, and the hardware shop zombies have already installed all the stuff I bought yesterday. I spend a while tinkering with the drill press and reading the manual for the arc-welding apparatus. Then I go and work out on the exercise device in the basement, grimly pretending that it's a torture machine for transferring physical stress to the bones of a human victim and that Jen's on the receiving end of it. After I've squished her into a bloody lump the size of a shopping bag, I feel drained but happier and ready to tackle difficult tasks. So I go looking for Sam.

He's in the living room, staring blankly at the TV screen with the volume turned off. I sit down next to him, and he barely notices. "What's wrong?" I ask.

"I'm—" He shakes his head, mute and miserable.

I reach for his hand but he pulls it away. "Is it me?" I ask.

"No."

I reach for his hand again, grab it, and hang on. He doesn't pull away this time, but he seems to be tense.

"What is it, then?"

For a while I think he isn't going to say anything, but then, just as I'm about to try again, he sighs. "It's me."

"It's—what?"

"Me. I shouldn't be here."

"What?" I look around. "In the living room?"

"No, in this polity," he says. Now I get it, it's not anger—it's depression. When he's down, Sam clams up and wallows in it instead of taking it out on his surroundings.

"Explain. Try and convince me." I shuffle closer to him, keeping hold of his hand. "Pretend I'm one of the experimenters, and you're looking to justify an early termination, okay?"

"I'm—" He looks at me oddly. "We're not supposed to talk about who we were before the experiment. It doesn't aid enculturation, and it's probably going to get in the way."

"But I—" I stop. "Okay, how about you tell me," I say slowly. "I won't tell anyone." I look him in the eye. "We're supposed to be a monadic couple. There aren't any negative-sum game plays between couples in this society, are there?"

"I don't know." He sniffs. "You might talk."

"Who to?"

"Your friend Cass."

"Bullshit!" I punch him lightly on the arm. "Look, if I promise I won't tell?"

He looks at me thoughtfully. "Promise."

"Okay, I promise." I pause. "So what's wrong?"

His shoulders are hunched. "I've just come out of memory surgery," he says slowly. "I think that's where Fiore and Yourdon and their crowd found most of us, by the way. A redaction clinic must be a great place to find experimental subjects who're healthy but who've forgotten everything they knew. People who've come adrift from the patterns of life, and who have minimal social connections. People with active close ties don't go in for memory surgery, do they?"

"Not often, I don't think," I say, vaguely disturbed by a recollection of military officers briefing me: trouble in another life, urgent plotting against an evil contingency.

"Not unless they're trying to hide something from themselves."

I manage to fake up an amused laugh for him. "I don't think that's very likely. Do you?"

"I'd . . . well. I'm pretty narrowly channeled emotionally. Narrow, but deep. I had a family. And it all went wrong, for reasons I can't deal with now, reasons I could have done something about, maybe. Or maybe not. Whatever, that's the bare outline of what I remember. The rest is all third-person sketching, reconstructed memory implants to replace whatever it meant to me. Because, I'm not exaggerating, it burned me out. If I hadn't undergone memory redaction, I'd probably have become suicidal. I have a tendency toward reactive depression, and I'd just lost everything that meant anything to me."

I hold his hand, not daring to move, suddenly wondering what kind of emotional time bomb I casually selected over the cheese and wine table half a week ago.

After about a minute, he sighs again. "It's over. They're in the past, and I don't remember it too clearly. I didn't have the full surgery, just enough to add a layer of fuzz so that I could build a new life for myself." He looks at me. "Do you know?"

Know what? I think, feeling panicky. Then I understand what he's asking.

"I had memory surgery, too," I say slowly, "but it wasn't for the first time. And it was thorough. I've—" I swallow. "I had to read an autobiography I wrote for myself." And did I lie when I was writing it? Did that other me tell the truth, or was he spinning a pretty tapestry of lies for the stranger he was due to become in the future? "It said I was mated once, long-term. Three partners, six children, it lasted over a gigasec." I feel shaky as I consider the next part. "I don't remember their faces. Any of them."

In truth I don't remember *any* of it. It might as well have happened to someone else. According to my autobiography it did. The whole thing ended more than four gigasecs ago—over a hundred and twenty years—and I went through my first memory reset early in the aftermath, and a much more thorough one recently. For more than thirty years those three mates and six children meant more to me than, well, anything. But all they are today is background color to the narrative of my life, like dry briefing documents setting up a prefabricated history for a sleeper agent about to be injected into a foreign polity.

Sam holds my hand. "I had surgery to deal with the pain," he says. "And I came out of surgery, and I found I probably didn't need it in the first place. Pain is a stimulus, a signal that the organism needs to take some kind of evasive action, isn't it? I don't mean the chronic pain caused by nerve damage, but ordinary pain. And emotional pain. You need to do something about it, not avoid it. Afterward, it was distant, but I felt empty. Only half-human. And I wasn't sure who I was, either."

I stroke his hand. "Was it the dissociative psychopathology?" I ask. "Or something deeper?"

"Deeper." He sounds absent. "I had such a void that I—well, I made the mistake of falling in love again. Too soon, with somebody who was brilliant and fast and witty and probably completely crazy. And they asked me about the experiment while I was miserable, trying to figure out whether I really *was* in love or was just fooling myself. We discussed the experiment, but I don't think they were too keen on the idea. And in the end it all got too much for me: I signed up, backed myself up, and woke up in here." He looks at me unhappily. "I made a mistake."

"What?" I stare at him, not sure what to make of this.

"It's not that I don't like sex," he says apologetically, "but I'm in love with someone else. And I'm not going to see them until—" He shakes his head. "Well, there it is. You must think I'm a real idiot."

"No." What I think is, I really have to rescue Cass, Kay, from that scumsucker who's got her locked up. "I don't think you're an idiot, Sam," I hear myself telling him. I lean sideways and kiss him on the cheek in friendly intimacy. He starts, but he doesn't try to push me away. "I just wish we weren't this messed up."

"Me too," he says sadly. "Me too." I lean against him for a while, words seeming redundant at this point. Then, because I'm becoming uncomfortably aware of his body, I get up and head back out to the garage. There's still daylight, and I've got an idea or two in my head that I'd like to work on. If it turns out I have to rescue Kay from Mick and he's violent, I want to be properly equipped.

ON Monday Sam goes to work. And the next day, and the one after that—every day of every week, except Sunday. He's being trained as a legal secretary, which sounds a lot more interesting than it is, although he's getting a handle on the laws and customs of the ancients—some big legal databases survived the dark ages almost untouched, and City Hall has to process a lot of paperwork. One result is that he wears the same dark suits every day, except at home, where it turns out to be okay for him to wear jeans and open-necked shirts.

I begin to get used to him leaving most days, and settle into a routine. I get up in the morning and make coffee for us both. After Sam heads for work I go down to the cellar and work out until I'm covered in sweat and my arms are creaking. Then I have another coffee, go outside, and run the length of the road between the two tunnels several times—at first I make it six lengths, as it's half a kilometer, but I begin to increase it after Tuesday. When I'm staggering with near exhaustion, I go back home and have a shower, another cup of coffee, and either put on something respectable if I'm heading downtown or something disrespectable if I'm going to work in the garage.

There are other unpleasantnesses, of course. About two weeks into our residence, I wake up in the middle of the night with an unpleasant belly cramp. The next morning I'm disgusted to discover that I'm *bleeding*. I'd heard of menstruation, of course, but I hadn't expected the YFH-Polity designers to be crazy enough to reintroduce it. Most other female mammals simply reabsorb their endometria, why should dark ages humans have to be different? I clean up after myself as well as I can, then find I'm still leaking. It's a miserable time, but when I break down and phone Angel to ask if there's any way of stopping it, she just suggests I go to the drugstore and look for feminine hygiene supplies.

Supplies come from the stores in the downtown zone. I get to shop a couple of times a week. Food comes in prepacked meal containers or as raw ingredients, but I'm a lousy cook and a slow learner so I tend to avoid the latter. This week I pull my routine forward—like, urgently—because feminine hygiene means the drugstore, where they sell pads to wear inside your underwear. The whole business is revolting. What's going to happen next? Are they going to inflict leprosy on us? I grit my teeth and resolve to buy more underwear. And pain medication, which comes in small bitter-tasting disks that you have to swallow and which don't work very well.

Clothing I've more or less sorted out. I've taken to asking Angel or sometimes Alice to choose stuff for my public appearances. This insures me against making a wrong choice and getting on anyone's shit-list. Jen points out that I've got lousy fashion taste, an accusation that might actually carry some weight if there were enough of us in this snow globe of a universe to actually *have* fashions, rather than simply being on the receiving end of a fragmentary historical clothing database that's advancing through the old-style 1950s at a rate of one planetary year per two tendays.

Other supplies . . . I haunt the hardware shop. Sam probably thinks I'm spending all the money he's earning on makeovers and hairdos or something, but the truth is, I'm looking to my survival. If and when the assassins find me, I'm determined they're going to have a fight on their hands. I don't think he's even looked in the garage once since we moved in. If he had, he'd probably have noticed the drill press, welding kit, and the bits of metal and wood and nails and glue and the workbench. And the textbooks: *The Crossbow, Medieval and Modern, Military and Sporting, Its Construction History and Management.* It's funny what's survived.

Currently I'm reading a big fat volume called *The Swordsmith's Assistant.* There's method in my madness. While there's no obvious way I can get my hands on a blaster or other modern weaponry, and I'm not suicidal enough to play with explosives inside a pressurized hab without knowing its physical topology, it occurs to me that you can still raise an awful lot of mayhem with the toys you can build in a dark age machine shop. My main headache with the crossbow, in fact, is going to be knowing the axis of rotation in each sector, so that I can correct my aim for Coriolis force. Which is where the plumb bob and the laser distance meter come in.

In public, I'm working hard at being a different person. I don't want anyone to figure out that I'm building an arsenal.

The ladies of our cohort—which means Jen, Angel, me, and Alice, because Cass still isn't allowed out in public by her husband—meet up for lunch three times a week. I don't ask after Cass because I don't want Jen to get the idea that I'm interested in her. She'd peg it as a weakness and try to figure out how to exploit it. I don't want her to get any kind of handle of me, so I dress up and meet them at a restaurant or cafe, and smile and listen politely as they discuss what their husbands are doing or the latest gossip about their neighbors. The nine other houses on my road are standing vacant, waiting for the next cohorts of test subjects to arrive, but that's unusual—I gather the others live near to people from other cohorts, and there's a rich sea of gossip lapping around the tide pools of suburban anomie.

"I think we can make some mileage against cohort three," Jen says one day, over a Spanish omelet dusted with paprika. She sounds cunning.

"You do?" Angel asks anxiously.

"Yes." Jen looks smug.

"Do tell." Alice puts her fork down in the wreckage of her Caesar salad. She's trying to look interested, but she can't fool me. Jen casts her a sharp look, then stabs her omelet.

"Esther and Mal live at the other end of Lakeside View from me and Chris." A piece of omelet quivers on the end of her fork, impaled for our attention. Jen chews reflectively. "I've noticed Esther watching me from their garden, some mornings. So I called a taxi to go shopping, then had it circle round and drop me off just beyond the tunnel at the other end of the road. Funny who you see in the area." She smiles, exposing perfect raptor-sharp teeth.

"Who?" asks Alice, obliging her with an audience.

"She goes in, and about ten minutes later Phil turns up by taxi. He sends it away and rings the doorbell. Leaves an hour or two later."

Angel tut-tuts disapprovingly. Alice just looks faintly disgusted.

"Don't you see?" asks Jen. "It's not public. That gives us leverage." She spears a broccoli stem, dismembers it a branch at a time, tearing with her teeth. "There's a word for it. Adultery. It's not negatively scored as such, as long as it's secret. But if it comes out—"

"*We* know," Angel interrupts. "So why—"

"Because we're not part of cohort three. Esther and Mal and Phil are all in cohort three. The, ah, peer pressure has to be applied by your peers. So this gives us leverage over Esther and Phil. If we tell Mal, they lose points big-time."

"I don't feel so good," I say, putting my knife down and pushing my chair back from the table. "Need some fresh air."

"Was it something I said?" asks Jen, casually concerned.

I'm getting better at lying with a straight face. I don't think I used to be good at it, but spending too much time around Jen is giving me a crash course in mendacity. "Nothing to do with you—must be something I ate," I say as I stand up.

I'm trying not to stand out, trying not to offend Jen or the others, and trying not to look eccentric in public, but there are limits to what I will put up with. Being tacitly enlisted in a conspiracy to blackmail is too much. I'll have to smile at them tomorrow or the day after, but right now I want to be alone. So I go outside, where a gentle breeze is blowing, and I walk to the end of the block and cross the road. There's very little traffic (none of us real humans drive vehicles—it's far too dangerous), and the zombies are configured to give right of way to pedestrians, so I manage to get into the park reasonably fast.

The park is a semidomesticated biome. The grass is neatly trimmed, the large deciduous plants are carefully pruned, and the small stream of water that meanders through it is tamed and can be crossed by numerous footbridges. It has the big advantage that at this time of day it's nearly empty, except for the zombie groundsman and perhaps a couple of wives with nothing better to do with their time. I walk along the stone path that leads from the edge of the downtown block toward the small coppice on the edge of the boating lake.

I gradually calm down as I near the side of the lake. It's simulating a sunny day with a little high cloud and a lazy breeze, just occasionally getting up enough speed to cool my skin through my costume. Apart from the incessant machinelike twitter of the fist-sized dinosaurs in the trees, it's quite peaceful. Sometimes I can almost bring myself to forget the perpetual simmering sense of anger and humiliation that Jen seems to thrive on inducing in the rest of us.

However much I try to, I can't put myself in their shoes. It's as if they don't realize that you can game the system by ignoring it, by refusing to participate, as well as by going along with the overt rewards and punishments. They've all unconsciously decided to obey the arbitrary pressure toward gender partitioning, and they won't be content unless everyone else conforms and competes for the same rewards. Was it like this for real dark ages females, created as random victims of genetic determinism rather than volunteers in an experiment enforced by explicit rewards and penalties? If so, I'm lucky: I've only got another three years of it.

Being a wife is a lonely business. Sam and I lead largely independent lives. He goes to work in the morning, and I only see him in the evenings, when he's tired, or on Sundays. On Sundays we go to Church, bound together by our mutual fear of being singled out for opprobrium, and afterward we go home together and try to remind each other that the score whores—who slavishly chase after every hint of right behavior that Fiore drops—are not the most intelligent or reasonable people. We have an uphill struggle at times.

It's a shame Sam's a male, and a shame that the internal dynamics of this compressed community have set up this artificial barrier between us. I have a feeling that if we weren't under so much external pressure, I could get to like him.

And then there's Cass, who was at Church last Sunday.

We live in a really small, tightly constrained and controlled synthetic world, and there are some aspects of the way it's organized that make its artificiality glaringly obvious. For example, we don't have fashions, not in the sense of spontaneous design creativity that spawns waves of imitation and recomplication. (Creativity is a scarce resource at the best of times, and with barely a hundred of us living here so far, there just isn't enough to go round.) What we do have is a strangely frenetic ersatz fashion industry, in the form of whatever's in the shops. Somewhere there's a surviving catalogue of styles from the dark ages, probably compiled from a museum, and the shops change their contents regularly, compelling us to buy new stuff every few cycles or fall out of date. (It's another conformity-promoting measure: forget to update your wardrobe contents, leave yourself open to criticism.) This month hats are in fashion, ridiculous confections with wide brims and net veils that shadow the face. I can cope with hats, although I don't like the brims or the veils—I keep catching them on things, and they get in the way.

But let me get back to Cass, the subject of my hopes and worries . . .

I'm standing beside Sam as usual, holding the hymnbook and moving my lips, letting my eyes rove around the other side of the aisle. A new cohort arrived last week and the Church is packed—they'll have to extend it soon. I'm trying to pick out the newcomers because I don't want to get them mixed up with the older cohorts. Maybe it's a bit of Jen's calculated cynicism rubbing off on me, but I'm learning to guess someone's degree of alienation by how long they've been around. I have a feeling I might be able to make some allies among the new intake as long as I look for them early in the conditioning cycle, before the score whores get their claws in.

For some reason Mick is sitting with—standing among—the new folks this week, and I automatically glance at the woman to his left. I do a double take. She's wearing a long-sleeved blue dress with a high collar, and a hat with a black veil that covers her face. She's got lots of makeup smeared around her eyes. Her mouth is a red slash, and her cheeks are colorless. But it's definitely Cass, and she's holding the hymnbook as if she's never seen one before.

Is that you, Kay? I wonder, tantalized by her presence. I've been holding on to that promise Kay extracted from me—"You'll look for me inside, won't you?" And Cass . . . she knows ice ghoul society. *If Mick wasn't so crazy with jealousy that he doesn't want her out in public, if—*

Sam nudges me discreetly in the ribs. People are closing their hymnbooks and sitting down. I hastily follow suit. (Don't want anyone to notice me, don't want to attract unwanted attention.)

"Dearly beloved," drones Fiore, "we are a loving congregation, and today we welcome to our bosom the new cohort of Eddie, Pat, Jon"—

and he names seven other fresh victims—"who I am sure you will take under your wings and strive to befriend in due course. We also offer a belated welcome to sleepyhead Cass, who has finally deigned to grace us with her fragrant presence . . ." He twitters on in like vein for some time, preaching a sermon of saccharine subordination illustrated periodically with some anecdote of misdoing. Vern, it seems, got falling-down drunk and vomited in Main Street two nights ago, while Erica and Kate had a stand-up fight so violent that it put Erica in hospital, along with Greg and Brook, who tried to pull Kate off her. Kate is now in prison, paying the price for her outburst in days on bread and nights on water, and by the time Fiore gets through excoriating her, there's an angry undercurrent of disapproval in the congregation. I glance sidelong at Cass, trying not to be too obtrusive about it. I can't make out her face—the veil shadows her expression effectively—but I'm pretty sure that if I could see her, she'd look frightened. Her shoulders are set, defensive, and she's hunched slightly away from Mick.

Once we go outside into the open air, I grab a glass of wine and down it rapidly, keeping close to Sam. Sam watches me, worried. "Something wrong?"

"Yes. No. I'm not sure." There are butterflies in my stomach. Cass is the most isolated of the wives in Cohort Four, the one who hasn't been allowed out anywhere—and could Sam stop me doing anything if I felt like it? Mick is poison, not the subtle social toxin of a Jen, but the forthright venom of a stinging insect, brutal and direct. "There's something I want to check out. I'll be back in a few minutes, okay?"

"Reeve—take care?"

I meet his eyes. *He's concerned!* I realize. Abashed, I nod, then slide away toward the front of the Church and the main entrance.

Mick is talking to a little knot of hard-looking men, wiry muscles and close-cropped hair—guys I see digging or operating incredibly noisy machinery, chewing up the roads then filling them in again—he's gesticulating wildly. A couple of the Church attendants stand nearby, and there're a couple of women waiting in the doorway. I sidle toward the front door and go inside. The Church has emptied out, and there's only one person still there, loitering near the back pew.

"Kay? Cass?" I ask.

She looks at me. "R-Reeve?"

It's dark, and I can't be sure but there's something about her heavy eye shadow that makes me think of bruising. Her dress would effectively conceal signs of violence if Mick's been beating her. "Are you all right?" I ask.

Her eyes turn toward the entrance. "No," she whispers. "Listen, he's—don't get involved. All right? I don't need your help. Stay away from me." Her voice quavers with a fine edge of fear.

"I promised I'd look for you in here," I say.

"Don't." She shakes her head. "He'll kill me, do you realize that? If he thinks I've been talking to anyone—"

"But we can protect you! All you have to do is ask, and we'll get you out of there and keep him away from you."

I might as well not have bothered talking to her: she shakes her head and backs toward the door, her shoes clacking on the stone floor. Behind the veil, her face isn't simply frightened, it's terrified. And the white powder on her cheek isn't quite enough to conceal the ivory stain of old bruising.

Mick is waiting outside. If he sees me emerging after Cass, he'll probably go nuts. And I'm beginning to wonder if I'm right about her. When I called her Kay, she showed no sign of recognition. But would she? Kay is an alias, after all, and with her being just out of memory surgery, and me not being Robin but Reeve in this hall of mirrors—if after these tendays someone called me Robin, would I realize they were talking to me at first?

I glance around frustratedly, wondering if there's a back exit. I'm alone in the Church nave. It's not my favorite place, you understand, but right now it lacks the almost palpable sense of hostility it exudes when we're all herded together in our Sunday best, wondering who's going to be today's sacrificial victim. Waiting for Mick to lose interest and leave, I walk around the front of the big room, trying to get a new perspective on things.

I've never been forward of the pews before. *What does Fiore keep in his lectern?* I wonder, walking toward the altar. The lectern, seen from behind, is quite disappointing—it's just a slab of carved wood with a shelf set in it. There are a couple of paper books filed there, but no robocatamite to account for Fiore's peculiar mannerisms. The altar is also pretty boring. It's a slab of smoothly polished stone, carved into neatly rectilinear lines. The symbols of the faith, the sword and the chalice, sit atop a metal rack in the middle of the purple-dyed cloth that covers the stone. I look closer, intrigued by the sword. It's an odd-looking thing. The blade is dead straight, with a totally squared-off tip, and it's about a centimeter thick. With no edge on it and no taper it looks more like a mirror-polished billet of steel than a blade. It's got a basket hilt and a gray, roughened grip, suggesting a functional design rather than a decorative one. Something nags at me, an insistent phantom memory stump itching where a real one has been amputated. I'm certain I've seen a sword like this before. There are faint rectangular grooves in the outer surface of the basket, as if something has been removed. And the flat "edge" of the blade isn't quite right—it shines with the luster of fine steel, but there's also a faint rainbow sheen, a diffractive speckling at the edge of my gaze.

I break out in a cold sweat. My blouse feels like ice against the chill of my skin as I straighten up and hastily head for the small door that's visible on this side of the organist's bench. I don't want to be caught here, not now! Someone is having a little joke with us, and I feel sick to my heart at the thought that it might be Fiore, or his boss, Yourdon the Bishop. They're *playing* with us, and this is the proof. Who can I tell? Most people here wouldn't understand, and those that did—we've got no way out, not unless the experimenters agree to release us early. But the exit leads straight back into the clinics of the hospitaler-confessors, and I have a horrible gut-deep feeling that they're involved in this. Certainly they're implicated.

I've got to get out of here, I realize, aghast. The thing is, I've seen swords like that before. Vorpal blades, they call them, I'm not sure why. This one's obviously decommissioned, but how did it get here? They don't rely on the edge or point to cut, that's not what they're for. They belonged to, to—*Who did they belong to?* I rack my brains, trying to find the source of this terrible conviction that I stand in the presence of something utterly evil, something that doesn't belong in any experimental polity, a stink of livid corruption. But my treacherous memory lets me down again, and as I batter myself against the closed door of my own history, I walk back into the light outside, blinking and wondering if I might be wrong after all. Wrong about Cass being Kay. Wrong about Mick being violent. Wrong about the sword and the chalice. Wrong about who and what I am . . .

7

Bottom

TIME passes glacially slowly. I don't say anything to Sam about the events in Church, not about Cass's black eye nor the Vorpal blade on the Church altar. Sam is comfortable to live with, happy to listen to my depressive chatter about the women's world, but there's always the worm of worry gnawing at the back of my mind: *Can I trust him?* I want to, but I can't be sure he isn't one of my pursuers. It's a horrible dilemma, the risk/trust trade-off. So I don't talk about what I do in the garage, or on the basement exercise machine, and he doesn't volunteer much information about what he does at work. A couple of the ladies who lunch are talking about organizing dinner parties, but if we invited ourselves into that kind of social circle they'd expect us to reciprocate and the stress would be—well, I don't think either of us is up to it. So we live our lonely lives in each other's back pockets, and I worry about Cass, and Sam reads a lot and watches TV, trying to understand the ancients.

When we get home after the abortive meeting in Church, I use my netlink to check our group's public points. Jen is leading on social connectedness, while Alice is second on that score—her helping me with clothes seems to be good for her. To my surprise I see that I'm at the bottom of the cohort. There's an activity breakdown and it looks like

everyone else is having sex with their partner: Forming stable relationships is a good way to jack up your score, easy points. I backtrack a
week or two and see that Cass is regularly active with Mick.

For some reason I find this unaccountably depressing. The others
are watching, and I'm *supposed* to be involved with Sam, and I don't
want to do anything that might give Jen any sense of satisfaction whatsoever. It's an immature attitude, but I'm really conscious of the fact
that they're keeping an eye on my score, waiting for me to surrender.
Waiting for me to give Sam what they think he ought to want. Too bad
they don't really know us.

ABOUT two weeks later I finally reach the end of my tether. It's a hot,
tiresome Tuesday evening. I've spent the morning exercising outdoors—
there are still no neighbors, although a couple of families are due to
move in when the next cohort arrives in a couple of weeks' time—and
then worked in the garage all afternoon. I'm trying to relearn welding
the hard way, and I'm lucky not to have burned my arm off or electro-
cuted myself so far.

I have vague recollections of having done this stuff a long time ago, in
gigaseconds past, but it's so long ago that the memories are all second-
hand and I've clearly forgotten almost everything I knew. There's something wrong with my technique, and the pieces of spring steel I'm trying
to make into a single fabrication are going brittle around the weld. I try
bending the last one in the vise and the join I've just spent an hour working on snaps and small fragments go flying. If I was standing a bit farther
over to the left, I could have got one in the eye. As it is, I get a nasty shock
and go inside to try to sort our dinner out, because Sam is usually back
from work around now, and if left to his own devices, he'll flop down in
front of the television rather than sorting out food for both of us.

So I'm in the kitchen all on my own, rummaging through the frozen
packages in the freezer cupboard for something we both eat, and I manage to drop a pizza box on the floor. It splits open and the contents spill
everywhere. It's one of those moments when the whole universe comes
spinning down on the top of your head, and you realize how alone and

isolated you are, and all your problems seem to laugh at you. *Who do I think I'm kidding?* I ask myself, and I burst into tears on the spot.

I'm trapped in a wholly inadequate body, with only patchy memories of whoever I used to be left to prod me along in search of a better life. I'm trapped in a fun-house mirror reflection of a historical society where everyone was crazy by default, driven mad by irrational laws and meaningless customs. Here I am, thinking I remember being in rehab, reading a letter written to myself by an earlier version—and how do I *know* I wrote the letter to myself? I don't even remember doing it! For all I know it's a confabulation, my own bored attempt to inject some excitement into a life totally sapped of interest. Certainly the rant about people who are out to kill me seems increasingly implausible and distant—outright unbelievable, if not for the man with the wire.

I can't remember any reasons why anyone would want me dead. And even a half-competent trainee assassin would find killing me a trivial challenge at best, right now. I can't even put a frozen pizza in a microwave oven without dropping it on the floor. I'm spending my spare hours in the garage trying to weld together a crossbow and busily planning to make myself a sword when the bad guys, if they're real, are running a panopticon—a total surveillance society—and have weapons like the one on the Church altar, edged with the laser-speckling strangeness of supercondensates, waveguides for wormhole generators. Knives that can cut space-time. They'll come for me in the clear light of day, and they'll be backed by the whole police state panoply of memory editors and existential programmers. There's nowhere for me to run, no way out except through the T-gates controlled by the experimenters, and no way in bar the same, and I don't even know if I've lost Kay, or if Kay is Cass or someone else entirely, and I'm not sure why I let Piccolo-47 talk me into coming here. All I've got are my memories, and I can't even trust *them*.

I feel helpless and lost and very, very small, and I stare at the pizza through a blurring veil of tears, and right then I hear the front door lock click to itself and footsteps in the front hall, and it's more than I can bear.

Sam finds me in the kitchen, sobbing as I fumble around for the dustpan.

"What's wrong?" He stands in the doorway looking at me, a bewildered expression on his face.

"I'm, I—" I manage to get the box into the trash, then drop the brush on top of it. "Nothing."

"It can't be nothing," he insists, logically enough.

"I don't want to talk about it." I sniff and wipe my eyes on the back of my sleeve, embarrassed and hating myself for this display of weakness. "It's not important—"

"Come on." His arm is around my shoulders, comforting. "Come on, out of here."

"Okay."

He leads me out of the kitchen and into the living room and over to the big glass windows. I watch, not really comprehending, as he opens one of them. Floor to ceiling, it forms a door in its own right, a door into the back garden. "Come on," he says, walking out onto the lawn.

I follow him outside. The grass is getting long. *What do you want?* I wonder.

"Sit down," he says. I blink and look at the bench.

"Oh, okay." I sniff again.

"Wait here," he says. He vanishes back into the house, leaving me alone with my stupid and stupefying sense of inadequacy. I stare at the grass. It's moist (we had a scheduled precipitation at lunchtime, water drizzling gently from a million tiny nozzles embedded in the sky), and a snail is inching its way laboriously up a stem, close to my feet. Not far away there's another one. It's a good time for mollusks, who haul their world around with them, self-contained. I feel a momentary flash of envy. Here I am, trapped inside the biggest snail shell anyone can imagine, a snail shell made of glass that exposes everything we do to the monitors and probes of the experimenters. And in my hubris I think I can actually crawl out of my shell, escape into my own identity—

Sam is holding something out to me. "Here, have a drink."

I take the tumbler. It's blue glass, with a fizz of bubbles trapped in the weighted base and a clear liquid half-filling it. I sniff a bouquet of bitters and lemon.

"Go on, it won't poison you."

I raise my glass and take a mouthful. *Gin and tonic*, some submerged ghost of memory tells me. "Thanks." I sniff. He pours himself one, too. "I'm sorry."

"What for?" he asks, as he sits down next to me. He's shed his jacket and necktie, and he moves as if he's weary, as if he's got my troubles.

"I'm a dead loss." I shrug. "It just got too much for me."

"You're not a dead loss."

I look at him sharply, then have to sniff again. I wish I could get my sinuses fixed. "Yes I am. I'm wholly dependent on you—without your job, what would I do? I'm weak and small and badly coordinated, and I can't even cook a pizza for supper without dropping it all over the floor. And, and . . ."

Sam takes another mouthful. "Look," he says, pointing at the garden. "You've got this. All day." He shakes his head. "I get to sit in an office full of zombies and spend my time proofreading gibberish. There's always more make-work for me, texts to check for errors. It makes my head hurt. You've at least got this." He looks at me, a guarded, odd look that makes me wonder what he sees. "And whatever it is you're doing in the garage."

"I—"

"I don't mean to pry," he says, looking away shyly.

"It's not secret," I say. I swallow some more of my drink. "I'm making stuff." I nearly add, *It's a hobby*, but that would be a lie. And the one person I haven't actively lied to so far is Sam. I've got a feeling that if I start lying to him now, I'll be crossing some sort of irrevocable line. With only myself for an anchor, and knowing how fallible my memories are, I won't be able to tell truth from fantasy anymore.

"Making stuff." He rolls his glass between his big hands. "Do you want a job to go to?" he asks.

"A job?" That's a surprise and a half. "Why?"

He shrugs. "To see people. Get out of the house. To meet people other than the score whores, I mean. They're getting to you, aren't they?"

I nod mutely.

"Not surprising." He stays tactfully silent while I drain my glass.

To my surprise, I feel a little better. *Get a job!* "How do I find a job?" I ask. "I mean, not being a man—"

"You phone the Chamber of Commerce and ask for one." He puts his glass down. I look at it, see the two snails climbing opposite sides of the same blade of grass, leaving their iridescent trails of slime. "It's as simple as that. They'll send a car to pick you up and take you somewhere with room for a body. They didn't run you through the induction course when you arrived, but it's easy enough. I don't know what they'll find for you or how much they'll pay you—I'd guess a lot less than they pay men, that seems to be how they did things in the dark ages—but if you find it too boring, you can always phone the CC again and ask for something else."

"A job," I say, trying the words out for sense. It's crazy, actually, but no more so than anything else in this world. "I didn't know I could get one."

He shrugs. "It's not illegal or anything." A sidelong look. "They just didn't set it up by default. It's another of those things we're allowed to game if we're smart enough to think of it."

"And I'll meet people."

"It depends where you work." Sam looks uncertain for a moment. "Most jobs, there are zombies around—but they try to keep at least two humans in every workplace. And there are visitors. But it's pretty boring. I really didn't think you'd be interested."

"It can't possibly be as mind-destroying as this!" I clench my hands.

"Don't bet on it." He shakes his head. "Dark ages work was often meaningless, unpleasant, and sometimes dangerous."

"Not as dangerous to my sanity as not doing anything."

"That's my Reeve." Sam smiles, a brilliant expression that I don't often see and that makes me really envy the lucky woman he left behind outside the experiment. "I'll get you another drink, then go fix dinner. How about we eat out here instead of inside? Just for once."

"I'd like that a lot," I say fervently. "Just for once."

· · ·

IN the early hours of the morning I'm awakened by one of my recurring nightmares.

I have several different bad dreams. What distinguishes this one is the quality of the imagery in it. I'm a neomorph, male again and roughly orthohuman in body plan, but extensively augmented with mechabolic subsystems from the cellular level up. Instead of intestines, I have a compact fusion gateway cell. I have three hearts to keep my different circulatory fluids moving, skin reinforced with diamond fiber mesh, and I can survive in vacuum for hours. These are all trappings of my role as a soldier in the service of the Linebarger Cats, because I am a tank.

But that's not what makes the dream a nightmare.

We're one-point-one megaseconds into the campaign, and even though we—my unit—don't normally sleep, we're all under the influence of fatigue poisons from nearly twelve consecutive diurns of high-speed maneuvers. Hostilities with this polity commenced as soon as High Command established the orbital elements on one of their better-connected real-space nodes. The Six Fingers Green Kingdom has been particularly tenacious in its attempts to hold on to its corrupt A-gates, which are still infected with Curious Yellow censorbots and contaminating everyone who passes through them. They're one of the last hold-outs on the losing side; they've survived long after the other censorship redoubts succumbed to our maneuvers by virtue of their fanatically obscurantist network topology and a cunning mesh of internal firewalls. But we've identified the real-space location of one of their main switches, and that means we've got a node with massive fan-out to exploit once we can get our people into it. My unit is on the sharp end.

The assault vector is one end of a T-gate ten meters in diameter, boosted up to about thirty percent of c and free-falling through the icy outer limits of the cloud of debris orbiting the brown dwarf Epsilon Indi B. EI-B is not much bigger than a gas giant planet, and has a surface temperature of under a thousand degrees absolute—by the time you get out to its halo, whole light minutes away, the star is almost invisible. Cometary bodies orbit it in chilly isolation, as cold as the depths of interstellar space.

Our assault gate is unpowered and stealthy. It drifts through the perimeter defense field of the Six Fingers Green Kingdom orbital in a matter of seconds and skims past the huge cylinder at a range of under fifty kilometers, preposterously close yet very hard to spot. As it flashes by, my unit is one of several who make a high-speed insertion through the distal end of the wormhole. As far as the defenders are concerned, we appear out of empty space right on their doorstep. And as far as we're concerned, it's a death trap.

It takes us fifty seconds to cover the fifty kilometers to the habitat, decelerating all the way, mashed flat in our acceleration cages as our suits jink and dodge and shed penaids and decoys and graser bombs. We lose eighty percent of our numbers to point defense fire in that fifty-second period. It's absolute carnage, but even so we're lucky—the only reason any of us survive at all is because we're working for the Linebarger Cats, and the Cats specialize in applied insanity. Everyone knows that only a lunatic would attack across open space, so the Green Fingers have concentrated ninety percent of their firepower on the inside of their orbital, pointing at the proximal ends of their longjump T-gates, rather than outside on the hub, covering the barren real-space approaches.

I'm unconscious for most of the approach, my memories of it spooled by sensors on my suit and buffered for instant recall once my meatbody unvitrifies so I can take over. One moment I'm lying down and the suit is closing around me, and the next I'm standing in the wreckage of a compartment aboard the Green Finger orbital, memories of the insane charge alive in my mind as I pull out my sword, slave my blaster nodes to my eyeball trackers, exude more ablative foam, and head for the inhabited spaces.

Fast forward:

Dealing with the civilians once we've taken the polity is going to be difficult because they've all been censored by Curious Yellow—the original version carrying the censorship payload, not the later hacked tools of various inquisitions and cognitive dictatorships. The censorship payload doesn't just delete memories of forbidden things—it tends to leave spores in its victims' brains and a boot loader in their netlinks, and if they upload into a vulnerable A-gate it can wake up and infect the gate firmware. So we have to round up everyone on board the hab we've just ripped through with swords and blasters, and recycle them through our own crude decontamination gates.

Now, here's where the dreamlike logic kicks in. *Their* assembler gates are the advanced, elegant products of a mature techgnosis. But *our* A-gates are crude lash-ups, hand-built in a matter of tens of megaseconds using what knowledge we could salvage. We threw them together in a blind hurry when we realized how far the contamination extended—throughout all the A-gates of the Republic of Is, basically—and they're messy and inefficient and slow. What we've built works, but it isn't fast. So we're running our assault gates in half-duplex mode, disassembling and storing the citizens for subsequent virus scanning and reincarnation. And because we haven't secured all approaches, and because other nodes within the Six Fingers Green Kingdom are fighting back with vicious desperation, we have to move *fast*.

After about five thousand seconds of collecting struggling civilians and feeding them into the gates, Group Major Nordak calls me with new orders. "The bodies are slowing us up," she sends. "Just harvest the heads. We'll resurrect them all when we've got the situation under control."

There's a huge crowd of civilians in a holding square on Deck J, milling around in confusion and fear. Two of us are pulling people out of the crowd through a door, telling them it's for outbound processing. Some of them don't want to go, but arguing with tankies in full armor is futile, and they end up coming to us whether they want to or not, contusions and broken limbs the only difference it makes to their eventual fate. We take them through the inner set of doors that don't open until the outer ones are closed. Then *all* of them get reluctant, when they see Loral and me waiting on the other side of the inner door, with the assault gate and our swords and the pile of discards.

We take it in turns, alternating, because it's hard, stressful work. I grab a struggling victim, maybe a plump female orthohuman or a scrawny guy who really needs a new body—some of them have been living feral, refusing to go through the A-gates for fear of Curious

Yellow, until they actually *grow old*—and I pinion the victims and lay them down on the slimy blood-slick floor of the room. They usually scream, and in many cases they piss themselves as Loral brings his Vorpal sword down on the back of their neck between the C7 and T1 vertebrae. A twitch on the power button and there's more blood squirting and splashing everywhere than you could imagine, and they stop screaming. Loral pulls her sword out and I get off the body and chase the head, which is usually soaking wet, the eyelids twitching with postamputation shock. I throw the head into the A-gate, low and fast as I can, and the gate swallows it and processes the skull and hopefully gets them logged before permanent depolarization and osmotically induced apoptosis can set in. Then Loral grabs the discarded body and slings it onto the heap in the corner, which one of our fellow special action troops carts away on a pallet loader every so often, while I flail at the floor with a broom in a losing battle to stop the blood puddling around our feet.

It's a disgusting and unpleasant job, and even though we've gotten into the swing of it and are working as fast as we can, we're only averaging one civilian every fifty seconds. We've been working for a hundred kiloseconds now, one of eight teams on the job—processing maybe sixteen thousand people a diurn between us. And it's just my bitter bad luck that when the doors open and the guys on the other side fling the next body at us, kicking and screaming at the top of their lungs, it's my turn to use the sword and Loral's to hold them down and I'm already raising the blade when I look at the terrified face and depending on which variation of the nightmare this is I see that it's my own, or worse—

— *Kay's*—

—and I'm sitting up swallowing a scream and someone is cradling me in his arms and I'm covered in chilly sweat and shuddering uncontrollably. I slowly realize I'm in bed, and I've just kicked off the comforter. There's moonlight outside the window, and I'm in YFH-Polity and no matter how bad things are by day, they can't hold a candle to how bad things get in my dreams, and I whimper softly in the back of my throat.

"It's all right now, you're awake, they can't hurt you." Sam strokes my shoulders. I lean against him and manage to turn the whimper into a sigh. My heart is pounding like one of the jackhammers they use to repair the roads, and my skin is clammy. His arm tightens around me. "Would you like to talk about it?" he murmurs.

"It's"—*awful*—"a recurring dream. Memories"—inadequately redacted, I think—"from an earlier life. What I wanted to be rid of, coming back to haunt me." I speak haltingly because my mouth feels musty, and I'm not entirely awake, just frightened out of sleep by the shadows of my own past. *What's he doing in here?*

"You were thrashing around, moaning and muttering in your sleep," he says. "I was worried you were having a seizure."

It's not unheard of, even in this age. I push myself up on one arm but don't pull away from him—instead I pull my right arm out from under the bedding and hold him tight.

"I lost a lot in surgery," I say slowly. "If this is part of it, I wish it would stay lost."

"It's gone now." He speaks soothingly, and I wrap my other arm round him and hold on tight. He's big, he's stable, he's serious, and he's *solid*. Serious Sam. I lean my face into the depression at the base of his throat and inhale deeply, once, twice. His arm around me feels good, secure. *Security Sam.* My ribs shake as I swallow a nervy chuckle. "What's that?" he asks.

"Nothing," I tell his throat. I'm awake enough now to realize that I'm not the only one in this house who sleeps naked. But I find that I don't care—I trust Sam not to try and overpower me, not to do anything I don't want. Sam has somehow stepped across the threshold from being a mistrusted stranger into a friend, and I never noticed it happening. And now I don't want to be left alone here, and it's the most natural thing in the universe to hold on to him and to run my hand up and down his spine and stick my face into the base of his throat and inhale his natural scent. "Do you mind staying? I don't want to be alone."

He tenses slightly, but then I feel his hand running down my back, caressing my spine. I lean into his embrace. He feels so *alive*, the antithesis of everything in my blood-drenched memory dream. I've been sleeping alone and not really touching anyone, much less fucking, for at least a month now, and therefore it doesn't surprise me in the slightest to find that I'm becoming aroused, sensual, needing more skin contact and more touch and more smell. I lick the base of his throat and move one hand between his legs, and what I find there is no surprise, because he's been living the same life of self-denial too.

"Don't—" he mutters, but I'm not listening. Instead, I'm running my face down his chest, kissing him as I fondle what's down below, giving the lie to his disinterest.

Sam's been holding back because of a lover stranded in the real world without him, and I've been holding back because of pride and the greedy eyes watching my social score. We'll probably regret this in the morning, but right now I'm drunk on touch. I rub my cheek against his thigh and lick him hungrily, feeling his hands in my hair—

"No." He sounds hesitant. I take him in my mouth as far as I can, and he sounds as if he's strangling. "No, Reeve, please don't—" I carry on sucking and licking and he draws breath to say something and instead gasps a little, and I finish him off with a sense of anticlimax. *That was too fast, wasn't it?* Then he's standing on the other side of the bed, his back turned and his shoulders hunched. "I *asked* you to stop," he says sullenly.

It's a while before I can talk. "I needed—" I stop. My mouth is acrid with the aftertaste. "I want you to be happy." If I'm going to give in and humiliate myself in front of the score whores, the least I can do is throw it back in their faces.

"Well, that's not the right way to do it." He's tense and defensive, as if I've hurt him. "I thought we had an understanding." He sidles around the bed and out the door before I can think of anything to say, refusing to meet my eyes, and a minute or so later I hear the shower come on.

I'm completely awake by now, so I pull on my bathrobe to go downstairs and make a mug of coffee by way of a substitute for mouthwash, because there's no way I'm going to go into the bathroom while Sam's busy trying to rinse my saliva away. I've got some pride left, and right now I don't think I could look at him without yelling, *What about your self-control, eh?* He moons incessantly over this amazing lover he met outside the polity, but he's not too proud to let me fellate him—until afterward, when suddenly I'm an un-person. I could really hate him for that. But instead I sit in the kitchen with my cooling coffee, and I wait for the noise of the shower to cease and the light upstairs to go out. Then I tiptoe back to my bed and lie brooding until near dawn, wondering what possessed me. In the end, I resolve not offer him any intimacies ever again, until I've had a chance to spit in his imaginary lover's face in front of him. Finally, I sleep.

THE next day I don't stir from bed until Sam has left for work. Once I'm up, I phone the Chamber of Commerce. The zombie who takes my call sounds only marginally sapient but agrees to send a taxi for me the next morning. I go outside and jog up and down the road until I'm exhausted—which takes a lot longer now—then take a shower. I spend the rest of the day in the garage trying to do some more work on the crossbow, which is not going well. I wonder why I'm bothering: It's not as if I'm going to shoot anyone, is it?

I leave Sam a half-defrosted pizza and a note explaining how to cook it in the kitchen. By the time I come indoors it's dark, Sam's holed up in the living room with the TV on, and I have no trouble sneaking upstairs and going to bed without seeing him. It's easy to do, now that we're both avoiding each other.

I am troubled in my sleep. It's a different bad dream, nothing like as vivid as the slaughterhouse nightmare, but even more disturbing in some ways. Imagine you're a detective, or some other kind of investigator. And you're looking for people, bad people who hide in shadows. They've committed terrible crimes but they've altered everyone's memories so that nobody can remember what they did or who they are. *You* don't know what they did or who they are, but it's your job to find them and bring them to justice in such a way that neither they, nor anyone else, can forget what they did and the consequences of their actions. So you're a detective, and you're walking through twilit polityscapes hunting for clues, but you don't know who you are or why you're charged with this mission. For all you know, you may even be one of the criminals. They've made everybody forget who they are and what they did. Who's to say that they didn't do it to themselves, too? You could be guilty of a crime so horrible that it has no name and everyone's forgotten it, and you'll find the irrevocable logic of detection drawing you to place yourself under arrest and hand yourself over to the courts of a higher power. And you'll be tried and sentenced for a crime you don't understand and don't remember committing, and the punishment will be beyond human comprehension and leave you walking the twilit polityscapes, a ghost shorn of most of your memories except for a faint indelible stain of original sin. And you'll be there because you've been sent looking for a master criminal by way of atoning for your past actions. And you'll be on their trail, and one day you will find them and, reaching out a hand to grab them by the shoulder, you'll find yourself looking at the back of your own head—

I wake up sweating and sick with my heart pounding in the night, and there is no Sam. For a moment I feel defiant and angry at his absence, but then I think: *What have I done to my only friend here?* And I roll over and wash the pillow in bitter tears before dawn.

But the next day I start my new job.

8

Child Thing

THE taxi that takes me to the Chamber of Commerce arrives about half an hour after Sam leaves for work. I'm ready and waiting for it but nervous about the whole idea. It seems necessary in some ways—to assert my independence from Sam, get an extra source of income, meet other inmates, break out of the lonely rut of being a stay-at-home wife—but in other respects it's a questionable choice. I have no idea what they're going to find for me to do, it's going to take up a large chunk of my time, it'll probably be boring and pointless, and although I'll meet new people, there's no way of knowing whether I'll hate them on sight. What seemed like a good idea at the time is now turning out to be stressful.

The taxi operator is no use, of course—he can't tell me anything. "Chamber of Commerce," he announces. "Please leave the vehicle." So I get out and head toward the imposing building on my right, with the revolving door made of wood and brass, hoping my uncertainty doesn't show. I march up to the clerk on the front desk. "I'm Reeve. I've got an appointment at, uh, ten o'clock with Mr. Harshaw?"

"Go right in, ma'am," says the zombie, pointing at a door behind him with a frosted-glass window and gold-leaf lettering stenciled along the top. My heels clack on the stone floor as I walk over and open it.

"Mr. Harshaw?" I ask.

The room is dominated by a wide desk made out of wood, its top inlaid with a rectangle of dyed, preserved skin cut from a large herbivore. The walls are paneled in wood and there are crude still pictures in frames hanging from hooks near the top, certificates and group portraits of men in dark suits shaking hands with each other. A borderline-senescent male in a dark suit, his head almost bereft of hair and his waistline expanding, sits behind the desk. He half rises as I enter, and extends a hand. *Zombie?* I wonder doubtfully.

"Hello, Reeve." He sounds relaxed and self-confident. "Won't you have a seat?"

"Sure." I take the chair on the other side of the desk and cross my legs, studying his face. Sure enough there's a slight flicker of attention—he's watching me, aware of my body—which means he's real. Zombies simply aren't programmed for that. "How come I haven't seen you in Church?" I ask.

"I'm on staff," he says easily. "Have a cigarette?" He gestures at one of the wooden boxes on his desk.

"Sorry, I don't smoke," I say, slightly stiffly. I hate the smell, but it's not as if it's harmful, is it?

"Good for you." He takes one, lights it, and inhales thoughtfully. "You asked about job vacancies yesterday. As it happens, we have one right now that would probably suit you—I took the liberty of looking through your records—but it specifically excludes smokers."

"Oh?" I raise an eyebrow. Mr. Harshaw the staffer isn't what I expected, to say the least; I was winding myself up to deal with a dumb zombie fronting a placement database.

"It's in the city library. You'd only be working three days a week, but you'd be putting in eleven-hour shifts. On the plus side, you'd be the trainee librarian there. On the minus side, the starting salary isn't particularly high."

"What does the job involve?" I ask.

"Library work." He shrugs. "Filing books in order. Keeping track of withdrawals and issuing overdue notices and collecting fines. Helping people find books and information they're looking for. Organizing the stacks and adding new titles as they come in. You'd be working under Janis from cohort one, who has been our librarian since the early days. She's going to be leaving, which is why we need to train up a replacement."

"Leaving?" I look at him oddly. "Why?"

"To have a baby," he says, and blows a perfect smoke ring up at the ceiling.

I don't understand what he's saying at first, the concept is so alien to me. "Why would she have to leave her job to—"

It's his turn to look at me oddly. "Because she's pregnant," he says.

For a moment the world seems to be spinning around my head. There's a roaring in my ears, and I feel weak at the knees. It's a good thing I'm sitting down. Then I begin to integrate everything and realize just what's going on. Janis is *pregnant*—she's got a neonate growing inside her body like an encapsulated tumor, the way humans used to incubate their young in the wild, back before civilization. Presumably she and her husband had sex, and she was fertile. "She must be—" I say, then cover my mouth. *Fertile.*

"Yes, she and Norm are very happy," Mr. Harshaw says, nodding enthusiastically. He looks satisfied with something. "We're all very happy for them, even if it means we do have to train up a new librarian."

"Well, I'd be happy to see, I mean, to try," I begin, flustered, wondering, *Did she ask the medics to make her fertile?* Or, a sneaking and horrible suspicion, *Are we* already *fertile?* I know menstruation was some kind of metabolic sign that went with being a prehistoric female, but I didn't really put it all together until now. Having a child is hard—you have to actively seek medical assistance—and having one grow inside your body is even harder. The idea that the orthohuman bodies they've put us in are so ortho that we could *automatically* generate random human beings if we have sex is absolutely terrifying. I don't think the dark ages medics had incubators, and if I got pregnant I might actually have to go through a live childbirth. *In fact, if Sam and I had—*

"Excuse me, but where's the rest room?" I ask.

"It's the second door through there, on the left." Mr. Harshaw smiles to himself as I make a dash for it. He's still smiling five minutes later as I make my way back into his office, forcing my face into a mask of composure, refusing to acknowledge the stomach cramps that took me to the stalls. "Are you all right?" he asks.

"I am, now," I say. "I'm sorry about that, must be something I ate."

"It's perfectly all right. If you'd like to come with me, perhaps we can visit the library and I can introduce you to Janis, see if you get along?"

I nod, and we head out front to catch a taxi. I think I'm doing pretty well for someone who's just had her worldview turned upside down and whacked on with a hammer. How long does a neonate take to grow, about thirty megs? It puts a whole new face on the experiment. I have a sinking sense that I must have implicitly agreed to this. Somewhere buried in the small print of the release I signed there'll be some clause that can be interpreted as saying that I consent to be made fertile and if necessary to become pregnant and bring to term an infant in the course of the study. It's the sort of shitty trick that Fiore and his friends would delight in slipping past us while we're vulnerable.

After a few minutes I realize that the oversight we were promised by an independent ethics committee isn't worth a bucket of warm— whatever. The extreme scenario would be for us females to *all* get pregnant and deliver infants, in which case the experimenters are going to be responsible for the care of about a hundred babies, none of whom gave their consent to be raised in a simulated dark ages environment without access to decent medical care, education, or socialization. Any responsible ethics oversight committee would shit a brick if you suggested running an experiment like that. So I suspect the ethics oversight committee isn't very ethical, if indeed it exists at all.

I'm thinking these thoughts as Mr. Harshaw tells our zombie driver to take us to the municipal library. The library is in a part of town I haven't visited before, on the same block as City Hall and what Mr. Harshaw points out to me as the police station. "Police station?" I ask, looking blank.

"Yes, where the police hang out." He looks at me as if I'm very slightly mad.

"I would have thought the crime rate here was too low to need a real police force," I say.

"So far it is," he replies, with a smile I can't interpret. "But things are changing."

The library is a low brick building, with a glass facade opening onto a reception area, and turnstiles leading into a couple of big rooms full of shelves. There are books—bound sheaves of dumb paper—on all the shelves, and there are a *lot* of shelves. In fact, I've never seen so many books in my life. It's ironic, really. My netlink could bring a million times as much information to me on a whim, if it was working. But in the informationally impoverished society we're restricted to, these rows of dead trees represent the total wealth of available human knowledge. Static, crude scratchings are all we're to be permitted, it seems. "Who can access these?" I ask.

"I'll leave it to Janis to explain the procedures," he says, running his hand over his shiny crown, "but anyone who wants can withdraw—borrow—books from the lending department. The reference department is a bit different, and there's also the private collection." He clears his throat. "That's confidential, and you're not supposed to lend it to anyone who isn't authorized to read it. That probably sounds dramatic, by the way, but it's actually not very romantic. We just keep a lot of the documentation for the project on paper, so we don't need to violate the experimental protocol by bringing in advanced knowledge-management tools, and we have to store the paper somewhere when it's not in use, so we use the library." He holds the door open. "Let's go find Janis, shall we? Then we'll have lunch. We can discuss whether you want to work here, and if so, what your pay and conditions will be, and then if you take the job, we can work out when you'll start training."

JANIS is skinny and blond, with a haggard, worried-looking expression and long, bony hands that flutter like trapped insects as she describes things. After having to put up with Jen's machinations, she's like a breath of fresh air. On my first day I arrive at my new job early, but Janis is already there. She whisks me into a dingy little staff room round the back of one of the bookcases that I'd never suspected existed on yesterday's tour.

"I'm so glad you're here," she tells me, clasping her hands. "Tea? Or coffee? We've got both"—there's an electric kettle in the corner and she switches it on—"but someone's going to have to run out and fetch some milk soon." She sighs. "This is the staff room. When there's nobody about, you can take your breaks here or go out for lunch—we close between noon and one o'clock—and there's also a terminal into the library computer." She points at a boxy device not unlike a baby television set, connected by a coiled cable to a panel studded with buttons.

"The library has a computer?" I say, intrigued. "Can't I just use my netlink?"

Janis flushes, her cheeks turning pink. "I'm afraid not," she apologizes. "They make us use them just like the ancients would have, through a keyboard and screen."

"But I thought none of the ancient thinking machines survived, except in emulation. How do we know what its physical manifestation looked like?"

"I'm not sure." Janis looks thoughtful. "Do you know, I hadn't thought of that? I've got no idea how they designed it! It's probably buried in the experimental protocol somewhere—the nonclassified bits are all online, if you want to go looking. But listen, we don't have time for that now." The kettle boils, and she busies herself for a minute pouring hot water into two mugs full of instant coffee granules. I study her indirectly while her back's turned. There's not much sign of her pregnancy yet, although I think there might be a slight bulge around her waist—her dress is cut so that it's hard to tell. "First, I want to get you started on how the front desk works, on the lending side. We've got to keep track of who's borrowed what books, and when they're due back, and it's the easiest thing to start you on. So"—she hands me a coffee mug—"how much do you know about library work?"

I learn over the course of the morning that "library work" covers such an enormous area of information management that back during the dark ages, before libraries became self-organizing constructs, people used to devote their entire (admittedly short) lives to studying the theory of how best to manage them. Neither Janis—nor I—is remotely qualified to be a real dark age librarian, with their esoteric mastery of catalogue systems and controlled information classification vocabularies, but we *can* run a small municipal lending library and reference section with a bit of scurrying around and a lot of patience. I seem to have some historic skills in that direction, and unlike my experience with arc welding, I haven't erased all of them. I can remember my alphabet and grasp the decimal classification scheme immediately, and the way each book has a ticket in an envelope inside the front cover that has to be retained when it's loaned out makes sense, too . . .

It's only by midafternoon, when we've taken a grand total of five returns and had one visitor who borrowed two books (on Aztec culture and the care and feeding of carnivorous plants), that I begin to wonder why YFH-Polity needs anything as exotic as a full-time librarian.

"I don't know," Janis admits over a cup of tea in the staff room, her feet stretched out under the rickety white-painted wooden table. "It can get a bit busy—wait until six o'clock, when most people are on their way home from work, that's when we get most of our borrowers—but really, they don't *need* me. A zombie could do the job perfectly well." She looks pensive. "I suspect it's more to do with finding employment for people who ask for it. It's one of the drawbacks of the entire experiment. We don't exist in a closed-circuit economy, and if they don't constantly provide jobs for people, it'll all fall apart. So what we're left with is a situation where they pretend to pay us and we pretend to work. At least until they merge the parishes."

"Merge the—there are more?"

"So I'm told." She shrugs. "They're introducing us in small stages, so that we know who our neighbors are before we get linked into a large community and everything goes to pieces."

"Isn't that a bit of a pessimistic attitude?" I ask.

"Maybe so." She flashes me a rare grin. "But it's a realistic one."

I think I'm going to like Janis, her ironic sense of humor notwithstanding: I feel comfortable around her. We're going to work well together. "And the other stuff? The restricted archive? The computer?"

She waves it off. "All you need to know is, once a week Fiore comes and we unlock the closed room and leave him alone in it for an hour or two. If he wants to take any papers away, we log them and nag him until he brings them back."

"Anyone else?"

"Well." She looks thoughtful. "If the Bishop shows up, you give him access to all areas." She pulls a face. "And don't ask me about the computer, nobody told me much about how to use it, and I don't really understand the thing, but if you want to tinker with it during a slack period, be my guest. Just remember everything is logged." She catches my eye. *"Everything,"* she repeats, with quiet emphasis.

My pulse quickens. "On the computer? Or off it?"

"Book withdrawals," she says. "Possibly even what pages people look at. You notice they're all hardcovers? You'd be surprised how small even the dark age technés could make a tracking device. You could build them into book spines, able to sense which pages the reader was opening the book to. All without violating protocol."

"But protocol—" I stop. The television doesn't look very complex, technically, but is it? Really? What goes into a machine like that? There must be either cameras or a really complex rendering system . . .

"The dark ages weren't just *dark,* they were *fast.* We're talking about the period when our ancestors went from needing an abacus to add two numbers together to building the first emotional machines. They went from witch doctors with poisonous chemicals—who couldn't even reattach a cleanly severed limb—to tissue regeneration, full control of the proteome and genome, and growing body parts to order. From using rockets to get into orbit to the first tethered lift systems. And they did all that in less than three gigs, ninety old-time years."

She pauses for a sip of tea. "It is *very* easy for us moderns to underestimate the dark age orthos. But it's a habit you'll shed after you've been here for a while, and to give them their due, the clergy—the experimenters—have been here longer than the rest of us. Even Harshaw, and he works for them." She pronounces his name with distaste, and I wonder what he's done to offend her.

"You think they've got more of a handle on this than we do?" I ask, intrigued.

"Damn right." (Yes, she says "damn": she's obviously getting into the spirit of things, speaking in the archaic slang the real old-timers would have used.) "I think there's more going on here than meets the eye. They've made a lot more progress toward stabilizing this society than you'd expect for just five megs of runtime." Her eyes flicker sharply toward a corner of the room right above the door, and I follow the direction of her gaze. "In part it's because they can see everything, hear everything, including this. In part."

"But surely that's not all?"

She smiles at me enigmatically. "Break's over, kid. Time to go back to work."

I get home late, bone-tired from filing returned books and standing behind a counter for hours. I have a gnawing sense of apprehension as I walk in the door. The lights are on in the living room and I can hear the television. I head for the kitchen first to get something to eat, and that's where I am when Sam finds me.

"Where've you been?" he demands.

"Work." I attack a tin of vegetable soup and a loaf of bread tiredly.

"Oh." Pause. "So what are you doing?"

He's put the butter in the refrigerator so it's as hard as a rock. "Training to be the new city librarian. Three days a week at present, but it's an eleven-hour day."

"Oh."

He bends over to put a dirty plate in the washing machine. I manage to stop him just in time—it's full of clean stuff. "No, you need to unload it first, okay?"

"Huh." He looks irritated. "So the city needs a new librarian?"

"Yes." I don't owe him any explanations, do I? Do I?

"Do you know Janis?"

"Janis—" He looks thoughtful. "No. I didn't even know we had a library."

"She's leaving in a couple of months, and they need someone to replace her."

He begins to remove plates from the bottom tray in the washing machine and stack them on the work-top. "She doesn't like the job? If it's so bad, why are you taking it?"

"It's not that." I finally get the soup out of the can and into a saucepan on the red-glowing burner. "She's leaving because she's pregnant." I turn round to watch him. He's focusing on the dishwasher, pointedly ignoring me. Still sulking, I suspect.

"Pregnant? Huh." He sounds a little surprised. "Why would anyone want to have a baby in—"

"We're fertile, Sam."

I manage to catch the plates he was unloading just in time. I straighten up, about half a meter from his nose, and he's too flustered to avoid my gaze.

"We're *fertile*?"

"That's what Janis says, and judging by her state, I think she's probably got the evidence to prove it." I scowl at him for a moment, then turn back to the soup pan. "Got a bowl for me?"

"Ye-yes." The poor guy sounds genuinely shaken. I don't blame him—I've had a few hours to think about it, and *I'm* still getting used to the idea. "I'll just find one—"

"*Think about it.* We signed up to join the study knowing it would run for a hundred megs, yes? Funny thing about libraries: You can look things up in them. The gestation time for a human neonate in a host body is twenty-seven to twenty-eight megs. Meanwhile, we're all fertile, and we've been told we can earn points toward our eventual termination bonuses by fucking. The historical conception rate for healthy orthos having sex while fertile is roughly thirty percent per menstrual cycle. What does that sound like to you?"

"But I, I—I mean, you could have—" Sam holds a soup bowl in front of himself as if it's some kind of shield, and he's trying to keep me at bay.

I glare at him. "Don't say it."

"I—" He swallows. "Here, take it."

I take the bowl.

"I think I know what you thought I was going to say and you're right and I take it back even though I didn't say it. All right?" He says it very fast, running the words together as if he's nervous.

"You didn't say it."

I put the bowl down very carefully, because there really is no need to throw it at his head, and also because, once I calm down a fraction, I realize that in point of fact he's right, and he *didn't* say that if I'd fucked him the other night and become pregnant it would have been all my own fault. *Smart Sam.*

"It takes two to hold a grudge match." I lick my lips. "Sam, I'm very sorry about the other night." What comes next is hard to force out. "I shouldn't have taken advantage of you. I've been going through a bad patch, but that's no excuse. I'm not—I've never been—particularly good at self-restraint, but it won't happen again." *And if it does, you won't get an apology like this, that's for sure.* "Much as I like you, you're not big on poly and this, this shit—" My shoulders are shaking.

"You don't have to apologize," he says, and takes a step forward. Before I know what's happening he's hugging me, and it really is good to feel his arms around me. "It's my fault, too. I should have more self-control and I knew all along you were getting interested in me, and I shouldn't have put myself in a position where you might have thought—"

I sniff. *"Shit!"* I yell, and let go of him then spin round.

The soup is boiling over and there's a nasty smell from the burner. I kill the power and grab the handle to shift it somewhere safe, then hunt around for something to mop it up with. While I'm doing that Sam, like a zombie with a priority instruction, keeps methodically unloading the washing machine and transferring crockery to the cupboards. Eventually I get what's left of my soup into a bowl and pile my slices of bread on a plate, wondering why I didn't just use the microwave oven in the first place.

"By the time I get to eat this, it'll all be cold."

"My fault." He looks apologetic. "If I'd let you get on with it—"

"Uh-huh." *We're apologizing to each other for breathing loudly, what's wrong with us?* "Listen, here's a question for you. You know the contract you, uh, signed—do you remember if there was a *maximum* duration on participation?"

"A *maximum*?" He looks startled. "It just said minimum one hundred megs. Why?"

"Figures." I pick up my plate and bowl and head toward the living room. "Human neonates hatched in the wild in primitive conditions took at least half a gigasec to reach maturity."

"Are you"—he's following me—"saying what I think you're saying?"

I put my bowl and plate down on the end table beside the sofa and perch on the arm, because if I sit on the sofa, it'll try to swallow me for good. "Why don't you tell me what you think I'm saying?"

"I don't know." Which means he doesn't want to say. He sits down at the other end of the sofa and stares at me. "We're being watched, aren't we? All the time. Do you think it's wise to talk about it?"

I blow on my soup to speed evaporative cooling. "No, but there's no point being paranoid, is there? There are going to be a hundred of us in here in time, at least. I suspect we outnumber the experimenters twenty to one. Are you telling me they're going to monitor the real-time take on everything we say to each other, as we say it? A lot of the netlink score incidents are preprogrammed—just events we happen to trigger. Someone has an orgasm in proximity to their spouse, netlink triggers. A bunch of zombies see someone damaging property or removing clothing in public, their netlinks trigger. It doesn't mean someone is sitting on the switch watching the monitors all the time. Does it?"

(Actually it's possible that this *is* the case, if we're in a panopticon prison run by spooks rather than half-assed academics, but I'm not going to tell *them* that I know this, assuming *they* exist. No way. Especially as I don't know *why* I know this.)

"But if we're being watched—"

"Listen." I put my spoon down. "We are here for a *minimum* of three years, maximum term unspecified, and we are *fertile*. That sounds to me like what they've got in mind involves breeding a population of genuine dark ages citizens. This is a separate polity, in case you'd forgotten, which means it has a defensible frontier—the assembler that generated these bodies we're wearing. Assemblers don't just make things, they filter things: They're firewalls. Polities are de facto independent networks of tightly connected T-gates defined by the firewalls that shield their edges from whatever tries to come in through their longjump T-gates. Their borders, in other words. But you can have a polity without internal T-gates; what defines it is the frontier, not the interior. We're functioning under YFH's rules. Doesn't that mean that anyone born into the place will be under the same rules, too?"

"But what about freedom of movement?" Sam looks antsy. "Surely they can't stop them if they want to emigrate?"

"Not if they don't know there's an outside universe to emigrate to," I say grimly. I take a spoonful of soup and wince, burning the roof of my mouth. "*Ouch.* We aren't supposed to talk about our earlier lives. What if they tighten the score system a bit more, so that mentioning the outside in front of children, or in public, costs us points? Then how are the nubes going to figure it out?"

"That's crazy." He jerks his head from side to side emphatically. "Why would anyone want to do that? I can understand the original purpose of the experiment, to research the social circumstances of the dark ages by experimental archaeology. But trying to create a whole population of orthos, stuck in this crazy dark ages sim and not even knowing it's a historical re-enactment rather than the real universe . . . !"

"I'm not sure yet," I say tiredly. "I'm not at all sure what it's about. But that's the point. We're missing essential data."

"Right, right." He looks pained. "Do you suppose it's anything to do with why they were picking people straight out of memory surgery?"

"Yes, that's got to be part of it." I gaze at him across a cold continental rift of sofa. "But that's only a part." I was going to say *we have to get out of here,* but that's not enough anymore. And despite what I've just said publicly, there's stuff that I'm not going to talk about. Like, I don't think we'll *ever* be allowed out. I don't know if this will ever end. If the child thing is true, they may be prepared to hold us here indefinitely, or worse. And that's leaving aside the most important questions: *Why?* And why us?

I go to work the next day, and the one after that, and by the end of my third day I am exhausted. I mean, *shattered.* Library work doesn't sound as if it should be hard, but when you're working for eleven hours with a one-hour break in the middle for lunch, it wears you down. The daytime is almost empty, but there's a small rush of custom every evening around six o'clock, and I have to scurry to and fro hunting for tickets, filing returned books, collecting fines, and getting things sorted out. Then in the morning I end up pushing a trolley loaded with books around the shelves, returning the borrowed items and sorting out anything that's been put back on a shelf out of sequence. If there's any time left over, I end up dusting the shelves that are due for cleaning.

"How do you know the books know when they're being read?" I ask Janis, halfway through my second morning. "I mean, take this one." I heft it where she can see it, a big green clothbound sheaf of papers with a title like *The Home Vegetable Garden.*

"Look." Janis takes it from me and bends the cover back, so that the plastic protective sleeve on the spine bends.

I look. "Aha." I can just see something like a squashed fly in there, two hair-fine antennae running up to the stitching atop the spine. "Those are . . . ?"

"Fiber optics. That's my guess." Janis hums to herself as she closes the book and slides it back into the trolley. "I don't think they can hear you, but they can sense which page is open and track your eyeballs. The experimenters have been careful to give us all different faces, and we all have two working eyes. That's no accident. Not all the ancients had that. If you want to read a book secretly, you need mirrored sunglasses and a timer, so you turn each page after the same amount of time."

"How do you know all this?" I ask admiringly. "You sound like a professional—" The word *spy* is on the tip of my tongue, but I swallow it with a little shiver.

"Before I checked into the clinic, I used to be a detective." She gives me a long look. "It's a skill set I didn't ask them to erase. Thought it might come in handy in my new life."

"Then what did you—" I stop myself just in time. "Forget I asked."

"By all means." She chuckles drily. "Listen, they tell me that it's normal for me to check into hospital a week or two before the delivery, and to stay there for a couple of weeks afterward. Can I"—she sounds tentative—"ask a big favor of you?"

"What? Sure," I say blankly.

"I figure I'm going to be in bed a lot of the time, bored out of my mind, and there's only so much television you can watch in a day, and Norm is working, so he can't keep me company. Would you mind visiting me and bringing me some library books? So I don't lose track?"

"Why, I'd be delighted to!" I say it with perfect sincerity, because I mean it. If *I* ever ended up in some kind of dark ages hospital for three or four cycles I'd want visitors. "You'll let me know what you want, all right?"

"Thank you." Janis sounds grateful. "Now if you could just get the footstool, these go on the top shelf and I can't reach as high as you can."

On my third day I'm due to meet up with Jen and Angel and Alice and do lunch. Jen's picked the Dominion Cafe as today's venue, and I walk there from the library, whistling tunelessly. I'm feeling unaccountably smug. I've found something new to do, I've got a source of income all of my own, I know things that the ladies who lunch haven't got a clue about, and if only I wasn't spending half my waking hours in fear of the future and wishing I could get out of this glass-walled prison and hook up with Kay again, I'd probably be quite happy.

The Dominion Cafe is a lot plusher than the name makes it sound, and I feel a bit underdressed as the maître d' ushers me to the booth where Jen is holding court. Here I am in a plain skirt and sweater, while Jen wears ever-more-exotic concoctions of spun bug spit and must spend three or four hours a day on her makeovers and hair. Angel isn't so much trying to ape her as getting tugged along in the undertow, and Alice looks a bit uncomfortable in their presence. But what do I care? They're people to talk to, and we're chained together by the mutual scorefile so I can't ignore them. This must be how the ancients used to feel about their families.

"Hello all," I say, pulling out a chair. "And how are you today?"

Jen waves at a metal bucket on a stand, with some kind of cloth draped over it. "Livin' large!" she announces. "Girls, a glass for Reeve. Won't you join us in a little Chateau Lafitte '59?"

"A little—" She whisks the cloth off the bucket, and I see it's full of ice packed around a green glass bottle.

"Champagne," Alice says, a little apologetically. "Fizzy wine."

"I wouldn't say no." Angel holds out a fluted glass while Jen picks up the bottle and pours.

"Why, is there something in particular to celebrate?" Jen and Angel don't normally do their drinking before sunset. So I figure it must be good.

"Well." Jen's eye sparkles wickedly. "You might think it was something to do with your correcting your last social shortcoming at long last." I feel my face heating. "But that's not it." *Bitch.* "It's just that this is Alice's last drink for some time."

"Excuse me?" I say, unsure what's going on.

"About eight months to go," Alice says, dabbing at her lips with a napkin. Her eyes flicker from me to Jen and back again, as if looking for an offer of help.

"I—" I stop. Lick my lips. "You're pregnant?"

"Yes." Alice nods, a quick up and down. She doesn't look happy Jen, however, looks ecstatic.

"Here's to Alice and her baby!" She raises a glass of bubbly, and I echo the gesture because it would be rude not to, but as I take a mouthful of the sweet, fizzy wine I catch Alice's eye, and it's like there's a static discharge—I can see exactly what she's thinking.

"To your very good health," I tell her over the rim of my glass, and I'm pretty sure she gets the unspoken message because her shoulders slump slightly, and she takes a small sip from her own glass. I look at Jen. "And you?" I ask, before I can apply the brakes to my motor mouth.

Jen doesn't crack a smile. "Shouldn't be too long now," she remarks, calmly enough. "Then you can buy me a bottle of champagne too, eh?"

I manage to summon up the ghost of a grin from somewhere. "You must want a baby badly."

"Of course! And I'm not just going to stop at one." Jen smiles at me sympathetically. "Of course, I heard all about your job. It must be very difficult."

"It's not so bad," I manage, before retreating into the glass. *Bitch.* "You know Janis is pregnant, too?" *I'll bet you do.* "I'm training to be her replacement." *What is this, let's all overload the life-support system week?* "It's going to mean more work for the rest of us."

"Oh, you'll be next," Jen says, with a casual, airy certainty that makes my blood run cold. "You'll see things differently when you've got one of your own. I say, waiter! Waiter! Where's our menu?"

9

Secret

TIME passes fast, mostly because I spend the afternoon with my nose buried in the encyclopedia, trying to remedy my desperate ignorance of dark ages reproductive politics. Which I sense is putting me at a dangerous disadvantage.

The next day is the first of four days off. I sleep until well after Sam's departed for the office. Then I go downstairs and work out. Of the nine other houses on our stretch of road, one is now occupied by Nicky and Wolf—but Wolf has a job and Nicky, who is lazy beyond my wildest aspirations, sleeps in until noon. So I get in a good hour-long run, by the end of which I'm sweated up but not breathless or aching anymore. It's spring in our biome, and the trees and flowers are beginning to blossom. The air is full of the airborne seminiferous dust shed by the hermaphroditic vegetation. It tickles my nose, making me sneeze, but some of the scents that accompany it—attractants for insects—are nice.

After exercise I shower, dress in respectable clothes, and head downtown to the hardware store to spend some of my money. I feel better about spending it, knowing it's not Sam's money, even though I realize this is stupid because it's just meaningless scrip issued to keep the experiment working, not real currency. I come away from the store with a brazing torch, flux, solder, lots and lots of copper wire, and some other odds and ends. Then I go shopping for domestic items.

I hit the drugstore first, armed with a shopping list of things I'd never heard of until yesterday—things the encyclopedia listed under sexual health. Unfortunately, just knowing what to ask for doesn't translate into being able to buy it, and I gradually figure out that the omissions make a pattern. I can understand them not having progestogen-based medications on general sale. But why are there no absorbent sponges? Or the plastic penile sheaths I read about? After about half an hour of searching I conclude that the drugstore is useless by design. I ran across a rather shocking article on religious beliefs about sex and reproduction, and it looks like our drugstore was stocked on the basis of instructions from eclecticist hierophants. Something tells me that the lack of contraceptives is not an accident. I'm just surprised I haven't already heard people grumbling about it.

I have better luck in the department store, where I buy a new microwave oven, some clip-on spotlights, and a few other items. Then I go hunting for a craft shop. It takes me a while to find what I'm looking for, but in the end I discover one tucked in a corner of the shop, inside a pulp carton—a small wooden loom, suitable for weaving cloth. I buy it along with a whole bunch of woolen thread, just so nobody raises any eyebrows. Then I catch a taxi home and install my loot in the garage, along with the unfinished crossbow and the other projects.

It's time to get things moving. It's time I stopped kidding myself that I can fight my way out of here, and time that I stopped kidding myself that they're going to let me go in (I checked the calendar) another ninety-four megaseconds. Forget the crossbow and the other toys I've been playing with. I've got a stark choice. I can conform like everyone else, go native in the pocket polity they've established, settle down and get on with the job of creating a generation of innocents who don't even know there's another universe outside. Who knows? After a gigasecond, will I even remember I had another life? It's not as if my presurgery self left me much to hold on to . . .

Or I can try to find out what's really going on. Fiore and his shadowy boss, Bishop Yourdon, are doing something with this polity, that much is clear. This isn't just a straightforward experimental archaeology commune. Too many aspects of the setup turn out to be just plain wrong when you examine them closely. If I can figure out what they're trying to do, maybe I can discover a way out.

Which is why I spend a personal infinity laboriously stripping reel after reel of copper wire of its insulation and threading it onto the loom. The first step in figuring out what's going on is to get myself some privacy. I need a shoulder bag lined with woven copper mesh to accompany the bug-zapper (my repurposed microwave oven), and there's no way I could order a Faraday cage from one of the stores without setting off alarms.

It takes me nearly two weeks to weave a square meter of copper wire broadcloth, working in darkness by touch alone. It's really fiddly stuff to work with. The strands keep breaking or bending, it takes ages to strip the insulation, and besides, I've got a day job to go to.

Janis is complaining about minor back pains and spending a lot of time in the toilet each morning, coming out looking pale. There are fewer wisecracks and jokes from her, which is a shame. She's beginning to bulge around the waist, too. She's putting a brave face on it, but I think underneath it all she's terrified. The prospect of giving birth like an animal (with all the attendant risk and pain) is enough to scare anybody, even if it didn't come with the added horror of being chained down in this place for the indefinite hereafter, the product of your blood and sweat held hostage against your cooperation. What I want to know is, why isn't there a resistance movement? I suppose in a panopticon anyone organizing such a thing would have to be very quiet about it— or very naive—but I can't help wondering why I haven't seen any signs of even covert defiance.

I checked the YFH-Polity constitution in the library (there's a copy on a lectern out front, for everybody to read) and what's missing from it is as important as what's there. There's a bill of rights that explicitly includes the phrase "right to life" (which, if you read some dark ages histories, doesn't mean what a naive modern would think it means), and it goes on to explicitly waive all expectations of a right to privacy, which means they can enforce it against my will. *Ick.* The constitution is a public protocol specification defining the parameters within which YFH's legal system operates. Before I came here, it seemed irrelevant, but now it terrifies me—and I notice that it says nothing about a commitment to freedom of movement. That's been an axiom for virtually all human polities, ever since the end of the censorship wars mopped up the last nests of Curious Yellow and the memetic dictatorships. Not that you'll find any such knowledge in our shelves; history stops in 2050, as far as your reading in this library goes, and anyway, everything after 2005 is accessible only via the computer terminals, using an arcane conversational text interface that I'm still fumblingly trying to explore.

I see relatively little of Sam during this time. After our argument, indeed ever since the halfhearted reconciliation, he's withdrawn from me. Maybe it's the shock of learning about his reproductive competence, but he's very distant. Before that nightmare, before I messed up everything between us, I'd hug him when he got home from work. We'd have a laugh together, or chat, and we were (I'm sure of this) growing close. But since that night and our argument, we haven't even touched. I feel isolated and a bit afraid. If we *did* touch I'd—I don't know. Let's be honest about this: I have an active sex drive, but the thought of getting pregnant in here scares the shit out of me. And while there are other things we could do if we were inclined to intimacy, I find the whole situation is a very effective turnoff. So I can't really blame Sam for avoiding me as much as he can. The sooner he gets out of here the sooner he can rush off in search of his romantic love—assuming the bitch didn't give up on him and go in search of a poly nucleus to joyfully exchange bodily fluids with about five seconds after he joined the experiment. Sam broods, and, knowing his luck, he's fixated on someone I wouldn't give the time of day to.

That's life for you.

FOUR weeks into my new job, twelve weeks before Janis is due to go on maternity leave, I have another wake-up-screaming nightmare.

This time things are different. For one thing, Sam isn't there to hold me when I wake up. And for another, I know with cold certainty that this one is true. It's not simply a hideous dream, it's something that actually happened to me. Something that wasn't meant to be erased back at the clinic.

I'm sitting at a desk in a cramped rectangular room with no doors or windows. The walls are the color of old gold, dulled but iridescent, rainbows of diffraction coming off them whenever I look away from the desk. I'm in an orthohuman male body, not the mecha battlecorpse of my previous nightmare, and I'm wearing a simple tunic in a livery that I vaguely recognize as belonging to the clinic of the surgeon-confessors.

On the desk in front of me sits a stack of rough paper sheets, hand-woven with ragged edges. I made the stuff myself a long time ago, and any embedded snitches in it have long since died of old age. In my left hand I hold a simple ink pen with a handle made of bone that I carved from the femur of my last body—a little personal conceit. There's a bottle of ink at the opposite side of the desk, and I recall that procuring this ink cost a surprising amount of time and money. The ink has no history. The carbon soot particles suspended in it are isotopically randomized. You can't even tell what region of the galaxy it came from. Anonymous ink for a poison pen. How suitable . . .

I'm writing a letter to someone who doesn't exist yet. That person is going to be alone, confused, probably very frightened indeed. I feel a terrible sympathy for him in his loneliness and fear, because I've been there myself, and I know what he's going through. And I'll be right there with him, living through every second of it. (*Something's wrong. The letter I remember reading back in rehab was only three pages, but this stack is much thicker. What's happening?*) I hunch over the desk, gripping the pen tightly enough that it forms a painful furrow beside the first joint of my middle finger as I scratch laborious tracks across the fibrous sheets.

As I remember the sensations in my fingers, the somatic memory of writing, I get a horrible sense of certainty, a deep conviction that I really *did* send myself a twenty-page letter from the past, stuff I desperately needed to see—of which only three pages were allowed to reach me.

Dear self:

Right now you're wondering who you are. I assume you're over the wild mood swings by now and can figure out what other people's emotional states signify. If not, I suggest you stop reading immediately and leave this letter for later. There's stuff in here that you will find disturbing. Access it too soon, and you'll probably end up getting yourself killed.

Who are you? And who am I?

The answer to that question is that you are me and I am you, but you lack certain key memories—most importantly, everything that meant anything to me from about two and a half gigaseconds ago. That's an awfully long time. Back before the Acceleration most humans didn't live that long. So you're probably asking yourself why I—your earlier self—might want to erase all those experiences. Were they really that bad?

No, they weren't. In fact, if I hadn't gone through deep memory surgery a couple of times before, I'd be terrified. There's stuff in here, stuff in my head, that I don't want to lose. Forgetting is a little like dying, and forgetting seventy Urth-years of memories in one go is a lot like dying.

Luckily forgetfulness, like death, is reversible these days. Go to the House of Rishael the Exceptional in Block 54-Honey-September in the Polity of the Jade Sunrise and, after presenting a tissue sample, ask to speak to Jordaan. Jordaan will explain how to recover my latest imprint from escrow and how to merge the imprint block back into your mind. It's a difficult process, but it's stuff that belongs to you and brought you deep happiness when you were me. In fact, it's the stuff that makes me myself—and the lack of which defines who you are in relation to me.

Incidentally, one of the things you'll find in the imprint is the memory of how to access a trust fund with a quarter million écus in it.

(Yes, I'm a manipulative worm: I want you to become me again, sooner or later. Don't worry, you're a manipulative worm, too—you must be, if you're alive to read this letter.)

Now, the basics.

You are recovering from deep memory erasure surgery. You are probably thinking that once you recover you'll go and spend the usual *wanderjahr* looking for a vocation, find somewhere to live, meet friends and lovers, and set up a life for yourself. *Wrong.* The reason you are recovering from memory erasure surgery is that the people you work for have noticed a disturbing pattern of events centered on the Clinic of the Blessed Singularity run by the order of surgeon-confessors at City Zone Darke in the Invisible Republic. People coming out of surgery are being offered places in a psychological/historical research project aimed at probing the social conditions of the first dark age by live role-play. Some of these people have very questionable histories: in some cases, questionable to the point of being fugitive war criminals.

Your mission (and no, you don't have any choice—I already committed us to it) is to go inside the YFH-Polity, find out what's going on, then come back out to tell us. Sounds simple, doesn't it?

There's a catch. The research community has been established inside a former military prison, a glasshouse that was used as a reprogramming and rehabilitation center after the war. It was widely believed to be escape-proof at the time, and it's certainly a very secure facility. Other agents have already gone in. One very experienced colleague of yours vanished completely, and is now over twenty megs past their criticality deadline. Another reappeared eleven megaseconds late, reported to the prearranged debriefing node, and detonated a concealed antimatter device, killing the instance of their case officer who was in attendance.

I believe that both agents were compromised because they were injected into the glasshouse with extensive prebriefing and training. We have no idea what to expect on the other side of the longjump gate into YFH-Polity, but their security is tight. We expect extensive border firewalls and a focused counterespionage operation supported by the surveillance facilities of a maximum-security prison. There is likely to be stateful examination of your upload vector, and careful background checks before you are admitted. This is why I am about to undergo deep memory excision. Simply put, what you don't know can't betray you.

Incidentally, if you're experiencing lucid dreams about this stuff, it means you're overdue. This is the secondary emergent fallback briefing.

I'm about to have these memories *partially* erased—unlinked, but not destroyed—before I go into the clinic in City Zone Darke. It's a matter of erasing the associative links to the data, not the data itself. They'll re-emerge given sufficient time, hopefully even after the surgeon-confessors go after the *other* memories that I'll be asking them to redact. They can't erase what I don't know I've already forgotten.

What is the background to your mission?

I can tell you very little. Our records are worryingly incomplete, and to some extent this is a garbage trawl triggered by the coincidence of the names Yourdon, Fiore, and Hanta cropping up in the same place.

During the censorship wars, Curious Yellow infected virtually every A-gate in the Republic of Is. We don't know who released Curious Yellow, or why, because Curious Yellow appears to have been created for the sole purpose of delivering a psywar payload designed to erase all memories and data pertaining to something or other. By squatting the assemblers, Curious Yellow ensured that anyone who needed medical care, food, material provisions, or just about any of the necessities of civilization, had to submit to censorship. Needless to say, some of us took exception to this, and the subsequent civil war—in which the Republic of Is shattered into the current system of firewalled polities—resulted in a major loss of data about certain key areas. In particular, the key services provided by the Republic—a common time framework and the ability to authenticate identities—were broken. The situation was complicated, after the defeat of the Curious Yellow censorship worm, by the emergence of quisling dictatorships whose leaders took advantage of the Curious Yellow software to spread their own pernicious ideologies and power structures. In the ensuing chaos, even more information was lost.

Among the things we know very little about are the history and origins of certain military personnel conscripted into sleeper cells by Curious Yellow once the worm determined it was under attack by dissidents armed with clean, scratch-built A-gates. The same goes for the dangerous opportunists who took advantage of Curious Yellow's payload capability in order to set up their own pocket empires. Yourdon, Fiore, and Hanta came to our attention in connection with the psychological warfare organizations of no less than eighteen local cognitive dictator-ships. They are extraordinarily dangerous people, but they are cur-rently beyond our reach because they are, to put it bluntly, providing some kind of service to the military of the Invisible Republic.

What we know about the sleeper cells is this: In the last few megasecs of the war, before the alliance succeeded in shattering and then sanitizing the last remaining networks of Curious Yellow, some of the quisling dictatorships' higher echelons went underground. It is now almost two gigaseconds since the end of the war, and most people dis-miss the concept of Curious Yellow revenants as fantasy. However, I don't believe in ignoring threats just because they sound far-fetched. If Curious Yellow really *did* create sleeper cells, secondary pockets of in-fection designed to break out long after the initial wave was sup-pressed, then our collective failure to pursue them is disastrously shortsighted. And I am particularly worried because some aspects of the YFH-Polity experimental protocol, as published, sound alarmingly amenable to redirection along these lines.

My biggest reason for wanting you to have undergone major memory erasure prior to injection into YFH-Polity is this: I suspect that when the incoming experimental subjects are issued with new bodies, they are filtered through an A-gate infected with a live, patched copy of Curious Yellow. Therefore preemptive memory redaction is the only sure way of preventing such a verminiferous gate from iden-tifying you as a threat for its owners to eliminate.

I watch myself writing this letter to myself. I can read it as clearly as if it's engraved in my own flesh. But I can't see any marks in the paper, because my old self has forgotten to dip his pen in the ink, and he's long since fallen to scratching invisible indentations on the coarse sheets. I seem to stand behind his shoulder although his head is nowhere in my field of vision, and I try to scream at him, *No! No! That isn't how you do it!* But nothing comes out because this is a dream, and when I try to grab the pen, my hand passes right through his wrist, and he keeps writ-ing on my naked brain with his ink of blood and neurotransmitters.

I begin to panic, because being trapped in this cell with him has brought memories flooding back in, memories that he cunningly suppressed in order to avoid triggering Curious Yellow's redaction factories. It's a movable feast of horrors and exultation and life in the large. It's too much to bear, and it's too intense, because now I remember the rest of my earlier dream of swords and armor and the reversible massacre aboard a conditionally liberated polity cylinder. I remember the way our A-gate glitched and crashed at the end of the rescue as we threw the last severed head into its maw, and the way Loral turned to me, and said, "Well *shit*," in a voice full of world-weary disgust, and how I walked away and scheduled myself for deep erasure because I knew if I didn't, the memory of it all would drag me awake screaming for years to come—

—And I'm *awake*, and I make it to the toilet just in time before my stomach squeezes convulsively and tries to climb up my throat and escape.

I *can't* believe I did those things. I don't believe I *would* have committed such crimes. But I remember the massacre as if it was yesterday. And if those memories are false, then what about the rest of me?

NOT entirely by coincidence, the next day is my first run with the shoulder bag. It started life as a rectangular green vinyl affair. It now sports a black nylon lining that I've stitched together with much swearing and sucking of pricked fingertips to conceal the gleaming copper weave glued to its inside. It looks like a shopping bag until I fold over the inner flap. Then it looks like a full shopping bag with a black flap covering the contents. Right now it contains a carton of extremely strong ground espresso, a filter cone, and several small items that are individually innocuous but collectively damning if you know what you're looking at. It's a good thing the bag looks anonymous, because unless I'm hallucinating all my memories, what I'm going to take home from work in that bag today will be a whole lot less innocuous than coffee beans.

I get in to work at the usual early hour and find Janis in the staff room, looking pale and peaky. "Morning sickness?" I ask. She nods. "Sympathies. Say, why don't you stay here, and I'll get the returns sorted out? Put your feet up—I'll call you if anything comes up that I can't handle."

"Thanks. I'll do just that." She leans back against the wall. "I wouldn't be here but Fiore's coming—"

"You leave that to me," I say, trying not to look surprised. I wasn't expecting him so soon, but I've got the bag, so . . .

"Are you sure?" she asks.

"Yes." I smile reassuringly. "Don't worry about me, I'll just let him in and leave him to get on with things."

"Okay," she says gratefully, and I go back out and get to work.

First I pile yesterday's returns on the trolley and push them around the shelves, filing them as fast as I can. It only takes a few minutes—most of the inmates here don't realize that reading is a recreational option, and only a handful are borrowing regularly. But then I skip the dusting and cleaning I'm supposed to do today. Instead, I grab my bag from behind the reception station, dump it on the bottom shelf of the trolley, and head for the shelves in the reference section next to the room where the Church documents are stored.

Into the bag goes a dictionary of sexual taboos, held in the reference shelves because some weird interpretation of dark age mores holds that libraries wouldn't lend such stuff out. It's my cover story in case I'm caught, something naughty but obviously trivial. Then I leave the trolley right where it is with the bag tucked away on the bottom shelf, where it's not immediately obvious. I head back to the front desk. My palms are sweating. Fiore is due to visit the archive, which means advancing my plans. Janis has always handled him before—but she's ill, I'm running the shop, and there's no point delaying the inevitable. I've got all my excuses prepared, anyway. I've barely been able to sleep lately for rehearsing them in my head.

Around midmorning a black car pulls up and parks in front of the library steps. I put down the book I'm reading and stand up to wait behind the counter. A uniformed zombie gets out of the front and opens the rear door, standing to one side while a plump male climbs out. His dark, oily hair shines in the daylight: The white slash of his clerical collar lends his face a disembodied appearance, as if it doesn't quite belong to the same world as the rest of his body. He walks up the steps to the front door and pushes it open, then walks over to the desk. "Special reference section," he says tersely. Then he looks at my face. "Ah, Reeve. I didn't see you here before."

I manage a sickly smile. "I'm the trainee librarian. Janis is ill this morning, so I'm looking after everything in her absence."

"Ill?" He stares at me owlishly. I look right back at him. Fiore has chosen a body that is physically imposing but bordering on senescence, in the state the ancients called "middle age." He's overweight to the point of obesity, squat and wide and barely taller than I am. His chins wobble as he talks, and the pores on his nose are very visible. Right now his nostrils are flared, sniffing the air suspiciously, and his bushy eyebrows draw together as he inspects me. He smells of something musty and organic, as if he's spent too long in a compost heap.

"Yes, she has morning sickness," I say artlessly, hoping he won't ask where she is.

"Morning sick—*oh*, I see!" His frown vanishes instantly. "Ah, the trials we have to suffer." His voice oozes a slug-trail of sympathy. "I'm sure this must be hard for her, and for you. Just take me to the reference room, and I'll stay out of your way, child."

"Certainly." I head for the gate at the side of the station. "If you'd like to follow me?" He knows exactly where we're going, the old toad, but he's a stickler for appearances. I lead him to the locked door in the reference section, and he produces a small bunch of keys, muttering to himself, and opens it. "Would you like a cup of tea or coffee?" I ask hesitantly.

He pauses and gives me the dead-fish stare again. "Isn't that against library regulations?" he asks.

"Normally yes, but you're not going to be in the library proper," I babble, "you're in the archive and you're a responsible person so I thought I'd offer—"

He stops being interested in me. "Coffee will be fine. Milk, no sugar." He disappears into the room, leaving his keys with the lock.

Now. Heart pounding, I head for the staff room. Janis is snoozing when I open the door. She sits up with a start, looking pale. "Reeve—"

"It's all right," I say, crossing over to the kettle and filling it up. "Fiore's here, I let him in. Listen, why don't you go home? If you're feeling ill, you shouldn't really be here, should you?"

"I've been thinking about thinking." Janis shakes her head. I rummage around for the coffee and filter papers and set the stand up over the biggest mug I can find. I scoop the coffee into the paper with wild abandon, stopping only when I realize that making it too strong for Fiore will be as bad as not getting him to drink it all. "You shouldn't think too much, Reeve. It's bad for you."

"Is it really?" I ask abstractedly, as I peel the foil wrapping from a small tablet of chocolate I bought at the drugstore and crumble half of it into the coffee grounds as the kettle begins to hiss. I wad the foil into a tight ball and flick it into the wastebasket.

"If you think about getting out of here," says Janis.

"Like I said, I'll call you a taxi—"

"No, I mean out of *here*." I turn round and she looks at me with the expression of a trapped animal. It's one of those moments of existential bleakness when the cocoon of lies that we spin around ourselves to paper over the cracks in reality dissolve into slime, and we're left looking at something really ugly. Janis has got the bug, the same one I've got, only she's got it worse. "I can't stand it anymore! They're going to put me in hospital and make me pass a skull through my cunt, and then they're going to have a little accident and I'll bleed out and they'll give me to Hanta to fix with her tame censorship worm. I'll come out of the hospital smiling like Yvonne and Patrice, and there won't be any *me* left, there'll be this thing that *thinks* it's me and—"

I grab her. "Shut *up*!" I hiss in her ear. "It's not going to happen!" She sobs, a great racking howl welling up inside her, and if she lets it out, I'm completely screwed because Fiore will hear us. "I've got a plan."

"You've—*what*?"

The kettle is boiling. I gently push away her groping hands and reach over to turn it off. "Listen. Go home. Right now, right this instant. Leave Fiore to me. *Stop panicking*. The more isolated we think we are, the more isolated we become. I won't let them mess with your head." I smile at her reassuringly. "Trust me."

"You." Janis sniffles loudly, then lets go of me and grabs a tissue off the box on the table. "You've got—no, don't tell me." She blows her nose and takes a deep breath, then looks at me again, a long, hard, appraising look. "Should have guessed. You don't take shit, do you?"

"Not if I can help it." I pick up the kettle and carefully pour boiling water into the funnel, where it will damp down the coffee grounds, extract the xanthine alkaloids and dissolve the half tab of Ex-Lax hidden in the powder, draining the sennoside glycosides and the highly diuretic caffeine into the mug of steaming coffee that, with any luck, will give Fiore a strong urge to take ten minutes on the can about half an hour after he drinks it. "Just try to relax. I should be able to tell you about it in a couple of days if things work out."

"Right. You've got a plan." She blows her nose again. "You want me to go home." It's a question.

"Yes. Right now, *without* letting Fiore see you here—I told him you were at home, sick."

"Okay." She manages a wan smile.

I pour milk into the coffee mug, then pick it up. "I'm just going to give the Reverend his coffee," I tell her.

"To give—" Her eyes widen. "I see." She takes her jacket from the hook on the back of the door. "I'd better get out of your way, then." She grins at me briefly. "Good luck!"

And she's gone, leaving me room to pick up the mug of coffee and the other item from the sink side and to carry them out to Fiore.

THE simplest plans are often the best.

Anything I try to do on the library computer system will be monitored, and the instant I try to find anything interesting they'll know I know about it. It's probably there as a honeypot, to snare the overly curious and insufficiently paranoid. Even if it isn't, I probably won't get anywhere useful—those old conversational interfaces are not only arcane, they're feeble-minded.

To put one over on these professional paranoids is going to take skill, cunning, and lateral thinking. And my thinking is this: If Fiore and the Bishop Yourdon and their fellow experimenters have one weak spot, it's their dedication to the spirit of the study. They won't use advanced but anachronistic surveillance techniques where nonintrusive ones that were available during the dark ages will do. And they won't use informational metastructures accessible via netlink where a written manual and records on paper will do. (Either that, or what they write on paper really *is* secret stuff, material that they won't entrust to a live data system in case it comes under attack.)

The ultrasecure repository in the library is merely a room full of shelves of paper files, with no windows and a simple mortise lock securing the door. What more do they need? They've got us locked down in the glasshouse, a network of sectors of anonymous orbital habs subjected to pervasive surveillance, floating in the unmapped depths of interstellar space, coordinates and orbital elements unknown, interconnected by T-gates that the owners can switch on or off at will, and accessible from the outside only via a single secured longjump gate. Not only that, but our experimenters appear to have a rogue surgeon-confessor running the hospital. Burglar alarms would be redundant.

After I knock on the door and pass Fiore his coffee, I go back to the reference section and while away a few minutes, leafing through an encyclopedia to pass the time. (The ancients held deeply bizarre ideas about neuroanatomy, I discover, and especially about developmental plasticity. I guess it explains some of their ideas about gender segregation.)

As it happens, I don't have to wait long. Fiore comes barging into the office and looks about. "You—is there a staff toilet here?" he demands, glancing around apprehensively. His forehead glistens beneath the lighting tubes.

"Certainly. It's through the staff common room—this way." I head toward the staff room at a leisurely pace. Fiore takes short steps, breathing heavily.

"*Faster,*" he grumbles. I step aside and gesture at the door. "Thank you," he adds as he darts inside. A moment later I hear him fumbling with the bolt, then the rattle of a toilet seat.

Excellent. With any luck, he'll be about his business before he looks for the toilet paper. Which is missing because I've hidden it.

I walk back to the door to the restricted document repository. Fiore has left his key in the lock and the door ajar. *Oh dear.* I pull out the bar of soap, the sharp knife, and the wad of toilet paper I've left in my bag on the bottom shelf of the trolley. *What an unfortunate oversight!*

I wedge my toe in the door to keep it from shutting as I pull the key out and press it into the bar of soap, both sides, taking care to get a clean impression. It only takes a few seconds, then I use some of the paper to wipe the key clean and wrap up the bar, which I stash back in the bag. The key is a plain metal instrument. While there's an outside chance that there's some kind of tracking device built into it in case it's lost, it *isn't* lost—it moved barely ten centimeters while Fiore was taking his ease. And I'm fairly certain there are no silly cryptographic authentication tricks built into it—if so, why disguise it as an old-fashioned mortise lock key? Mechanical mortise locks are surprisingly secure when you're defending against intruders who're more used to dealing with software locks. Finally, if there's one place that won't be under visual surveillance, it's Fiore's high-security document vault while the Priest is busy inside it. This is the chain of assumptions on which I am gambling my life.

I make sure my bag is well hidden at the bottom of the trolley before I slowly make my way back to the staff room. And I wait a full minute before I allow myself to hear Fiore calling querulously for toilet paper.

The rest of the day passes slowly without Janis to joke with. Fiore leaves after another hour, muttering and grumbling about his digestion. I transfer the soap bar to the wheezing little refrigerator in the staff room where we keep the milk. I don't want to risk its melting or deforming.

That evening, I lock up and go home with my heart in my mouth, sweat gluing my blouse to the small of my back. It's silly of me, I know. By doing this, I risk rapid exposure. But if I don't do it, what will happen in the longer term is worse than anything that can happen to me if they catch me with a library book from the reference-only collection and a distorted bar of soap. It won't be just me who goes down screaming. Janis knew about Curious Yellow and was afraid of surveillance. I don't know why, or where from, but it's an ominous sign. Who *is* she?

Back home, I head for the garage before I go indoors. It's time to power up the bug zapper in anger for the first time. The bug zapper is the cheap microwave oven I bought a few weeks ago. I've had the lid off, and I've done some creative things with its wiring. A microwave oven is basically a Faraday cage with a powerful microwave emitter. It's tuned to emit electromagnetic energy at a wavelength that is strongly absorbed by the water in whatever food you put inside. Well, that's no good for me, but with some creative jiggery-pokery, I've succeeded in buggering up the magnetron very effectively. It now emits a noisy range of wavelengths, and while it won't cook your dinner very well, it'll make a real mess of any electronic circuits you put in it. I open the door and shake my copper-lined bag's contents into it, then reach through the fabric to retrieve the bar of soap. I really don't want to fry *that*—Fiore might get suspicious if he got the shits every time he went to the library while I was on duty.

I drop the oven door shut and zap the book for fifteen seconds. Then I push a button on the breadboard I've taped to the side of the oven. No lights come on. There's nothing talking in the death cell, so it looks like I've effectively crisped any critters riding the book's spine. Well, we'll see when I take it back to the library, won't we? If Fiore singles me out in Church the day after tomorrow, I'll know I was wrong, but sneaking a dirty book out of the library for an evening isn't in the same league as stealing the keys to—

The plaster of paris! Mentally, I kick myself. I nearly forgot it. I tip the right amount into an empty yoghurt pot with shaky hands, then measure in a beaker of water and stir the mass with a teaspoon until it begins to get so hot that I have to juggle it from hand to hand.

Ten minutes pass, and I line a baking tray with moist whitish goop (gypsum, hydrated calcium sulphate). Hoping that it has cooled enough, I press both sides of the soap bar into it a couple of times. I have a tense moment worrying about the soap's softening and melting, and I make the first impression too early, while the plaster's so soft and damp that it sticks to the soap, but in the end I think I've probably got enough to work with. So I cover the tray with a piece of cheesecloth and go inside. It's nearly ten o'clock, I'm hungry and exhausted, tomorrow is my day off, and I am going to have to go in to work anyway to visit Janis and make sure she's all right. But next time Fiore visits the repository, I'm going to be ready to sneak in right after he's left. And then we'll see what he's hiding down there . . .

10

SUNDAY dawns, cool and mellow. I groan and try not to pull the bed-clothes over my head. By one of those quirks of scheduling, yesterday was a workday for me, tomorrow is another, and I'm feeling hammered by the prospect of two eleven-hour days. I'm not looking forward to spending half my day off in forced proximity to score whores like Jen and Angel, but I manage to force myself out of bed and rescue my Sunday outfit from the pile growing on the chair at the end of the room. (I need to take a trip to the dry-cleaners soon, and spend some time down in the basement washing the stuff I can do at home. More drudgery on my day off. Does it ever stop?)

Downstairs, I find Sam laboriously spooning cornflakes into a bowl of milk. He looks preoccupied. My stomach is tight with anxiety, but I force myself to put a pan of water on the burner and carefully lower a couple of eggs into it. I need to make myself eat: My appetite isn't good, and with the exercise regime I'm keeping up, I could start burning muscle tissue very easily. I glance inward at my mostly silent netlink to check my cohort's scores for the week. As usual, I'm nearly the bottom-ranked female in the group. Only Cass is doing worse, and I feel a familiar stab of anxiety. I'm nearly sure she isn't Kay, but I can't help feeling for her. She has to put up with that swine Mick, after all. Then my stomach does another flip-flop as I remember something I have to do before we go.

"Sam."

He glances up from his bowl. "Yes?"

"Today. Don't be surprised if—if—" I can't say it.

He puts his spoon down and looks out the window. "It's a nice day." He frowns. "What's bugging you? Is it Church?"

I manage to nod.

His eyes go glassy for a moment. Checking his scores, I guess. Then he nods. "You didn't get any penalties, did you?"

"No. But I'm afraid I—" I shake my head, unable to continue.

"They're going to single you out," he says, evenly and slowly.

"That's it." I nod. "I've just got a feeling, is all."

"Let them." He looks angry, and for a moment I feel frightened, then I realize that for a wonder it isn't me—he's angry at the idea that Fiore might have a go at me in Church, indignant at the possibility that the congregation might go along with it. *Resentful.* "We'll walk out."

"No, Sam." The water is boiling—I check the clock, then switch on the toaster. Boiled eggs and toast, that's how far my culinary skills have come. "If you do that, it'll make you a target, too. If we're both targets . . ."

"I don't care." He meets my gaze evenly, with no sign of the reticence that's been dogging him for the past month. "I made a decision. I'm not going to stand by and let them pick us off one by one. We've both made mistakes, but you're the one who's most at risk in here. I haven't been fair to you and I, I"—he stumbles for a moment—"I wish things had turned out differently." He looks down at his bowl and murmurs something I can't quite make out.

"Sam?" I sit down. "Sam. You can't take on the whole polity on your own." He looks sad. *Sad?* Why?

"I know." He looks at me. "But I feel so helpless!"

Sad and angry. I stand up and walk over to the burner, turn the heat right down. The eggs are bumping against the bottom of the pan. The toaster is ticking. "We should have thought of that before we agreed to be locked up in this prison," I say. I feel like screaming. With my extra-heavy memory erasure—which I have a sneaking suspicion exceeded anything my earlier self, the one who wrote me the letter and then forgot about it, was expecting—I'm half-surprised I got here in the first place. Certainly if I'd known Kay was going to dither, then pull out, I'd probably have chosen to stay with her and the good life, assassins or no.

"Prison." He chuckles bitterly. "That's a good description for it. I wish there was some way to escape."

"Go ask the Bishop; maybe he'll let you out early for bad behavior." I pop the toast, butter it, then scoop both eggs out of the water and onto my plate. "I wish."

"How about we walk to Church today?" Sam suggests hesitantly, as I'm finishing breakfast. "It's about two kilometers. That sounds a long way, but—"

"It also sounds like a good idea to me," I say, before he can talk himself out of it. "I'll wear my work shoes."

"Good. I'll meet you down here in ten minutes." He brushes against me on his way out of the kitchen, and I startle, but he doesn't seem to notice. Something's going on inside his head, and not being able to open up and ask is frustrating.

Two kilometers is a nice morning walk, and Sam lets me hold his hand as we stroll along the quiet avenues beneath trees suddenly exploding with green and blue-black leaves. We have to walk through three tunnels between zones to get to the neighborhood of the Church—there are no lines of sight longer than half a kilometer, perhaps because that would make it obvious that our landscapes are cut from the inner surfaces of conic sections rather than glued to the outside of a sphere by natural gravity—but we see barely anyone. Most folks travel to Church by taxi, and they won't be leaving their homes until we're nearly there.

The Church service starts out anticlimactic for me, but probably not for anyone else. After leading the congregation into a tub-thumping rendition of "First We Take Manhattan," Fiore launches into a long peroration on the nature of obedience, crime, our place in society, and our duties to one another.

"Is it not true that we were placed here to enjoy the benefits of civilization and to raise a great society for the betterment of our children and the achievement of a morally pure state?" he thunders from the pulpit, eyes focused glassily on an infinity that lurks just behind the back wall. "And to this end, isn't it the case that our social order, being the earthly antecedent of a Platonic ideal society, must be defended so that it has room to mature and bear the fruit of utopia?" *A real tub-thumper*, I realize uneasily. I wonder where he's going? People are shuffling in the row behind me; I'm not the only one with a guilty conscience.

"This being the case, can we admit to our society one who violates its cardinal rules? Must we forebear from criticizing the sins out of consideration for the sensibilities of the sinner?" He demands. "Or for the sensibilities of those who, unknowing, live side by side with the personification of vice incarnate?"

Here it comes. I feel a mortal sense of dread, my stomach loosening in anticipation of the denunciation I can feel coming. There's got to be more to this than a furtive library book, and I have a horrible sinking feeling that he's figured out the soap impression and the plaster of paris and the mold I'm preparing for the duplicate keys—

"No!" Fiore booms from the pulpit. "This cannot be!" He thumps the rail with one fist. "But it grieves me to say that it *is*—that Esther and Phil are not merely adulterating their souls by sneaking their vile intimacies behind the backs of their ignorant and abused spouses, but are adulterating the fabric of society *itself*!"

Huh? It's not me that he's going after, but the thrill of relief doesn't last long: There's a loud grumble of rage from the congregation, led by cohort three, whose members are the ones Fiore is accusing. Everyone else looks round and I turn round with them—not to go with the crowd could be dangerous right now—and see a turbulent knot a couple of rows back, where well-dressed churchgoers are turning on each other. A frightened female and a defensive-looking male with dark hair are looking around apprehensively, not making eye contact, but trying to—yes, they're looking for escape routes as Fiore continues. Something tells me they're too late.

"I would like to thank Jen in particular for bringing this matter to my attention," Fiore says coolly. My netlink dings, registering the arrival of more points than I'd normally rack up in a month, an upward adjustment I can blame on the fact that I'm in the same cohort as the little snitch. She's scored big-time with this accusation of adultery. "And I ask you, what are we going to do about the sickness in our midst?" Fiore scans the audience from his pulpit. "What is to be done to cleanse our society?"

My sick sense of dread is back with a vengeance. This is going to be a whole lot worse than anything I'd anticipated. Normally, Fiore singles a handful out for ridicule, laughter, the pointed finger of contempt—a minor humiliation for sneaking a library book out of the reference section would be nothing out of the ordinary. But this is big bad stuff, two people caught subverting the social foundations of the experiment. Fiore is on a roll of righteous indignation, and the atmosphere is getting very ugly indeed. A roar goes up from the back benches, incoherent rage and anger, and I grab Sam's hand. Then I check my netlink and freeze. *He's fined cohort three all the points he's just given to Jen!* "Let's get out of here before it turns nasty," I mutter into Sam's ear, and he nods and grips my hand back tightly. People are standing up and shouting, so I sidle toward the side of the aisle as fast as I can, using my elbows when I have to. I can see Mick on the other side, yelling something, the tendons on the sides of his neck standing out like cables. I don't see Cass. I keep moving. There's a storm brewing, and this isn't the time or place to stop and ask.

Behind me Fiore shouts something about natural justice, but he's barely audible over the crowd. The doors are open, and people are spilling out into the car park. I gasp with pain as someone stomps on my left foot, but I stay upright and sense rather than see Sam following me. I make it through the crush in the doorway and keep going, dodging small clumps of people and a struggling figure, then Sam catches up with me. "Let's *go*," I tell him, grabbing his hand.

There are people in front of us, clustered around—it's Jen. "Reeve!" she calls.

I can't ignore her without being obvious. "What do you want?" I ask.

"Help us." She grins widely, her eyes sparkling with excitement as she spreads her arms. She's wearing a little black-silk number that displays her secondary sexual characteristics by providing just a wisp of contrast: her chest is heaving as if she's about to have an orgasm. "Come on!" She gestures at the dark knot near the Church entrance. "We're going to have a party!"

"What do you mean?" I demand, looking past her. Her husband, Chris, is conspicuously absent. Instead, she's acquired a cohort of her own, followers or admirers or something, Grace from twelve and Mina from nine and Tina from seven—all of them are from newer cohorts than our own—and they're watching her, looking to her as if she's a leader . . .

"Purify the polity!" she says, almost playfully. "Come on! Together we can keep everyone in line and hold everything together—and earn loads more points—if we make a strong enough statement right now. Send the deviants and perverts a message." She looks at me enthusiastically. "Right?"

"Uh, right," I mumble, backing away until I bump into Sam, who's come up behind me. "You're going to teach them a lesson, huh?"

I feel Sam's hand tightening on my shoulder, warning me not to go too far, but Jen's in no mood to pick up minor details like sarcasm: "That's right!" She's almost rapturous. "It's going to be real fun. I got Chris and Mick ready—"

There's a high-pitched scream from somewhere behind us. "Excuse us," I mumble, "I don't feel so good." Sam shoves me forward, and I stumble past Jen, still stammering out excuses, but the situation isn't critical. Jen doesn't have time to waste on broken reeds and moral imbeciles, and she's already drifting toward the group in the Church door, shouting something about community values.

We make it to the edge of the car park before I stumble again and grab hold of Sam's arm. "We've got to stop them," I hear myself saying. I wonder what that toad Fiore thought he was unleashing when he transferred so many points from one cohort to another. Doing that to the score whores is only going to have one result. At the very least, cohort three is going to rip the shit out of Phil and Esther—but now we've got Jen, trying to spin the whole thing as social cleansing in order to position herself at the head of a mob. I can see a hideous new reality taking shape here, and I want nothing to do with it.

"Not sensible." He shakes his head but slows down.

"I mean it!" I insist. I swallow, my throat dry. "They're going to beat Phil and Esther—"

"No, it's already gone past that point." There's an ugly quaver in his voice.

I dig my heels in and stop. Sam stops, too, of necessity—it's that, or shove me over. He's breathing heavily. "We've got to do something."

"Like. What?" He's breathing deeply. "There're at least twenty of them. Cohort three *and* the idiots who've gotten some idea that they can parade their virtue by joining in. We don't stand a chance." He glances over his shoulder, seems to shudder, then suddenly pulls me closer and speeds up. "Don't stop, don't look round," he hisses. So of course I stop dead and turn around to see what they're doing behind us.

Oh shit, indeed. I feel wobbly, and Sam catches me under one arm as I see what's happening. There are no more screams, but that doesn't mean nothing's going on. The screaming is continuing, inside the privacy of my own skull. "They *planned* this," I hear myself say, as if from the far end of a very dark tunnel. "They prepared for it. It's not spontaneous."

"Yes." Sam nods, his face whey-pale. There's no other explanation, crazy as it seems. "Ritual human sacrifice seems to have been a major cultural bonding feature in pretech cultures," he mutters. "I wonder how long Fiore's been planning to introduce it?"

They've got two ropes over the branches of the poplars beside the Church, and two groups are busy heaving their twitching payloads up into the greenery. I blink. The ropes seem to curve slightly. It might be centripetal acceleration, but more likely it's because my eyes are watering.

"I don't care. If I had a gun, I'd shoot Jen right now, I really would." I suddenly realize that I'm not feeling faint from fear or dread, but from anger: "The bitch needs killing."

"Wouldn't work," he says, almost absently. "More violence just normalizes the killing, it doesn't put an end to it: They're having a *party* and all you could do is add to the fun . . ."

"Yeah, I—but I'd feel better." Jen had better have bars on her windows and sleep with a baseball bat under her pillow tonight, or she's in trouble. And she royally deserves it, the mendacious bitch.

"Me too, I think."

"Can we do anything?"

"For them?" He shrugs. There's no more screaming, but a tone-deaf choir has struck up some kind of anthem. "No."

I shiver. "Let's go home. Right now."

"Okay," he says, and together we start walking again.

The singing follows us up the road. I'm terrified that if I look back, I'll break down: There's absolutely nothing I can do about it, but I feel a filthy sense of complicity with them. As for Fiore . . . he's got it coming. Sooner or later I'll get him. But I'm going to bite my tongue and not say a word about that for now, because I've a feeling he staged this little show to teach us a lesson about the construction of totalitarian power, and right this moment all the spies and snitches are going to be wide-awake, looking for signs of dissent.

A kilometer up the road and ten minutes away from the ghastly feeding frenzy, I tug at Sam's arm. "Let's slow down a little," I suggest. "Catch our breath. There's no need to run anymore."

"Catch our—" Sam stares at me. "I thought you were mad at me."

"No, it's not you." I carry on walking, but more slowly.

His hand on my arm. "We didn't join in."

I nod, wordlessly.

"Three-quarters of the people there were as horrified as we were. But we couldn't stop it once it got going." He shakes his head.

I take a deep breath. "I'm pissed at myself for not making a stand

while there was time. You can game a mob if you know what you're doing. But once people get moving in groups like that, it's really hard to
contain them. Fiore didn't need to set that off. But he did, like pouring
gasoline on a barbecue." Both of which are items I've only lately become acquainted with. "And after that sermon and the score transfer,
he couldn't have stopped it even if he wanted to."

"You sound like you think it's a matter of choice." I glance sidelong
at him: Sam's not stupid, but he doesn't normally talk in abstractions.
He continues: "Do you really think you could have stopped it? It's implicit in this society, Reeve. They set us up to make it easy to make people kill for an abstraction. You saw Jen. Did you really think you could
have stopped her, once she got going?"

"I should have stuck a knife in her ribs." I trudge on in silence for a
few seconds. "I'd probably have failed. You're right, but that doesn't
make me feel better."

We walk slowly along the road, baking beneath the noonday heat of
an artificial late-spring sun in our Sunday outfits. The invertebrates
creak in the long, yellowing grass, and the deciduous trees rustle their
leaves overhead in the breeze. I smell sage and magnolia in the warm
air. Ahead of us the road dives into a cutting that leads to another of the
tunnels with built-in T-gates that conceal the true geometry of our inside-
out world. Sam pulls out his pocket flashlight, swinging it from his wrist
by a strap.

"I've seen mobs before," I tell him. *If only I could forget.* "They
have a peculiar kind of momentum." I feel weak and shaky as I think
about it, about the look on Phil's face—I hardly knew him—and the
hunger stalking the shadow of the crowd. Jen's malicious delight.
"Once it gets past a certain point, all you can do is run away fast and
make sure you have nothing to do with what happens next. If everybody did that, there wouldn't be any mobs."

"I guess." Sam sounds subdued as we walk into the penumbra of
the tunnel. He switches his flashlight on. The cone of light bobs around
crazily ahead of us as the road swings to the left.

"Even a sword-fighting fool of a hero can't divert a mob like that on
their own once it gets going," I tell him, as much for my own benefit as

anything else. "Not without battle armor and some heavy weaponry, because they're going to keep coming and coming. The ones behind can't see what's happening up front, and the fool who stands in the way without backup is going to end up a dead fool really fast, even if he kills a whole load of them. And anyway, your sword-fighting fool, he's no smarter than any of them in the mob. The time to stop the mob is before it gets started. To stand up in front of it first, and tell it no."

We're walking into the dark curve of the tunnel, out of sight of either entrance. Sam sighs.

"I knew someone who'd do that," he says wistfully. "The man I fell in love with. He wasn't a fool, but he'd know how to handle a situation like that."

The *man*? Sam doesn't seem like the type to me—until I remember that I'm seeing him through gender-trapped eyes, the same way he's looking at me, and that I've got no way of knowing who or what Sam was before he volunteered for the experiment. "Nobody could do that," I tell him gently.

"Maybe so. But I think I'd trust Robin's judgment before I'd trust—"

I stop as suddenly as if I have just walked into a wall. The hairs on the back of my neck are all standing on end, and my stomach is knotting up again as if I'm going to be sick.

"What's wrong?" asks Sam.

"The person on the outside you've been pining after," I say carefully. "He's called Robin. Is that right?"

"Yes." He nods. "I shouldn't have said, we'll get penalized—"

I grab his hand like it's a floatation aid and I'm drowning. "Sam, Sam." *You idiot! Yes, you!* (I'm not sure which of us I mean.) "Did it ever occur to you to ask if maybe I *knew* Robin?"

"Why? What good would that have done?" His pupils are huge and dark in the twilight.

"You are the biggest—" I don't know what to say. Truly, I don't. *Stunned* is the mildest word that describes how I feel. "The name you gave Robin was Kay, right?"

"You—"

"Kay. Yes or no?"

He tenses and tries to pull his hand away. "Yes," he admits.

"O-kay." I don't seem to be able to get enough air. "Well, Sam, we are going to continue on our way home, now, aren't we? Because who we were before we came here doesn't make any difference to where we are now, does it?"

His expression is impossible to read in the darkness. "You must be Vhora—"

I nearly slap him. Instead, I reach out with the index finger of my free hand and touch his lips. "Home first. Then we talk," I tell him, stomach still churning, aghast at my own stupidity and willful blindness. *Okay, so I walked right into this one.* And I think I just sprained my brain. *Now what?*

He sighs. "All right." He still doesn't use my name. But he turns to shine the flashlight ahead of us. And that's when I see the outline of the door in the opposite wall.

IT'S funny how the more we travel the less we see.

Traveling via T-gates, we avoid the intervening points between the nodes because the gate is actually a hole in the structure of space, and in a very real sense there are no intervening points. And it's not much different in a car. You get in, you tell the zombie where to take you, and he steps on the gas. Not that there's a machine under the bonnet that clatteringly detonates liquid distilled from ancient fossilized biomass (just a compact gateway generator and a sound effects unit), but it feels the same, in terms of your interaction with your surroundings.

Meanwhile, outside the cars and the corridors and the gates and the head games we deny playing with each other, there's a real universe. And sometimes it smacks you in the face.

Like now. I have known all along, in an abstract kind of way, that we're living in a series of roughly rectangular terrain features laid out on the curved inner surface of several huge colony cylinders, spinning to provide centripetal acceleration (a substitute for gravity), in orbit around who-knows-what brown dwarf stars. The sky is a display screen, the wind is air-conditioning, the road tunnels are a necessary part of the illusion, and if you go for a walk in the overgrown back lot you'll find a steep hill or cliff that you can't climb because it goes vertical only a few meters up. I haven't given much thought to how it's all stitched together, other than to assume there are T-gates in each road tunnel. *But what if there's another way out?*

I clutch his hand. "Stop! Turn your flashlight back. Yes, there, right there."

"What is it?" he asks.

"Let's see." I tug him toward it. "Come on, I need the light."

The tunnel walls are made of smoothly curved slabs of concrete set edge to edge, forming a hollow tube maybe eight meters in diameter. The road is a flat sheet of asphalt, its edges meeting the walls of the tube just under the halfway point up its sides. (Now that I think about it, what could be running under the road deck? It might be solid, but then again, there could be just about anything down there.) What I've noticed is a rectangular groove in the opposite wall. Close up I can see it's about a meter wide and two meters high, a plain metal panel sunk into one side of the tunnel. There's no sign of any handle or lock except for a hole a few millimeters in diameter drilled halfway up it, just beside one edge.

"Give me the flashlight."

"Here." He passes it without argument. I get as close to the wall as I can and shine the light into the crack. Nothing, no sign of hinges or anything. I crouch down and shine it into the hole. Nothing there, either. "Hmm."

"What is it?" he asks anxiously.

"It's a door. Can't say more than that." I straighten up. "We can't do anything about it right now. Let's go home and think about this."

"But if we go home, we won't be able to talk!" In the dim light of the flashlight, his eyes look very white. "They'll overhear everything."

"They don't see everything," I reassure him. "Come on, let's go home. This afternoon I want you to mow the lawn."

"But I—"

"The lawn mower is in the garage," I continue implacably. "Along with other things."

"But—"

"If they're not waiting for us when we get home, they're not monitoring the tunnels, Sam. Noticed your netlink recently? No? Well, we don't seem to have lost any points just now. There are gaps in the surveillance coverage. I think I know somewhere else they're not monitoring, and you ought to know we're not the only people who want out."

I feel safe telling him that much, even though if they brainscoop me and feed me to Curious Yellow right now, it'll take down three of us: me and Sam and Janis. Kay may be in denial right now but she—*No, you've got to keep thinking of him as Sam,* I tell myself—isn't, I think, going to sell me to the bad guys. I am pretty sure I can read Sam well enough now to know what's bugging him. It's funny how I was in lust with Kay but couldn't tell if I trusted her. Now I trust Sam, but I doubt I'll ever fuck him again. Life is strange, isn't it? "You *do* want out, don't you?" I ask.

"Yes." He sounds tremulous.

"Then you're going to have to trust me for a little bit longer because I don't have an escape plan yet." I squeeze his hand. "But I'm working on it."

Together, we walk toward the light.

THAT afternoon Sam changes into jeans and a T-shirt and mows the lawn. I'm in the garage wearing overalls and safety goggles, because I've made a mold from the plaster of paris dies and I'm pouring solder into it, casting a lead copy of the key to Fiore's cabinet of curiosities. The lead key won't turn in the lock, but it'll do okay as a template for the engraving disk and the small bar of brass I've got waiting.

To confuse anyone who's watching, I've got some props sitting around—a wooden wall plaque purchased from the fishing store, a plate to engrave with some meaningless dedication. When I showed Sam what I was up to he blinked rapidly, then nodded. "It's for the women's freehand cross-stitch club," I said, pulling the explanation right out of my ass. There is no such club, but it *sounds* right, a backup explanation that will trigger a reflex in whatever watcher is scanning us for anomalous behavior.

We may be living in a glass jar with bright lights and monitors trained on us the whole time, but it's not likely that everything we do is being watched by a live human being in real time. We massively outnumber the experimenters, and they're primarily interested in our public socialization. (At least, that's the official story.) To monitor an intelligent organism properly requires observers with a theory of mind at least as strong as the subject. We subjects outnumber the experimenters by a couple of orders of magnitude, and I've seen no sign of strongly superhuman metaintelligences being involved in this operation, so I think the odds are on my side. If we *are* up against the weakly godlike, I might as well throw in the towel right now. But if not . . . You can delegate all you want to subconscious mechanisms, but you run the risk of them missing things. *Sic transit gloria panopticon.*

The Church services are almost certainly monitored in every imaginable way. But after Church, Fiore and his friends will be too busy rerunning the lynching from every imaginable angle and trying to figure out how the social dynamics of a genuine dark ages mob operate. They won't be watching what I get up to in the garage until much later, probably just a bored glance at a replay to make sure I'm not fucking my neighbor's husband or weeping hysterically in a corner. Because they're used to using A-gates to fab any physical artifacts they need, they probably look at what I'm doing as some sort of dark ages hobby and view me as a slightly dull but basically well-adjusted wife. I even gained a couple of points last week for my weaving. I laboriously hand-wove a Faraday cage lining for my shoulder bag right under their noses, and they treated it as if I was diligently practicing a traditional feminine craft! There are gaps in their surveillance and bigger gaps in their understanding, and those gaps are going to be their downfall.

Concentrating on making the key and thinking about how much I am beginning to hate them is a good way for me to avoid confronting what happened outside the Church this morning. It's also a good distraction from the wall I walked into in my head, or the door in the tunnel, or any of the other troubling shit that's happened since I woke up this morning and thought it was going to be just another boring Sunday.

After what feels like a few infinitely tense minutes—but the lying clock insists it's been the best part of four hours—I emerge from the garage. The hot morning sunlight has softened into a roseate afternoon glow, and insects creak beneath a turquoise sky. It looks like I've missed an idyllic summer afternoon. I feel shaky, tired, and very hungry indeed. I'm also sweating like a pig, and I probably stink. There's no sign of Sam, so I go indoors and hit the bathroom, dump my clothes and dial the shower up to a cool deluge until it washes everything away.

When I get out of the shower I rummage around in my wardrobe until I find a sundress, then head downstairs with the vague idea of sorting out something to eat. A microwave dinner perhaps, to eat on the rear deck while the illusory sun sets. Instead, I run into Sam coming in through the front door. He looks haggard.

"Where've you been?" I ask. "I was going to sort out some food."

"I've been with Martin and Greg and Alf, down at the churchyard." I look at him, closer. His shirt is sweat-stained, and there's dirt under his fingernails. "Doing the burying."

"Burying?" For a moment I don't get what he's talking about, then it clicks into place and I feel dizzy, as if the whole world's revolving around my head. "The—you should have told me."

"You were busy." He shrugs dismissively.

I peer at him, concerned. "You look tired. Why don't you go have a shower? I'll fix you some food."

He shakes his head. "I'm not hungry."

"Yes you are." I take hold of his right arm and lead him toward the kitchen. "You didn't eat any lunch unless you sneaked a snack while I wasn't looking, and it's getting late." I take a deep breath. "How bad was it?"

"It was—" He stops and takes a deep breath. "It was—" He stops again. Then he bursts into tears.

I am absolutely certain that Sam has seen death before, up close and personal. He's at least three gigs old, he's been through memory surgery, he's experienced the psychopathic dissociation that comes with it, he's hung out with dueling fools like me in my postsurgery phase, and he's lived among pretech aliens for whom violent death and disease are all part of life's unpalatable banquet. But there's an enormous difference between the effects of a semiformal duel between consenting adults, with A-gate backups to make resurrection a minor headache, and cleaning up after a random act of senseless brutality in a Church parking lot.

Forget about no backups, no second chances, nobody coming home again scratching their heads and wondering what was in the two kiloseconds of their life that's just vanished. The difference is that *it could have been you.* Because, when you get down to it, the one thing you know for sure is that if the toad in the pulpit had got the wrong name, it would have been *you* up there in the branches, choking and twitching on the end of a rope. It could have been you. It wasn't, but that's nothing but an accident of fate. Sam's just back from the wars, and he's definitely got the message.

Maybe that's why we end up on the wooden bench on the back deck, me sitting up and him with his head in my lap, not crying like a baby but sobbing occasionally between gasping breaths. I'm stroking his hair and trying not to let it get to me either way—the jagged razor edge of sympathy, or the urge to tell him to pull himself together and get with the program. Judgment hurts, and he'll talk it out in his own way if I just lend him an ear. If not—

Well, I could have used a listener the other night, but I won't hold that against him.

"Greg rang while you were in the shed," he says eventually. "Asked if I'd help clean up. What I was saying this morning. Not letting them give me any shit. I figured part of that was, if I couldn't do anything at the time I could maybe do some good afterward." And he's off again, sobbing for about a minute.

When he stops, he manages to speak quietly and evenly, in thoughtful tones. It sounds as if he's explaining it to himself, trying to make sense of it. "I caught a taxi to Church. Greg told me to bring a shovel, so I did. I got there and Martin and Alf were there, along with Liz, Phil's—former wife. Mal is in hospital. He tried to stop them. They hurt him. The mob,

I mean. There are other decent people here, but they're mostly too frightened to even help bury the bodies or comfort the widow."

"Widow." It's a new word in our little prison, like "pregnant" and "lynch mob." It's an equally unwelcome arrival. (Along with "mortal" if we stay here long enough, I guess.)

"Greg got a ladder from inside the Church hall, and Martin went up to cut down the bodies. Liz was very quiet when we got Phil down, but couldn't take it when he was lowering Esther. Luckily Xara showed up with a bottle of rye and sat with her. Then Greg and Martin and Alf and me started digging. Actually, we started on the spot, but Alf said it was Fiore's fault, and we should use the graveyard. So we did that, while Alf got some boards. I think we did it deep enough. None of us has ever done this before."

He goes silent for a long time. I stroke the hair back from the side of his face. "Twenty cycles," he says after a while.

"Seven months?"

"Without backups," he confirms.

It's a frightening amount of time to lose, that's for sure. Even more frightening is the fact that their last backups are locked up in the assembler firewall that isolates YFH-Polity from the outside world—while I'm not certain it's infected with Curious Yellow, I have my suspicions. (CY copies itself between A-gates via the infected victims' netlinks, doesn't it? And the suspiciously restricted functionality of our netlinks inside YFH worries me.) There might not be any older copies of Phil or Esther on file elsewhere. If that's the case, and if we can't phage-clean the infected nodes, we might lose them for good.

Sam is silent for a long time. We stay there on the bench as the light reddens and dims, and after a while I just rest my hands on his shoulder and watch the trees at the far end of the garden. Then, with absolutely no buildup, he murmurs, "I knew who you were almost from the beginning."

I stroke his cheek again, but don't say anything.

"I figured it out inside a week. You were spending all your time talking about this friend you were supposed to be looking out on the inside for. Cass, you thought."

I keep stroking, to calm myself as much as anything else.

"I think I was in shock at first. You seemed so dynamic and confident and self-possessed before—it was bad enough waking up in that room and finding I was this enormous bloated shambling thing, but then to see you like that, it really scared me. I thought at first I was wrong, but no. So I kept quiet."

I stop moving my hands around, leaving one on his shoulder and one beside his head.

"I nearly killed myself on the second day, but you didn't notice."

Shit. I blink. "I was dealing with my own problems," I manage to say.

"Yes, I can see that now." His voice is gentle, almost sleepy. "But I couldn't forgive you for a while. I've been here before, you know. Not here-here, but somewhere like here."

"The ice ghouls?" I ask, before I can stop myself.

"Yes." He tenses, then pushes himself upright. "A whole planet full of pre-Acceleration sapients who probably aren't going to make it without outside help because they took so long bootstrapping their techné that they ran out of easily accessible fossil fuels." He swings his legs round and sits upright, next to me but just too far away to touch. "Living and breeding and dying of old age and sometimes fighting wars and sometimes starving in famines and disasters and plagues."

"How long were you there, again?" I ask.

"Two gigs." He turns his head and looks straight at me. "I was part of a, a—I guess you'd call it a reproductive unit. A family. I *was* an ice ghoul, you know. I was there from late adolescence through to senescence, but rather than let them nurse me, I ran out onto the tundra and used my netlink to call for upload. Nearly left it too late. I was terminally ill and close to being nestridden." Sam looks distant. "All the pre-Acceleration tool-using sapients we've seen use K-type reproductive strategies. I'd outlived my partners, but I had three children, their assorted *cis*-mates and *trans*-mates, and more grandchildren than—"

He sighs.

"You seem to want me to know this," I say. "Are you sure about that?"

"I don't know." He looks at me. "I just wanted you to know who I am and where I come from." He looks down at the stones between his feet. "Not what I am now, which is a travesty. I feel dirty."

I stand up. He's gone on for long enough, I think. "Okay, so let me get this straight. You're a former xeno-ornithologist who got way too close to your subjects for your own emotional stability. You've got a bad case of body-image dysphoria that YFH failed to spot in their excuse for an entry questionnaire, you're good at denial—self and other—and you're a pathetic failure at suicide." I stare at him. "What am I missing?" I grab his hands: "*What am I missing?*" I shout at him.

At this point I realize several things at once. I am really, *really* angry with him, although that's not all I feel by a long way, because it's not the kind of anger you feel at a stranger or an enemy. And while I've been working out like crazy and I'm in much better physical shape than I was when I came here, Sam is standing up, too, and he has maybe thirty centimeters and thirty kilos on me because he's male, and he's built like a tank. Maybe getting angry and yelling in the face of someone who's that much bigger than I and who's shocky right now from repeated bad experiences isn't a very wise thing to do, but I don't care.

"* * *," he mumbles.

"What?" I stare at him. "Would you care to repeat that?"

"* * *," he says, so quietly I can't hear it over the noise of the blood pounding in my ears. "That's why I didn't kill myself."

I shake my head. "I don't think I'm hearing you properly."

He glares at me. "Who do you think you *are*?" he demands.

"Depends. I was a historian, a long time ago. Then there were the wars, and I was a soldier. Then I became the kind of soldier who needs a historian's training, then I lost my memory." I'm glaring right back at him. "Now I'm a ditzy, ineffectual housewife and part-time librarian, okay? But I'll tell you this—one day I'm going to be a soldier again."

"But those are all externals! They're not *you*. You won't tell me anything! Where do you come from? Did you ever have a family? What happened to them?"

He looks anxious, and suddenly I realize he's afraid of me. *Afraid?*

Of me? I take a step back. And then I register what my face probably looks like right now, and it's like all my blood is replaced with ice water of an instant, because his question has dredged up a memory that was, I think, one of the ones my earlier self deliberately forgot before the surgery, because he knew it would surface again and forgetting it hurt but knowing it might be erased by crude surgical intervention was even worse. And I sit down hard on the bench and look away from him because I don't want to see his sympathy.

"They all died in the war," I hear myself saying woodenly. "And I don't want to talk about it."

WHEN I sleep, another horror story dredges itself up from my suppressed memories and comes to visit. This time I know it's genuine and true and really happened to me, and there's nothing I can do to change it in any detail—because that's what makes it so nightmarish.

The ending has already been written, and it is not a happy one.

In the dream, I am a gracile male orthohuman with long, flowing green hair and what my partners describe as a delightful laugh. I am a lot younger—barely three gigs—and I'm also happy, at least at first. I'm in a stable family relationship with three other core partners, plus various occasional liaisons with five or six fuckbuddies. We're fully bisexual, either naturally or via a limbic system mod copied from bonobos. My family has two children, and we're thinking about starting another two in half a gig or so. I'm also lucky enough to have a vocation, researching the history of the theory of mind—an aspect of cultural ideology that only became important after the Acceleration, and which goes in and out of fashion, but which I hold to be critically important. The history of my field, for example, tells us that for almost a gigasecond during the old-style twenty-third century, most of humanity-in-exile were zimboes, quasi-conscious drones operating under the aegis of an overmind. How that happened and how the cognitive dictatorship was broken is something I'm studying with considerable interest and not a few field trips to old memory temples.

One of these visits is the reason I am not at home with my family when Curious Yellow comes howling out of nowhere to erase large chunks of history, taking with it an entire interstellar civilization, and (to make things personal) my family.

I'm visiting a Mobile Archive Sucker in the full physical flesh when Curious Yellow first appears. The MASucker is a lumbering starship, effectively a mobile cylinder habitat, powered by plasma piped from the interior of a distant A0 supergiant via T-gate. It wallows along at low relativistic speeds between brown dwarf star systems, which in this part of the galaxy are spaced less than a parsec apart. During the multigigasecond intervals between close encounters, the crew retreats into template-frozen backup, reincarnating from the ship's assemblers whenever things get interesting. The ship is largely self-sufficient and self-maintaining (apart from its stellar tap, and a tightly firewalled T-gate to the premises of the research institute that created it centuries ago). Its internal systems are entirely offnet from the polity at large because it's designed for a mission duration of up to a terasecond, and it was envisaged from the start that civilization would probably collapse at least once within the working life of the ship. That's why I've come out here in person to interview Vecken, the ship's Kapitan, who lived shortly after the cognitive dictatorship and may have recollections of some of the survivors.

Now here's a curious thing: I can't remember their faces. I remember that Lauro, Iambic-18, and Neual were not simply important to me, not just lovers, but in a very real way defined who I was. A large chunk of my sense of identity was configured around this key idea that I wasn't solitary: that I was part of a group, that we'd collectively adjusted our neuroendocrinology so that just being around the others gave us a mild endorphin rush—what used to be a haphazard process called "falling in love"—and we'd focused on complementary interests and skills and vocations. It wasn't so much a family as a superorganism, and it was a fulfilling, blissful state of affairs. I think I may have had a lonely earlier life, but I don't remember much of that because I guess it paled into insignificance in comparison.

But I can't remember their faces, and even now—a lifetime after the grief has ebbed—that bugs me.

Neual was quick with hands and feet, taking slyly sarcastic delight in winding me up. Lauro had perfect manners but lost it when making love with us. Iambic-18 was a radical xenomorph, sometimes manifesting in more than one body at the same time when the fancy took it. Our children . . .

Are all dead, and it is unquestionably my fault. The nature of Curious Yellow is that it propagates stealthily between A-gates, creating a peer-to-peer network that exchanges stegged instructions using people as data packets. If you have the misfortune to be infected, it installs its kernel in your netlink, and when you check into an A-gate for backup or transport—which proceeds through your netlink—CY is the first thing to hit the gate's memory buffer. A-gate control nodes are supposedly designed so that they can't execute data, but whoever invented CY obviously found a design flaw in the standard architecture. People who have been disassembled and reassembled by the infected gates infect fresh A-gates as they travel. CY uses people as a disease vector.

The original CY infection that hit the Republic of Is installed a payload that was designed to redact historical information surrounding some event—I'm not sure what, but I suspect it's an aftershock left by the destruction of one of the old cognitive dictatorships—by editing people as they passed through infected gates. But it only activated once the infection had spread across the entire network. So Curious Yellow appeared everywhere with shocking abruptness, after spreading silently for hundreds of megasecs.

In my memory-dream, I am taking tea in the bridge of the *Grateful for Duration,* which in that time takes the form of a temple to a lake kami from old Nippon. I'm sitting cross-legged opposite Septima (the ship's curator) and waiting for Kapitan Vecken to arrive. As I spool through some questions I stored offline, my netlink hiccups. There's a cache-coherency error, it seems—the ship's T-gate has just shut down.

"Is something going on?" I ask Septima. "I've just been offlined."

"Might be." Septima looks irritated. "I'll ask someone to investigate." She stares right through me, a reminder that there are three or four other copies of this strange old archivist wandering the concentric cylinder habs of the ship.

She blinks rapidly. "It appears to be a security alert. Some sort of intruder just hit our transcription airgap. If you wait here a moment, I'll go and find out what's going on."

She walks over toward the door of the teahouse and, as far as I can reconstruct later, this is the precise moment, when a swarm of eighteen thousand three hundred and twenty-nine wasp-sized attack robots erupt from the assembler in my family's home. We live in an ancient dwelling patterned on a lost house of old Urth called Fallingwater, a conservative design from before the Acceleration. There are doors and staircases and windows in this house, but no internal T-gates that can be closed, and the robots rapidly overpower Iambic-18, who is in the kitchen with the gate.

They deconstruct Iambic-18 so rapidly there is no time for a scream of pain or pulse of netlinked agony. Then they fan out through the house in a malignant buzzing fog, bringing rapid death. A brief spray of blood here and a scream cut short there. The household assembler has been compromised by Curious Yellow, our backups willfully erased to make room for the wasps of tyranny, and, although I don't know it yet, my life has been gracelessly cut loose from everything that gave it meaning.

After the executions, they eat the physical bodies and excrete more robot parts, ready to self-assemble into further attack swarms that will continue the hunt for enemies of Curious Yellow.

I know about this now because Curious Yellow kept logs of all the somatic kills it made. Nobody knows why Curious Yellow did this—one theory is that it is a report for CY's creators—but I have watched the terahertz radar map of the security wasps eating my family and my children so many times that it is burned into my mind. I'm one of the rare survivors among the millions targeted as somatic enemies, to be destroyed rather than edited. And now it's as if I'm watching it again for the first time, reliving the horror that made me plead with the Linebarger Cats to take me in and turn me into a tank. (But that was half a gigasecond later, when the *Grateful for Duration* made contact with one of the isolated redoubts of the resistance.)

I realize I'm awake, and it's still nighttime. My cheeks itch from the salty tracks of tears shed in my sleep, and I'm curled up in an uncomfortable position, close to one edge of the bed. There's an arm around my waist, and a breathing breeze on the back of my neck. For a moment I can't work it out, but then it begins to make sense to me. "I'm awake now," I murmur.

"Oh. Good." He sounds sleepy. How long has he been here? I went to bed alone—I feel a momentary stab of panic at the thought that he's here uninvited, but I don't want to be alone. Not now.

"Were you asleep?" I ask.

He yawns. "Must have. Dozed off." His arm tenses, and I tense, too, and push myself back toward the curve of his chest and legs. "You were unhappy."

"What I didn't tell you earlier." And I'm still not sure it's a good idea to tell him. "My family. Curious Yellow killed them."

"What? But Curious Yellow didn't kill, it edited—"

"Not everyone." I lean against him. "Most people it edited. Some of us it hunted down and murdered. The ones who might have been able to work out who made it, I think."

"I didn't know that."

"Not many people do. You were either directly affected, in which case you were probably dead, or it happened to someone else, and you were busy rebuilding your life and trying to make your struggling fire-walled micropolity work without all the external inputs provided by the rest of Is-ness. A gig after the end of the war it was old news."

"But not for you."

I can feel Sam's tension through his arm around me.

"Look, I'm tired, and I don't want to revisit it. Old pains, all right?" I try and relax against the side of his body. "I've become a creature of solitary habits. Didn't do to get too close to anyone during the war, and since then, haven't had the opportunity."

His breathing is deep and even. Maybe he's already asleep. I close my eyes and try to join him, but it takes me a long time to drift off. I can't help wondering how badly he must have been missing contact with another human being, to share my bed again.

11

Buried

MONDAY is a working day, and it's also usually a lunch date, but I'm not about to break bread with Jen after yesterday's events. I head for work with the brass key hidden in my security bag. Once inside I rip into the filing and cleaning immediately. It's midmorning before I realize that Janis hasn't arrived yet.

I hope she's all right. I don't remember seeing her yesterday, but if she's heard about what happened—well, I don't know how close to the victims she was, but I can only imagine what she must be going through if she knew them well. She was feeling ill a couple of days ago—how is she now?

I head for the front desk. Business is dead today, and I haven't had a single visitor, so I have no qualms about flipping the sign on the door to CLOSED for a while. In the staff room there's a file of administrative stuff, and after leafing through it for a bit, I find Janis's home number. I dial it, and after a worryingly long time someone answers the telephone.

"Janis?"

Her voice sounds tired, even through the distortion the telephone link seems to be designed to add. "Reeve, is that you?"

"Yes. I was getting worried about you. Are you all right?"

"I've been sick today. And to tell the truth, I didn't feel like coming in. Do you mind?"

I look around. "No, the place is dead as a—" I stop myself just in time. "Listen, why don't you take a couple of days off? You were going to be leaving in a couple of months anyway, there's no point overdoing it. If you want, I'll drop round with some books on my next day off, day after tomorrow. How about that?"

"That sounds great," she says gratefully, and after a bit more chat I hang up.

I'm just shifting the CLOSED sign back to OPEN when a long black limousine draws up at the curb outside. I manage a sharp intake of breath—*What's Fiore doing here today?*—before the Priest gets out, and then, uncharacteristically, holds the door open for someone else. Someone wearing a purple dress and a skullcap. I realize exactly who it must be—the Bishop: Yourdon.

The Bishop turns out to be as cadaverously thin and tall as Fiore is squat and bulbous. A stork and a toad. There's a peculiarly sallow cast to his skin, and his cheekbones stand out like blades. He wears spectacles with thick hornlike rectangular frames, and his hair hugs his scalp in lank swatches the color of rotten ivory. He strides forward, skeletal-looking hands writhing together, as Fiore bumbles along huffing and puffing to keep up in his wake. "I say, I say!" Fiore calls. "Please—"

The Bishop pushes the library door open, then pauses. His eyes are a very pale blue, with slightly yellowish whites, and his gaze is icily contemptuous. "You've fucked up before, Fiore," he hisses. "I do wish you'd keep your little masturbatory fantasies to yourself in future." Then he turns round to face me.

"Hello?" I force a smile.

He looks at me as if I'm a machine. "I am Bishop Yourdon. Please take me to the document repository."

"Ah, yes, certainly." I hurry out from behind the desk and wave him toward the back.

Fiore harrumphs and breathes heavily as he waddles after us, but Yourdon moves with bony grace, as if all his joints have been replaced with well-lubricated bearings. Something about him makes me shudder.

The look he gave Fiore—I can't remember having seen such an expression of pure contempt on a human face in a very long time. I lead them to the room; the Grim Reaper stalking along behind me in angry silence, followed by a bumbling oleaginous toad.

I stand aside as we reach the reference section, and Fiore fumbles with his keys, visibly wilting under Yourdon's fuming gaze. He gets the door open and darts inside. Yourdon pauses, and fixes me with an ice-water stare. "We are not to be disturbed," he informs me, "for *any* reason whatsoever. Do you understand?"

I nod vigorously. "I, I'll be at the front desk if you need me." My teeth are nearly chattering. *What is it with this guy?* I've met misanthropes before, but Yourdon is something special.

Fiore and the Bishop hang out in the archive, doing whatever it is they do in there for almost three hours. At a couple of points I hear raised voices, Fiore's unctuous pleading followed by the Bishop hissing back at him like an angry snake. I sit behind the desk, forcing myself not to look over my shoulder every ten seconds, and try to read a book about the history of witch-hunts in preindustrial Europa and Merka. It contains disturbing echoes of what's going on here, communities fractured into mutually mistrustful factions that compete to denounce one another to greedy spiritual authorities drunk on temporal power. However, I find it hard to concentrate while the snake and the toad in the back room are making noises like they're trying to sting each other to death.

It's well into my normal lunch hour when Fiore and Yourdon surface. Fiore looks subdued and resentful. Yourdon appears to be in a better mood, but if this is his good humor, I'd hate to see him when he's angry. When he smiles he looks like a skull someone's stretched a sheet of skin over, colorless lips peeling back from yellowing teeth in a grin completely bereft of amusement. "You'd better get back to work then," he calls to Fiore as he strides past my desk without so much as a nod in my direction. "You've got a lot of lost headway to make up." Then he barges out through the front door as the long black limousine cruises round the edge of the block, ready to convey its master back to his usual haunts.

A few minutes later Fiore bumbles past me with a sullen glare. "I'll be round tomorrow," he mutters, then stomps out the door. No limousine for the Priest, who staggers off on foot in the noonday heat. *My, how the mighty are fallen!*

I watch him until he's out of sight, then walk over and flip the sign on the door to CLOSED. Then I lock up and take a deep breath. I wasn't expecting this to happen today, but it's too good an opportunity to miss. I go fetch my bag from the staff room, then head for the repository.

It's time for the moment of truth. Less than a hundred seconds after Fiore left the building, I slide the laboriously copied key into the lock. My heart is pounding as I turn it. For a moment it refuses to budge, but I jiggle it—the teeth aren't quite engaging with the pins—and something falls into position and it squeals slightly and gives way. I push the door wide, then reach for the light switch.

I'm in a small room with no windows, no chairs, no tables, one bare electric bulb dangling on a wire from the ceiling, bookshelves on three walls, and a trapdoor in the middle of the floor.

"What *is* this shit?" I ask aloud, looking round.

There are box files on all the shelves, masses of box files. But there are no titles on the spines of the boxes, just serial numbers. Everything's dusty except the trapdoor, which has been opened recently. I inhale, then nearly go cross-eyed trying not to sneeze. If this is Fiore's idea of housekeeping, it's no wonder Yourdon was pissed at him.

I look at the nearest shelf and pull down one of the files at random. There's a button catch and I open it to find it's full of paper, yellowing sheets of the stuff, machine-smooth, columns of hexadecimal numbers printed in rows of dumb ink. There's a sequence number at the top of each sheet, and it takes me a few seconds to figure out what I'm looking at. It's a serialized mind map, what the ancients would have called a "hex dump." Pages and pages of it. The box file probably holds about five hundred sheets. If all the others I see contain more of this stuff, then I'm probably looking at about a hundred thousand sheets, each containing maybe ten thousand characters. Whatever is stored in this incredibly inefficient serial medium, it isn't very big—about the same size as a small mammal's genome, maybe, once you squeeze out all the redundant exons. It's three or four orders of magnitude too small to be a map of a human being.

I shake my head and put the box file back. From the level of dust on top of it, it hasn't been touched for quite a time. I don't know what this stuff is, but it isn't what Fiore and Yourdon came here to look at. Which leaves the trapdoor.

I bend down and grab the brass ring, then lift. The wooden slab hinges up at the back, and I see a flight of steps leading down. They're carpeted, and there are wooden handrails to either side. Okay, so there's a secret basement under the library, I tell myself, trying not to giggle with fear. What have I been working on top of?

Of course I go downstairs. After what Fiore did to Phil and Esther, I'm probably dead if they find me in the repository. Taking the next step is a logical progression, nothing more.

The steps go down into twilight, but they don't go down very far. The floor is three meters below the trapdoor, and there's a light switch on the rail at the bottom. I flick it and glance around.

Guess what? I'm not in the dark ages anymore.

If I was still in the dark ages, this would be a musty basement with brick walls and wooden lath ceiling, or maybe poured concrete and steel beams. They weren't big on structural diamond back then, and their floors didn't grow zebrastripe fur, and they used short-lived electrical bulbs instead of surfacing their ceilings with fluorescent paint. There's a very retro-looking lounger in a mode that I'm sure went out of fashion some time between the end of the Oort colonial era and the first of the conservationista republics, and some weird black-resin chairs that look like the skeletons of insects, if insects grew four meters tall and supported themselves with endoskeletons. *Hmm.* I glance over my shoulder. Yes, if Yourdon and Fiore were having a knockdown shouting match in here with the hatch open, I might just about have heard it at the front desk.

The other items in the basement are a lot more disconcerting.

For starters, there's something that I am almost certain is a full military A-gate. It's a stubby cylinder about two meters high and two meters in diameter, its shell slick with the white opacity of carbonitrile armor. There's a ruggedized control workstation next to it, perched on a rough wooden plinth—you use those things in the field when you're operating under emission control, to make field expedient whatever it is you need in order to save your ass. *Got plutonium? Got nuke.* Not that I've got the authentication ackles to switch the thing on—if I mess with it I'll probably set off about a billion alarms—but its presence here is as incongruous as a biplane in the bronze age.

For seconds, the walls are lined with racks of shelving bearing various pieces of equipment. There's what I'm fairly certain is a generator pack for a Vorpal sword, like the one on the Church altar. That brings back unpleasant memories, because I remember those swords and what you can do with them—blood fountaining out into a room where the headless corpses are already stacked like cordwood beside the evacuation gate—and it makes me feel nauseous. I take a quick breath, then I look at the shelves on the other side of the room. There are lots of them, some of them stacked with the quaint rectangular bricks of high-density storage, but most of the space is given over to ring binders full of paper. This time, instead of serial numbers on the spines, there are old-fashioned human-readable titles, although they don't mean much to me. Like *Revised Zimbardo Study Protocol 4.0,* and *Church Scale Moral Delta Coefficients*, and *Extended Host Selection Criteria*—

Host selection criteria? I pull that one off the shelf and begin reading. An indeterminate time later I shake myself and put it back. I feel dirty, somehow contaminated. I really wish I didn't understand what it said, but I'm afraid I do, and now I'm going to have to figure out what to do with the knowledge.

I stare at the A-gate, speculating. There's a very good chance that it's not infected with Curious Yellow, because they wouldn't want to risk infecting themselves. But it still won't help me escape, and it probably won't work for me anyway unless I can hold a metaphorical gun to Fiore's head, threaten him with something even more frightening than the prospect of Yourdon's revenge—and if I've got the measure of Yourdon, any revenge he'd bother to carry out would truly be a worse fate than death.

Shit. I need to think about this some more. But at least I've got until tomorrow, when Fiore returns.

• • •

BUSINESS is dead, literally dead. After I go back up top and lock the repository, I flip the door sign to OPEN and sit at the front desk for a couple of hours, waiting tensely to see if the zombies are going to come and drag me off to prison. But nothing happens. I haven't tripped any alarms by my choice of lunchtime reading matter. With hindsight it's not too surprising. If there's one place Fiore and Yourdon and the mysterious Hanta won't want under surveillance, it's wherever they're hiding their experimental tools. Their kind doesn't thrive in the scrutiny of the panopticon. Which, as it happens, gives me an idea.

Midway through the afternoon I lock up for half an hour and hit the nearest electronics shop for a useful gadget. Then I spend a nervous hour installing it in the cellar. Afterward, I feel smug. If it works, it'll serve Fiore and Yourdon right for being overconfident—and for making this crazy simulation too realistic.

Business is so dead that I go home half an hour early. It's a warm summer evening, and I've got about two kilometers to walk. I barely see anyone. There are some park attendants out mowing the grass, but no ordinary folks. Did I miss a holiday or something? I don't know. I put one foot in front of the other until I hit the road out of the town center, follow it down into a short stretch of tunnel, then back into daylight and a quiet residential street with trees and a lazy, almost stagnant creek off to one side.

I hear voices and catch a faint smell of cooking food from one of the houses as I walk past. People are home—I haven't mysteriously been abandoned all on my own. *What a shame.* I briefly fantasize that the academicians of the Scholastium have figured out that all is not well in YFH-Polity and arrived to evacuate all of us inmates while I waited behind the library counter. It's a nice daydream.

Pretty soon I come to the next road tunnel linking hab segments. This time I pull out a flashlight as I pass out of sight of the entrance. Yes, just as I guessed—there's a recessed doorlike panel in one wall of the tunnel. I pull out a notepad and add it to my list. I'm slowly building up a map of the interrelated segments. It looks like a cyclic directed graph, and that's exactly what it is, a network of nodes connected by lines representing roads with T-gates along their length. Now I'm adding in the maintenance hatches.

You can't actually see a T-gate—it's just that one moment you're in one sector and the next moment you've walked through an invisible brane and you're in another sector—but the positioning of the hatches can probably tell me something if I'm just smart enough to figure it out. Ditto the order of the network: if it's left-handed or right-handed, or if there's a Hamiltonian path through it. In the degenerate case, there may be no T-gates at all; this might actually be a single hab cylinder, divided up by bulkheads that can be sealed against loss of pressure. Or all the sectors may be in different places, parsecs apart. I'm trying to avoid making assumptions. If you don't search with open eyes, you risk missing things.

I get home at about my usual time, tense and nervous but also curiously relieved. What's done is done. Tomorrow Fiore will either notice my meddling, or he won't. (Or with any luck he'll assume Yourdon did it, which I think is equally likely. There's no love lost between those two, and if I play my cards right, I can exploit their division.) Either way I should learn something. If I don't . . . well, I know too much to stop now. If they knew how much I've figured out about their little game, they'd kill me immediately. No messing, no ritual humiliation in front of the score whores in Church, just a rapid brainsuck and termination. Fiore's playing with fire.

Sam is in the living room, watching TV. I tiptoe past him and head upstairs, badly in need of a shower. When I get to my room I shed my clothes, then go back to the bathroom and turn the water on, meaning to wash today's stresses away.

Seconds after I get in I hear footsteps, then the bathroom door opening. "Reeve?"

"Yeah, it's me," I call.

"Need to talk. Urgently."

"After I finish," I say, nettled. "Can't it wait?"

"I suppose."

Small torments add up; I'm now in a thoroughly bad mood. What's life coming to, when I can't even take a shower without interruption? I soap myself down methodically then wash my hair, taking care to rub the inefficient surfactant gel into my scalp. After a couple of minutes of rinsing, I turn off the water and open the door to reach for my towel, to be confronted by a surprised-looking Sam.

"Pass me the bath sheet," I tell him, trying to make the best of things. He complies hastily. Months of living in this goldfish bowl society have done strange things to my body-sense, and I feel surprisingly awkward about being naked in front of him. I think he feels it, too. "What's so important?" I step out of the shower as he holds the towel for me.

"Phone call," he mumbles, trying to look away—his eyes keep drifting back toward me.

"Uh-huh. Who from?" He folds me in the towel as if I'm a delicate treasure he's trying not to touch. I shiver and try to ignore it.

"From Fer. He and El, they've heard something bad from Mick, and they're talking about sorting it out."

"Bad." I try to concentrate. The water on my skin is suddenly cold. "What kind of bad?"

"It's Cass, I think." I tense up inside. "Mick gave them some crazy story about hearing from Fiore. Said the Priest told him that one of the rules in here is, what was it, 'be fruitful and exponentiate.' That you can get a gigantic score bonus for having children."

"That's not good," I say carefully, "but it might just be Mick acting in character."

"Well, yes, that's what Fer said, but then Mick told El he was going to get that bonus whether or not Cass wanted it." He sounds apprehensive. "El wasn't sure what that meant."

My mind races. "Cass wasn't at Church yesterday, Sam. Last time I saw her she wouldn't talk—she seemed afraid." I have a nasty feeling that I know what's going on. I really don't want it to be true.

"Yes, well, Fer called me when El told him Mick had made some kind of joke about stopping Cass trying to escape for good. He wasn't sure just what it was but said it didn't sound right. Reeve, what's going on? What are we going to do if it turns out he's been tying Cass up while he's been at work, or using physical force, or something?"

For someone living in a dark ages sim, Sam can be heartbreakingly naive at times. "Sam, do you know what the word 'rape' means?"

"I've heard it," he says guardedly. "I thought it had to involve strangers, and usually killing. Do you think—"

I turn round. "We've got to find out what's going on, and we've got to get her out of there if it's true. I don't think we can count on the police zombies, or Fiore for that matter, to help. Fiore's messed up in the head anyway, even Yourdon thinks so." I pause. "This is very bad."

The thought of what Cass might be going through horrifies me, especially as I can guess how some of our cohort will react if we try to rescue her. Before last Sunday I might have been more hopeful, but now I know better than to expect anything but gruesome savagery from our neighbors if they think their precious points are at risk. "I think Janis would help, but she's ill. Alice, maybe. Angel is scared but will probably follow if we approach her right. Jen—I don't want Jen around. What about you guys?"

"Fer agrees," Sam says simply. "He doesn't like the idea either. El, maybe not. I think if I ask, I can get Greg and Martin and Alf involved. A team." He looks at me oddly.

"No killing," I say, warningly.

He shudders. "No! Never. But—"

"Someone's got to go find out if it's true, or if it was just Mick making a joke in bad taste. Right?"

He nods. "Right. Who?"

"I'll do it," I say flatly. "Tonight. I'm going to get dressed. You get on the phone to people. Get them round here. I want to sort out what we're doing before I go in, that way there won't be any nasty surprises. All right?"

He nods then looks at me, an odd expression in his face. "Anything else?"

"Yes." I lean forward and kiss him quickly on the lips. "Get moving."

THREE hours later, we're holed up in a vacant house on a quiet residential side street across the road from what we now know is Cass and

Mick's home, thanks to an obliging zombie taxi driver. This street is still three-quarters unoccupied. We pile out of our three taxis at five-minute intervals and go to ground. Fer was among the first to arrive. He got us into the empty house with a crowbar. There's not a lot of furniture, and everything is dusty—not to mention dark, because we don't want to turn on the lights and risk alerting Mick—but it's better than trying to hide in the front garden for a couple of hours.

There are only five of us—me, Sam, Fer, Greg, and Greg's spouse, Tammy. Tammy is determined and very quietly furious—I think it's because she didn't realize how bad things really were until Sam phoned Greg. It's nearly midnight, and we're all tired, but I run through the plan once again.

"Okay, one more time. I'm going to go across the road and ring the doorbell. I'll ask to see Cass. Depending how Mick reacts, Sam and Fer, you'll rush him or hang back. I've got the whistle. One whistle means come in and get me, I need help. Two means get Mick." I stop. "Greg, Tammy, you take the stockings, pull them over your heads. We don't want him to recognize you if you have to take Cass and look after her."

"I hope you're wrong about this," Tammy says grimly.

"So do I, believe me. So do I." I glance sidelong at Fer.

"Mick's not been right in the head since I've known him," Fer mutters.

"Anything else before we go?" I ask, standing up.

"Yes," says Fer. "If you don't whistle, and you don't come out within ten minutes, I'm going in anyway." He grips his crowbar.

"I should hope so." I nod, then get up and head across the road.

Mick's garden is overgrown with weeds, and the grass is long. There are no lights in the windows, but that doesn't mean anything. Like our house, there's a conservatory at the front. The door stands open. I step inside and look at the front door. There's a new lock drilled into it, big and chunky-looking. I ring the doorbell. Nothing happens. I ring it again, and a light comes on in the hall. I tense up, ready for it as I hear a key turn in the lock, then another key, and the door opens.

"You." It's Mick. He belches at me, and I smell sour wine on his breath. He's wearing a dirty T-shirt and boxers, and he's clutching a metal canister with an open top. "What do you want?" He leers at me. "Din't I tellya not to bug me?"

"I want to see Cass," I say evenly. There's *stuff* piled in the hall. Looks like empty food cartons, rubbish. It smells sickly sweet. "She wasn't at Church on Sunday."

"Yeah?" He raises the can and takes a drink from it, then looks at me slyly. "Come in."

I step over the threshold as he backs into the house. It looks like it started out as a mirror image of the one Sam and I live in, but it's been trashed. The hall is stacked with ripped boxes of ready meals and bits of decaying food. Something upstairs has leaked, and there's a smelly stain spreading down one wall. "She's upstairs, resting," he says, gesturing at the staircase. "Whyn't you go up an' see her?"

I stare at him. "If you think she won't mind."

"She won't."

As I set foot on the staircase he sidles round below and closes the door, then twists both keys in the locks. "Go on," he tells me, "nothin' to worry about." He giggles.

That does it. I've got the whistle on a cord round my neck, hidden under the jumper I'm wearing. I pull it out and blow two sharp blasts as I take the steps two at a time. Mick winces, then turns to look up at me, his face a picture of confusion slowly turning into anger. "Whatyuh do *that* for?" he shouts. Then there's a loud thump from behind him as someone hits the door.

I make the top step and glance round quickly. The master bedroom is on the left, just like in my own house. There are piles of filthy clothing mounded up along one wall, and I take in the sick-but-sweet stench of blocked drains overlying something else, something less identifiable. I dart into the bedroom, and my hand goes to the light switch. Something squeals.

There's a splintering crash downstairs and a bellow of inarticulate rage, but I'm too busy staring at the bed to pay attention. Most of the furniture in the room has been trashed, like someone threw it about or took an axe to it. The bed is the sole exception, but it's been stripped down to the mattress. It stinks of excrement and stale urine, there are flies buzzing about, and it's occupied: Cass is lying on it naked. Her arms are tied to the headboard, and her legs to either corner of the bottom of the bed. She's filthy and there are bruises on her thighs and her face looks like she's been repeatedly punched. That's where the squealing noise is coming from. I think he's broken her jaw.

"Up here," I yell through the doorway. I turn back to her. "We'll get you out of here, my friend." I bend over her and pull out the switchblade I brought along for emergencies. "This is going to hurt." I begin sawing on the cord around her arms and she whimpers. As she moves there's a horrible stench from the encrusted mattress and I realize she isn't just skinny, she's half-starved, and there are sores on her arms, angry red rope burns.

I hear more crashes and bangs from downstairs, then an angry yell. Cass whimpers, then moans loudly as the last cord parts; her arms flop limply, and she moans some more. Her hands are puffy and bruised-looking, and I've got a bad feeling about them, but there's no time to waste. I move to the foot of the bed and start sawing away at the rope around her right ankle, and that's when she screams and I see what he's done to stop her from running away. There's blood on the rope because he's slashed the big tendon on her ankle, and her foot flops uncontrollably, and every time it moves, she tries to scream, gurgling around her broken jaw. *He said you get lots of points for having a baby.* I yell with fury, then there's someone in the doorway. I look up and see it's Sam. There's a cut on his cheek that's bleeding, and one eye is half-closed. That gets my attention, and I'm in control again. "Over here," I say tensely. "I need you to hold her leg still . . ."

When we go downstairs, Greg phones a number I don't know about and calls an ambulance. Everyone is a bit the worse for wear, except for Greg and Tammy. Sam is going to have a beautiful black eye tomorrow, and Fer caught a kick in the ribs while he and Sam and Greg were taking down Mick. They've laid him out on the floor of the conservatory while we figure out what to do with him. I'm really regretting my earlier stand against lynching, but the first priority is to get Cass to safety. We'll have plenty of time to deal with Mick later, assuming he doesn't choke on his own vomit while he's unconscious. That would make things easier all round.

"How is she?" asks Tammy. "I'd better—"

"No." I stop her by standing in the way. "Trust me. We need to get her to the, the hospital. This isn't something you can do at home."

"How bad?" Tammy demands.

"*Hospital.*" I don't want her to see what Mick did to Cass's legs. I don't want to be responsible tonight.

The ambulance arrives within five minutes, a boxy white vehicle with stylized red crescents on it. Two polite zombies in blue uniforms come up to the front door. "This way," I say, leading them upstairs. For once I'm glad there are zombies everywhere—they won't ask the kind of awkward questions someone with cognitive autonomy might raise. Sam is up there with Cass, and a minute later the zombies pile back downstairs to fetch a folding wheeled platform for her.

"Who is next of kin?" asks one of the zombies as they come down the stairs with Cass lying on the stretcher.

Fer begins to point toward Mick, and Tammy bats his hand away. "I am!" she says. "Take me with you."

"Request approved," says one of the zombies. "Ride up front, please." They wheel Cass out toward the back of the vehicle, and Tammy follows them.

Greg watches her for a moment, then turns to look back at Mick. "What are we going to do with him?" he asks.

There's a hard expression on Fer's face. "Nothing," I say quickly, before Fer can open his mouth and stick his foot in it. "Remember what we agreed? No lynching." I pause. "What we do tomorrow is another matter."

"Will the police do anything?" Fer asks after a moment.

"I don't think so," says Sam, coming downstairs. He's holding a damp towel to his eye. "I really don't think they're programmed for this sort of thing. If we're unlucky, they'll come after us for trampling on the flower bed and breaking down the door, but I don't think you can really expect a zombie to cope with this sort of . . . thing." He looks very sober as he stares at Mick's prostrate form.

"Let's go home," I suggest. "How about we meet up tomorrow evening to talk about it?"

"That works for me," says Greg. Sam nods.

I eye Mick's prostrate form. "If he tries to come after any of us, I think we should kill him."

"You sound as if you're not certain." That's Fer.

"Certain?" I stare at him: "Shit, I've got half a mind to cut his throat right here! Except, Sunday"— I swallow—"has kind of put me off." I stare at him some more. "You kicked the shit out of him. Think he'll come back for more?"

Greg shakes his head. "I hope he tries something," he says, a curious half smile on his lips. I shiver. Just for a moment he reminds me of Jen.

"Come on, let's go." I take Sam's free hand. "Fer, would you call two taxis?

It's close to one in the morning when Sam and I get home, filthy and tired and bruised. "Go on in," I say, pausing in the conservatory. "This shirt's going in the trash." Sam nods wordlessly and goes indoors, leaving me to strip off under the cool moonlight. I feel numb and tired, but also satisfied with the night's work. I correct that—mostly satisfied. I unzip my trousers in case any of the crap on the bed rubbed off on them, then I follow him inside.

Sam's standing in the living room doorway, holding a bottle of vodka and two tumblers. He hasn't turned the lights on, but he's shed his shirt, and the moonlight shining through the tall glass windows outlines his bare shoulders in silver. "I do not want to dream tonight," he says, holding the bottle out to me.

"Me neither." I take one of the glasses, then brush past him into the living room. I'm tired, I realize, but I'm also wired with excitement and tension and apprehension about tomorrow, and a burning hot anger for Cass—*Why didn't I go round to see her before?*—and a fresh hatred for Fiore and Yourdon, and the faceless scum who created this nightmare and expect us to live in it. "What are you waiting for?" I drop onto the sofa and hold my glass out. Sam tips colorless spirit into it. "C'mon."

He sits down next to me and fills his own glass, then caps the bottle. "I should have listened to you earlier," he says, taking a mouthful.

"So?" I raise my glass. "I hope the hospital can help. She was—"

There's a long moment of silence. It's probably only a couple of seconds, but it feels like hours.

"I didn't know."

"None of us did." But these sound like feeble excuses to me right now, so I take another mouthful of vodka in order to have something else to occupy my mouth with.

"R-Reeve. There's something else I want you to know." I look at him sharply. He's looking right back at me, and I'm suddenly conscious that I'm nearly naked. And he's not wearing that much either, now I allow myself to notice it.

"Go ahead," I say, trying to keep my voice neutral.

"I'm. Oh." He looks away, looking pained. Inexpressive. "Yesterday I said some things I didn't really mean. Hurtful things, some of them. I want to apologize."

"No apology needed," I say, my heart beating painfully fast.

"Oh, but there is. You see, I didn't mean everything I said. But when I said * * * I was telling the—"

"Stop right there." I raise a hand. "Those words. You, uh, oh *shit*." My head's spinning. It's late at night, I've been through a lot, I've been drinking vodka, and Sam's saying words to me that my ears refuse to listen to. "I didn't hear you just now, and I know for sure you said the same thing before, and I didn't hear the words." He looks puzzled, even offended. "I mean, I *heard* you speak, but I couldn't understand them." I'm beginning to worry. "You used the same phrase, didn't you? *Exactly* the same words? Could there be something wrong with my—" He stands up and strides over to the sideboard to retrieve his tablet, which has been lying there gathering dust for some time. "What?"

He says something to it, then holds it up in front of me. Dim letters glow on the screen:

I LOVE YOU

"You *what*?" I say, "You're trying to say * * *—" And I *know* I'm saying the words, but I can't *hear* them. "Shit." I shake my head. "It's me.

Sam, I'm so sorry." I stand up and hug him. "* * *, too. It's just, there's something really flaky up with my language module. Is that what you've been trying to tell me?" I lean back far enough to see his face. "Is it?"

"Yes," he admits. His face is a picture of worry. "I don't say that easily. And *I* can't hear it either, Reeve, I thought I was going nuts."

"I guess not." I'm close enough to feel his crotch. "And I guess you only say that to people you're serious about." He nods. "And maybe you're close enough that I can tell you that I'm flattered, and very happy, and, and—" I pause. I feel as if I ought to know what this weird inability to understand those three happy words means, but I can't quite recall it. "We've got to get out of here."

He nods. "I really don't like this," he says, miserably, a wave of his hand encompassing everything from his body outward. "I've—they should have spotted it. I don't feel right when I'm big and slow and *fixed*. I mean, they can patch it temporarily but I don't like that, either, it's easier just not to be. Only they didn't even give me a, a—" He's breathing too fast.

I feel a stab of anger, not at Sam but at Fiore and the other idiots. "You've got a big-body dysphoria, haven't you?" He nods. "Figures." Kay spent a whole lifetime as an alien, didn't she? And kept changing bodies, as if she couldn't quite settle on a form that she felt comfortable in. Doubtless it's fixable with therapy, but fixing people's problems isn't exactly what this polity is about. "Sam." I kiss him on the cheek. "We've got to get out of here. Where's your tablet?"

"Over there."

"I need to show you something." I let go of him and fetch it, intending to point out to him the myriad ways in which the polity constitution turns us into victims of a biologically deterministic tyranny. "Here—" I page through it quickly. "Hey, I didn't see this before!"

"What?" He looks over my shoulder.

"List of revealed behavioral scores. Gender-based. Huh." I stare. Sex with your partner gets five points for the very first occurrence, dropping off to one point each time after a while. In other words, it's a decay function. "Adultery," that bad word, gets minus one hundred. There are some other crazy items. Getting pregnant brings fifty points, bringing the baby to term brings another fifty. What's abortion? Whatever it is, it gets hammered as hard as adultery, which is what got Esther and Phil into—let's not go there. There are other things here, the most improbable activities, that get huge penalties. But rape isn't mentioned. Murder loses you just seventy points. What kind of sense does that make? It's ludicrous! "Either they're trying to generate a psychotic polity, or the people in the society they derived these scores from were off their heads."

"Or possibly both." Sam yawns. "Listen, it's late. We need to get some sleep. Why don't we go to bed and chew this over tomorrow? With the others?"

"Yes." I put the tablet down, not mentioning that tomorrow I've got other plans because Fiore is visiting the library again. "Tomorrow is going to be a very interesting day."

12

Bag

I spend a long time lying in bed awake, fantasizing about what I'd like to do to Mick, about what I think he deserves to have done to him—but which isn't going to happen. I finally drift into sleep after a particularly brutal fantasy, and I dream again, but this time it's no nightmare. Rather, it's a flashback to how I started my life as a tank. I guess these flashbacks *would* be nightmarish, if they were still invested with any emotional impact—instead they're grisly and freighted with significance, but drained of immediacy by time and necessity.

I stay aboard the MASucker *Grateful for Duration* for almost a gigasecond as it crawls slowly through interstellar space. There's not really anything else I can do—we've been offlined by Curious Yellow, which appears to have targeted the ship for special treatment on the basis of its self-contained systems. Half-crazy with worry for my family, tempered by apprehension about my situation, I check myself into one of the ship's assemblers when it becomes clear that this isn't a temporary outage, that something vast and extremely ugly has overcome the Republic of Is and there's no way around it. We won't find out what's happening until the *Grateful for Duration* reaches its next destination, an obscure religious retreat in orbit around a small and very cold gas giant that orbits a brown dwarf about thirty trillion kilometers away. I extract a promise from Kapitan Vecken that he'll unserialize me if anything interesting happens, then archive myself to backup storage for the duration.

When I blink and awaken in the A-gate, the universe has changed around me. I've been asleep for a gigasecond while we crawled across almost three Urth-style "light years," then spent a megasec decelerating under high-gee conditions to a rendezvous with Delta Refuge. The contemplatorian monastery has been erased and filed in deep storage, bits and atoms reconfigured into the sinister angled constructs of a military-industrial complex. Kapitan Vecken is reluctant to lend his ship to the resistance cabal, but he's happy to run off a clone of his stand-alone A-gate to help speed their botched, jerry-built attempts at constructing a sterile, uninfected nano-ecosystem. And he's happy to put me ashore. So I meet the resistance.

At that time—when I first join them—the Linebarger Cats are an informal group of refugees, dissidents, and generally uncooperative alienists who resent any attempt to dictate their conscious phase space. They live in a few cramped habs with little attempt to conceal the artificiality of the environment. In my first few kiloseconds the close-lipped paramilitaries who insist on searching me as I climb out of the transfer pod explain what I've missed. The infection is a history worm. It infiltrates A-gates. If you go into an infected A-gate, it crudely deletes chunks of your memory (mostly at random, but if you remember anything from before the Republic of Is, you're likely to lose it). Then it copies its own kernel into your netlink. There are some bootstrap instructions. If you find an uninfected gate, there's a compulsion to put it into operator debugging mode, enter commands via the conversational interface, then upload yourself. At which point the A-gate executes the infected boot loader in your netlink, copies it into its working set, and—bang!—another infected gate.

Assemblers are an old established technology, and for many gigaseconds they've been a monoculture, best-of-breed, all using the same subsystems—if you want a new A-gate, you just tell the nearest assembler to clone itself. Where Curious Yellow got started we do not know, but once it was in the wild, it spread like an ideal gas, percolating through the network until it was everywhere.

It takes a while for a worm to overrun an A-gate network while in stealth mode, using human brains as the infective vector, but once the infection reaches critical mass, it's virtually impossible to stop it spreading throughout an entire polity.

Once the activation signal is sent, everything speeds up. Suddenly, there are privileged instruction channels. Infected A-gates sprout defenses, extrude secure netlinks to the nearest T-gates, and start talking to each other directly to exchange orders and information. Here's the fun thing about Curious Yellow—A-gates that are infected can send each other message packets, peer to peer. If you've got the right authentication keys, you can send a distant gate running Curious Yellow instructions to make things. Or modify things. Or change people as they pass through it. It's an anything box.

Fearful weapons appear, seemingly at random, engaged on search and destroy missions for who knows what. Someone, somewhere, is writing the macros, and the only way to stay clear is to sever all T-gate connections, shutting the rogue assemblers off from their orders. But the A-gates are still infected, still running Curious Yellow. And if you use them to make more A-gates, *those* will be infected, too, even if you write complete new design templates—Curious Yellow's payload incorporates a pattern recognizer for nanoreplicators and inserts itself into anything that looks even remotely similar. The only solution is to drop back to prereplicator tech, use the infected gates to make dumb tools, then try to rebuild a sterile assembler from the wreckage of post-Acceleration technosystems.

Or you can surrender to Curious Yellow and try to live with the consequences, as the Linebarger Cats explain to me in words of one syllable. Then they ask me what I intend to do, and I ask if I can sign up.

Which explains *how* I ended up as a tank, but not really *why*.

I wake up as the bright light of dawn crosses the edge of my pillow. I stretch and yawn and look at Sam sleeping beside me, and for a heart-stoppingly tender moment I long to be back on the outside, where I'm Robin and she's Kay and we're both properly adjusted humans who can be whoever we want to be and do whatever we want to do. For a moment I wish I'd never found out who he was . . .

So I force myself to get out of bed. It's a library day, and I need to be there because I've got at least one customer to deal with—Fiore. I'm tired and apprehensive, wondering in the cold light of day if I've blown everything. The idea of going through a normal working cycle after what happened last night feels bizarre, the sort of thing a zombie would do—as if I'm entirely a creature of unconscious habit, obedient to the commands of an unknown puppeteer. But there's more to it than just doing the job, I remind myself. I've got a different goal in mind, something else that the day job is just a cover for. I'm still not entirely sure what's going on here, why I was sent, and who Yourdon and Fiore are, but enough stuff has surfaced that I can make an educated guess, and the picture I'm piecing together isn't pretty.

I'm fairly sure that from the outside YFH-Polity must appear to be a successful social psychology experiment. It's a closed microcosm community with its own emergent rules and internal dynamics that seem to be eerily close to some of the books I've been reading in my spare hours in the library. It's got to be providing great feedback on dark ages society for Yourdon and Fiore to wave under the noses of the academic oversight committee appointed by the Scholastium. But on the inside of the glasshouse, things are changing very rapidly. When Yourdon and Fiore and the mysterious Hanta announce a continuation, and say that all the inmates have agreed to extend their consent, nobody's going to look too deeply. By then, the experimental population will have nearly doubled. Half the inmates will be newborn citizens, unknown to the oversight committee on the outside. Maybe it's even worse than that— I ought to go to the hospital and visit Cass, nose around, and see what their maternity facilities are like. I'll bet they're pretty advanced for a dark ages facility. And that they're expecting plenty of multiple births.

There's also the question of the box files in the document repository. I figure they contain about a billion words of data, committed to a storage medium that is stable for tens of gigasecs, potentially even for hundreds. *Spores.* That's what they need the babies for, isn't it? I can't remember why we don't have repeated outbreaks of Curious Yellow anymore, it's one of those memories that's buried too deeply for me to retrieve. But there's got to be a connection, hasn't there? The original Curious Yellow infection spread via human carriers, crudely editing them to insert its kernel code and making them issue debugger commands to load and execute on each assembler they found. It spread via the netlink. Our netlinks don't work properly, do they? *Hmm*. The new A-gates are different, but they're equally a monoculture, just one that's designed to resist Curious Yellow's infection strategy. I can't help thinking about that MilSpec assembler in the library basement. There's something I'm missing here, something I don't *quite* have enough data for—

I'm dressed for work, standing in the kitchen holding a mug of coffee, and I don't remember how I got here. For a moment I shudder, in the grip of an anonymous sense of abstract horror. Did I just get dressed, walk downstairs, and make coffee in an introspective haze as I tried to get to grips with the real purpose of this facility? Or is something worse happening? The way I can read the words "I love you" but hear them as "* * *" suggests something's not quite right in my speech center. If I'm suffering memory dropouts, I could be quite ill. I mean, *really* ill. The small of my back prickles with cold sweat as I realize that I might be about to unravel like a knit jumper hooked by a nail. I know my memory's full of gaps where associations between concepts and experiences have been broken, but what if too much has gone? Can the rest of me just disappear spontaneously, speech and memory and perceptions falling victim to an excess of editing?

Not knowing who you are is even worse than not knowing who you were.

I get out of the house as fast as I can (leaving Sam asleep upstairs in the bedroom) and walk to work. The weather is as hot as usual—we seem to be moving into a scheduled "summer" season—and I make good time even though I set off in the opposite direction from normal, intending to loop around the back way and come into the downtown district where the library is via a different road.

I open up the library. It's neat and tidy—when neither Janis nor I are there I guess there's probably a zombie janitor on staff duty. I head to the back room to fortify myself with another coffee before Fiore arrives, and as I'm waiting for the kettle to boil I get a surprise.

"Janis! What are you doing here? I thought you were ill."

"I'm feeling a lot better," she says, summoning up a pale smile. "Last week I was getting sick a lot, and the lower back pain was getting to me, but I'm less nauseous now, and as long as I don't have to do a lot of bending or lifting, I should be all right for a while. So I thought I'd come in and sit in on the front desk for a bit."

Shit. "Well, it's been very quiet for the past few days," I tell her. "You don't have to stay." A thought strikes me. "You heard about Sunday."

"Yes." Her expression closes up. "I knew something bad was going to happen—Esther and Phil were too indiscreet—but I didn't expect anything like . . ."

"Would you like some coffee?" I extemporize, trying to figure out how to get her out of here while I do things that could get me into deep shit if they go wrong.

"Yes, please." She's got that brooding look, now. "I could strangle the greasy little turd."

"Fiore's visiting this morning," I say, managing to pitch my voice as casually as I can, hoping to get her attention.

"He is, is he?" She looks at me sharply.

I lick my lips. "Something else happened last night. I—it would really help if you could do me a favor."

"What kind of favor? If it's about Sunday—"

"No." I take a deep breath. "It's about one of my cohort. Cass. Her husband, Mick, he's been, uh, well, some of us went round yesterday night, and we took her to the hospital. We're making sure he doesn't go anywhere near her, and meanwhile—"

"Mick. Short guy, big nose, eyes as mad as a very mad thing indeed. That him?"

"Yes."

Janis swears, quietly. "How bad was it?"

I debate how much to tell her. "It's about as bad as it can get. If he finds her again, I'm afraid he'll kill her." I stare at her. "Janis, Fiore *knew*. He had to! And he didn't do anything. I'm half-expecting him to nail us all for a ton of points next Sunday for intervening."

She nods thoughtfully. "So what do you want me to do?"

I switch the kettle off. "Take today off sick, like you have for the past few days. Go to the hospital, visit Cass. If they've wired her jaw, she might be able to talk. We can't be with her all the time, but I think she'll need someone around. And someone who'll be there to call the police if Mick shows up. I don't know if the hospital zombies will do that."

"Forget the coffee, I'm out of here." As she stands up she looks at me oddly. "Good luck with whatever you're planning for Fiore," she says. "I hope it's painful." Then she heads for the door.

AFTER Janis leaves, I go and wait behind the front desk. Fiore shows up around midmorning and pointedly ignores me. I offer him a coffee and get a fish-eye stare instead of a "yes"—he seems suspicious. I wonder if it's because of what happened last night? But he's here alone, with no police and no tame congregation of score whores to back him up, so he pretends he didn't see me at all, and I pretend I don't know anything's wrong. He heads for the locked door in the reference section, and I manage to hold back the explosive gulp of air my lungs are straining for until he's gone.

My hands keep tensing and kneading the handles of my bag as if they belong to someone else. There's a carving knife in the bag, and I've sharpened the blade. It's not much of a dagger, but I'm betting that Fiore isn't much of a knife fighter. With any luck he won't notice anything, or he'll assume Yourdon is the author of my little modification to the cellar and, therefore, leave it alone. The knife is for the worst case, if I think Fiore has realized what I'm up to. It's piss poor compared to the kit I used to work with, but it's better than nothing. So I sit behind this desk like a prim and proper librarian, entertaining mad fantasies about sawing off the Priest's head with a carving knife while I wait for him to emerge from the repository.

Sweat trickles down the small of my back as I look out across the forecourt toward the highway, watching the pattern of light and shade cast by the leaves of the cherry trees on either side of the path shift and recombine on the concrete paving stones. My head hurts as I run through my fragmentary information again. Are my intermittent disconnects hiding things from me that I need to know?

Riddle me this: Why would three missing renegade psyops specialists from the chaos that followed the fall of the Republic of Is surface inside an experiment re-enacting an historical period about which we know virtually nothing? And why would the filing cupboard at the library contain what looks like a copy of the bytecode to Curious Yellow, printed on paper? Why can't I hear the spoken words "I love you," and why am I suffering from intermittent memory blackouts? Why is there a stand-alone A-gate in the basement, and what is Fiore doing with it? And why does Yourdon want us to have lots and lots of babies?

I don't know. But there's one thing I'm absolutely clear about: These scumsuckers used to work for Curious Yellow or one of the cognitive dictatorships, and this is all something to do with the aftermath of the censorship war. I'm here because old-me, the Machiavellian guy with the pen whittled from his own thighbone, harbored deep suspicions along these very lines. But in order to get me in through the YFH firewalls he had to erase the chunks of his memories that would give him away—and those are the very pieces of me that I need in order to understand the situation!

It's frustrating. It's also immensely worrying because there's more at risk here than simple personal danger—whether from the experimenters or the other victims. I have a faint inkling of the pain and suffering Curious Yellow caused the first time it got out, and of the terrible struggle it took to chop up the worm's Chord-type network and sterilize every single assembler. It ruptured what was once an integrated interstellar civilization, smashing it into a mess of diamond-shard polities. How *did* we stop it . . . ?

Footsteps. It's Fiore, looking curiously self-satisfied as he heads toward the library doors.

"Finished, Father?" I call.

"Yes, that is all for today." He inclines his head toward me, a gesture that's evidently intended to be gracious but that comes over as a pompous bob. Then his eyebrows furrow in a frown. "Ah yes, Reeve. *You* were involved in the business last night, I believe?"

My left hand tightens on the knife handle inside my bag. "Yes." I stare him down. "Do you know what Mick was doing to Cass?"

"I know that"—something seems to occur to him, and he changes direction in midsentence—"it is a most serious thing indeed to interfere in the holy relation between husband and wife. But in *some* circumstances it may be justifiable." He stares at me owlishly. "She was pregnant, you know."

"And?"

He must think my expression is one of puzzlement, because he explains, "If you hadn't intervened, she might have lost the child." He glances at his watch. "Now, you must excuse me—I have an appointment. Good day." And he's off through the door again like a shot, leaving me watching him from behind, mouth agape with disbelief.

Why is Fiore concerned with the health of a fetus, but not about its mother being assaulted, repeatedly raped, held prisoner for weeks, maimed in such a way that she may never walk again? *Why?* He's got all the human empathy of a zombie. What's wrong with him? And why did he suddenly change his tune? I'd swear he was about to denounce what we did last night, but then he moderated his line. Fear of what the Bishop might say if he incited another near riot over the way we rescued Cass, or something else?

They want us to have lots of children. But why is that important to them? Is it something to do with Curious Yellow?

I grind my teeth until Fiore is out of sight, then I hop down from my stool, hang up the CLOSED sign, and head for the lock-up. The secret basement downstairs is as I left it except for the assembler, which is chugging to itself and gurgling as it loads feedstock or coolant or something through pipes in the floor. I guess Fiore's set it running some kind of long batch job. But checking up on it isn't why I'm down here right now—I'm here to retrieve the video cartridge from the camcorder I left running on the equipment shelf.

The camcorder is a small metal box with a lens on one side and a screen covering the other. I don't know what's going on inside it. It certainly isn't an original dark ages artifact—I've seen pictures of them in the library books—but it does the same job. Along with all the other tech artifacts in this polity, some set designer probably slaved over it for hours trying to figure out how to give it the right functionality without adding too much. They got it wrong, but not *too* wrong. The original machines used things called "tapes" or "disks," but this one just writes everything it sees onto a memory diamond the size of a sand grain that's good for a gigasec of events.

I go sit down on the sofa to play with the 'corder. Putting my bag down next to me, I poke at the display until I've zapped back an hour or three. Then I fast-forward through darkness until the light comes on and Fiore comes in. At triple normal speed I watch as he goes over to the bookshelves and leafs through a couple of folders. I pause and zoom in to see what he was reading: POLICY ON SEXCRIME, followed by a glance at FAMILIAL STABILITY INDEX, whatever that is. Next, he trots over to the A-gate and chatters to it, gesturing at the terminal. I don't see any sign of biometric authentication, no retinal scan or anything, but he may have used a password. The gate cylinder rotates around its long axis, and he steps inside. *Fast-forward* and about a kilosecond later he steps out again, blinking. So he's just backed himself up, has he?

Back at the control terminal Fiore issues some more commands, and the gate begins chugging to itself. I glance over my shoulder. Yes, it's still doing that—just some kind of long synthesis job. He heads for the staircase and—

Shit! I whip round and reach for my bag. The A-gate cylinder is opening.

Knife in left hand, bag in right hand. Everything is crystal clear. *Fiore suspected.* He backed himself up, then set an ambush, and I've blown it. The cylinder turns and the interior cracks into view. White light, a smell of violets and some kind of weird volatile organics, a bit of steam. There's someone/something in there, moving.

I dart forward, bag raised, knife ready to block. They're sitting up, head turning. I'll only get one chance to do this. Heart pounding, I upend the empty shoulder bag over the head, lank black hair—fat jowls wobbling indignantly hands coming up—and I shove the knife blade up against his throat and yell, *"Freeze!"*

The duplicate Fiore freezes.

"This is a knife. If you move or make a sound or try to dislodge the bag over your head, I will cut your throat. If you understand, say yes."

His voice is muffled, but sounds almost amused. "What if I say no?"

"Then I cut your throat." I move the knife slightly.

"Yes," he says hurriedly.

"That's good." I adjust my grip. "Now let me tell you something. You are thinking you have a working netlink and you can call for help. You're wrong, because netlinks work via spread spectrum, and you're wearing a Faraday cage over your head, and although it's open at the bottom you're standing in a cellar. The signal's attenuated. Do you understand?"

Pause. "There's nobody there!" He sounds slightly panicky. Clever fellow.

"I'm glad you said that because if you hadn't, I'd have cut your throat," I tell him. "Like I said earlier, if you try and lose the bag, I'll kill you immediately."

He's shaking. Oh, I shouldn't be enjoying this, but I am. *For everything you've done to us I ought to kill you a hundred times over. What have I turned into?* I'm almost shaking with the intensity of—it's like hunger, the yearning. "Listen to these instructions. I will shortly tell you to stand up. When I do so, I want you to *slowly* rise, keeping your arms by your sides. If at any point you can't feel the knife, you'd better freeze, because if you keep moving, I'll kill you. When you're on your feet, you will step fifty centimeters forward, then slowly move your hands behind your back. You will then lace your fingers together. Now, slowly, stand up."

Fiore, to give him his due, has a cool enough head to do exactly as I tell him with no hesitation and no hysterics. Or maybe he just knows exactly what he can expect if he doesn't obey. He can't be under any illusions about how hated he is, can he?

"Forward one pace, then hands behind back," I say. He steps forward. I have to stretch to keep the knife around his neck, but I reach down with my free hand and follow his right arm round. Now is the moment of danger—if he were to kick straight back while blocking with his left shoulder he could hurt me badly and probably get away. But I'm betting Fiore knows very little indeed about serious one-on-one physical mayhem, and the bag over his head should keep him disoriented long enough for me to do this. I step to one side, reach into my pocket with my right hand until I find what I'm after, then squeeze the contents of the tube over his hands and fingers. Cyanoacrylate glue—the librarian's field-expedient handcuffs. "Don't move your hands," I tell him.

"What is it—" He stops. Of course he can't help moving his hands and the stuff flows into small cracks. It's less viscous than water but it polymerizes in seconds. I move the knife round to the side of his neck and examine my handiwork. He might be able to get his hands apart if he's willing to leave skin behind, but he won't be able to take me by surprise while he's doing it.

"Okay, we're now going to take three slow steps forward. Yes, you can shuffle. I'll tell you when to stop—easy, easy, stop!"

I stop him in the middle of an open patch of floor. I need to think. He's breathing hoarsely inside the improvised hood, and he stinks of fear-sweat. Any moment now, he'll realize that I can't let him live, then he'll be uncontrollable. I've got maybe twenty seconds—

"When my husband says * * * I can't hear him," I say conversationally. "What does that mean?"

"It means you're infected with Curious Yellow." He sounds oddly placid.

"You ran off a duplicate of yourself as a guard to see who was coming in here," I tell him. "That was smart. Were you afraid I was using the A-gate?"

"Yes," he says tersely.

"It's immune to the strain I'm infected with, isn't it?" I ask.

I can feel his muscles tensing. "Yes," he says reluctantly.

"And Yourdon didn't insist it was locked to your netlinks?" I ask, tensing as I gamble everything on the right answer.

He doesn't give it to me verbally, but he grunts and begins to pull his hands apart and I *know* I'm right, but I also know I've got about three seconds left. So I step in close behind him and run my right hand down his chest, caressing, and he freezes when I get to his crotch. A moment of relief—he's anatomically orthohuman, and male. I grab his balls and squeeze viciously. He jackknifes forward, speechless and gasping, almost knocking me over with the violence of it, and the bag goes flying. But that's okay, because a moment later I grab his hair and while he's preoccupied with the terrible breath-sucking pain, I pull his head up and run the knife blade smoothly through his carotid artery and thyroid cartilage, just below the hyoid bone.

See, the difference between me and Fiore is that I don't enjoy killing, but I know how to do it. Whereas Fiore gets off on control fantasies and watching his score whores lynch lovers, but it didn't occur to him to tell the assembler to restore him holding a weapon, and it took him almost twenty seconds to realize that I was going to have to kill him regardless of anything he did or said. Basically, Fiore is your bureaucrat-type killer who runs push-button experiments by remote control, while I'm—

I blank again.

THE civil war lasts two gigasecs, nearly sixty-four years by the reckoning of long-lost Urth. It's probably still raging in some far-flung corners of human space. When the longjump network was shattered in an attempt to firewall the damage, it split the interstellar net into disjoint domains separated by lightspeed communications lag. Isolated pockets of Curious Yellow are probably still running, out beyond the liberated light cone, in the eternal darkness and cold—just as there may be outposts of free posthumanity who dropped off the net when the Republic of Is disintegrated. Redaction, the deletion of memory, is Curious Yellow's deadliest weapon—some of those polities might have been deliberately forgotten, their proximal T-gate endpoints dropped into stars and the memories of their existence erased from everyone who used an infected A-gate. The true horror of Curious Yellow is that we have no way of knowing how much we have lost. Entire genocidal wars could have been wiped from our memories as if they never happened. Perhaps this explains the worm's peculiar vendetta against practicing historians and archaeologists. It, or its creator, is afraid we will remember something . . .

I spend my first gigasec among the Cats being a tank. There's very little that is human left in me once I get a clear picture of what's going on. It's not hard to generalize from the tales of random atrocities committed against people who specialize in the past; besides, the gigasecond of nonexistence I spent aboard *Grateful for Duration* is a small death in its own right—time enough for children to mature as adults, for spouses to despair, mourn, and move on. Even if by some miracle my family hasn't been targeted for liquidation because of my career, they're still lost to me. That sort of experience tends to make one bitter. Bitter enough to give up on humanity as a bad job, bitter enough to experiment with other, more sinister, identities.

About my body: I mass approximately two tons and stand three meters high at the shoulder. My nervous system is nonbiological—I'm running as a real-time sim with sensory engagement through my panzer's pain nerves. (The long-term dangers of complete migration into virtch are well understood, but avoidable to some extent by maintaining a somatotype and staying anchored in the real world. Besides which, there's an emergency to deal with.) If I have to, I can accelerate my mind to ten times normal speed. My skin is an exotic armor, pebbled with monocrystalline diamonds held in a shock-absorbent quantum dot matrix that can be fast-tuned to match the color of any background from radio frequencies through to soft X-rays. For fingernails I have retractable diamond claws, and for fists—clench and point—I have blasters. I don't eat, or breathe, or shit, but take power from a coil wrapped around an endless stream of plasma gated from the photosphere of a secret star.

As a callout sign I adopt the name *liddellhart*. The other Cats don't know what this signifies. Maybe that explains why over the bloody course of four hundred megs and sixteen engagements I end up being promoted to template-senior sergeant and replicated a hundredfold. Unlike Loral and some of the others, I don't freeze up when there's a problem. I don't experience shock and dissociation when I realize we've just decapitated twelve thousand civilians and shoved their heads into a tactical assembler that is silently failing to back them up. I do what's necessary. I don't hesitate when it's necessary to sacrifice six of me in a suicide attack to buy time for the rest of the intrusion team to withdraw. I don't feel anything much except for icy hatred, and while I appreciate in the abstract that I'm sick, I'm not willing to ask for medical attention that might impair my ability to fight. Nor do our shadowy directors, who are watching over us all, see fit to override me.

For the first gigasec, we pursue the war by traditional methods. We find half-forgotten T-gates leading into polities under the control of Curious Yellow. We go through, shoot up the assemblers they're using as immigration firewalls, establish a toehold, fight our way in, install sanitized A-gates of our own, and forcibly run the civilian population through them to remove the Curious Yellow taint from their heads. The ones who survive usually thank us afterward.

At first it's relatively easy, but later we find we are attacking polities where the defenses are heavier, and later still Curious Yellow starts programming the civilians to fight bitterly and without quarter. I've seen naked children, shaking in the grip of an existential breakdown, walking toward panzers with Vorpal blades clutched inexpertly in both hands. And I've seen worse things than that. The idea of Curious Yellow, of surrender to a higher cause, seems to appeal to a certain small subset of humanity. These people manipulate the worm, customizing its payload to establish quisling dictatorships in its shadow, and the horrors these gauleiters invent in its service are far worse than the crude but direct tactics the original worm used.

Quite late on in the campaign I realize this and, in a fitful flashback to my earlier self, I begin to spend some of my spare time thinking about the implications. My study of the psychology of collaboration becomes one of the most heavily accessed stacks in the Cats' internal knowledge base. So it probably shouldn't come as a surprise when I receive a summons to headquarters, combined with orders to converge my deltas and revert to orthohuman skin before transit.

At first I'm apprehensive. I've grown used to being an armored battalion, spending most of my seconds between action in icy orbit around a convenient failed star or exoplanet. *Breathing* and *eating* and *sleeping* and *emoting* are worrying, senseless handicaps. I recognize that they are of interest in comprehending the enemy motivational framework, and allowances must be made for them among the people we liberate, but why should I subject myself to the frailties of flesh? But eventually I realize that it's not about me. I need to be able to work with the headquarters staff. So I reconverge my various selves, erasing my identity from the kilotons of heavy metal that have until so recently been my limbs, and I report to the nearest field command node for up-processing.

WHEN I come to, I find I'm leaning over the A-gate control panel. In my left hand I'm clutching a dripping knife so tightly that my fingers are close to cramping. There's blood halfway across the room, forming an obscene lake.

If I got it right, he won't have had time to use his netlink. He'll have been in acute physical agony as his head came out of the bag, then he'll have blacked out because of blood loss. Unconsciousness within ten seconds: It's more than he deserved.

But now I've got a huge problem, namely a hundred and ten kilos of dead meat lying in about ten liters of gore in the middle of a grass carpet that's already dying. Is this incriminating or what? Oh, and my sweater and skirt and sensible shoes are covered in blood. This does not look good.

I laugh, and it comes out as a hysterical giggle with more than a little madness in it. *This is bad,* I think. *But there's got to be something—*

For a moment I flash back to the time with the malfunctioning A-gate, the pools of fluid and lumps of deanimated meat. That helps stabilize me, in a way: It makes it clear what I have to do. I pick up Fiore's arm and give it an experimental tug. His sallow flesh ripples, and when I put my back into it, he jerks free of the carpet and skids a few centimeters toward me. I grunt and tug again, but it's not easy to move him so I pause for a bit and look around. There's some kind of cabling on one of the tool shelves, so I go over and grab a couple of meters of wire, twine it around his torso under the arms, and use it to pull him toward the A-gate. Finally, I get him into position, back inside the gate chamber.

It's hard to keep him inside—one leg keeps flopping out—but eventually I figure out that I can hold him in if I use the rest of the cable to truss him up.

"Okay, take five," I tell myself breathlessly, bending over the field terminal. *Talking to yourself, Reeve?* I ask ironically. *Are we going mad, yet?* My fingers leave sticky reddish smears on it as I prod at virtch controls, but eventually I manage to bring up the conversational interface. The gate seems to have a load of scheduled background synthesis jobs queued up, but it's multitasking, and this is an interrupt: "Gate accept raw waste feedstock for disassembly okay."

"Okay," says the gate, and the door whines slightly as it seals around the evidence.

"Gate select template cleaning systems index that there, I want one of them, *make me one of them* okay."

"Okay, fabricating," says the gate. "Time to completion, three hundred and fifty seconds after end of current job." Ah, the conveniences of modern life.

I go upstairs to the common room and make myself a cup of tea.

While it's brewing, I strip off my outer clothes and drop them in the sink. We've got some basic cleaning equipment, and the detergent is pretty good at getting out stains, probably better than anything they had in the real dark ages. A couple of rinses, and my skirt and sweater are simply soaking wet, so I wring them out and drape them over the thermal vent and dial up the air temperature.

Back downstairs, I find the A-gate gaping open and the stuff I asked for sitting inside it. Fiore has been transformed into a carpet cleaning machine and a bunch of absorbent towels. It takes another trip upstairs to fill its tank with water. The smell of solvents makes me dizzy, but after half an hour I've gotten the visible bloodstains out of the carpet and off the walls and shelves. I can't easily do anything about the ceiling tiles, but unless you knew someone had been killed in here you'd just mistake the spots for a leak upstairs. So I put the carpet cleaner back in the gate and talk to myself.

"It's a blind," I say, then yawn. It must be the adrenaline rush finally subsiding. "Fiore, Yourdon, and the other one. Psywar specialists working on emergent group behavior controls." The blackouts seems to have jostled free some more fragmentary memories, dossiers on—"War criminals. Ran the security apparat for the Third People's Glorious Future Sphere. When the vermifuge was released, they went on the run. They've spent the past gigasecs working on a countervermifuge, then on a way to harden Curious Yellow."

I blink. Is this me, talking? Or a different me, using my speech centers to communicate with the rest of—whoever I am?

"Priority. Exfiltration. Priority. Exfiltration." My hands are moving over the gate control systems even without me willing them. "Shit!" I yelp. But there's no stopping them, they know what they're doing. They seem to be setting up an output program.

"System unavailable," says the gate, its tone of voice flat and unapologetic. "Longjump grid connectivity unavailable."

Whatever my hands are doing, it doesn't seem to work. Something has shaken loose inside my memory, something vast and ugly. "You must escape, Reeve," I hear my own voice telling me. "This program will auto-erase in sixty seconds. Network connectivity to external manifold is not available from this location. You must escape. Auto-erase in fifty-five seconds."

Even though I'm only wearing clothes-liners, I break out in a cold sweat up and down my spine. "Who are you?" I whisper.

"This program will auto-erase in fifty seconds," something inside me replies.

"Okay, I hear you! I'm going, I'm going already!" I'm terrified that when it says *this program* it means *me*—obviously it's some kind of parasite payload, like the Curious Yellow boot kernel. But where can I escape to? I look up, at the ceiling, and it clicks into place. I need to go *up*, through the walls of the world. Maybe, just maybe, this polity is interleaved with others—if so, if I can just break into an upper or lower deck, there may be a way to get to a T-gate and rejoin the manifold of the Invisible Republic. "Going up, right?"

"This program will auto-erase in thirty seconds. Escape vector approved. Conversational interface terminated."

It goes very quiet in my head; I stand over the assembler terminal shivering, taking rapid shallow breaths. A shadow seems to have passed from my mind, leaving only a cautious peace behind. The horror I feel is hollow, now, an existential dread—*So they hid zombie code inside me? Whoever they were?*—but I'm back, I'm still *me*. I'm not going to suddenly stop existing, to be replaced by a smiling meat puppet wearing my body. It was just an escape package, configured to report home after a preset period or some level of stress if I couldn't figure out what to do. When it couldn't dial out, it issued a callback to me, the conscious cover, and told me what it wanted. Which is fine. If I do what it wants and escape, then I can get any other little passengers dug out of my skull and everything will be great! And I want to escape anyway, don't I? *Don't I?* Think happy thoughts.

"Fuck, I just killed Fiore," I whisper. "I've got to get out of here! What am I *doing*?"

Upstairs, the common room is as steamy as a sauna. Coughing and choking I dial down the heat, grab my damp clothes, and pull them on, then head for the door. Then—this is the hardest part—I pat my hair into order, pick up my bag, and calmly walk across the front lot toward the curb to hail a passing taxi.

"Take me home," I tell the driver, teeth nearly chattering with fear.

Home, the house I've shared with Sam for long enough to make it feel like somewhere I know, is a scant five minutes away by taxi. It feels like it's halfway to the next star system. "Wait here," I tell the driver. I get out and head for the garage. I don't want to see Sam, I really hope he's at work—if he sees me, I might not be able to go through with this. Or even worse, he might get dragged in. But he's not around, and I manage to get into the garage and pick up my cordless hammer drill, a bunch of spare bits, and some other handy gadgets I laid aside against a rainy day. I go back to the taxi, and I'm still tightening the belt to hang everything off when it moves away.

We cruise up a residential street, low houses set back from the road behind white picket fences, separated by trees. It's hot outside, loud with the background creaking of arthropods. We drive into a tunnel entrance. I take a deep breath. "New orders. Stop right here and wait sixty seconds. Then drive through the tunnel and keep going. Keep your radio turned off. At each road intersection, pick a direction at random and keep driving. Do not stop, other than to avoid obstructions. Accept one thousand units of credit. Continue driving until my credit expires. Confirm." I bite my lower lip.

"Wait sixty seconds. Drive, turning randomly at each intersection, until credit limit exceeded. Avoid obstacles. Confirm?"

"Do it!" I say, then I open the door and pile out into the tunnel mouth with my kit. I wait tensely as the zombie drives off, then I start walking back into the blackness.

The tunnel darkens as it curves, and I pull the big metal flashlight out. Like everything else here, it's probably not authentic, no electro-chemical batteries—the same infrastellar T-gate that powers cars or starships will suffice to provide a trickle of current to a white diode plate. Right now, that's good news. I shine it at the walls to either side as I walk, until I come to one of the recessed doors. Unlike the last time I came this way, I'm prepared for it. Out comes the hammer drill, and I only spend a few seconds sliding a stone bit into it—all that time in the garage has paid off, I guess. The racket it makes as it bites and chews at the concrete next to the door is deafening, but chunks of synrock fall away, and the air fills with acrid dust that bites at my lungs when I inhale. *Should have brought a mask*, I realize, but it's a bit late now, and anyway, the sound and feel of the drill is changing as the bit skitters across bright metal. "Hah!" I mutter, resisting the frantic itch that keeps prodding me to look over my shoulder.

It takes me a couple of minutes to get enough of the surface of the doorframe exposed to be sure what I'm looking at, but the more I see, the happier I am. The concrete tunnel is a hollow tube, and the door is some kind of inspection hatch near a join. If I'm right, the join isn't a T-gate, it's a physical bulkhead designed to seal segments off in event of a pressure breach, which means this is part of a larger physical structure. This door will lead into the pressure door mechanism, and maybe via an airlock into other adjacent segments—up and down as well as fore and aft, I hope. The only problem is, the door's locked.

I dig around in my pockets for one of the toys I took from the garage. Chopped-up magnesium from a block the hiking shop sold me, mixed with deliberately rusted iron filings in a candle-wax base—a crude thermite charge. I stick a gobbet of the stuff above the lock mechanism (which is annoyingly anchored in the concrete), flick my lighter under it, then jerk my hand back and turn away fast. Even with my eyelids tightly shut the flare is blindingly intense, leaving purple afterimages of the outline of my arm. There's a loud hissing sputter, and I wait for a slow count of thirty before I turn round and push hard on the door. It refuses to budge for a moment, then silently gives way. The lock is a glowing hole in the partially exposed doorframe—I hope we don't have a pressure excursion anytime soon.

I step through the door and glance around. I'm in a small room with some kind of crude-looking machine occupying most of it. Gas bottles, axles, physical valves. It looks as if it was built during the stone age and designed to be maintained using tools from the hardware store. *Maybe it was?* I scratch my head. If this hab was originally configured for some kind of paleo cult, made to resemble one of the polities of old Urth, it would be relatively easy for Yourdon and Fiore to tailor to their purposes, wouldn't it? Maybe that's what old-me meant about this place having unique features suiting it to their needs. There's a ladder, of all things, bolted to the wall, and a hatch in the floor. I go over to the hatch in the floor, which is secured by a handwheel. Turning the wheel isn't too hard, and after a moment there's a faint breeze as the hatch rises and rotates out of the way.

Hmm. There's a pressure imbalance, but it's nothing major. That means open doorways, maybe a whole deck down below. But I said I'd go up, didn't I? I start to climb. The hatch in the ceiling has another wheel, and it takes me longer to rotate it, but there's some sort of spring mechanism inside it that raises it out of the way. That's smart design for you. They assume that pressure breaches come from outside, which in a rotating cylinder hab like this means *down,* so you have to exert force to open a hatch leading down. But hatches leading up have a passive power assist to make it easy to get away from the blowout. I like that philosophy: It's going to make life ever so much easier.

I climb into the tunnel, then pause to pull my headlamp on. Getting it lit, I climb up above the hatch. Then I step sideways off the ladder and close it behind me. I'm now at the bottom of a dark tunnel occupied only by the ladder, punctuated by shadows far above me, and the trail I've left leads down instead of up. I hope there are doors up there. It would be really shitty luck to have gotten this far only to find they're all jammed or depressurized or something.

13

Climb

BATTALION HQ doesn't send me direct to Staff. Instead, they put me through an A-gate, and I come out wearing my original ortho body. I feel small and incredibly fragile and alive. It's an alarming experience that later reminds me of my arrival in YFH-Polity. After my reanimation, they disassemble me and split me into about 2^{24} separate stripes of data and zap it off over quantum-encrypted links via different T-gates. I don't feel this process, of course. I just get into an A-gate and wake up sitting in another one. But along the way I've been fed through a cryptographic remixer circuit, combined and recombined with other data streams with serial numbers filed off, so that even if a couple of the nodes have fallen into enemy hands, they won't be able to work out where I'm coming from, where I'm going, or who I am.

I blink and come alive again, then open the door of the booth. A tense moment—I'm about to enter the semimythical head office of the Linebarger Cats. A compactly built female xeno with feline features is waiting for me, tapping her claw-tipped fingers. "You're Robin, aren't you?" She says. "I love you."

"I'm sorry, are you sure you've got the right person?" I ask.

She bares needle-sharp fangs at me in something approximating a smile: "In your dreams. It's just a diagnostic test patched into your new netlink—if you can hear the words, it means you're not carrying a copy of Curious Yellow. Welcome to the crazy camp, Sergeant-Multiple. I'm Captain-Doctor Sanni. Let's go find an office and I'll explain what's going on."

Sanni is an odd mixture of sly articulacy and shy secretiveness, but she's read my paper and decided I'm wasted on line ops, and she's got the clout to make it stick. When she tells me why, I'm inclined to agree. This problem is a whole lot more interesting than blowing holes in defensive perimeters, and much more important in the long term.

"Curious Yellow can be broken," she explains. "All we have to do is to fracture enough network links that the cost of maintaining internal coherency among the worm farms exceeds their available bandwidth. When that happens, it'll lose the ability to coordinate its attacks, and we can then defeat it in detail. But the problem is what happens afterward."

"After." I shake my head. "You're already thinking about the post-war situation?"

"Yes. See, Curious Yellow isn't going to go away. We could replace all the A-gates in human space with another monoculture, and they'll still be just as prone as the last set to infestation by another coordinated worm attack. And running a polyculture is going to be expensive enough that local monocultures will have a competitive edge . . . In the long run, it'll evolve back toward a state that is vulnerable to similar infestations. What we need is an architectural solution—one that locks Curious Yellow out by design. The best way to do that is not to eliminate the worm, but to repurpose it."

"Repurpose it?"

"As an immune system."

It takes our team, which is one of about fifty groups working under General-Dean Aton, nearly a gigasec to work out the details of that single short sentence and turn it into a weapon. We methodically iterate through hundreds of possibilities, researching the effects on a firewalled experimental network of worm-infested gates before the final working solution is clear, and it takes hundreds of megs to implement and distribute it. But when the main operations group is ready to launch the brutal physical assaults on a thousand network junctions that will ultimately bring down Curious Yellow, the vaccine is waiting for them.

Curious Yellow is a *coordinated* worm. It accepts instructions from remote nodes. It compares instructions with its neighbors, and if they look right, it executes them—this keeps any single worm-infested gate from being easily subverted. By simultaneously assaulting thousands, we convince them that our new instructions are valid and to be obeyed, and they begin to spread out through the network. The vermifuge is a hacked version of Curious Yellow, equipped with a new payload. It does several tasks that, in combination, should suffice to keep a new infestation down. When humans go through a 'fuged A-gate, the gate installs Sanni's diagnostic patch in their language centers, while purging any Curious Yellow infection already present. The diagnostic patch is a simple dyslexic loop—if you're also infested with Curious Yellow you won't be able to hear the words "I love you." The final stage of the operation is that once the vermifuge is in place in a wormed gate, it will refuse to accept new instructions broadcast by Curious Yellow's creators.

We spend a gigasec working all this out and applying it. Tens of thousands of unique soldier-instances die, assaulting hardened positions in order to load copies of the vermifuge into the first gates they capture. Civilian losses are scary, too, millions dying as the embattled and increasingly disconnected Curious Yellow nodes take random defensive measures, and their quislings lash out at their invisible tormentors. But in the end resistance virtually collapses in the space of a single tenday. There's chaos everywhere, atrocities and score-settling and panic. There are even some cases of starvation and life-support collapse, where all the assemblers stopped working throughout an entire polity. But we've won, and the factional groups in the alliance either disband or become petty governments, starting the long process of rebuilding their little defensible corners of the former megapolity.

The Linebarger Cats mostly go back to their prewar activities, a troupe of historic re-enactment artists in the pay of a retiring metahuman power who has spent the past gigasecs sleeping through the chaos. But not all of us can let go and forget . . .

ONCE upon a time, when I was young and immortal, I jumped off a two-kilometer-high cliff on a partially terraformed moon orbiting a hot Jupiter. There was a fad for self-sustaining biospheres and deep gravity wells and it was selling itself as a resort—that's my excuse. I did it without a parachute. Gravity was low, about three meters per second squared, but it was still a two-kilometer drop toward a waterfall that obscured the jungle canopy far below with a haze of rainbow fog. I was trying on a mythopoeic body, and as I dropped I spread my wings for the first time, feeling the tension in the enormous thin webs between the fingers of my middle-hands. As experiences go I would heartily recommend it to anyone—right up until the point where an updraft caught my left wing and flipped me tumbling toward a ridge, which I bounced off with a broken finger that folded horribly backward, wrapping me in a caul of my own wingskin as I fell spinning toward my death.

Back at the top of the cliff they insisted on making me watch the last half minute of my life over and over again. I shook my head and went into the A-gate to revert to my orthobody back down at the coffeehouse on the rocky shore beside the lake at the bottom of the waterfall. I stayed there for a long time. I couldn't stop wondering what it must have been like to be there. The hot dull pain in my mid-hand, the tumbling and whipping chill of the wind, the certainty that I'm going to die—

I wondered if I'd ever find out.

It happened a long time ago. Since then, hair-raising topological exploits with the Linebarger Cats—not to mention age and cynicism—have shown me how the way we warp and twist space-time has impaired our ability to comprehend the structures we inhabit. Architecture has always influenced or controlled social organization, but in a polity connected by T-gates, it has become more than influential—architects have become our dictators.

The vast majority of us live in the frigid depths of space, in spinning cylinders of archaic design that orbit brown dwarf stars or the outer gas giants of solar systems in which no world remotely like long-dismantled Urth could ever form. For the most part we pay no attention to the underpinnings of our human-habitable spaces, save when they inconvenience us and we need to repair or replace them. They're the empty stages upon which we parade the finery of our many-roomed mansions, interlaced by holes in space that annul the significance of the dark light years between . . .

. . . Until you try to climb one of the emergency maintenance shafts. *Then* you know about it.

The ladder rungs are anchored to the antispinward wall of the shaft, rising toward the infinity of darkness that swallows my flashlight beam whenever I look up. Below me there's a long drop to a floor as unforgiving as the rocks at the foot of that waterfall. I climb steadily, pacing myself. The radius of curvature of the hab segments in YFH-Polity is small enough that if this is a single cylinder, it must be several kilometers in diameter. The roof of our hab is too high to touch from on top of a four-story building—the tallest structures in downtown—but I'm already far above that, with no sign of any openings.

At two hundred rungs I stop and rest. My arms are already feeling sore, muscles complaining. If I hadn't been working out for weeks, I'd be half-dead by now. I have no way of knowing how much farther I'll have to climb, and a dull worry gnaws at my stomach. *What if I'm wrong?* I'm assuming YFH-Polity is what it appears to be—a bunch of hab sectors spliced together with T-gates, interleaved among other self-contained polity segments across a multiplicity of real-space habitats. But what if they've gone further than simply blocking access to the rest of the network? It used to be the glasshouse, after all. What if my embedded passenger got it critically wrong, and we're actually stranded in a single location? There might be no way out.

But I can't go back. Yourdon must have figured out I'm on the loose by now. He'll mobilize the zombies and hunt me down like a rat cornered by army ants. Sam will be alone, wondering what happened, getting lonelier and crazier and more depressed. Sooner or later Mick will get his hands on Cass again. Jen will continue to play her malignant head games with Alice and Angel. Fiore will slowly turn the entire community into festering hate-filled puppets dancing to the tune of a dark ages culture based on insecurity and fear. And I'm fairly certain I know what their game is.

This isn't an archaeology experiment, it's a psychological warfare laboratory. They're testing out their design for an emergent behaviorally controlled society. YFH-Polity is a prototype for the next generation of cognitive dictatorship. Because, when they surface to release their new and improved version of Curious Yellow upon an unsuspecting net, it won't be to install a crude censorship regime. The payload they're planning will subtly impose behavioral rules on its victims, and the resulting emergent society will be one designed for their exploitation. A future of Church every Sunday, sword and chalice on the altar, a pervert in every pulpit preaching betrayal and distrust. Score whores in your neighborhood twitching panopticon curtains to enforce an existential fascism—and that's just the beginning. If the population of unvaccinated loyal carriers that Yourdon and Fiore are breeding up are destined to be carriers of the next release of Curious Yellow, the whole of human space will end up looking like a bunch of postop cases from the surgeon-confessor's clinic.

I can't afford to fail.

Minutes trickle away in silence before I start moving again, putting one hand above the other, then one foot, then the next hand, then the next foot. Repeat five times, then rest five beats. Repeat five times, then rest five beats makes *ten*. Repeat *that* another nine times, and I'm a hundred rungs farther up this tube of torments. Morbid thoughts plague me. I could hit a patch of grease and slip. Or just . . . not reach the top. The rungs are about twenty centimeters apart. I'm nearing five hundred, now, a hundred meters straight up. I'd hit the bottom so fast I'd splash. (Banging off the ladder on the way down, of course, gently drifting in the grip of Coriolis force. If I'd remembered to bring a plumb bob and a long enough string, I could figure out roughly how large this hab cylinder is, but I didn't think that far ahead.) My shoulders and elbows ache like they're in a vise. I've spent ages pulling and pushing on that stupid weight machine in the basement, but there's a difference between a half-hour workout and hanging on for life. If I have another memory fugue, I'm toast. How high can I go? How far apart are the inhabitable decks? If I'm unlucky, it could be kilometers—

I can't fail; I owe it to what Lauro, Iambic-18, and Neual used to mean to me not to let this happen. If I forget, then it might as well never have happened. Memory is liberty.

Six hundred rungs and my arms are shrieking for mercy. My thigh muscles aren't too happy, either. I'm gritting my teeth and hoping for mercy when I see a shadow above me. I stop and pant for a while, studying the outline. Rectangular, set into the wall. *Could it be?* I resume climbing, doggedly putting one hand in front of the other until I get there, close to nine hundred rungs up.

The shadow turns out to be the entrance to a short human-height tunnel leading away from beside the ladder. It runs two meters into the wall, then there's a thick, curved pressure door with another handwheel set in it. *I'm there!* I'd dance for joy except my arms feel as if they'd fall off. I step into the tunnel and switch my big flashlight to candle mode, then sit down and lean back against the wall and close my eyes for a count of a hundred. I think I've earned it. Besides, I don't know what'll be waiting on the other side of the door.

My arms feel like rubber, but I don't dare hang around. After a couple of minutes I force myself to my feet and inspect the handwheel. It looks workable, but when I try to turn it, it won't budge. "Shit," I mutter aloud. These are desperate straits. *Maybe if I had a lever,* I think, then I remember the flashlight. It's a big aluminum bar with a light at one end. I stick it through the spokes of the wheel and lean my weight on it, pushing against the wall, putting everything I've got into trying to make the thing turn.

After a couple of minutes I admit to myself that the wheel is not going to budge. It occurs to me that the builders of this hab were hot on fail-safes—what if it isn't turning because there's hard vacuum on the other side? Either it's got a deadlock triggered by too high a pressure differential, or it's just been in vacuum for so long that it's welded shut. "Shit," I mutter again. This could be another of Yourdon and Fiore's half-assed security measures. What good does it do me to get into an access tunnel if the other floors are all open to space? Assuming they know about these access tunnels in the first place, of course.

I wipe the sweat from my face and lean against the wall. "Up or down?" I ask aloud, but nobody's answering. Down, at least there's another level with air. Up, and . . . well, there might be nothing. Or there might be a whole damn orbital habitat that the bad guys don't know about. I could step out into a city boulevard in Old Paradys, or the back of a brasserie in Zhang Li. If I get lucky. If I'm not just imagining those places.

I stow the big flashlight in my belt loop and head back toward the ladder. If I don't get somewhere in another thousand rungs, I'm going to have to rethink my escape plan. Two thousand rungs total will be nearly half a kilometer. If I'd realized I was in for something like this, I would have bought climbing equipment, a winch, even a rope I could sling around myself so I could rest on the ladder. I fantasize briefly about rocket packs and elevator cars. Then I grab the next rung and begin to climb again.

Another nine hundred rungs up the ladder I become half-certain that I'm going to die. My arms are screaming at me, and my left thigh has started threatening to cramp. I pause for breath, my heart hammering. It's like being on the cliff again. This hab has got to be kilometers in radius—the gravity here feels about the same as it did when I started out. I'm in a tube with Urth-standard gee, air: terminal velocity will be about eighty meters per second. If I were to let go, the Coriolis force would rub me against the ladder like a cheese grater at two hundred kilometers per hour, leaving a greasy red smear. I can keep climbing, sure, but how easy is it going to be to climb back down if I keep going up until I'm exhausted? Thinking about it, I'm not sure going down is any better than going up. Less lifting, but still flexing a left elbow that feels about twice the size it should be, hot and throbbing as I raise it—

There's another platform ahead. Twenty rungs up. Roughly four hundred meters from the bottom. "What?" I'm talking to myself—that's not good news. I raise my right hand. Yes, it's a platform.

The next thing I know, I'm sitting on the platform, my legs dangling over the abyss, and I have no clear recollection of how I got here. I must have had another fugue moment. I shudder, my blood running cold at the realization.

I look round. This platform is just like the last one, right down to the door with the handwheel set in it two meters up the tunnel. Which means either I'm shit out of luck, or—well, I can try the door, at least. If it doesn't work, I can rest up. Then it's either up or down, heads or tails. I really don't think I can make another climb until my abused muscles have had some time to recover, and I didn't bring water or food. So I guess it's down, and down and down and back into the depths of Yourdon's little totalitarian fantasy.

Unless I let go of the ladder.

Or the door opens.

I take a kilosecond to rest up before I approach the door. When I spin the wheel one-handed, it smoothly winds up momentum, then there's a sigh of long-seated gaskets as it pulls away from the frame and swings out to one side. I look through the opening and see a universe that doesn't make any kind of sense to my eyes.

The floor in front of the doorway is flat, slightly rough, with a grayish stippled regularity typical of a high-grip paving system. The segments are Penrose tiles, presumably laid out by a walking assembler that crawled across the inner surface of this gigantic cylindrical space, never recrossing its own path as it vomited out the floor. Above my head there's a grayish ceiling that curves in the far distance to meet the upturned bowl of the horizon. Fine needles of diamond stab from the floor to the roof, holding heaven and earth apart. The door I've just stepped out of is set in the base of one of the needles—they're huge, and they're a long way apart.

This is probably an interdeck, an interstitial support space between the inhabited floors. Or it's a deck that hasn't been linked into the manifold of T-gates, terraformed and tamed and occupied. At a guess I've climbed right through Yourdon's security cordon, a level left open to vacuum. If I'd gone down I'd have found . . . what? Maybe a level where the experimenters live, where they're working on the upgraded *Curious Yellow*. Or just as likely, another vacuum level.

My knees feel like rubber. I lean against the outer wall of the radial tube I've just climbed, feeling completely exhausted. I look up at the ceiling, almost half a kilometer up, and realize just how little it curves and how wide the basin of reality is. There are clouds in here, collecting near the tops of some of the needles. The air is slightly misty and smells of dry yeast. Strange monochromatic humps in the floor suggest hills and berms—mass reserves waiting for the giant habitat assemblers to go to work on them. I try to identify the end caps of the cylinder, but they're lost in the haze, several tens of kilometers away. The light is coming from thousands of tiny bright points in the ceiling.

I could starve to death in this place long before I could walk out of it.

I try to rest up for a while, but unease prods me into premature motion. I know I need to try and accommodate this fatigue, but there's an edge of panic whenever I think about Kay, or the consequences of the thing lurking in my head that (I'm half-convinced) is causing these blackouts. There's not a lot I can do, except stay with the ladder and hope to find something more promising on the next deck up—almost a kilometer above my head. But I don't think I'd make it.

I stumble away from the ladder, heading toward the nearest berm. Maybe there'll be some emotional machinery near there that I'll be able to communicate with, something from outside YFH-Polity's frontier that'll be able to put me in touch with reality. I try my netlink, but it's dull and frozen, showing nothing but a crashed listing of point scores allocated to my cohort. *Curious Yellow*, I think dully. *That's why I can't hear Sam when he says* * * *: *the score-tracking system is based on Curious Yellow.*

A couple hundred meters from the berm I see signs of life. Something about the size of a taxi, consisting of loosely coupled rods and spheres, is hunching up over the crest of the deposit. It extends tubular sensors in my direction, then vaults over the crest of the hill, sensors blurring into iridescent disks, ball-and-rod assemblies spinning on its back. The balls are growing and thinning, unfolding like cauliflower heads that glow with a diffractive sheen. I stop and wait for it to arrive. I guess it's some kind of specialized biome construction supervisor, an intelligent gardener. There is absolutely nothing I could do to stop it from killing me if it's hostile—I might as well attack a tank with a blunt carving knife—but that's relatively unlikely. Knowing that doesn't make waiting easy, though.

It closes intimidatingly rapidly but rolls to a stop about three meters away from me. "Hello," I say, "do you have a language facility?"

The gardener draws itself up until it looms over me. Florets open and close, buzzing faintly. "Who are you and what are you doing here?"

I relax very slightly. "I'm Robin." The name feels odd, unfamiliar. "What polity is this?"

It buzzes and clicks to itself, flattening slightly at the top like a puzzled cobra. "Hello, Robin. This zone is no polity. It is ballast sector eighty nine, aboard the MASucker *Harvest Lore*. It is not an inhabitable biome. What are you doing here?"

No polity. I'm on a MASucker. Which means there'll probably only be one longjump gate on the whole ship, heavily firewalled . . . I close my eyes and try not to sway on my feet. "I am trying to locate legal authorities to whom I can report a serious crime. Mass identity theft. If this isn't a polity, what is it?"

"I am not authorized to tell you. You are Robin. I am required to ask you: How did you get here? You are showing signs of physical distress. Do you require medical attention?"

I attempt to open my eyes, but they're not responding. "Help," I try to say. Then my eyes open, and I'm back on the ladder, hanging off it by one hand, feet dangling over the abyss of an infinite cylinder, but there are no rungs and there's another tube nested inside this one, stippled with a myriad of tiny points of light, and something is coming out of the wall to lean over me. "Help," I repeat, as the thing bends toward me.

"I will alert the Kapitan's lodge."

Darkness.

WE declared victory within the local manifold ten megasecs ago, and the magnitude of the reconstruction headache is just beginning to sink in. We've driven Curious Yellow back into its box and broken up the quisling dictatorships that thrived under it. But the war isn't over until a restart is out of the question. And that's an entirely different matter.

"The problem is, about half of the Provisional Government have vanished," Sanni—now a very senior colonel—tells me. (We're in a staff meeting room in MilSpace, cramped and beige and securely anonymized.) "The high-profile arrests are all very well, but where are the others?" She doesn't sound happy.

"They can't just vanish. Not without leaving some kind of traces, surely?" That's Al, the long-suffering gofer who keeps our research team in touch with the operational requirements group and headquarters' Received Instructions Interpretation Unit, whose job is to make sense of the oracular statements our Exultant patron occasionally offers. "There are a lot of scores to settle."

"It's a lot easier to slip through the cracks than it used to be," Sanni explains patiently. "Back when the Republic was unitary it could track identities effectively. But since the end of Is, we've been left with a myriad of self-contained polities, not all of which will talk to each other. Their internal data models aren't transitive. There could be any number of inconsistencies out there, and we can't normalize for them."

What she means is, the Republic of Is provided the most important common services a post-Acceleration civilization needs: time and authentication. Without time, you can't be sure that the same financial instrument isn't being executed in two different places at once. And without authentication, you can't be certain that the person in Body A is the owner of Identity A, rather than an interloper who has stolen a copy of Body A. Time was easy before spaceflight because it was a function of geography, not network connectivity, and tracking people was easy because people couldn't change species and sex and age and whatever on a whim. But since the Acceleration, the prevention of identity theft has become one of the core functions of government, *any* government. It's not just a matter of preventing the most serious of crimes against the person; without time and authentication little things like money and law enforcement stop working.

Now the Republic of Is has fragmented, and its successor polities aren't all running on the same time base. It's possible to slip between the cracks and vanish. It's possible for a hapless emigrant to leave Polity A for Polity B and arrive with a different mind directing their body, with all the authentication tokens that travel with them still pointing at the original identity. If your A-gate firewalls don't trust each other implicitly, you've got a huge problem. Which is why we're holed up here in a dingy cubicle in MilSpace discussing it, rather than returning to business as usual on the outside.

"We're going to have a huge problem with revenants," Sanni adds. "Not the solo ones who just want to hide. They'll mostly go to ground, set up a new identity, erase their memories of the war, build a new life. A whole bunch of dog-fucking criminals are going to think: Hey, I could be anyone tomorrow! And the dilemma we face is, is there really any point persecuting a former collaborator if they don't even remember what they did anymore? I figure we're best leaving the deserters to lie. But the organized groups are going to be a real headache. If they stay organized and hang on to their memories, they could try to start it all up again. We might be able to nail a bunch of them through traffic analysis, but what if they set up an identity remixer somewhere? If they can get lots of clean identities going into an isolated polity where they mingle with the criminals, bodies go in, bodies come out, and how would we know what's happening in the middle? If they're in charge of the firewall, they can play any number of tricks. A shell game."

"So we look out for things like that," Al suggests.

I stare at him, and force myself to wait for a couple of seconds before

I open my mouth: Al isn't always fast on the uptake. "That's a fair description of any modern polity," I point out. "And we haven't consolidated control everywhere—we've only broken CY's coordination capability within all the networks we're in direct communication with. If we want to clean up, we've got to go further."

"So?" Al glyphs amusement in lieu of having a face to smile with. "It's an ongoing process. Maybe you need to think about what you're going to do with the bad guys when you've rounded them up?"

14

Hospital

I hear dryness, and there's a taste of blue in my mouth, and I have an erection. I lick my lips and find my mouth is dry and tastes like something died in it. And I don't have an erection because I don't have a penis to have one with. What I've got is a bad case of, of—*memory fugue*, I realize, and my eyes click open.

I'm lying between harshly starched white sheets, facing a white wall with strange sockets in it. Pale green hangings form a curtain on either side of my bed. Someone's put me in an odd gown with a slit running right up the back. The gown is also green. *This must be the hospital,* I think, closing my eyes and trying not to panic. *How did I get here?* Trying not to panic is a nonstarter. I gasp and try to sit up.

A few seconds later the dizziness subsides and I try again. My heart's pounding, I'm queasy, and the front of my head aches; I feel as weak as a jellyfish. Meanwhile the panic is scraping at my attention again. *Who brought me here? If Yourdon finds me, he'll kill me!* There's some kind of box with buttons on it hanging from a hook on the bed frame. I pick it up and stab a button at semirandom, and my feet come up. *Other way!* Ten seconds later I'm sitting up uncomfortably, the bed raised behind my back. It puts an unpleasant pressure on my stomach, but with verticality comes a minute degree of comfort—I've got some control over my environment—before the greater unease sneaks up on me again.

Okay, so the gardener—I trail off, my internal narrative stuck in a haze of incomprehension. *It brought me here? Where is here, anyway?* This bed—it's one of a row, spaced alongside one wall in a huge, high-ceilinged white room. There's an array of windows set high up in the opposite wall, and I can glimpse blue and white sky through it. Incomprehensible bits of equipment are dotted around. There are lockers next to some of the beds—and I see that one of the beds at the other end of the room looks to be occupied.

I close my eyes, feeling a deadweight of dread. *I'm still in the glasshouse*, I realize sickly.

But I'm too weak to do anything, and, besides, I'm not alone. I hear the clack of approaching heels and the sound of voices coming my way. "Hours end at four o'clock," says a female voice with the flattening of affect I've come to expect of zombies. "The consultant will visit in the evening. The patient is weak and is not to be disturbed excessively." The curtain twitches back, and I see a female zombie wearing a white dress and an odd hair adornment. The zombie looks at me. "You have a visitor," she intones. "Do not overexert yourself."

"Uh," I manage to say, and try to turn my head so I can see who it is, but they're still half-concealed behind the curtain. It's like a nightmare, when you know some kind of monster is creeping up on you—

"Well, if it isn't our little librarian!"

And I think, *Fuck, I know that voice!* And simultaneously, almost petulantly, *But you can't be here*, just as Fiore steps around the curtain and leans over the rail alongside my bed, an expression of bemused condescension on his face. "Would you like to tell me where you think you were going?"

"No." I manage to avoid gritting my teeth. "Not particularly." The nightmare has caught up, and the well of despair is threatening to swallow me down. They've caught me and brought me back to play with me. I feel sick and hot.

"Come now, Reeve." *Unctuous, that's the word.* Fiore plants one plump hand on my forehead, and I realize he feels clammy and cold. "Oh dear. You *are* in a state." He removes the hand before I can shake it off, and I shiver. "I can see why they brought you straight here."

I clamp my teeth shut, waiting for the coup de grâce, but Fiore seems to have something else in mind. "I have to look after the pastoral well-being of *all* my flock, little lady, so I can't stay too long with you. You're obviously *ill*"—he puts some kind of odd emphasis on the word—"and I'm sure that's the explanation for your recent erratic behavior. But next time you decide to go climbing in the walls, you should come and talk to me first"—for a moment his expression hardens—"you wouldn't want to do anything you might regret later."

Between shivers, I manage to roll my eyes. "I have no regrets." *Why is he playing with me?*

"Come now!" Fiore clucks disapprovingly for a moment. "Of course you have regrets! To be human is to be regretful. But we must learn to make the most of what we have to work with, mustn't we? You've been slow to settle in and find your place in our little parish, Reeve, and that's been causing some concern to those of us who keep an eye on such things. I have—may I be frank?—been worried that you might be an incorrigibly disruptive influence. On the other hand, you obviously mean well, and care for your neighbors—" An unreadable expression flits across his jowls. "So I'm trying to give you the benefit of the doubt. Rest now, and we'll continue our little chat later, when you're feeling better."

He straightens up in his portly manner and begins to turn away. I shiver again, a chill running up my spine. *It's like he doesn't know I killed him!* I realize. I can see Fiore running multiple instances of himself, but surely they'd be aware of each other, by way of their netlink? *Why, doesn't he—*

"You," I manage to say.

"Yes?"

"You." It's hard to form words. I'm really feeling feverish. "What's the, the . . ."

"I don't have all day!" His voice rises when he's irritated, in an annoying whine. He straightens his robe. "Nurse? I say, nurse!" In a quieter voice, to me: "I'll have them send for your husband. I'm sure you'll have a lot to talk about." Then he turns on his heel and bumbles away down the ward toward the other occupied beds.

I realize my teeth are chattering: I'm not sure whether from fever or black helpless rage. *I killed you! And you didn't even notice!* Then the nurse comes stomping along in her sensible shoes, clutching some kind of primitive diagnostic instrument, and I realize that I'm feeling extremely unwell.

NURSE Zombie gives me a test that involves sliding a cold glass rod into my ear and staring into my eyes from close range, then she pulls out a jar and gives me what I assume at first is a piece of candy, except that it tastes vile. The hospital is set up to resemble a real dark ages installation, but luckily they seem to draw the line at leeches or heart transplants and similar barbarism. I guess this is some sort of drug, synthesized at great expense and administered to have some random weird systemic effect on my metabolism. "Try to sleep," Nurse explains to me. "You are ill."

"C-cold," I whisper.

"Try to sleep, you are ill." But Nurse bends down and pulls out a loose-weave blanket. "Drink lots of fluids." The glass on the table next to me is empty, and in any case, I feel too shivery to pull an arm out from under the blanket. "You are ill."

No shit. It's not just my arms and legs—all my joints are screaming at me in chorus with a whole load of muscles I wish I didn't have right now—but my head's throbbing and I feel like I'm freezing to death and my stomach's not so good either. And the blackouts and memory fugues are still with me. "What's wrong with, me?" I ask, and it takes a big effort to get the words out.

"You are ill," the zombie repeats. It's useless arguing with her—nobody home, no theory of mind, just a bunch of reflexes and canned dialogues.

"Who can I ask?"

She's turning away, but I seem to have tripped a new response. "The consultant will visit at eight o'clock tonight, all questions must be addressed to the consultant. The patient is weak and must not be disturbed excessively. Drink lots of fluids." She picks up an empty jug that was out of view a moment ago and whisks it away toward one end of the ward. A moment later she's back with it. "Drink lots of fluids."

"Yeah . . ." I shudder and try to work myself into a smaller volume under the blanket. I dimly realize I ought to be asking lots of questions—actually I ought to be forcing myself out of bed and running like my hair's on fire—but right now, just pouring myself a glass of water seems like an heroic task.

I lie back and stare at the ceiling, incoherent with anger and embarrassment. Did I imagine myself killing Fiore in the library? I don't think so; the memories are vivid. But so are all my other memories, the massacres and the endless years of war. And not all my memories are real, are they? The bootstrap memory, talking to another voice in my own larynx—if it's not just a false memory of a false memory, then it certainly wasn't me: It was a customized worm running on my implant. I can't—this is getting difficult—trust myself, especially while I keep going into fugue.

"Can I?" I ask, and I open my eyes again, and Sam startles.

He's leaning over me where Fiore was, and I realize immediately that I've been in fugue for some time. I'm cold, but I'm no longer feverish; the sheets are damp with sweat, and the light visible through the windows is dimming toward evening. "Reeve?" he asks anxiously.

"Sam." I lift my hand and reach for him. He wraps my fingers in his. "I'm ill."

"I came as soon as I heard. Fiore telephoned the office." He sounds slightly shocky, his eyes haunted. "What happened?"

I shiver again. The damp sheets are getting to me. "Later." Meaning: *Not where the walls have ears.* "Need water." My mouth's really dry. "I keep having fugues."

"The nurse said something about a consultant," says Sam. "Dr. Hanta. She said he'd be coming to look at you later. Are you going to be all right? Why are you ill?"

I clutch Sam's hand as hard as I can. "I don't know." He offers me the water glass, and I swallow. "Suspect . . . not. Not sure. How long was I . . . asleep . . . for?"

"You didn't recognize me when I came in," Sam says. He's holding on to my hand as if he's afraid one of us is drowning. "You didn't recognize me."

"Memory fugue's getting much worse," I say. I lick my lips. "Three"—*no, four*—"today. I'm not sure why. I keep remembering stuff, but I'm not sure how much of it is real. Thought I'd"—I stop before I say *killed Fiore*, just in case I really did and there's some other reason the priest doesn't know about it—"escaped. But I woke up here." I close my eyes. "Fiore says I'm ill."

"What am I meant to do?" Sam asks plaintively. "How do I fix you? There's no A-gate here . . ."

"Dark ages tech." My hand aches from gripping him. I force it to relax. "They didn't disassemble people and rebuild them, they used medicine, drugs, and surgery. Tried to repair damaged tissue in situ."

"That's insane!"

I chuckle weakly. "You're telling me? That's what the consultant is, he's a doctor." One of those weird, obsolescent words that doesn't mean what it used to—in the real world outside this prison, a doctor is a scholar, someone who investigates stuff, not a wetware mechanic. I suppose it may have meant the same back in the real dark ages, when nobody really knew how self-replicating organisms functioned and there was an element of research involved. "I think he's meant to figure out what's wrong with me and repair it. Assuming they don't just have a medical assembler down in the basement here—" I clutch his hand, because a horrible thought's just struck me. If they've got a medical A-gate, won't it be infected with Curious Yellow? "Don't let them put me in it!"

"Put you in—what? What is it, Reeve? Reeve, are you having another fugue?"

Things are going gray around me. He leans close, and I whisper, "* * *," in his ear. Then—

• • •

DESPERATION is the engine of necessity.

It's two hundred megs since that committee meeting with Al and Sanni and a lot of things have changed. Me, for example: I'm not in military phenotype anymore. Neither is Sanni. We're civilians now, corpuscles of military experience discharged into the circulating confusion of reconstruction that has become the future of Is.

I'm not used to being human again, ortho or otherwise—bits of me are missing. When the war exploded, trapping me on the MASucker for almost a generation, I was reduced to what I was carrying on my person and in my head. Then when I militarized myself, I had to let component aspects of my identity go. I'm not sure why, in all cases. Some things make sense (when at war, one's scruples about inflicting pain and injury on the enemy faction must be suppressed), but there are gaps that follow no obvious rhyme or reason. According to my written notes from the period on the *Grateful for Duration*, I used to have an abiding and deep interest in baroque music of the preindustrialized age, but now I can't recall even a scrap of melody. Again, I used to be married, with children, but I am mystified by my lack of memories from the period, or feelings. Maybe that was a reaction to grief, and maybe not— but now I've been demobilized, I find myself out of reaction mass and adrift along an escape vector diverging from all attachments. Only my new job retains any hold over me.

The Linebarger Cats emerged from the coalition with significant assets. To my surprise I received a credit balance that with careful management might mean I never need to work again—at least for a few gigasecs. It seems that warfare pays, if you're on the winning side and manage not to misplace your mind in the process.

When I left MilSpace (a convoluted process involving numerous anonymous remixer networks and one-way censorship gates to strip me of my military modules before my reintegration into civil society), I had myself reassembled as a louche young man in the Cognitive Republic of Lichtenstein. There's a lot to be said for being louche, especially after you've spent several hundred megaseconds with no genitals.

Lichtenstein is a vivid and cynical colony of artistic satirists, so sophisticated they've almost circled back into primitivism. By convention we use visual field filters that limn everything in dark strokes, filling our bodies with color. Life aspires toward a state of machinima. It's a strange way to be, but familiar and comfortable after the unsleeping hyperspectral awareness of a tankie. So I hang around in the galleries and salons of Lichtenstein, exchanging witty repartee and tall stories with the other habitués, and in my copious free time I pay frequent trips to the bathhouses and floataria. I make a point of never sleeping with the same person twice in the same body, although I discover that even such anonymous abandon doesn't protect me from my lovers' tears: It seems half the population have lost someone and are wandering, searching the world over.

My life is outwardly directionless for the first four or five megs. In private I work on something that might eventually turn out to be a memoir of the war—an old-fashioned serialized text provocatively promoting a single viewpoint, without any pretense at objectivity—while in public I live on my savings. DeMob gave me a reasonably secure cover identity as a playboy remittance man from a primogeniture polity, sent to while away his youth in less hidebound (and politically loaded) biomes, and it's not hard to keep up appearances. But deep down, the insignificance and lack of meaning of such a life chafes; I want to be doing something, and while the project I've been working on under Sanni's auspices for the past couple of years fits the bill, it is, perforce, anonymous. If I make a mark, it will be by my deeds, not my name. And so, as my debauch intensifies, I slip into a kind of melancholic haze.

Then one morning I am awakened by a brassy flare of trumpets from the bedside orrery, which announces that I have a visitor.

I realize who and where I am—and that I am desperately sick—at the exact moment that Dr. Hanta presses a small, freezing cold brass disk against the bare skin between my breasts. "Ow!"

"Breathe slowly," she orders, not unkindly, then blinks like a sleepy owl from behind her thick-lensed glasses: "Ah, back in the realm of the conscious, are we?"

By way of an answer I go into a hoarse coughing fit, my muscles locking in spasms that leave my ribs aching. Hanta recoils slightly, removing the stethoscope. "I see," she says. "I'll just wait a moment— glass of water?"

I realize she's jacked the back of my bed up as the coughing subsides. "Yes. Please." I'm shivery and weak but not freezing anymore. She holds out a glass, and I manage to accept it without spilling anything, although my hand shakes alarmingly. "What's wrong with me?"

"That's what I'm here to find out." Hanta is a petite female, shorter than I am, her skin a shade darker, although not the aubergine-tinted brown of Fiore. Her short hair is dusted with the silver spoor of impending senescence, and there are laugh-lines around her face. She wears an odd white overcoat buttoned up the front and carries the arcane totems of her profession, the caduceus and stethoscope—the bell of the latter she rubs upon my chest. She looks friendly and open and trustworthy, the antithesis of her two clerical colleagues: but beauty is not truth, and some gut instinct tells me never to let my guard down in her presence. "How long have you been febrile?"

"Febrile?"

"Hot and cold. Chills, shivers, alternating with too hot. Night sweats, anything like that."

"Oh, about—" I feel my forehead wrinkling. "What day is it? How long have I been in here?"

"You've been here six hours," Dr. Hanta says patiently. "You were brought in around midafternoon."

I shiver convulsively. My skin is icy. "Since an hour or two before then."

"The Reverend Doctor Fiore tells me you were climbing." Her tone is neutral, professional, with no note of censure.

I swallow. "Since then."

"You're a lucky lady." Hanta smiles enigmatically and moves her stethoscope to the ball of my left shoulder, pulling open my hospital gown to get at it. "I'm sorry, I'll be quick. Hmm." She stares into the stethoscope's eye crystal and frowns. "It's a long time since I've seen that . . . sorry." She straightens up. "It's not safe to climb around in the walls here; some of the neighboring biomes aren't biomorphically integrated. There are replicators in the mass fraction reserve cells that will eat anything based on a nucleotide chassis that doesn't broadcast a contact inhibition signal, and you're not equipped for that."

I swallow again—my mouth is unnaturally dry. "What?"

"Somehow or other you've managed to get yourself infected with a strain of *pestis mechaniculorum*. You're feverish because your immune system is still just about containing it. It's a good thing for you that we found you before mechanotic cytolysis set in . . . Anyway, I'll fix you up just as soon as I finish sequencing it."

"Um." I shudder again. "Oh, okay."

"'Okay' indeed. Do I have to tell you not to go climbing around inside the walls again?" I shake my head, almost embarrassed by my own fear of discovery. "Good." She pats me on the shoulder. "At least if you're going to do it again, come to me first, please? No more unfortunate accidents." She carefully disconnects the stethoscope and wraps it around her caduceus. It makes soft clicking noises as it fuses with the staff. "Now I'll just run you off a little antirobotic, and you'll be up and about in no time."

Dr. Hanta hitches up her coat, then perches on a stool next to my bed. "Isn't this a bit out of character?" I ask her, throwing caution to the winds. I suspect if I asked Fiore or Yourdon that question, they'd bite my head off, but Hanta seems more approachable, if not more trustworthy.

"We all make mistakes." It's that smile again: It's slightly fey and very sincere, as if she's laughing at a joke that I'd laugh along with, if I only knew what it was. "You leave worrying about the integrity of the experiment to me, dear." She waves a dismissive hand. "Of course you worry about it when the priests' backs are turned. Of course people try to game the system—it's only to be expected. Probably some people don't even want to be here. Maybe they changed their minds after signing the waiver. All I can say is, we'll do our best to make sure they're not unhappy with the outcome." She raises an eyebrow at me speculatively. "It's not easy to run an experiment on this scale, and we make mistakes, what else can I say? Some of us make more mistakes than others." And now she pulls an expression of mild distaste, which seems to say it all. She's inviting my agreement, and I find myself nodding along despite my better judgment.

"But those mistakes . . ." I stop, unsure if I should continue.

"Yes?" She leans forward.

"How's Cass?" I force myself to ask.

Dr. Hanta's face, which up until now has been open and friendly, closes like a trapdoor. "Why do you ask?"

I lick my lips again. "I need something to drink." She slides off her stool and paces round my bed, pours what's left of the water jug into my cup, and hands it to me without a word. I swallow. "One of Fiore's little mistakes, I suppose." I aim to say it lightly, but it comes out dripping with sarcasm.

"Oh yes." Dr. Hanta looks round, toward the far end of the ward—at something hidden from me by the curtain. I shudder, and this time it's not from the fever chills. "I wouldn't say one of his *little* mistakes." Her tone of voice is dry, but there's something behind it that makes me glad I can't see her face. But when she turns back to me, her expression is perfectly normal. "Cass will be all right, dear."

"And Mick?" I prompt.

"That is under discussion."

"Under discussion. Was what happened to Esther and Phil discussed ahead of time?"

"Reeve"—she actually has the gall to look upset—"no, it wasn't. Someone miscalculated badly. They've gone back to the primary sources and discovered that what, what Esther and Phil were doing wasn't so very unusual. And you're right, the weighting attached to, uh, what they did—Major Fiore misjudged the mood of the crowd. It won't happen again, we've learned from that experience, and from—" She swallows, then nods minutely at the curtain. "If a couple doesn't get on, there's going to be a procedure to go through to obtain formal social approval of the separation. We're not evil. We're in this for the long haul, and if you're unhappy, if everyone's unhappy here, the polity won't gel, and the experiment can't work."

The experiment can't work. I look at her and find myself wondering, *Does she mean it?* Fiore and Yourdon are so cynical I find myself startled to be in the presence of a member of their team who seems to believe in what she's doing. I'm suddenly appalled, as badly taken aback by her honesty as the police zombies are by a stripper. "Uh. I think I see." I shake my head, then wince. My neck aches. "But as long as Mick stays here, some of us won't be happy at all."

"Oh, Mick will be dealt with one way or another, dear." Her caduceus trills for attention, and she fidgets with it as she talks. "I don't think the psychological damage is irremediable—we probably won't have to restore from backup, which is a good thing right now. But I'm going to have to redesign his motivational parameters from the ground up." She frowns at the serpent heads but doesn't explain herself further. "Cass will be . . . well, I'm attending to the physical damage right now, and when she's better, I'll ask her who she wants to be." She falls silent for a few seconds. "Most medical fraternities, confronted by a patient with this level of damage, would prescribe gross memory surgery—or simply terminate the instance and restore from backup. I don't believe in authorizing such a serious step without taking her wishes into account."

She falls silent again. After a moment I realize she's staring at me. "What is it?"

"We need to talk about your blackouts."

"My what?" I bite my tongue, but it's a bit late to play dumb.

Dr. Hanta raises one eyebrow and crosses her arms. "I'm not stupid, you know." She looks away, as if she's speaking to someone else. "Everyone in here has been through redactive reweighting and experiential reduction before we recruit them. One of the reasons this polity needs a medical supervisor is to be ready for identity crises. Most people have some inkling of who they used to be and why they wanted memory surgery. Occasionally, we get someone who doesn't remember—there's something they wanted to bury so deep that they wouldn't even know what it was about. Something painful. But I don't normally see . . . well! You've gone into fugue twice since you were admitted to this ward, did you know that? I checked with your husband during your last one, and he said you've been having them more frequently."

She leans toward me, keeping her hands sandwiched in her armpits as if she's hugging herself. "I don't like to intrude where I'm not wanted, but by the sound of it, you need help very badly indeed. You seem to have had a bad reaction to the suppressants the clinic used on you, and while I can't be sure without making a detailed examination, there is a risk that you could be heading for some kind of crisis. I don't want to overstate things, but in the worst-case scenario you could lose . . . well, everything that makes you *you*. For example, if it's an autoimmune re-action—according to your file you've got a heuristic upgrade to your complement system, and sometimes the Bayesian recognizers start firing off at the wrong targets—you could end up with anterograde amnesia, a complete inability to lay down any new mnemostructures. Or it might just be a sloppy earlier edit bleeding through and triggering random in-tegration fugues, in which case things will ease off after a while, al-though you won't enjoy the ride. But I can't tell you what to expect, much less treat you, if you won't even admit you've got a problem."

"Oh." It takes me a while to absorb this, but Hanta is remarkably patient with me and waits while I think about things. If I didn't know better, I'd swear she actually liked me. "A problem," I echo, uncertain how much I can let slip, before a cold chill runs its icy fingers up my spine, and I shudder uncontrollably.

"Speaking of problems . . ." Hanta raises her caduceus: "This will hurt, but only momentarily and a lot less than being eaten alive by a mechaplague." She smiles faintly as she points it at my shoulder, and I wince as the asps strike at me. There's a toothy little prickling as they begin pumping adjuvant patches into my circulation, upgrading my prosthetic immune system so that it can deal with the *pestis*. I try not to wince.

"The infection will take some time to die off, and there's a risk that it's adaptable enough to out-evolve the robophages, so I'm going to keep you here overnight—just for observation. Hopefully you'll be well enough to go home tomorrow, and I'm going to write you up for a week off work while you recover. In the meantime, have a think about what

I said concerning your memory problem, and we can talk about it in the morning when I check on your progress."

The snake-heads let go of me and wrap themselves back around the staff as Hanta stands up. "Sleep well!"

NATURALLY, I don't sleep well at all.

At first, I spend an indeterminate time shuddering with cold chills and occasionally forgetting to inhale until some primitive reflex kicks me into sucking in great rasping gasps of air. Sleep is out of the question when you're afraid you'll stop breathing, so I amuse myself to the point of abject terror by rolling the events of the day over in my mind. Great arterial gouts of blood project like ghosts upon the wall, shadows of my guilt over killing Fiore . . . Fiore? But he doesn't know I killed him! Did I hallucinate the whole thing? Obviously not the mad scramble up the shaft, arms burning with overstressed muscles. The priest and the doctor both knew about it. Assuming I didn't imagine their visits, I remind myself. I'm fighting off a mecha infection and an obscure neurological crisis at the same time. Wouldn't it be reasonable to suspect I might just be out of my skull?

The lights on the ward have dimmed, and the glimpse of sky I can see through the windows is deepening toward purple, fly-specked with burning pinpricks of luminescence that glitter oddly, as if refracted through a deep pool of water. Maybe they don't know I know about Curious Yellow and the assembler in the library basement, I tell myself. They just think I'm having a mental breakdown, and I went for a little climb. *Dissociative fugue, isn't that what the ancients called it?* I got myself infected with compost nano and Fiore called Hanta in to patch me up, and he won't mention it in Church because it would undermine the integrity of the experiment. Maybe they're right, and I just imagined killing Fiore. I'm not simply remembering fragments of badly suppressed memories, I'm confabulating out of fragments, synthesizing false memories from the wreckage of a failed erasure job. The memories of my time in the Cats, could they simply be recollections from a game I used to play? Multiplayer immersive worlds with a plot and an identity model—

I don't remember being a gamer, but if I wanted to get rid of an addiction, mightn't I have tried to flush it out with a lightweight round of memory surgery?

I can't ask anyone, I realize. If I ask Sam, and he hasn't heard of the Linebarger Cats, it doesn't mean they weren't real—everyone here's been through memory excision! I'd giggle if my throat wasn't so dry. *I am Reeve! Watch me fake up a bunch of memories to haunt myself with!* Was the guy who stalked me through the hallways of the Invisible Republic real? What about the mad bitch with the sword who called me out? I've been running from enemies I never actually saw—only glimpsed out of the sides of my eyes. It's like I'm suffering from blindsight, the strange neurological trauma that leaves its victims unable to see but able to sense events in their visual field by guessing. Maybe I'm an intelligence agent trying to track down a dangerous nest of enemies . . . and maybe I'm just a sad, sick woman who used to substitute game play for living a real life and who's now paying the price.

I lie awake in the twilight and eventually I realize that the shivering has gone. I ache, and I'm feeble, but that's to be expected after the long climb. And as I lie there I become aware of the subtle noises on the ward, the soft white noise of the air-conditioning, the tick of a clock, the quiet sobbing of—

Sobbing?

I sit bolt upright, the sheet and blanket falling away from me. My thoughts churn in parallel with a sense of dread and a numinous awareness of relief. *Rescuing Cass* and *If Cass is here, then that memory was real* with *Still doesn't mean everything else was real* and finally *If it was real, Cass must be . . .*

"Shit," I hear myself mutter. I pull the bedding up and clutch it like a frightened child. "I can't deal with this." I feel like sucking my thumb. "I am not ready for this." I'm subvocalizing, so low I make no sound. I have to talk softly when I'm telling myself the truth, because the truth is embarrassing and hurtful. I flash back to what Hanta said: When she's better, I'll ask her who she wants to be, and that's a comfort because I certainly don't have anything better to offer her. *Is Hanta up to doing memory surgery properly?* I ponder. It would surprise me if they didn't have a full surgeon-confessor along for the ride—it's the ultimate prophylactic for those little ethical embarrassments that an experimental polity might suffer. (Or for those little infiltration-level embarrassments that a secret military installation might encounter, a lying, cynical part of me that I'm no longer entirely sure I believe in adds.)

I lie down again. The sobbing continues for a while, then I hear the clacking heels of a nursing zombie converge on the bed. Quiet voices and a sigh, followed by snores. The white ghost of a nurse pauses at the foot of my bed, its face a dim oval. "Do you need anything?" It asks me.

I shake my head. It's a lie, but what I need they can't provide.

Eventually I doze off.

15

Recovery

THE next morning starts badly, shattered into fragments like a
dropped vase:

"More fugues. Reeve, you're getting worse."

His large hand enfolding my small one. Weak and pale. He strokes
the back of my wrist with his thumb. I look into his eyes and see sadness there and wonder why—

Two liquid-metal snake-heads bite at my wrist, and I cry out,
pulling away as they inject soothing numbness. The woman who carries
them is a goddess, golden-skinned with burning eyes.

I'm a tank again, a regiment of tanks, dropping through the freezing night toward an enemy habitat—or did this come later? I disconnect
from the virtch interface and shake my head, look around at the other
players in the game arcade, and hear myself whisper, *"But it wasn't
like that—"*

Scratch of a carved goose feather on rough paper, body of a pen made
from a human bone. You will remember nothing at first. If you did, they
could parse your experience vector and identify you as a threat.

"She's really bad this morning. The adjuvants have worked—that
infection is definitely on the mend—but she's no use to us like this."

"What do you expect me to do? She's in danger of sliding into full-blown anterograde—"

A suffocating stench of bowels as I slide my rapier back out of his guts. He lies among the rosebushes in a dueling zone, beneath the shadow of a marble statue of an extinct species of flying mammal. A sudden stab of horror, because this is a man I could have loved.

"Fix her."

"I can't! Not without her consent."

Hand tightening around someone's wrist until it's almost painful. "She's in no condition to give it—look at that, what are you going to do if she starts to convulse?"

I'm a tank again, looping in a pool of horrors, blood trickling beneath my gridded toes as I swing my sword through the neck of another screaming woman while two of my other instances hold her down.

I'm flying, tumbling arse over wing as my thumb sings a keening pain of broken bone, and I smell the fresh water of the roaring waterfall beneath me.

"Make it stop," I hear someone mumble, and there's blood on my lips where I've almost bitten through them. It's me who's being held down by the tanks, facing a woman with burning eyes, and behind her is a man who loves me, if I could only remember what his name was.

The snakes bite again and drink deep, and the sun goes dark.

RESTART:

I become aware that someone is holding my right hand.

Then, a timeless period later, I realize that he's still holding my hand. Which implies he's very patient, because I'm still lying in bed, and it's very bright. "What time is it?" I ask, mildly panicky because I need to get to work.

"Ssh. It's around lunchtime, and everything's all right."

"If it's all right"—Sam squeezes my hand—"how long have you been sitting there?"

"Not long."

I open my eyes and look at him. He's on the stool beside my bed. I pull a face, or smile, or something. "Liar."

He doesn't smile or nod but the tension drains out of him like water and he sags as it runs away. "Reeve? Can you remember?"

I blink rapidly, trying to get some dust out of a corner of my left eye. *Can I remember—*"I remember lots," I say. How much of what I remember is true is another matter. Just trying to sort it out makes my head hurt! I'm a tank: I'm a dissolute young bioaviator with a death wish: Maybe I'm a sad gamer case instead, or a deep-cover agent. But all of these possibilities are a whole lot sillier and less plausible than what everything around me is saying, which is that I'm a small-town librarian who's had a nervous breakdown. I decide I'll go with that version for the time being. I hold Sam's hand tight, like I'm drowning: "How bad was it?"

"Oh Reeve, it was bad." He leans across me, and hugs me and I hug him back as tight as I can. "It was bad as can be." He's shaking, I realize with a sense of growing awe. *He feels for me that deeply?* "I was afraid I was going to lose you."

I nuzzle into the base of his neck. "That would be bad." It's my turn to shudder with a frisson of existential dread at the thought that *I* could have lost *him*. Somewhere in the past week Sam has turned into my anchor, my refuge in the turbulent waters of identity. "I've got . . . well. Things are a bit jumbled today. What happened? When did you hear . . . ?"

"I came as soon as I could," he mumbles in my ear. "Last night they called but said I couldn't visit, it was too late." He tenses.

"And?" I prompt. I feel as if there should be something more.

"You were fitting." He's still tense. "Dr. Hanta said it's an acute crisis; you needed a fixative, but she couldn't do it without your permission. I told her to give it anyway, but she refused."

"A fixative? What for?"

"Your memories." He's even tenser. I let go of him, feeling cold.

"What does this fixative do?"

Dr. Hanta answers from behind me as I turn round to look at her. "Memory is encoded in a number of ways, as differential weightings in synaptic connections and also as connections between different nerves. The last excision and redaction you underwent was faulty. You began to experience breakthrough. In turn, that was triggering alerts in your enhanced immune system, and then you got yourself exposed to a mechanocytic infestation, which made things much worse. Whenever new associative traces would start integrating, your endogenous robophages would decide it was a mechanocyte signal and kill the nerve cells. You were well on your way to losing the ability to form new long-term associative traces—progressive brain damage. The fixative is normally used as the last step in redactive editing. I used it to renormalize, erase, the old memories that were breaking through. I'm sorry, but you won't be able to access them now—you keep those that you've already integrated, but the others are gone for good."

Sam has loosened his grip on me, and I lean against him as I stare at the doctor. "Did I give you permission to mess with my mind?" I ask.

Hanta just looks at me.

"Did I?" I echo myself. I feel aghast. *If she did it against my will, that's—*

"Yes," says Sam.

"What?"

"She—you were pretty far gone." He hunches over again. "She was describing the situation to you, and me, and I was asking her to do it, and she said she couldn't—then you were delirious. You began mumbling and she asked you, and you said yes."

"But I don't remember . . ." I stop. I think I do remember, sort of. *But I can't be sure, can I?* "Oh."

I stare at Hanta. I recognize the expression in her eyes. I stare at her for a long time—then I manage to make myself nod, just a quick jerk really, but it's enough to break contact, and I think we all breathe out simultaneously. Meanwhile I'm thinking, *Shit, I'll never be able to figure out where I've come from now, will I?* But it's not as bad as what was going to happen otherwise. I don't remember the attacks, exactly, but I remember what happened between them, the consequences—it's a consistent story. A new story of my life, I suppose. "I feel much better," I say cautiously.

Sam laughs, and there's a raw edge in it that borders on hysteria. "You feel better?" He hugs me again, and I hug him right back. Hanta is smiling, with what I think is relief at a difficult situation resolved. The suspicious paranoid corner of me files it away for future reference, but even my secret-agent self is willing to concede that Hanta might actually be what she seems, an ethically orthodox practitioner with only the best interests of her patients at heart. Which is a big improvement on Fiore or the Bishop, but at least one out of three isn't bad.

"So when can I go home?" I ask expectantly.

IT turns out that I'm stuck in hospital for the rest of the day and the next night, too. Hospital life is tedious, punctuated by the white-clad ghosts wheeling around trolleys of food and different things, instruments and dark age potions.

I still ache from the fever, and I feel weak, but I'm well enough to get up and go to the bathroom on my own. On my way back I notice that the curtains around the other occupied bed on the ward are drawn back. I glance around, but there are no nurses present. Steeling myself, I approach.

It is Cass, and she's a mess. Her legs are encased in bright blue polymer tubes from toe to thigh, and raised by wires so that the bedding dangles across her in a kind of valley. The bruises on her face have faded to an ugly green and yellow except around her eye sockets, which look simultaneously puffy and hollow, her eyelids sagging closed. She's still thin, and a translucent bag full of fluid is slowly draining into her wrist through a pipe.

"Cass?" I say softly.

Her eyes open and roll toward me. "Guuh," she says.

"What?" She flinches slightly. I hear footsteps behind me. "Are you all right?"

The nursing zombie approaches. "Please step away from the patient. Please step away from the patient."

"How is she?" I demand. "What have you done to her?"

"Please step away from the patient," says the nurse, then a different reflex triggers: "All questions should be addressed to medical authorities. Thank you for your compliance. Go back to bed."

"Cass—" I try a last time. Gross memory surgery falls through my mind like a snowflake, freezing everything it touches. I feel awful. "Are you there, Cass?"

"Go back to bed," says the nurse, a touch threateningly.

"I'm going, I'm going," I say, and I shuffle away from poor, damaged Cass. Cass who I thought was Kay, obsessing over her, when all the time Kay was sleeping in the next room, and Cass was living in a nightmare.

I have a problem with the ethics here, I think. Hanta's not bad. But she collaborates with Fiore and Yourdon. What kind of person would do that? I shake my head, wincing at the cognitive dissonance. One who'd perform illegal memory surgery then implant the recollection of giving informed consent in the victim's mind? I shake my head again. I don't really think Hanta would do that, but I *can't* be sure. If the patient agrees with the practitioner afterward, is it really abuse?

IT'S a bright, sunny Thursday morning when Hanta comes and sits by my bedside with a clipboard. "Well!" Her smile is fresh and approving. "You've done really well, Reeve. A splendid recovery. I think you're about well enough to go home." She uses her pen to scribble an annotation on her board. "You're still convalescent, so I advise you to take it very easy for the next few days—certainly you shouldn't go back to work until this time next week at the earliest, and ideally not until the Monday afterward. Take this note and give it to Janis when you return to work, it's a certificate of exemption from employment. If you feel at all unwell, or have another dizzy spell, I want you to telephone the hospital immediately, and we'll send an ambulance for you."

"Will the ambulance be much use if I'm incoherent or hallucinating?" I ask doubtfully.

Hanta shoves an unruly lock of hair back into place: "We're still populating the polity," she says. "The paramedics aren't due to arrive until next week. They have to have additional skill set upgrades to their implants. But in two weeks' time if you call an ambulance or see a nurse or need a police officer, you won't be dealing with a zombie." She glances along the ward. "Can't happen soon enough, if you ask me."

"I was meaning to ask . . ." I trail off, unsure how to raise the subject, but Dr. Hanta knows what I'm talking about.

"You did the right thing when you called the ambulance," she says firmly. "Never doubt that." She touches my arm for emphasis. "But zombies are no use for nonroutine circumstances." A little sigh. "It'll be much easier when I have human assistants who can learn on the job."

"How big is the polity going to grow?" I ask. "The original briefing said something about ten cohorts of ten, but if you're going to have police and ambulance crews, surely that's not enough?"

She looks surprised. "No, a hundred participants is just the size of the comparison set for score renormalization, Reeve, a single parish. We introduce participants to each other in a controlled manner, ten cohorts to a parish, but you're nearly all settled in now. Next week is when we open the manifold and link all the neighborhoods together. That's when YFH-Polity actually comes into existence! It's going to be quite exciting—you're going to meet strangers, and there'll be far fewer zombies."

"Wow," I say, my voice hollow and my head spinning. "How many, uh, neighborhoods, are you planning to link in?"

"Oh, thirty or so parishes. That's enough to form one small city, which is about the minimum for a stable society, according to our models."

"Keeping track of that must be a big job," I say slowly.

"You can say that again." Dr. Hanta stands up and straightens her white coat. "It takes at least three of me to keep track of everything!" Another errant curl gets tucked behind her collar. "Now, if you don't mind, I'm going to leave you. You're ready for discharge whenever you want to go home; just tell the nurse on the front desk that you're leaving. Is there anything else?"

"Yes," I say hastily. Then I pause for a moment. "When I was having my crisis, were you tempted to . . . you know, change anything? Apart from administering the fixative algorithm, that is?"

Hanta stares at me with her big brown eyes. She looks thoughtful. "You know, if I tried to change the minds of everyone who I thought needed changing, I'd never have time to do anything else." She smiles at me, and her expression turns chilly. "And besides, what you're asking about is highly questionable behavior, ethically questionable, Mrs. Brown. To which I have two responses. Firstly, whatever I might think of a patient, I would *never* act in a manner contrary to their best interests. And secondly, I expected better of you. Good day."

She turns and stalks away. *I've really put my foot in it now*, I think, feeling sick with embarrassment. *Me and my big mouth* . . . I want to run after her and apologize, but that would be asking to compound the misunderstanding, wouldn't it? *Idiot,* I tell myself. She's right, they couldn't run the polity without having a medical supervisor who has the subjects' best interests in mind; and I've just pissed off the only member of the experimental team who might be on my side. She could have helped me figure out how to fit in better, and instead . . . *Shit. Shit. Shit.*

There's really nothing left to do here. I stand up and rummage through the carrier bag Sam left for me last night. There's underwear, a floral print dress, and a pair of strappy sandals, but he forgot my handbag. Oh well, he gets high marks for trying. I make myself decent then, after waiting long enough for Dr. Hanta to leave the ward, I head down to reception. On the way I pass the other ward, signposted MATERNITY. I guess it'll be getting busy in a few months, but right now it's depressingly empty. There's a spring in my step as I reach the front desk. "Checking out," I say.

The zombie on the desk nods. "Mrs. Reeve Brown leaving the institution of her own volition," she drones. "Have a nice day."

The hospital faces onto Main Street, sandwiched between a run of shops and a stretch zoned for offices. It's a sunny, warm day, and my spirits rise as I go outside. I feel airy and empty, light as a feather, not a care in the world! *At least, not for now*, a stubborn part of me mutters darkly. Then I get the impression that even the part of me that's always alert shrugs its shoulders and sighs. *Still, might as well take the day off to recover.* Fiore has actually let me off the hook, for which I can thank Dr. Hanta; so I've got an actual choice. I'm free to keep on kicking and struggling against the inevitable, or I can go home and relax for a few days, just play the game and settle down. (It'll avoid attracting unwelcome attention from Fiore or the score whores, and I can pretend I'm having fun while I'm about it; I'll treat it like a game. Plus, it occurs to me that if I want to get back at Jen, the best way to do it is to defeat her on her own terms. I can always go back to figuring out how to escape later.) Meanwhile, I really ought to try to sort things out with Sam because I don't like the way paranoia and dread seems to have been levering us apart.

It takes me three hours to catch a taxi home, mostly because I pass the Lady's Lodge Beauty Parlor and stop to get my hair tidied up, and then the department store. The staff in the salon and the store are still all zombies, which is annoying, but at least they don't get in the way. I need some more clothes, anyway—I have no idea what happened to what I was wearing the other day, plus, dressing à la mode is a good, easy way to boost your score, and I can use that right now—and in between buying a couple of new outfits I fetch up at the cosmetics counter. The store is deserted, and I figure I'll give Sam a surprise, so I wait while the zombie assistant applies a makeover with inhuman speed. Those dark ages folks may not have had much by way of reconstructive nano, but they knew a lot about using natural products to change they way they looked: I barely recognize myself in the mirror by the time she's finished.

I'm still not very well, and find myself flagging much sooner than I expected. So I finish off in the shop, arrange to have my purchases delivered, and catch a taxi home. Home is much as I expected—a mess. The cleaning service I commissioned when I got the library job has been round, but they only come once a week, and Sam has been letting the dirty dishes pile up in the kitchen and leaving the glasses in the living room. I try to ignore it and put my feet up, but after half an hour it's too much. If I'm going to settle down a bit, I need to take care of that—it's part of the role I'm playing—so I move everything to the kitchen and start cycling them through the dishwasher. Then I go and lie down for a while. But a pernicious demon of dissatisfaction has gotten into my head, so I get up and start on the living room. It comes to me that I really don't like the way the furniture is laid out, and there's something about the sofa that annoys me unaccountably. The sofa will have to go.

In the meantime I can rearrange where everything is, and then I realize it's nearly six. Sam will be home soon.

I'm a very poor cook, but I manage to puzzle my way through the instructions on the cartons, and I'm just laying out the cutlery on the dining table in the dayroom when I hear the door rattle.

"Sam?" I call. "I'm home!"

"Reeve?" He calls back.

I step into the hall, and he does a double take. "Reeve?" He gapes at me: It's a priceless moment.

"I had a little accident at the cosmetics counter," I say. "Like it?"

He goes cross-eyed for a moment, then manages to nod. In addition to the makeover I'm wearing the sexiest, most revealing dress I could find. I'll take my praise where I find it. Sam's never been a great one for expressing his emotions, and this is going pretty far for him. Come to think of it, he looks tired, sagging inside his suit jacket.

"Hard day?" I ask.

He nods again. "I, uh"—he draws breath—"I thought you were ill."

"I am." I'm more tired than I want to admit in front of him. "But I'm glad to be home, and Dr. Hanta's given me the next week off work, so I figured I'd lay on a little surprise for you. Are you hungry yet?"

"I missed lunch. Didn't feel much like eating back then." He looks thoughtful. "That wasn't such a good idea, was it?"

"Come with me." I lead him into the dayroom and sit him down, then go back to the kitchen and switch on the microwave, then pick up the two glasses of wine I'd poured and take them back to the table. He doesn't say anything, but he's agog, eyes tracking me like an incoming missile. "Here. A toast—to our future?"

"Our . . . future?" He looks puzzled for a moment, then something seems to clear in his mind, and he raises his glass and finally smiles at me, surrendering some inner doubt. "Yes."

I hurry back to sort out our supper, and we eat. I don't taste much of the food because, to tell the truth, I'm watching Sam. I came so close to losing him that every moment feels delicate, like glass. A huge and complex tenderness is crystallizing in me. "Tell me about your day," I ask, to draw him out, and he mumbles through an incoherent story about missing papers for a deed of attainder or something, watching my face all the time. I have to prompt him to eat. When he's done, I walk round the table to fetch his plate, and I can feel the heat of his gaze on me. "We need to talk," I say.

"We need." His voice is congested with emotion. "Reeve."

"Come with me," I say.

He stands up. "Where? What is this about?"

"Come on." I reach out and take his necktie and gently tug. He follows me into the hallway. "This way." I take the steps slowly, going up, listening to his hoarse breathing deepen. He doesn't try to pull away until I reach the bedroom door.

"We shouldn't be doing this," he says hoarsely. "I don't know why you're doing this, but we mustn't."

"Come on." I give him a little tug and he follows me into the bedroom and I finally let go and turn to face him. I feel a looseness in my innards as I look up at his face, a warmth at my crotch. "Kay. Sam. Whoever you are. I love you."

I freeze, my eyes wide as I see his pupils dilate and he looks puzzled: I realize he didn't hear me! "The magic phrase, Sam." And I realize that I mean it. This isn't the stinger-ampoule side effect of Jen's malice, it's something more profound. "What you said to me the other day, I'm saying it right back to you." His expression clears. "Come here."

He looks confused, now. "But if we—"

"No buts." I reach over to him and tug at the knot on his necktie. It unclips from his collar, and I fumble at the top button. He chews his upper lip, and I can feel him trembling under my fingers, warm and immensely solid and reassuring. I take a step closer until I'm leaning up against him, and I feel through his clothes that he's as excited as I am. "I want you, Sam, Kay. I don't want to have any barriers between us, it hurts too much. I've nearly lost you twice now, I'm not going to lose you again."

His hands on my shoulders, huge and powerful. His breath on my cheek. "I'm afraid this isn't going to work, Reeve."

"Life's frightening." I get another button undone, then I look up to see his face above me, and I stop. I was about to stretch up to kiss him, but something about his expression isn't right. "What is it?"

"What's *wrong* with you?" he hisses. "This isn't like you, Reeve, what's happening?"

"I'm doing what I should have done last week." I wrap my arms around him and lean my forehead against his shoulder. But he's started a train of thought going, running on rails right through my lust simple: "I've had a bad experience. It put a lot of things into a new perspective, Sam. You ever had one of those? Done something stupid and crazy and maybe a bit evil and only realized afterward that you'd jeopardized everything you ever cared about? Been there, done that—more than once—most recently the day before yesterday, and I don't want to be defined by my mistakes. So I'm walking away from them. I want us to work, I don't want to—"

"Reeve, stop it. *Stop* this. You're scaring me."

Huh? I pull back and stare at him, offended. It's like a bucket of ice water in the face.

"This isn't you speaking, is it?" he asks. He sounds certain.

"Yes it is!" I insist.

"Really?" He looks skeptical. "You wouldn't have thrown yourself at me like this last week."

"Yes I would! In a moment, if I wasn't so conflicted." Then what he's trying to tell me without actually saying it in so many words sinks in, and I jam one hand across my mouth to keep from screaming in frustration.

"So you're not conflicted now," he says, gently leading me over toward the bed and pushing me down on the edge of it, sitting next to me so we're shoulder to shoulder. "But you were conflicted when you went into the hospital, Reeve. You've been conflicted as long as I've known you. So you'll pardon my momentary suspicion when, the moment you get home, you throw yourself at me? After swearing off sex entirely just a week ago."

It's there in front of me, a yawning abyss of my own making, no longer avoidable since Dr. Hanta applied her fixative. I am stuck with the me that I have become, unable to restore that which is missing. "I'm not who I was a week ago," I say tightly. "She fixed the memory leak-age, for one thing. And I've acquired a restored sense of my own mor-tality from somewhere I don't want to talk about, except it's not anything that they did to me. I think." But a cynical corner of my mind says, *You said "I love you," didn't you? Last time you did that, your CY-hack was triggered. Someone's tweaked your netlink, haven't they?*

The cold horror that steals over you when you wake up unsure whether you died in the night has just stroked its bony hand along my spine. Somewhere between the cooling puddle of blood in the library basement and Dr. Hanta's sly consent, I seem to have lost something. Sam's right, old-me wouldn't be doing this. Old-me would be scared of different things, and rightly so—and I'm still scared of Fiore and Yourdon, and I still want out of their perverse managed society, but we're on board a MASucker, and I know what that means.

"I still want you," I tell him. Although a worm of doubt adds, "I'm just not sure I want you for the same reasons I wanted you last week."

"They've gotten to you."

I laugh shakily. "They got to me a long time ago. I just didn't notice until now." I clutch at him, but as much from terror as lust. "Why are you here, Kay? Why did you sign up for the experiment?"

"I followed you."

"Bullshit!" I can see it now. "That's not enough. And don't tell me it was to get away from your time with the ice ghouls. Why did you go there? What were you running away from?"

Sam is silent and unresponsive for a while. "If I tell you, you'll prob-ably hate me."

"So?" I see an opportunity. Shuffling up onto the bed I pull my legs up under my dress and sit cross-legged with my hands in my lap. "If I listen to your story and I don't hate you afterward, will you let me fuck you?"

"I don't see what that's got to do with—"

"Let me be the judge of my motives, Sam." *Even if they're contam-inated.* "You keep trying to second-guess me. It's getting to be a bad habit. Before, I didn't want to sleep with you for reasons that made sense at the time. Then when the reasons no longer apply, you say I'm acting out of character. You don't give me credit for being able to change of my own volition."

He shakes his head.

"Have you any idea how insulting that is?"

"That's not what I meant—"

"I am capable of change, that's why I'm here!" I draw a deep breath. "I'm not who I was during the war, Sam, or before it, or even after it. I'm who I am now, which is the end product of all those other people becoming one another. They can put you into the dark ages, but they can't put the dark ages into you, not short of truncating your life expectancy to about three gigasecs or erasing so many memories you might as well be . . ." I trail off. I've got a strange feeling that I just realized something vitally important, but I'm not sure what.

He looks at me oddly. "You'll hate me," he says. "I did terrible things."

"So?" I shrug. "I did bad things, too. People out there wanted to kill me, Sam. I thought it was something to do with a mission I was on and had accidentally erased, but now I'm not so sure; maybe they were just after me because of, well, one of the people I used to be. A person who fought in the war. A combatant."

He rocks back and forth thoughtfully. "Nobody here but us war criminals," he says.

It is very interesting to discover that the phrase "my blood runs cold" actually reflects a physical sensation. It is much less pleasant to do so while sitting next to someone you love unconditionally and currently can't share a room with without needing a change of underwear, and who's just triggered that sensation in your head. And it's even worse when you realize that what he said applies to you, too. "Nobody here but us monsters," I say, trying to be flippant. "Or amnesiacs haunted by the ghosts of their past lives."

"Has it occurred to you that YFH-Polity might be very convenient for a certain type of person?" Sam asks slowly.

I'm getting impatient. "Are you going to lay me down on this bed and have sex with me after you finish lecturing me to death?"

He turns a funny color. "If we both still want to."

If we both still want to. Well, I guess you just have to work with what you've got. "I'm all ears," I say.

He shudders. "Don't say that."

"Well it's"—*not literally*—"true. Sort of."

"Where were you when the war broke out?" he asks.

Oops. I didn't expect him to ask that. Revealing that kind of thing would be a big no-no under normal circumstances—a breach of operational security that could allow an opponent to work out exactly who you are and thereby figure out all sorts of useful things about you, enough to endanger you operationally, because virtually everything you ever did in public is stored in a database somewhere. But—we're in the guts of a MASucker, and if I'm not mistaken, there's only one data channel in or out, and Sam isn't part of the cabal, and I reckon the current risk of our being eavesdropped on is low. Nor are these normal circumstances.

"I was aboard a MASucker, interviewing the crew," I admit. "We were cut off for more than a gig after the net went down." Sam makes a thoughtful noise. "Your turn," I prompt, trying to change the subject.

"I was an auditor." Sam is silent again. "That's why they drafted me."

"They?"

"The Solipsist Nation: Third Unforgivable Thoughtcrime Battalion, to be precise. They were doing a search and sweep for unsecured memory temples through the disconnected segment I was stranded in, less than a hundred kilosecs after Curious Yellow cut loose. I'd already been censored and compromised, and they just grabbed me and added me to their distributed denial of consciousness array. I spent the next couple of megs scrambling graveyards beyond retrieval, then they got around to actually in-processing me and assigned me to erasing archive trails."

Ugh. And I thought what I did in the Linebarger Cats was ugly? I must shiver or give some other cue because Sam pulls away from me slightly. "What clades did the Solipsist Nation align with?" I ask, trying to distract him.

"What clades?" He shakes his head. "It was us against everyone,

Reeve. You think anybody in their right minds would ally themselves with an aggressively solipsistic borganism?"

"But you"—I force myself to lean closer as I ask; he's tense and unhappy—"you were just a component, weren't you?"

He shakes his head. "I had some degree of autonomy, by the time the war ended the Nation had taken to investing us with a modicum of free will. I was . . . well. Before the war, I looked pretty much the way you do right now. The Nation upgraded me, turned me into a combat ogre—and put me on occupation duty. You know what they called us? Rape machines. If you want to break someone's will to resist, you can go via the brain, but if the netlink's been fried by EMP, you have to get physical. They gave us penises with backward-facing spines, you know that? We did . . . terrible things. Eventually we were overrun—my segment was overrun—by a consortium of enemies, and they offlined us and when I woke up I was back to being me again, but a *me* with memories and a large chunk of the Nation wedged in my head. I spent half a meg in my cell disbelieving in the walls and floor before I realized that they had to exist for the same reason *I* had to exist. And while I was part of the Nation I did things." Deep breath. "Things that left me ashamed to be human. Or male."

"Yeah, but." I stall. "You weren't yourself. Right?"

"I wish I could believe that." He sounds forlorn. "I wouldn't do that kind of thing now, but then—I remember believing in what I was doing. That was part of why I did the ice ghoul thing, I didn't want to be part of a species that could dream something like the Solipsist Nation into existence. I wanted—we wanted—to think every thought in the human phase-space. Do you know what it's like to be hungry and always eating and never full? Solipsist Nation wrecked memory temples out of spite because they contained thoughts we hadn't originated. And I contributed to that. I enthusiastically optimized the processes. I did it because I wanted to." He takes a deep breath. "I killed people, Reeve. I killed people permanently."

"Then we're not so different."

"You?" He stares. "But you said you'd . . ."

"I started the war on a MASucker; I didn't stay there." I take a deep breath, because I don't think I can dodge this one. "I volunteered. Joined the Linebarger Cats, combat operations. Spent nearly a gigasec being an armored regiment. Ended up in Psyops."

"Well." His voice is shaky. "I didn't expect *that*."

"What proportion of the people here do you think fought in the wars?"

"I haven't thought about it."

"People who were there don't want to remember it. Almost as soon as we'd got a local cease-fire established, people were slinking off to the surgeon-confessors."

"Yes." He pauses. "But Reeve, I'm a monster. There are things in my head—even after excision—that I don't like to visit. You don't want to get too close to me."

"Sam." I shift toward him. "I'm . . . There are things I tried to bury, too. I could say the same. Do you care?"

"What, about what you did?"

"Yes."

"No."

"Well, then." It's my turn to sound shaky. "What I said earlier stands. A bargain, and you agreed to it, hmm?"

He shrinks away. "I didn't know."

I swallow to try and clear my dry mouth. "I don't mean right now," I say. To my surprise, I mean it. "But I still want you, just as soon as you get used to the idea that I want you and I'm still me. You don't have to project your hatred of what you were forced to do onto me. And besides, I didn't see any barbs on your cock the other night."

"But you've changed too much!" He bursts out, like an iced-over air valve finally cutting loose. "Since Dr. Hanta saw you. Before that, you were *you*: You were moody and thoughtful, you were cynical, you were funny—I don't have the words for it. Whatever she did, it's *changed you*, Reeve. You'd refuse to do something just because it was expected of you; now you're trying to make me fuck you! Do you really want to get trapped in YFH for the foreseeable future? Trapped and pregnant, too?"

I think about it for a moment. "What's the problem?" Hanta is a more than conscientious doctor, and I'm confident I can survive a pregnancy—after all, every female mammal in my family tree did it before me, didn't they? How bad can it be?

"Reeve." Now he's looking at me as if I've morphed into battle-form, sprouting spikes and guns and armor before his eyes. I giggle. It's like he's seen a ghost! "What have they done to you?"

"Offered me a way out of having been a monster." I lean toward him hopefully. "Give me a kiss?"

DESPITE my best planning, we do not make love in the end.

In fact, when I finish the cleaning up and come to bed, Sam gets up and, with sleepy dignity, insists he's sleeping alone.

I am so angry and frustrated that I could cry. My problem is easily defined—it's the solution that eludes me. It's not that I've changed a lot, but—with or without Hanta's prompting—I've decided to take some time out of struggling, and the outward manifestation looks like a huge switch. Sam simply hasn't caught up with me yet. It's very disturbing to be around someone who seems to have inverted all their values and beliefs, and I know if it was Sam who'd been in hospital and come home glassy-eyed and different, I'd be incredibly upset. But I wish he wouldn't project his anxiety onto me—I'm all right, in fact I'm better than I've been at any time since I first woke up in the custody of the surgeon-confessors.

Yes, there's a problem here: Fiore and Yourdon are doing something very dubious with a serialized copy of Curious Yellow, they've figured out a way to defeat the security patch in everyone's implants; and they seem to be researching how to use social control rules installed via CY to create an emergent dictatorship. But—and this is the important question—*why should I care?* Haven't I been through enough already? I don't have to let myself be tortured by my own memories; I've already nearly killed myself trying to do what Sanni and the others in Security Cell Blue wanted. I've done my duty, and failed. And now . . .

My dirty little secret is that while I was in hospital I realized that I could give up. I've got Sam. I've got a job that has the potential to be as interesting as I want it to be. I can settle down and be happy here for a while, even though the amenities are primitive and some of the neighbors are not to my taste. Even dictatorships need to provide the vast majority of their citizens with a comfortable everyday life. I don't have to keep fighting, and if I give up the struggle for a while, they'll leave me alone. I can always go back to it later. Nobody will scream if I stop, except maybe Sam, and he'll adapt to the new me eventually.

All of which is great in theory, but it doesn't help when I'm crying myself to sleep, alone.

16

Suspense

THE next day is Friday. I wake up late, and by the time I get downstairs, Sam has already gone to work. I feel drained, enervated by the aftereffects of my infection and the stupid climbing attempt, so I don't do much. I end up spending most of the day shuttling between the bedroom and the kitchen, catching up on my reading and drinking cups of weak tea. When Sam comes home—really late, and he's already eaten at the steak diner in town and had a glass or three of wine—I demand to know where he's been, and he clams up. Neither of us wants to back down, so we end up not talking.

On Saturday I come downstairs in time to find him putting the lawn mower away. "You'll need to tidy up in the garage," he says by way of greeting.

"Why?" I ask.

"I need to stash some stuff."

"Uh-huh. What stuff?"

"I'm going out. See you later."

He means it—ten minutes after that he's gone, off in a taxi to who knows where. And it's our most significant communication in two days.

I kick myself for being stupid. *Stupid* is the watchword of the day.

So I go into the garage and look for stuff to throw out. It's a scrapyard of unfinished projects, but I think the welding gear can go, and the half-finished crossbow, and most of the other junk I've been tinkering with under the mistaken idea that what I need to escape from is *where* I am, rather than *who* I am. Some bits are missing anyway; I guess Sam's already made a start on clearing it out to make room for his golf clubs or whatever. So I heap my stuff in one corner and pull a tarpaulin over it. *Out of sight, out of mind, out of garage,* that's what I say.

Back inside, I try to watch some TV, but it's inane and slow, not to mention barely comprehensible. Bright blurry lights on a low-resolution screen with a curving front, slow-moving and tedious, with plots that don't make sense because they rely on shared knowledge that I just don't have. I'm steeling myself to turn it off and face the boredom alone when the telephone rings.

"Reeve?"

"Hi? Who—Janis! How are you?" I clutch the handset like a drowning woman.

"Okay, Reeve, listen, do you have anything on today?"

"No, no I don't think so—why?"

"I'm meeting a couple of friends in town this afternoon to try out a new cafe near the waterfront that's just appeared. I was wondering if you'd like to come and join us? If you're well enough, that is."

"I'm"—I pause—"supposed to take it easy for a few days. That's what Dr. Hanta said." Let her chew on that. "Is there a problem with work?"

"Not so you'd notice." Janis sounds dismissive. "I'm catching up on my reading, to tell the truth. Anyway, I got the note from the hospital. Don't worry on my part."

"Oh, okay then. As long as I'm not going to have to run anywhere. How do I get to this place?"

"Just ask a taxi to take you to the Village Cafe. I'll be there around two. I was thinking we could try out the cafe and maybe chat."

I am getting an itchy feeling that Janis isn't telling me everything, but the shape of what she's not telling me is coming through clearly enough. I shiver a bit. *Do I really want to get involved?* Probably not—

but they'll start talking if I don't, I think. Besides, if they're planning something stupidly dangerous, I owe it to Dr. Hanta to talk them out of it, I suppose. I glance at the TV set. "All right. Be seeing you."

It's already one o'clock, so I change into a smarter outfit and call a taxi to the Village Cafe. I've no idea what friends Janis might have in mind, but I don't think she'd be tasteless enough to invite Jen along. Beyond that, I don't want to risk making a bad impression. Appearances count if you're trying to up your score, and other people pay attention to that kind of thing. And I don't expect Janis would be organizing anything like this if it wasn't important.

It's a wonderful day, the sky a deep blue and a warm breeze blowing. Janis is right about one thing—I don't remember ever seeing this neighborhood before. The taxi cruises between rows of clapboard-fronted houses with white picket fences and mercilessly laundered grass aprons in front of them, then hangs a left around a taller brick building and drives along a tree-lined downhill boulevard with oddly shaped buildings to either side. There are other taxis about, and people! We drive past a couple out for a stroll along the sidewalk. I thought Sam and I were the only folks who did that. Who am I missing?

The taxi stops just before a cul-de-sac where a semicircle of awnings shield white tables and outdoor furniture from the sky. A stone fountain burbles wetly by the roadside. "Village Cafe," recites the driver. "Village Cafe. Your credit score has been debited." Blue numerals float out of the corner of my left eye as I open the door and step out. There are people sitting at the tables—one of them waves. It's Janis. She's looking a lot better than the last time I saw her: She's smiling, for one thing. I walk over.

"Janis, hi." I recognize Tammy sitting next to her but don't know what to say. "Hello everybody?"

"Reeve, hi! This is Tammy, and here's Elaine—"

"El," El mumbles.

"And this is Bernice. Have a chair? We were just trying to work out what to order. Would you like anything?"

I sit down and see printed polymer sheet menus sitting in front of each chair. I try to focus on them, just as a box with a grille on it above the door to the cafe crackles and begins to shout: "Good afternoon! It's another beautiful day . . ."

"I think I'll have a gin and tonic," I say.

"Your attention please, here are two announcements," continues the box. "Ice cream is now on sale for your enjoyment. The flavor of the day is truffle and banana. Here is a warning. There is a possibility of light showers later in the day. Thank you for your attention."

Tammy pulls a face. "It's been doing that every ten minutes since we arrived. I wish it'd shut up."

"I asked at the counter," Janis says apologetically. "They say they can't shut it off—it's everywhere in this sector."

"Yes? What is this sector, anyway? I don't remember it." I bury my nose in the menu immediately in case I've just made a faux pas.

"I'm not sure. It appeared yesterday, so I thought we should go look at it."

"Consider it looked at," says Bernice. Who is dark and slightly plump and wears a perpetual expression of mild disgust: I think I've seen her at Church, but that's about it. "Mine's a mango lassi."

A zombie, male, wearing a dark suit and a long, white apron, shuffles out of the cafe. "Are you ready to order?" he asks in a high, nasal voice.

"Yes, please." Janis rattles off a list of drinks, and the waitron retreats indoors again. The drinks are mostly alcohol-free: I seem to be one of the odd ones out. *Oops*, I think. "Tammy and El and I have been meeting up every Saturday for the past few weeks," she adds in my direction. "We tell our husbands we're a sewing circle. It's a good excuse to gossip and drink, and none of them would know a real sewing circle if one bit him on the toe, so . . ."

"What *is* a sewing circle?" asks Bernice.

El reaches diffidently into a huge bag and pulls out a thing that looks like an airlock cover made of cloth. There are pins stuck in it, and colored thread. "Something like we all get together to do embroidery. Like this." She pulls a needle out and manages to stab herself in the ball of one thumb with it. "I'm not very good yet," she adds mournfully.

"Count me out of the sewing," I say. "But the drinks and gossip are another matter."

"That's what she said you'd say." Tammy flashes me an apologetic smile. "Besides, I was wondering if you knew what had happened to Mick."

Oops again. "I'm not sure. I asked Dr. Hanta about him, and she said it was *under discussion*, whatever that means. I know Cass is still in the hospital."

"Ah, right." Tammy leans back. "Ten dollars says they both retire from the experiment within a week."

I shiver. There's only one way in or out of a MASucker, for reason of security—to let the flight crew barricade the door if the civilization on the other side of it collapses. "I'm not sure how likely that is," I say. "But Dr. Hanta has a way of straightening things out. I'm sure she'll be able to do something for Cass, and I know Mick hasn't visited her since . . . well."

"What about Fiore?" asks Janis.

I am getting the distinct feeling that they've invited me here to pump me for information, but what do I care? They're buying the drinks. "I ran into him after the business with Cass," I say. Then the cafe door opens, and the waitron returns with our drinks. I shut up until his back's turned. "He, um, I get the feeling he doesn't approve of us doing anything unpredictable, but at the same time Mick went too far. We solved a problem for him."

"Oh." Janis looks disappointed, and I mentally kick myself. What she's really asking about is what happened in the library the day she was off sick.

"I got talking to Dr. Hanta in hospital," I offer. "She said, uh, well, she doesn't approve of the business with Esther and Phil at all. I got the impression she was yelling at the Bishop about it. They're going to add rules for divorce proceedings to the score system to stop it happening again. And rape, to stop anyone getting ideas from Mick."

"Hmm." Janis looks thoughtful. "If they stick to a strict dark ages re-creation, they'll make rape a serious penalty score, but only if the male gets caught."

"Eh?" Tammy looks indignant. "What good will that do?"

"What good does *any* of this do?" Janis asks drily. She reaches into her handbag and pulls out a piece of knitting, which she passes to me. "I think this is yours, you left this in the library," she tells me.

I gulp and hastily stuff the Faraday cage lining of my botched experimental carrier into my handbag. "Thanks, I sure did," I babble.

Janis smiles slowly. "It's a bit scratchy, but it catches the light just so."

Wheels within wheels. "It needs a bit more work," I extemporize. "Where did you find it?"

"In the back office. I was just tidying up."

My heart seems to be pounding, but nobody else has noticed. Janis looks at me, then looks at El. "What do you think?" she asks.

El looks up from her embroidery, harried. "I think I feel a little sick," she says, and reaches for her pink lemonade. "Church is going to be bad tomorrow."

"Lots of developments," Tammy agrees.

"What are you talking about?" I ask.

Janis nods at me: "Yes, that's right, you've been in hospital all week. Since Tuesday, anyway."

Tammy pulls out a tablet and puts it on the table. "Lots of new stuff in here," she says, tapping the screen. "You'll want to know about it."

"About what?" I ask.

"For starters, it seems our last cohort is in place here."

"But they said there were another fourteen after mine"—I do the math—"so we're six short. At least?"

Tammy taps her tablet. "They've been running multiple sections of YFH-Polity in parallel. We're just one subsector, a parish, they call it. From Monday they're all going to be linked up, so we've got lots of new neighbors."

So far this is what Dr. Hanta told me. "And?"

Janis gives me a long, appraising look. "It's a lot bigger than they told you outside when you were signed up. What does that suggest to you?"

I look at her belly. It's not much of a bump yet. Then, almost involuntarily, my eyes slide sideways. "El, are you, I mean I hope I'm not prying here, but are you by any chance—"

"Pregnant?" El looks at me with her baby-blue eyes and puts one hand on her stomach. "Whatever gave you that idea?"

I try not to wince too obviously. "My period's overdue," says Bernice. *Permanence.* "What else are they doing?" I probe.

"There are a lot of new facilities opening up," Tammy explains enthusiastically. "There's a kinematoscope, and a swimming pool and gymnastic coliseum, and a theatre. More shops, too. And City Hall will be open for business."

Bernice cracks before I do. "Whoa. That's a new one on me!"

"I think they're trying to make us *comfortable*," says Janis.

"Us?" I ask. "Or them?" My eyes take in bellies around the table, occupied bellies. In fact, mine is the only *un*-occupied one here. Thanks to Sam.

"Does it make any difference? I'm pretty sure most of us will be too busy changing nappies soon to worry about anything else."

Janis has a tone of voice that she uses when she means to convey the exact opposite of the literal meaning of her words. She's using it now, laying on the sarcasm with a trowel.

I smile brightly. "Then I suppose you think we should lie back and enjoy these wonderful new recreational resources!"

"Reeve," Tammy says warningly, "this is serious."

"Oh, you bet," I agree enthusiastically. "Absolutely!" I finish my drink. "I'm sure you ladies have got lots of important things to be talking about, but I just remembered I haven't finished washing the dishes, and I've got to clear out the garage before my husband gets home." I stand up. "Thanks for the weaving, Janis. See you later?"

The rest of the soi-disant ladies' sewing circle look dubious, but Janis smiles back at me, then winks. "Be seeing you!"

I beat a hasty retreat. I like Janis, but this sewing circle of hers frightens me. She's unhappy here, that much is clear, and I don't think she'll want Dr. Hanta to help her over it. I'm going to have to tell Fiore about Janis, I realize. She needs help. *After Church tomorrow?*

THE journey to Church the next day is strained and tense. We dress in our Sunday best and call a taxi as usual, but Sam doesn't say anything—he's taken to communicating in grunts—and keeps casting me odd sidelong looks when he thinks I won't notice. I pretend not to see. In truth I'm tense, too, winding myself up for the inevitable and unpleasant conversation with Fiore after the service. Church is packed these days, and we're lucky to get a seat. At least there are other churches in the other parishes (and presumably other instances of Fiore to preach in them), so it's not likely to get any more crowded. "We'll have to leave earlier in future," I tell Sam, and he stares at me.

Fiore walks in and goes to the front, and the music strikes up, a catchy brassy little number by (my netlink tells me) a composer named Brecht. Then Fiore starts the service proper. "Dear congregants, we are gathered here today in unity to recognize our place in the universe, our immutable roles in the great cycle of life, which none shall take from us. Let us praise the designers who have given us this day and all the days before us a role to fulfill! Praise the designers!"

"*Praise the designers!*" echoes the congregation.

"Dear congregants, let us remember that true meaning and happiness in life can be found through complying with the great design! A round peg in a round hole!"

"*A round peg in a round hole!*" rolls the response.

"Let us also give thanks for the happiness that has come to Mrs. Reeve Brown, who is now most certainly a round peg in a round hole, and for the solace and comfort that members of our congregation's away team have brought to Mrs. Cassandra Green, now recovering in hospital! Happiness, comfort, and solace!"

"*Happiness, comfort, and solace!*"

I shake my head, happy but confused. I can't figure it out, why is Fiore holding me of all people up as an example to the rest of the congregation? I glance round and see Jen, a couple of aisles away, staring snake eyes at me.

"It is our duty to care for our neighbors, to help them conform to the ways of our society, to join with them in their joy and their sorrow, their acceptance and their forgiveness. If your neighbors need you, go unto them and give them the benefit of your generosity. We are all neighbors, and those of us who are not in need this week may be among the neediest next week. Guide and care for them, and chide them when it is appropriate . . ."

I begin to zone out. Fiore's voice is hypnotic, his tone rising and falling in a measured cadence. It's warm and stuffy in Church with the doors shut, and it seems Fiore isn't going to divert from his sermon to condemn a sinner this week. For which I should be grateful—Fiore could have decided to wreck my score for what I did last week. Despite the warmth, I find myself shivering. He's shown more forbearance than I expected. Should I follow his example, and instead of telling him about Janis, try to set her straight myself?

". . . For remember, you are your brother's keepers, and by the behavior of your brethren shall you be judged. Voyage without end, amen!"

"Voyage without end!" echoes the chorus. *"Amen!"*

We stand, and there's another sing-along, clap-along number—this time in a language I don't understand, about marching and freedom and bread according to the psalm book—and then the priest and his attendants leave the front, and the service is over.

I'm a bit disappointed, but also relieved as we file out of the Church into the bright daylight, where a buffet is waiting for us. Sam is even quieter than usual, but right now I don't care. I snag a glass of wine and a plate with a wheatmeal and fungus confection on it and wander over to the vicinity of our cohort.

"Decided to settle down, have we?" asks a voice at my left shoulder. I manage to suppress a frown of distaste. It's Jen, of course.

"I care for my neighbors," I say, squeezing every gram of sincerity I can muster into it; then I make myself smile at her.

She beams back at me, of course. "Me too!" She trills, then glances round. "I'm glad Fiore was merciful today, though. I gather some of us might have been in for a rough ride!"

Sly little bitch. "I've no idea what you're talking about," I begin, but it's impossible to go on because the Church bells have begun to ring. Normally they clang in a vague semblance of rhythm, but now they're jarring and clattering as if something's caught up among them. People are turning and looking up at the tower. "That's odd."

"Yes, it is." Jen sniffs dismissively and begins to turn toward a nearby knot of males.

"I haven't finished with you."

"In your dreams, darling." A broad grin, and she slips away.

Irritated, I look up at the tower. The door below it is ajar. *Odd*, I think. It's not strictly my business, but what if something's come loose? I ought to get help. I deposit my glass and plate with a passing waitron and walk toward the door, taking care to stay off the grass in my high heels.

The clashing and clattering of disturbed bells is getting louder, and there's something dark on the front step, under the door. As I make my way to it I look down and an unpleasantly familiar stink infiltrates my nostrils, bringing tears to my eyes. I turn round, and yell, "Over here! Help!" Then I push the door open.

The bell tower is a tall space illuminated by small windows just below the base of the spire. The daylight spilling down from them casts long shadows across the beams and the bells that dangle from them, jostling and clashing above the whitewashed floor, staining the spreading pool of dark liquid. Spreading black, the gray of shadows, and a pale pendulum swinging across the floor. It takes a second for my eyes to grow accustomed to the dimness, and another second before I understand what they're showing me.

Mick, of all people, is the one playing the endless atonal carillon that summoned me. It is immediately obvious that his mastery of music is involuntary. He hangs from a bell-rope by the ankles, his head tracing an endless pendulous circuit across the floor in twin tracks of blood. Someone has taped his arms to his body, gagged him, and rammed hypodermic needles into each ear. The cannulae drip steadily, emptying what's left of his blood supply from his purple and congested head. Loops and whorls and spirals of blood have trickled in a delicate filigree, but some unevenness in the ground leads the runnels to flow toward a pool on the inside of the door.

I'm simultaneously appalled, dumbstruck with admiration for the artistic technique on display, terrified that whoever did it might still be lurking at the scene, and utterly nauseated at my satisfaction at Mick's end. So I do the only sensible and socially expedient thing I can think of, and scream my lungs out.

The first fellow to arrive on the scene—a couple of seconds after I get started—isn't much use: He takes one look at the impromptu chandelier, then doubles over and adds his lunch to the puddle. But the second on the scene turns out to be Martin, one of the volunteer gravediggers. "Reeve? Are you all right?"

I nod and manage to take a sobbing breath. I feel unstable, and my vision is watery. "Look." I point. "Better get the . . . the . . . Fiore. He'll know what to do."

"I'll call the police." Martin walks around the pool of blood and vomit carefully and picks up the telephone handset that's fastened to the wall by the vestry entrance. "Hello? Operator?" He jiggles the switch on top of the handset. "That's odd."

My brain is slowly beginning to work again. "What's odd?"

"The telephone. It's not making any noise. It doesn't work."

I snuffle, wipe my nose on the sleeve of my jacket, and stare at him. "That's very odd." *Yes*, a quiet corner of my mind reminds me, *that's odd, and not in a good way.* "Let's go outside."

Andrew—the guy who's throwing up—has just about finished, and is down to making choking, sobbing noises. Martin pulls him up by one arm, and we walk outside together. There's a growing crowd on the porch, curious to know what's going on. "Someone call the police," Martin shouts. "Get the Reverend if you can find him!" People are pushing past him to look inside the doorway, yelling in disbelief and coming back out again.

Somebody is sending us, the congregation, a message, aren't they? I stumble but make it down onto the grass. Sam's there, looking concerned. "You were with me during the service," I hiss. "You were next to me the whole time. You know where I was."

"Yes?" He looks puzzled. So do I. *I'm not sure why I'm doing this, but . . .*

"I spoke to Jen briefly, then heard the bells and went to see. Then I screamed. I was only inside for a second on my own. Wasn't I?"

Sam gets it: His shoulders tense suddenly. "How bad is it?"

"Mick." I gasp quietly, then run out of words. I can't continue just now because I had to look; I saw how his killer fastened him to the bell-rope by his ankles, cutting him and running the thick rope through the meaty gap between the bone and the thick tendon. I'm half-afraid that when they cut him down, they'll discover he was raped first, while paralyzed, before his killer strung him up to drain like a slab of flesh. A moment later I'm leaning on Sam's shoulder, sobbing. He doesn't pull away, but holds me in silence while all around us the crowd throbs and chatters. I've seen many horrible things in my life, but there was a judicial deliberation implicit in what was done to Mick—a hideous moral statement, blindly confident in its own righteousness. I know exactly who did it, even though I spent the entire service next to Sam; because for hours on end I lay awake and fantasized about doing that to Mick, the night we took Cass away.

"WELL, Mrs. Brown, how fascinating to see you here! Always in the thick of things, I see."

His Excellency smiles like a skeleton, jaw agape at some private joke. Sam shuffles next to me but holds his peace. You do not talk back to the Bishop, especially when it's clear that his humor is a mercurial thing, a butterfly floating above a blast furnace of rage at the intrusion that has spoiled his Sunday.

Fiore clears his throat. "She is not a suspect," he says stiffly.

"What?" Yourdon's head whips round like a snake's. The police zombies around us tense as if nervous, hands going to the batons at their belts.

It's been half an hour since I opened the door, and the cops have surrounded the churchyard. They're not letting people go until Yourdon says so. He's clearly in a foul mood. Cold-blooded murder isn't something our community has had to deal with so far, and if we're to stay in the spirit of the experiment, we must remember that to the ancients it was as grievous a crime as identity theft or relational corruption. It's at this point that the deficiencies of our little parish become apparent. We have no real chief of police, no trained investigators. And so the Bishop is forced to tend his flock in person.

"I saw her arrive with her husband, she was present throughout the service, and numerous witnesses saw her approach the door and go inside, then heard her scream. She was alone inside for all of ten seconds, and if you think she could have committed the offense in that space of time . . ."

"I'll ask for you to second-guess me when I can't be bothered to make up my own mind." Yourdon's cheek twitches, then he switches his attention to Martin so abruptly I feel my knees weaken. An invisible pressure has come off my skull. "You. What did you see?"

Martin clears his throat, and is stuttering into an account of finding me screaming before a corpse when a cop walks up to Fiore for a brief, mumbled conversation.

Yourdon glares at his subordinate. "Will you stop that?"

Fiore shuffles. "I have new information, Your Excellency."

"Yes? Well, out with it! I haven't got all day."

Fiore—the bumptious, supercilious buffoon of a priest who likes nothing more than to lord it over his congregation—wilts like a punctured aerostat. "A preliminary forensic examination appears to have revealed DNA traces left by the killer."

Yourdon snorts. "Why did we wait to commission a squad of detectives? Come on, don't waste my time."

Fiore takes a sheet of paper from the cop. "PCR amplification in accordance with—no, skip that—determines that the fingerprint on file is congruent with, uh, myself. And nobody else in YFH-Polity."

Yourdon looks furious. "Are you telling me that you strung him up to bleed out?"

To his credit, Fiore holds his ground. "No, Your Excellency, I'm telling you that the murderer is playing with us."

I lean against Sam, feeling nauseous. *But that was my fantasy, wasn't it? About how to deal with Mick. And I never told anyone about it. Which means, I must be the killer! Except I didn't do it. What's going on?*

"That's it." Yourdon claps his hands together. "Action this day—you, Reverend Fiore, will coordinate with Dr. Hanta to select, train, and augment a chief police constable. Who in turn will be empowered and authorized to induct four citizens into the police force at the rank of sergeant. You will also discuss with me at a later date the selection of a judge, procedures for arraigning criminals before a jury, and the appointment of an executioner." He glares at the priest. "Then you will, I trust, return your chapel to the pristine condition it was in before I entrusted it to you—and see to the pastoral care of your flock, many of whom are in dire need of direction!"

The Bishop turns on his heel and sweeps back toward his long black limousine, trailed by a trio of police zombies bearing primitive but effective automatic weapons. I sag against Sam's arm, but he keeps me upright. Fiore waits until the Bishop slams his door shut, then takes a deep breath and shakes his head lugubriously. "No good will come of this," he grumbles in our direction—us, the proximate witnesses, and the zombies who discreetly hem us in. "Police: dismissed. Citizens, you should attend to the state of your consciences. At least one of you knows exactly what happened here today, before the service, and staying silent will not be to your benefit."

The police zombies begin to disperse, followed by a gaggle of curious parishioners. I approach Fiore cautiously. I'm very disturbed, and I'm not sure this is the right time, but . . .

"Yes, what is it, my child?" He narrows his eyes and composes his face in a smile of benediction.

"Father, I, I wonder if I can have a word with you?" I ask hesitantly.

"Of course." He glances at a police zombie. "Go to the vestry, fetch a mop and bucket and cleaning materials, and begin cleaning up the floor of the bell tower."

"It's about . . ." I trail off. My conscience really is pricking me, but I'm not sure how to continue. I feel eyes on me from across the yard, curious eyes wondering what I'm saying.

"Do you know who did it?" Fiore demands.

"No, I wanted to talk to you about Janis, she's been very strange lately—"

"Do you think Janis killed him?" Bushy elevated eyebrows frame dark eyes that stare down his patrician nose at me, a nose that doesn't belong to the same face as those wattles of fatty tissue around his throat. "Do you?"

"Uh, no—"

"Some other time, then," he says, and before I realize I'm dismissed, he's calling out to another police zombie, "You! You, I say! Go to the undertaker depot and bring a coffin to the bell tower—" And a moment later he's walking away from me, cassock flapping around his boots.

"Come on," says Sam. "Let's go home right now." He takes me by the arm.

I screw up my eyes to keep from crying. "Let's."

He leads me across the car park toward the waiting queue of taxis. "What did you try to tell Fiore?" he asks quietly.

"Nothing." If he wants to know so badly, he can talk to me the rest of the time, when I'm lonely.

"I don't believe you." He's silent for a minute as we get into a taxi.

"Then don't believe me." The taxi pulls away from the curb without asking us where we want to go. The zombies know us all by sight.

"Reeve." I look at him. He stares at me, his expression serious.

"What?"

"Please don't make me hate you."

"Too late," I say bitterly. And right then, for exactly that moment, it's true.

17

Mission

IT'S raining when I wake up the day after the murder. And it rains—
gently, lightly, but persistently—every day for the rest of the week, mir-
roring my mood to perfection.

I've got the run of the house and doctor's orders to take things
easy—no need to go in to work in the library—so I should be happy. I
made up my mind to be happy here, didn't I? But I seem to have messed
things up with Sam, and there are dark, frightening undercurrents at
work around me—people who've made the opposite choice and who'll
pounce on me in an instant if I don't tread a careful line. Now that I
have time to think things through, I'm profoundly glad that Fiore wasn't
paying attention when I tried to tell him about Janis. Life is getting
cheaper by the week, and there are no free resurrections here—no home
assemblers to back up on daily.

Am I really that worried?

Yes.

I manage to make it through to Thursday morning before I crack. I
wake up with the dawn light (I'm not sleeping well at present), and I
hear Sam puttering around the bathroom. I look out the window at the
raindrops that steadily fall like a translucent curtain before the vegeta-

tion, and I realize that I can't stand this any more. I don't want another day on my own in the house. I know Dr. Hanta said to take the whole week off to recover, but I feel fine, and at least if I go in to work, there'll be something to do, won't there? Someone to talk to. A friend, of sorts, even if she's behaving weirdly these days. And even if I feel uncomfortable about what I'll say when I see her.

I dress for work, then head downstairs and call a taxi, as usual. I'm half-tempted to walk, but it's raining, and I've neglected to buy any waterproof gear. *Rain aboard a starship, who'd have imagined it?* I wait just inside the front porch until the taxi pulls up, then rush over to it and pile in on the backseat. "Take me to the library," I gasp.

"Sure thing, ma'am." The driver pulls away, with a bit more acceleration than I'm used to. "Wonder when this weather will stop?"

Huh? I shake myself. "What did you say?"

"I heard from Jimmy at the public works department that they're doing it because they discovered a problem with the drainage system—need to flush out the storm sewers. I'm Ike, by the way. Pleased to meet you."

I just about manage to recover gracefully: "I'm Reeve. Been driving cabs long?"

He chuckles. "Since I got here. You're a librarian? That's a new one on me. I can get you downtown from here, but you'll need to show me which block it's on."

"The merger," I manage to say.

"Yeah, that's the deal." He taps a syncopated rhythm on the steering wheel, keeping time with the windscreen wipers, then hauls the cab through a sharp turn. "What does a librarian do all day?"

"What does a cab driver do?" I counter, still shaken. *Those are manual controls! They put one of us in charge of a machine like that* . . . They must be serious about turning this into a functioning polity. Which means they probably figure they've got the scoring levels loaded into our implants just about right. "People come in and they ask for books and we help them find them." I shrug. "There's more to it than that, but that's it in a nutshell."

"Uh-huh. Me, I drive around all day. Get a call on the wireless, go find the fare, take them where they want to go."

"Sounds boring. Is it?"

He laughs. "Finding books sounds boring to me, so I guess we're even! Downtown square, City Hall coming up. Where do you want to go from here?"

It's not raining in the downtown district. "Drop me off here and I'll walk the rest of the way," I offer, but he's having none of it.

"Naah, I need to learn where everything is, don't I? So where is it?"

I surrender. "Next left. Go two blocks, then take the first right and park. You're opposite it."

I arrive at my workplace thoroughly shaken and not quite sure why. I already heard Yourdon talking about police sergeants and judges. Are we going to end up without any zombies at all, doing everything for ourselves? That would be how you'd go about running an accurate dark ages social simulation, I realize, but it means things are happening on an altogether larger scale than I'd imagined.

I'm a little late—the library is already open—but there are no customers, so I walk straight up to the counter and smile at Janis, who is nose-down in a book. "Hi!"

She jerks upright, then looks surprised. "Reeve. I wasn't expecting you today."

"Well, I got bored sitting around at home. Dr. Hanta said I could come in to work today if I wanted to and, well, it beats watching the rain, doesn't it?"

Janis nods, but she looks unamused. She closes her book and puts it down carefully on the desk. "Yes, I suppose it does." She stands up. "Want a cup of coffee?"

"Yes please!" I follow her back into the staff room. It feels really good to be back—this is where I belong. Janis is feeling low, but I can help sort that out. Then we've got a library to run! And what could be better than that? Ike can keep his smelly, dangerous cab.

"Well then." Janis switches the kettle on and looks me up and down critically. "I may have to go out for a couple of hours. You going to be all right running the place on your own?"

"No problem!" I straighten my skirt. Maybe it was some lint?

She winces, then rubs her forehead. "Please, not so much enthusiasm this early in the morning. What's gotten into you?"

"I've been bored!" I manage to keep myself from squeaking. "It's been boring at home, and it's been raining all week long." I pull out the other chair and sit down. "You can't go shopping every day of the week, there's only so much cleaning and tidying you can do in one house, the television is boring, and I should have stopped here to borrow some books but I thought . . ." I wind down. *What* have *I been thinking?*

"I think I see." A wan smile tugs at the corners of her eyes. "How's Sam?"

I tense. "What makes you ask?"

The smile fades. "He was here yesterday. Wanted to talk about you, wanted to know my opinion . . . He doesn't feel he can talk to you, so he has to let it out with someone else. Reeve, that's *not* good. Are you all right? Is there anything I can do to help?"

"Yes, you can change the subject." I say it lightly, but she just about freezes right up on the spot. "Sam's taken offense to something I said, and we need to sort it out between us." My stomach churns with anger and guilt, but I bite back on it. It's not Janis's fault after all, but Sam should know better, the pig. "We'll sort it out," I add, trying to reassure her.

"I . . . see." Janis looks as if she's sucking on a slice of lemon. Right then the kettle comes to a boil, so she stands up and pours the hot water into two mugs, then scoops in the creamy powder and mixes it up. "I hope you won't take this the wrong way, Reeve, but you seem to have changed since you came out of hospital. You haven't really been yourself."

"Hmm? What do you mean?" I blow on my coffee to cool it.

"Oh, little things." She raises an eyebrow at me. "You've gained a certain enthusiasm. You're more interested in exteriors than interiors. And you seem to have lost your sense of humor."

"What's humor got to do with it?" I glare at my mug, willing myself not to get angry. "I know who I am, I know who I was."

"Forget I said it." Janis sighs. "I'm sorry, I don't know what's gotten into me. I'm getting really bitchy these days." She falls silent for a while. "I hope you don't mind my leaving you for a few hours."

I manage a forced laugh. Janis's issues aren't my business, strictly speaking, but—"What are friends for?"

She looks at me oddly. "Thanks." She takes a mouthful of her coffee and makes a face. "This stuff is vile, the only thing worse that I can think of is not having it at all." Her frown lengthens. "I'm running late. See you back around lunchtime?"

"Sure," I say, and she stands up, grabs her jacket from the back of the door, and heads off.

I finish my coffee, then go back to the front desk. There's some filing to do, but the cleaning zombies have been thorough—they didn't even leave me any dusty top shelves to polish. A couple of bored office workers drop in to return books or browse the shelves for some lunchtime entertainment, but apart from that the place is dead. So it happens that I'm sitting at the front desk, puzzling over whether there's a better way to organize the overdue returns shelf, when the front door opens, and Fiore steps in.

"I wasn't expecting you," he says, pudgy eyes narrowing suspiciously.

"Really?" I hop off my stool and smile at him, even though all my instincts are screaming at me to be careful.

"Indeed not." He sniffs. "Is the other librarian, Janis, in?"

"She's out this morning, but she'll be back later." I get a horrible sense of déjà vu as I look at him, like a flashback to a bad dream.

"Hmm. Well, if I can trouble you to turn your back, I have business in the repository." His voice rises: "I don't want to be disturbed."

"Ah, all right." I take an involuntary step back. There's something about Fiore, something not quite right, a feral tension in his eyes, and I'm suddenly acutely aware that we're alone, and that he outweighs me two to one. "Will you be long?"

His eyes flicker past my shoulder. "No, this won't take long, Reeve." Then he turns and lumbers toward the reference section and the secure document repository, not bothering to look at me. For a moment I don't believe my own instincts. It's a gesture of contempt worthy of Fiore, after all, a man so wrapped up in himself that if you spent too long with him, you'd end up thinking you were a figment of his imagination. But then I hear him snort. There's the squeak of the key in the lock, and a creak of floorboards. "You might as well come with me. We can talk inside."

I hurry after him. "In what capacity am I talking to you?" I ask, desperately racking my brains for an excuse not to join him. "Is it about Janis?"

He turns and fixes me with a beady stare. "It might be, my daughter." And that's pure Fiore. So I follow him through the door and down the steps into the cellar, a hopeless tension gnawing at my guts, still unsure whether I'm right to be worried or not.

Fiore pauses when we get to the strange room at the bottom of the stairs. "What exactly do you think of Dr. Hanta?" he asks me. He sounds tired, weighed down with cares.

I'm taken aback. What is this, some kind of internal politicking? "She's"—I pause, biting my tongue, acutely aware who I'm talking to— "refreshingly direct. She means well, and she's concerned. I trust her," I add impulsively, resisting the urge to add, *unlike you*. I manage to maneuver so my back is to the storage shelves on one wall. *If I have to grab something—*

"That's not unexpected," Fiore says quietly. "What did she do to you?"

"She didn't tell you?"

"No, I want you to tell me in your own words." His voice is low and urgent, and something in my heart breaks. I can't pretend this isn't happening anymore, can I? So I play for time.

"I was having frequent memory fugues, and I picked up a nasty little case of gray goo up top in the ship's mass fraction tankage. That set my immune system off, and it began taking out memory traces. Dr. Hanta had to put me on antirobotics and give me a complete memory fixative in order to stop things progressing." I move my hands behind my back and slowly shuffle backward, away from him and toward the wall. "I'd say she's a surprisingly ethical practitioner, given the way everyone else here carries on in secret. Or do you know differently?"

"Hmm." Fiore—fake-Fiore—leans over the assembler console and taps in some kind of code. "Yes, as a matter of fact I do."

While he isn't watching I take another step back until I bump up against shelves. *Good.* I'm already mentally preparing what I need to do next.

Fiore continues, implacably. "One of your predecessors here—yes, they're still around in deep cover—got it worked out. Dr. Hanta isn't her real name. She, or rather it, used to be a member of the Asclepian League." I give a little gasp. "Yes, you do remember them, don't you? She was a Vivisector, Reeve. One of the inner clade, dedicated to pursuing their own vision of how humanity should be restructured."

"Thanks for reminding me what I came here to get away from," I say shakily. "I'm going to be having nightmares about that for the next week."

He turns and glares at me. "Are you stupid, or—" He stops himself. "I'm sorry. But if that's all it means to you, you *really* are beyond—" He stabs at the console angrily. "Shit. I thought you'd be at least vaguely concerned for the rest of us in here."

I take a deep breath, trying to get my nausea under control. The Asclepians were another of the dictatorship cults, a morphological collective. Much worse than the Solipsist Nation. They restructured polities one screaming mangled body at a time. If Dr. Hanta is an Asclepian, and she's working with Yourdon and Fiore, the future they're trying to sculpt is a thing of horror. "She can't be. She just can't."

"And I suppose you think Major-Doctor Fiore is just a fat, egocentric psychiatrist?" He grins at me humorlessly. "Stop that, Reeve, I know what you're up to. Hanta fucked with your head really well, didn't she? Probably got you to give your consent first, too. They're hot on formalities, Asclepians. Fiore and Yourdon are war criminals, too. Shit, most of the people here did things so nasty they want to forget everything. Do you remember why this is an *experimental* polity?"

"Remember?" That's a new one on me.

"Oh. A memory fixative, that makes sense." He takes a final poke at the console. It dings and turns luminous green. "Where would dictators be without our compliant amnesia? Make the collective lose its memory, you can conceal anything. 'Who now remembers the Armenians?'" He takes a step back. "Listen, we'll have to break whatever conditioning she loaded your implant with."

My stomach churns for real this time. I feel sick. He's a monster, and he wants to drag me back down into the turmoil I was in before Hanta sorted me out. And I've been up the ladder now, I know there's no way out. We're stuck here. Resistance is futile. I really ought to run for it, call the Bishop and get the police to take him away. But that'd be like betraying myself, too, wouldn't it? "Did you kill Mick?" I whisper. "How did you get in that body?"

"Will you feel better if I say yes?" His voice is surprisingly gentle. "Or will you feel worse?"

"I'll—" I take another gulp of air. "I want to know."

Fake-Fiore, Robin, blinks slowly, pudgy eyes closing: I tense but he opens them again before I can gather my wits to move. "It was after you killed Fiore," he says. "I got into the assembler and backed myself up, programmed in a body merge and neural splice, so I'd come out in Fiore's skin instead of like . . ." He nods at me. "I put a two-hour hold on it to give you time to get the mess sorted out, but you must have blanked in between. So I wake up inside the gate and find the basement has been partially cleaned, and you're missing, and I had to finish the job. Fiore's backed up in the gate, and I've got his biometrics, so I manage to get a dump of his implant, and when one of him showed up to check on you, I told him you'd just gone missing. He believed me. He's not very good at handling multiplicity.

"On Sunday morning I went to visit Cass in the hospital," he says quietly. "It turns out I wasn't her first visitor that morning. I haven't heard anything about it through the rumor net, but it was pretty bad: I think Hanta covered it up afterward but if you were wondering . . . I caught Mick. He'd been living in the basement of an empty house, stealing stuff from folks' kitchens while they were at work—we're a trusting bunch, have you noticed that? We leave our back doors unlocked. He'd gagged her and you saw the tissue scaffolds Hanta had her legs in. She couldn't do anything. I mean, she was trying to get away, but not getting very far. He was raping her again, Reeve, and you know what I think about third chances."

I nod, gulping for breath. The horror of it is that I can see everything in my mind's eye: me-in-Fiore's-flesh creeping up on Mick as he humps away, Cass thrashing around helplessly—Mick's probably tied her arms out of the way—and me-in-Fiore's-flesh saps Mick at the base of the skull. He doesn't do it very carefully, because he's beyond fury at this point; beyond caring about inflicting subarachnoid hemorrhages. He doesn't care at all whether Mick wakes up again. In fact he thinks Mick's waking up would be a very bad idea, at least for Cass, and maybe come to think of it he can use Mick to send a message to any borderline sociopaths who are thinking about following his example—

It's very me. Me as I used to be, not me as I was before (quiet, peaceful historian, devoted family man) or me as I am now (slightly squirrelly, evanescent with the joy of discovering what it's like to surrender after fighting for what seems like my entire life), but me as I was in the middle, the grim-faced killing machine. But then I meet his eyes, and I see an awful sadness in them, a sick sense of guilt that mirrors what I feel at the knowledge that I'm absolutely going to have to shop him to the Bishop because we can't afford to have a murderous doppelganger of one of our most respected citizens running around—

I grab the first thing my fingers scrabble across: a heavy file of paper hardcopy, part of the dump of Curious Yellow from the closet upstairs. I take two brisk paces forward as I raise it and bring it down on top of his head as hard as I can. He sags and falls over, but I don't stick around to finish the job. Instead, I turn and run for the stairs. If I can make it to the top and slam the door, he'll be trapped down here for long enough to call—

"Going somewhere?" drawls Janis, pointing a stungun at me from the top step. I can see her trigger finger whitening behind the guard.

I start to raise my hands. "Don't—"

She does.

I groan and reach up to touch my head, which hurts like hell where Reeve thumped me. Someone grabs my wrist and tugs experimentally, and I open my eyes. It's Janis. She looks concerned. "What happened?" I ask.

"I caught her running up the stairs, in a real hurry to get somewhere." Janis peers at me. "What about you?"

I touch my head finally and wince at the sharp pain. "She thumped me with something, a box file I think. I fell over." *Stupid, stupid.* I feel a bit sick. Looking round brings a stab of pain to my neck. "Hit my head on the A-gate plinth."

"Then it was lucky I was in time."

"Huh. There's no such thing as luck where you're involved."

"That was in another life," she says pensively. "Are you going to be all right on your own? I need to close up shop."

"Get it closed, already." I wince and push myself upright, breathing heavily. This body has a lot of momentum, and a lot of insulation, but it's not built for bouncing around. "If anybody finds us—"

"I'll sort them out."

Janis vanishes upstairs. I sit up and manage not to retch. Reeve almost ruined it for both of us, and I'm horrified at how close I came to blowing it. If I hadn't figured out who Janis was, I'd be on my own down here and Reeve would have killed me without blinking. *Doctor's orders.*

I'm going to have to do something about Reeve, and I'm not looking forward to this. Surely Hanta—let's make that Colonel-Surgeon Vyshinski, to give her her real name—got to her, but losing a week isn't something that I take lightly, and besides, she knows stuff that might come in useful. *Dilemmas, dilemmas.* If there was some way to trivially reverse the brainwashing that Hanta's applied . . . *shit.* Hanta's an artist, isn't she? It'll be some sort of motivational/value abreactive hack, subtle as hell, leaves the personality intact but tweaking the gain on a couple of traits, just enough to turn Reeve into a good little score whore.

I sit with my legs apart, panting a trifle heavily over my enormous wobbling gut-bucket, and try to come to terms with the fact that I'm going to have to kill my better half. It's upsetting, however often you've done it before.

There's some clattering upstairs. I stand up, wheezing, and waddle over to see what's going on. I hate this body, but it's been useful for getting me into places none of us could otherwise go—they've been letting their internal security get sloppy, forgetting the authenticator rhyme: *something shared, something do, something secret, something you?* I suppose settling for *something you* is sufficient if you've got control over all the assemblers in a polity, but still. I wait at the bottom of the stairs. "Who is it?" I call quietly.

"Me," says Janis. "I need a hand with her."

"Humph." I haul myself up the steps. Janis is waiting at the top with Reeve, whose wrists and ankles she's trussed together with a roll of library tape. Reeve is twitching a little and showing signs of coming to. "What are you thinking we should do with her?" I ask.

"Can you get her downstairs?" Janis asks breathlessly.

"Yes." I lean forward and grasp Reeve by the ankles: For all that this body is grotesquely overweight, it's not weak. I lift and drag, and Janis holds Reeve's arms up enough to stop her head banging on the steps. At the bottom I pull her toward the A-gate. By this time her eyes are rolling, and she's turning red in the face. Hating myself, I lean forward. "What would *you* do?" I ask her.

"Mmph! Mmmph."

Defiant to the end—that's me. I look up at Janis. "Why didn't you kill her?"

"I didn't want to," says Janis.

"What, you're going to just—"

"Just put her in the gate!" She sounds stressed.

I get my hands under Reeve's armpits and lift. She goes limp, trying to deadweight on me. "I don't like this any more than you do," I tell her. "But this town's too small for both of us."

As I dump her into the A-gate, she kicks out with both legs, but I'm expecting that, and I punch her over the left kidney. That makes her double up. I swing the door shut. "Well?" I glare at Janis. "What now?" I feel like shit. Killing myself *always* makes me feel like shit. That's why I'm deferring to Janis, I think. Pushing the tough choice off onto someone else's shoulders.

Janis is bending over the control station. "Figuring this out," she murmurs. "Look, I'm going to lift a template from her, okay?"

"Fuck." I shake my head, a parody of resignation. There's a thud from inside the A-gate, and I wince. I feel for Reeve: I can see myself in her place, and it's horrifying. "Why?"

"Because." Janis looks up at me. "Fiore's going to suspect if we keep you running around in drag. Don't you think it's time for you to go back?"

"Back?"

"To being Reeve," she says patiently.

"Oh," I echo. "*Oh*, I see." Being thumped on the head has left me sluggish and stupid. Janis is right, we don't have to kill her. And suddenly I feel a whole lot better about punching Reeve and dumping her into a macro-scale nanostructure disassembler, for the same reason that punching yourself in the face never feels quite as bad as having someone else do it for you.

"I'm going to template from her, and then you're going to follow her, and I'm going to take a delta from your current neural state vector and overlay it on Reeve. You'll wake up back in her body, with both sets of memories, but you're going to be the dominant set. Think that'll work?"

There's another muffled thump from inside the A-gate, then muffled retching noises—Janis has triggered the template program, paralyzing Reeve via her netlink, and the chamber is filling with ablative digitizer foam. "It had better," I say.

"I'm worried Fiore may suspect what's going on. The thing with Mick could blow it completely if he puts two and two together."

I sigh heavily. "Okay, I'll go back to being Reeve. I suppose that makes sense."

"You agree?" She looks haggard in the dim light from the ceiling bulbs. "Good, then it's not entirely stupid. What then . . . ?"

"Then we sit down and figure out how to nail down the lid on this mess. Once I know what she knows."

"Right." Her lips quirk in a faint smile. "Your direct, no-nonsense approach is always like a breath of fresh air."

"Once a tank, always a tank," I remind her.

"Right," she echoes, and for a moment I can see a shadow of her former self. That sends a pang through my chest.

"The sooner I'm myself again, the better."

We sit in silence for long minutes while the gate chugs to itself, then finally the console chimes, and there's a click as the door unlatches. I walk over and swing it open: as usual, the chamber is bare and dry. I glance over and see that she's watching me.

"Ready?" she asks.

"See you on the other side, Sanni," I say as I close the door.

That's all.

SECURITY Cell Blue used to be part of the counterespionage division

of the Linebarger Cats. It was supposedly disbanded, all memory traces erased, at the end of the censorship wars. I know this is not the case because I'm a member. We didn't disband, we went underground—because our mission wasn't over.

This is a risky business. Our job is to do unpleasant things to ruthless people. Covering our tracks costs money—lots of it, and it isn't always fungible across polity frontiers these days. Local militias and governments have reinvented exchange rates, currency hedges, and a whole host of other archaic practices. Some polities are relatively open, while others have fallen into warlordism. Some place great stock on authentication and uniqueness tracking, while others don't care who you think you are as long as you pay your oxygen tax. (The former make great homes; the latter make great refuges.) As a consequence of the postwar fragmentation, we end up moving around a lot, shuffling our appearances and sometimes our memories, forking spares and merging deltas. At first we live off the capital freed up by the Cats' liquidation; later we supplement it by setting up a variety of business fronts. (If you've ever heard of the Deadly Viper Assassination Squad, or Cordwainer Heavy Industries, that's us.) Operationally, we work in loosely coupled cells. I'm one of the heavy hitters, my background in combat ops meshing neatly with my intelligence experience.

About fifty megs after the official end of hostilities, I receive a summons to the Polity of the Jade Sunrise. It's a strictly tech-limiting polity, and I'm in ortho drag, my cover being a walkabout sword-fighting instructor. I've got access to enough gray-market military wetware that I can walk the walk as well as slice the floating hair, and my second-level cover is as a demilitarized fugitive from summary justice somewhere that isn't tech-limited—which sets me up for the Odessa Introduction if I see a target of opportunity and need to run a Spanish Prisoner scam on them. I've been doing a lot of that kind of job lately, but I'm not sure what this particular one is about.

The designated rendezvous is the public bathhouse on the Street of Orange Leaves. It's a narrow, cobbled, mountainside road, running from near the main drag with the silversmith's district down toward the harbor. It's a fine spring afternoon, and the air is heavy with the smell of honeysuckle. A gang of kids are playing throw-stick loudly outside the drunkenly leaning apartment buildings, and the usual light foot traffic is laboriously winding its way up and down the middle of the road, porters yelling insults at rickshaw drivers and both groups venting their spleen on the shepherd who's trying to drive a small flock of spidergoats uphill.

I've been here long enough to know what I'm doing, more or less. I spot a boy who's hanging back on the sidelines and snap my fingers. He comes over, not so much walking as slithering so that his friends don't see him. Grubby, half-starved, his clothes faded and patched: perfect. A coin appears between two of my fingers. "Want another?" I ask.

He nods. "I don't do thex," he lisps. I look closer and realize he's got a cleft palate.

"Not asking you to." I make another coin appear, this time out of reach. "The teahouse. I want you to look round the back alley and see if there are any men waiting there. If there are, come and tell me. If not, go in and find Mistress Sanni. Tell her that the Tank says hello, then come and tell me."

"Two coin." He holds up a couple of fingers.

"Okay, two coin." I glare at him, and he does the disappearing trick again. The kid's got talent, I realize, he does that like a pro. Sharp doubts intrude: *Maybe he is a pro?* We rounded up the easy targets a long time ago—the ones who're still running ahead of us tend to be a lot harder to nail.

I don't have long to wait. A cent or so passes, then lisp-boy is back. "Mithreth Thanni thay, the honeypot ith overflowing. I take you to her."

The honeypot is overflowing: doesn't sound good. I pass him the two coins. "Okay, which way?"

He does a quick fade in front of me, but not too fast for me to follow. We're round the back of a dubious alleyway, then into a maze of anonymous backyards in a matter of seconds. Then he goes over a rickety wooden fence and along another alley—this one full of compost, the stink unbelievable—and up to an anonymous-looking back door. "The'th here."

My hand goes to my sword hilt. "Really?" I stare at the kid, then at the two dead thugs leaning against each other beside the back step. The kid flashes a lightning grin at me.

"You *did* thay to check the back alley for muggerth, Robin."

"Sanni?"

He sketches a bow, urchin-cool. I raise an eyebrow. The muggers look as if they're sleeping, if you ignore the blood leaking from their noses. Very good work, for an intel type who isn't a wet ops specialist. "We don't have long. Authenticate me."

We do the routine, something shared, something do, something secret, something you—all the stuff the Republic of Is used to do for us. "Okay, boss, why did you call me?" Sanni isn't my boss these days, but old habits die hard.

"The honeypot is leaking." He drops the lisp and stands tall, Sanni's natural presence shining through the bottleneck of his three-hundred-meg body. "We—Vera Six, that is—got word about twenty megs ago that a bunch of familiar spooks were haunting the Invisible Republic. It all snowballed really fast. Looks like several of the memory laundries have been infiltrated and the glasshouse has been taken over."

I lean against the wall. "The *glasshouse*?"

Sanni nods. "Someone's going to have to go in and polish the mirrors. Someone else. I forked an instance five megs ago, and she hasn't reported back yet. It's going to be deep cover, I'm afraid."

"Shit and pig-fucking shit." I glare at the dead muggers as if it's their fault.

The glasshouse is a rehab center for prisoners of war. The setup is designed to encourage resocialization, to help integrate them back into something vaguely resembling postwar society; it's a former MASucker configured as a compact polity with with just one T-gate in or out. Bad guys go in, civilians come out. At least, that was the original theory.

"What's going on?" I ask.

"I think someone's broken our operational security," says Sanni. I shudder and stare at the muggers. "Yes," he says, seeing the direction of my gaze. "I said we don't have long. A group drawn from several of our operational rivals have infiltrated the Strategic Amnesia Commissariat of the Invisible Republic and taken over the funding and operational control of the glasshouse. They discharged all the current inmates, and we no longer know what's going on inside. The glasshouse is under new management."

"I'm the wrong person, and in the wrong place. Can't you send Magnus? Or the Synthesist? Do an uplevel callback to descendant coordination and the veterans' association and see if anybody—"

"I don't exist anymore," Sanni says calmly. "After my delta went in and didn't report back, the bad guys came after my primary and killed me repeatedly until I was almost entirely dead. This"—he taps his skinny chest—"is just a partial. I'm a ghost, Robin."

"But." I lick my lips, my heart pounding with shock. "Won't they simply kill me, too?"

"Not if you're identity-dead first." Sanni-ghost grins at me. "Here's what you're going to have to do . . ."

Connections

I am me. Joints creak, heart pumps. It's warm and dark, and I'm sleepy. It slowly comes to me that I'm squatting with my arms wrapped around my knees and my chin—oh. So I'm not passing as Fiore? Right. That's satisfying to know. One more fact to add to the pile. Roll the dice, see what comes up on top.

I've been in two places at once for most of the past two weeks. I've been in hospital, recovering at home. Talking to Dr. Hanta, being horrified in the bell tower, trying to tell the Reverend about Janis. And another me has been living in the library, sleeping in the staff room, cautiously exploring off-limits sections of the habitat, and latterly conspiring with Janis. *Sanni.* A doubled moment of eternal jarring shock—meeting her head-on up the stairs with a gun in her hand, just as startled as a week ago, stumbling across her in the basement with a knife. She broke down and cried, then, when she realized she wasn't the only one anymore. I wouldn't have credited it if I hadn't been there myself. Hard-as-diamonds Sanni, reduced to this? Isolation does strange things to people . . .

"Come on, Reeve. Talk to me! Please. Are you all right in there?" There's a note of desperation in her voice. "Say something!" She leans over me anxiously. "How does it feel?"

"Let's see." I blink some more then unwrap my arms and push myself upright. I'm Reeve again. *Damn, but I feel so light!* After being tied down by the centripetal chains fastened to Fiore's flesh for more than a tenday, it's an amazing sensation. I could drift away on a light breeze. I find myself grinning with delight, then I look up at her and my face freezes. "I—she—nearly shopped you to Fiore."

Janis blanches. "When?"

"After we disposed of Mick. Let me think." I close my eyes. I need to get rid of the sudden storm surge of adrenaline. "Low risk. I—she—was uncertain, and she misjudged her timing. She didn't know who you are, she just thought you were up to no good, so she tried to shop you for your own protection. Fiore was preoccupied and told her to get lost. As long as nothing reminds him, you're clear."

"Shit." Janis takes a step back, and I see that she's still holding the stunner, but she's got it pointed at the floor. She's swaying slightly, with relief or shock. "That was close."

I take a deep breath. "I've never been brainwashed before." A little part of me still thinks Dr. Hanta is a sympathetic and friendly practitioner who only means the best for me, but it's outvoted by the much larger part of me that is eager to use her intestines as a skipping rope. "I am"—*breathing too fast, slow down*—"not amused."

"Let's try a ping test." Janis hesitates for a moment. "Do you love me?"

"I love you." My heart speeds up again. "Hey, I heard that!"

"Yes." Janis nods. "I didn't, though. You know what? I think the diff-merge must have scribbled over part of the CY load in your netlink."

"No." I step out of the assembler and carefully close the door. "It happened earlier. I heard it earlier"— I frown—"talking to Sam, after I got out of hospital. I mean, she heard it."

"Curious." She cocks her head to one side, a very Sanni-like gesture that looks totally out of place on the Janis I've gotten to know over the past few months. "Maybe if she—" Janis snaps her fingers. "They've repurposed CY, haven't they? The bit we're carrying around in here, it's used for loading behavior scorefiles and such, but if Hanta's been modifying it to work as a general-purpose boot loader . . ."

I shudder. The consequences are clear enough. The original Curious Yellow used humans as an infective vector, but only really ran inside A-gates that it had infected. A modified CY that can actually run and do useful stuff inside a host's netlink, and which doesn't trigger the detection patch, is a whole lot scarier. You can do things with it like—"The zombies?"

"Yes." Janis looks as if she's seen a ghost. "Are we still in the glasshouse? Or have they relocated us?"

"We're still in the glasshouse," I reassure her. It's the first bit of good news I've been able to piece together so far. "MASucker *Harvest Lore,* if what she remembers seeing upstairs is anything to go by. I mean, we might have been on a different MASucker, but I thought you accounted for them all?"

"I think so." She nods, increasingly animated. "So that locked area you found in City Hall"—when I was being Fiore—"is probably the only T-gate on-site. Right?"

"There are the short-range gates to the individual residences." I shiver again: Getting into City Hall and out again without being identified was a matter of sheer brazen luck. Ten minutes later I'd have run into the real Fiore. "They're definitely switched off a hub at City Hall; I found the conference suite they inducted us through. As I recall, on the *Grateful for Duration* the longjump T-gate was connected to the flight control deck by a direct short-range gate, but was itself stored in a heavily armored pod outside the main pressure hull, in case someone tried to throw a nuke through. So, if we assume they haven't rebuilt the *Harvest Lore* in flight, there's going to be a way to get to the longjump node from either City Hall or the cathedral, which is just over the road."

"Right." She nods. "So. If this is the *Harvest Lore,* we're about two hundred years from next landfall. If we assume exponentiation at, say, five infants per family, there's time for ten generations . . . right, they're looking to breed up about twenty thousand unauthenticated human vectors. Hanta's got time to implant netlinks in them all. So when we arrive, she can flood the network with this new population of carriers—"

"That's not going to happen." I smile, baring my teeth. "Never doubt that. They think they've got us trapped. But the *right* way to view it is, we can't retreat."

"You think we can take them on directly?" Sanni asks, and for a moment she's entirely Janis—isolated, damaged, frightened.

"Watch me," I tell her.

THE rest of the day passes uneventfully. I say goodbye to Janis and go home as usual. At least, that's what it must look like to anyone who's watching me. I've spent the past few hours in an absentminded reverie, rolling around irreconcilable memories and trying to work out where I stand. It's most peculiar. On the one hand, I've got Reeve's horror at finding Mick dead, her apprehensive fear that Janis might be "untrustworthy" and a hazard to the friendly and open Dr. Hanta. And on the other hand, I've got Robin's experiences. Sneaking around City Hall on tiptoe, finding locked areas and avoiding Fiore by the skin of my teeth. Coming across Mick in the hospital, with Cass. Dropping in on Janis in the library, her initial guilty fear and the slowly growing conviction—on my part—that she wasn't just a bystander but an ally. Recognition protocols and the shock of mutual recognition.

Janis has been on her own in here for almost half a year longer than I have. When she realized she wasn't alone, she broke down and cried. She'd been certain it was only a matter of time before Dr. Hanta got around to her. Terror, isolation, fear of the midnight knock on the door: They wear you down after a while. She got pregnant before anyone had figured out that part of the scheme. I'm surprised she's still functioning at all.

The score system and the experimental protocols are a real obstacle to us: For all we know, half the population of YFH-polity could be cell members of one faction or another, blundering around in the dark, unwilling to risk revealing themselves. But unless we can somehow kick over the superstructure of artifice that the cabal have established, we won't be able to link up with our potential allies and identify our real enemies. Divide and conquer: You know it makes sense.

I get home in due course, by way of the hardware store. Sam is absent, so I go straight into the garage to see what I can do. This isn't the time for recrimination, but I'm really pissed at myself. I was going to get rid of this stuff! If nothing else, I found making historic weapons fascinating. I may end up doing it as a hobby, when all this is over, if there's scope for such luxuries.

Still, I guess I won't be needing the crossbow now. Or the sword I was trying to temper. Sanni and I have got a sterile assembler with full military scope. We left it cooking last night, slowly and laboriously building a stockpile of polynitrohexose bricks. Making weapons by A-gate is a slow process, and the higher the energy density the longer it takes, so we compromised and opted for chempowered weapons. The first batch of machine pistols will be ready when we go in to work tomorrow. Which leads to the next logical question—where's my Faraday cage bag gotten to in this pile?

I'm hopping around on top of a pile of scattered steel bar stock and spilled screwdrivers, cursing up a blue streak and clutching my left foot when some change in the light alerts me to the fact that the garage door is open. "What the fuck—"

"Reeve?"

"*Fuck!*" I howl. "Shit. Dropped my hammer and—"

"Reeve? What's going on?"

I force myself to calm down. "I dropped my hammer and it landed on this pile of bar stock and it bounced on my toe." I hop some more. The pain is beginning to subside. "The hammer is evil and must be punished."

"*The hammer?*" He pauses. "Have you been drinking?"

"Not yet." I lean against the wall and experimentally put my foot on the floor. "Ouch. I just decided to turn over a new—heh—leaf again. A girl needs a hobby and all that." I raise an eyebrow.

He looks at me skeptically. "Bad day at the office?"

"It's always a bad day at the office, insofar as the office exists in the first place."

He frowns. "What's this about a hobby?"

"Extreme metalworking, or something like that. Have you seen my copy of *The Swordsmith's Assistant*? I was going to throw it out when I wasn't feeling myself, but I never got round to it."

You can almost see the light come on above his head. "Reeve? Is that you?"

"I had a crap day at the office, too. Reading poetry out of boredom, you know? 'Last night I met upon the stair, a big fat man who wasn't there; he wasn't there again today: inside my head he'll have to stay.' Ogden Nashville. Apparently, the ancients seem to have liked him for some reason. C'mon, let's go and round up some supper."

Sam retreats back into the house ahead of me, lips moving sound-lessly as he turns it over in his head. I *have* been reading poetry at work, I just hope my improvised doggerel gets through. (Poetry really gums up conversational monitoring systems. Parsing metaphor and emotional states is an AI-complete problem.)

We end up in the kitchen. "Were you thinking about cooking again?" Sam asks cautiously. Thinking back to days past, I suspect he wasn't too enthusiastic about being subjected to some of my experiments.

"Let's just order a pizza instead, hmm? And a flask of wine."

"Why?" He stares at me.

"Do you have to turn every suggestion for what to do of an evening into an impromptu therapy session?"

He shrugs. "Just asking." He begins to turn away.

I grab his shoulder. "Don't do that."

He turns back sharply, looking surprised. "What?"

" 'Last night I met upon the stair, a big fat man who wasn't there; he wasn't there again today: inside my head he'll have to stay' . . . I haven't been myself lately, Sam, but I'm feeling *a lot better* today." I frown at him, willing the words to sink in.

"Oh, you mean . . ."

"Shh!" I hold up a warning finger. "The walls have ears."

Sam's eyes widen, and he begins to pull away from me. I grab at his shoulder, hard, then step in close and wrap my arms around him. He tries to push back, but I lean my face against his shoulder. "We need to talk," I whisper.

"About what?" he whispers back. But at least he stops pushing.

"What's going on." I lick his earlobe, and he jolts as if I've stuck a live wire in it.

"Don't *do* that!" he hisses.

"Why not?" I ask, amused. "Afraid you might enjoy it?"

"But we, they—"

"I'm going to order food. While we're eating, let's keep things light, okay? Afterward we'll go upstairs. I've got a trick or two to show you. *For avoiding eavesdroppers.*" I add in a whisper: *"Smile, please."*

"Won't it be obvious?" He's lowered his arms and is holding me loosely around the waist. I shiver because I've been wanting him to do that so badly for the past week—no, let's not go there.

"No it won't be. They use low-level monitors to track normal behavior. They call in high-end monitors only if we act funny. So don't act funny."

"Oh." I look up as he looks down for a startled instant, and I kiss him. He tastes of sweat and a faint, musty aroma of dust and paperwork. A moment passes, then he responds enthusiastically. "This is normal?" he asks.

"Whoa! Dinner first." I laugh, pulling back.

"Dinner first." He looks at me with a dark, serious expression.

I phone for a pizza and a couple of glass jars of wine, and while Sam heads for the living room, I try to catch my breath. Things are moving too fast for comfort, and I'm suddenly having to deal with a mass of conflicted emotions at a time when all I was wanting to do was recruit another dissatisfied inmate to the campaign. The thing is, Sam and I have too much history for anything between us to be simple—even though we haven't actually done very much together. We haven't had *time*, and Sam's got big body-image issues, and then she/me nearly fucked everything between us completely while under the influence of the pernicious Dr. Hanta—oh, hindsight is a wonderful tool, isn't it? Thinking about it, Sam's dissatisfaction and passivity has been a running sore between us, and I half suspect it took my apparent co-option to kick him into doing something about it.

I feel guilty as I remember what I was thinking at the time. *I can surrender . . .* yes, and they'll make my life a living hell, won't they? Did I really want to hand complete control over my life to the likes of Fiore, Yourdon, and Hanta? I don't think I explicitly intended to do that, but it amounted to the same thing. It feels like a moment of cowardice in my own past, a *voluntary* moment of cowardice, and I feel oddly dirty because of it. Because it's not far out of my normal character to feel that way inclined—Hanta didn't rebuild her/me, she just tweaked a few weightings in my mind map. "The only thing necessary for the triumph of evil is that good men do nothing" in spades. And Sam got to see that side of me. *Ick.*

The closet bings for attention and I take the pizza tray and wine out of it. On my way through to the living room I kick my shoes off, strewing them in the hallway. "Sam?" He turns round. He's nesting in the sofa again, the television turned to some sports channel. "Turn the volume up."

He raises an eyebrow at me but does as I ask, and I sit down next to him. "Here. Garlic and tofu with deep-fried lemon chicken steak." I open the box and pull out a slice, then hold it in front of his mouth. "Eat?"

"What is this?"

"I want to feed you." I lean against him and hold the pizza in front of his face, just out of reach. "Go on. You're begging for it really, aren't you?"

"Gaah." He leans forward and takes a bite at it—I try to pull my hand back, but I'm just too late and he gets a mouthful. I laugh and lean closer and find his arm is around my shoulders. Chewing: "You. Are. Intolerable."

"Manipulative," I suggest. "Annoying."

"All of the above?"

"Yes, all of it by turns." I feed him another mouthful, then change my mind about letting him have the whole slice and eat the rest of it myself.

"Every time I think I understand you, you change the rules," he complains. "Give me another . . ."

"Not my fault. I don't make the rules."

"Who does?"

I point a finger at the ceiling, waggle it about. "Remember our chat in the library?" After I came out to Janis, last Tuesday, she phoned Sam and asked him to come visit. He was very surprised to see me-as-Fiore, almost as much as when we showed him the basement and the A-gate. "Remember my face?" He nods, looking dubious. "Janis and I sorted everything out. Settled the slight difference of opinions. I'm feeling a lot better now, and less inclined to give up on things."

His arm tightens. Warm, comforting, presence. "But why?"

I take a deep breath and offer him another slice of pizza. Better keep it short. At this rate he's going to eat it all. "You don't want to live like this."

"But I—" He stops.

"Do you?" I prod him.

He looks at me. "Watching you, this past week—" He shakes his head. "I'd *love* to be able to settle in like that." He shakes his head again, underscoring the ironic tone in his voice. "What alternative is there?"

"We're not supposed to talk about where we came from." I pause to chew for a moment. "And we can't go back." I flick a warning glance his way. "But we can make ourselves more comfortable here if we re-arrange our priorities." *Will he get it?*

Sam sighs. "If only we could do that." He glances down at his lap.

"I've got a new priority for you," I say, my heart beating faster.

"Really?"

"Yes." I put the pizza box down and plaster myself against him. "We can start right here by you picking me up and carrying me upstairs to the bathroom."

"The *bathroom*?"

"Yep." I kiss him again, and suddenly I'm not sure this is a good idea at all. "Where we're going to get in the shower together, and wash each other, and talk. Can't go to bed smelling of office work, can we?"

"Shower—" His monosyllables aren't his most appealing attribute: I kiss him into silence, shivering with alarm at my own responses.

"Now."

THINGS do not go according to plan.

The plan seemed simple enough. Get Sam on board again. Doing that, holding a proper conversation with him, was another matter with the ever-present risk of being overheard. But if you disguise your suspicious activities as something expected of you, while only the dumb listener bots are online, you've got a good chance of doing it undetected. The dumb listeners aren't good for much more than keyword monitoring, and the cabal is sufficiently short on spare bodies that they can't monitor everything we say all the time.

So call me naive, if you like. I figured that as a married couple, one of us pretending to seduce the other and then dragging them into a shower—lots of nice white noise to confuse audio tracking, sheets of water to make it hard to lip-read, and an excuse to stand really close together—would be a pretty good way of evading surveillance.

What I didn't consider was that when I stand too close to Sam my skin tingles, and I feel warm and needy in intimate places. And what I especially didn't consider is that Sam is horribly conflicted but has corresponding urges. He's human, too, and we both have certain needs, which we've been trying to ignore for much too long.

Sam does as I ask him, and about halfway up the stairs I realize that I'm going to lose control if we do this. I nearly tell him to stop, but for some reason my mouth doesn't want to open. He puts me down on the bathroom carpet and stands too close. "What now?" he asks, a quiet tension in his voice.

"We, um, undress." Without realizing quite how, I find my hands are already working on his trouser belt. When I feel him begin to unbutton my blouse, I shudder, and not with fear. "Shower."

"This isn't such a good—"

"Shut up."

"You'll become, uh, pregnant."

"Won't." *Worry about it later.* I run my hand around his back, feeling the thin man-fur that runs up the base of his spine, and I lean closer. "Not worried anymore."

"But." I feel him unzip my skirt. Hands on my thighs. "Surely."

I kiss him to make him stop. We're down to underwear. "Shower. *Now.*" My teeth are chattering with a rising tide of need that threatens to wreck what's left of my self-control.

We're in the shower cubicle, wearing our underwear, and I dial the pressure up to maximum and the temperature to fusion. His tongue—

garlic and honey and a hint of something else, of him. Arms around each other, we stand under the spray, and I feel the tension in his back. He's got an erection, of course. Why am I still wearing anything? Moments later I'm not. And a moment after that I'm crunched against the wall, my knees drawn up, gasping at the size of him inside me.

"You want to talk . . ."

The entire universe is in here. I wrap my arms around him and latch on to his lips, hungrily. I *want* to talk, but right now I've got higher priorities.

"Opening ceremony."

"Yes?"

"On a MASucker. Yes!"

"Yes . . ."

"Only one T-gate out. Six gigs to next star system. If we break connection, bad guys can't pay up on scorefiles. Breaks carrot side of dictatorship, no payoff for compliance. Yes . . ."

"Overthrow the—the?"

He heaves like the wild sea. I'm lost on him, abandoned. At first when I was Reeve, the idea of pregnancy horrified me. Then Hanta tweaked something, and it was no big deal. Now I just don't *care* anymore: It's survivable, and if it's the cost of having Sam right now, I'll pay. I want to focus, to plan, but we've gotten carried away. Sam is pounding away with no subtlety, and he knows better, which means he's lost on the ocean, too. If we can find each other and cling together through the night, who knows? "Sam, I, I want you to—"

"Oh!" A moment later, a quieter "oh!" And a sensation of spreading warmth that drives me to grind against him until everything goes away, and I become the ocean for a few eternal seconds.

THINGS don't go according to plan, but they go strangely well. After the first mad flush of lust, we collapse in the shower, then soap each other off thoroughly. Sam doesn't cringe away from my hands this time but seems quiet, thoughtful. I kiss him, and he responds. After a while I begin to feel as if my skin's about to fall off: I can barely see the bathroom for steam. "Let's dry off and go to bed," I suggest, feeling another little jolt of worry.

"Okay." Sam turns the shower head to OFF and opens the cubicle door. It's cold out there. I shiver, and for a wonder he wraps his arms around me.

"Are you feeling comfortable?" I ask hesitantly. "I mean, with this?"

He thinks for a moment. "I'm comfortable with you."

"But—"

He kisses the back of my head. "It's you. That makes it easier."

There's nothing left to divide us: We know exactly how fucked up we are. We've had such disastrous misunderstandings already that there's nothing left to come. Sam freaks at the idea of being human and male and large? Yes. I have problems with the idea of pregnancy, and there're no contraceptives in YFH-Polity? Sure. We're past all that. It's all going to be very simple from now on.

So we towel each other dry and I take his hand and together we go to the bedroom, where presently we make love again, tenderly and slowly.

THE next morning, I stumble downstairs late, disheveled and happy, to find there is a letter waiting for me on the front hall carpet. It's like a bucket of cold water in the face. I pick it up and carry the piece of paper into the kitchen and read it while the coffee machine gurgles and chugs to itself.

To: Mrs. Reeve Brown
From: The Polity Administration Committee

Dear Mrs. Brown

It is now four months since your arrival in YFH-Polity. In this time, numerous changes have taken place in our little community, and we will shortly be commencing Phase Two of the experiment in which you agreed to participate.

Accordingly, may I extend to you an invitation to our first Town Meeting, to be held at City Hall on Sunday morning in place of the regularly scheduled Sunday Service. The meeting will explain the forthcoming Phase Two changes, and will be followed by a service of thanksgiving, to be conducted by the Very Reverend Dr. H. Yourdon in the cathedral.

Yours truly . . .

This puts a new perspective on things, doesn't it? I shake my head, then take the two coffee mugs back upstairs. On my way I snag the identical-looking letter with Sam's name on it.

"What do you think?" he asks, when he's had time to read it.

"I think it's exactly what it sounds like." I shrug. "Things are getting bigger, new faces, new scenery—this 'cathedral' they're opening! You can't run a town the way you run a parish of a couple of hundred people, can you? No way can everybody know each other. So they'll need a different intergroup score mechanism to keep people behaving themselves. To account for the anonymity of cities, the sight of familiar strangers."

His cheek twitches. "I'm not sure I like the sound of that."

"Oh, it can't be that bad," I assure him, rolling my eyes.

"Can't it?"

I nod. "No." A thought strikes me. "Listen, can you get away from the office for lunch?"

"What, you mean . . . ?"

"Yes. Drop by the library about one o'clock, and we'll go eat together." I smile at him. "How does that sound?"

"You want me to—" He works it out. "Yes, I can do that."

"Good." I lean close and kiss him on the cheek. "Be seeing you."

I arrive at work fifteen minutes early, clutching my bag—not, in and of itself, an unusual variation—but the place is unlocked because Janis is already in. "Janis?" I poke my head round the office door.

She's not there. I sigh and head for the depository.

Down in the basement I find Janis loading magazines into box files. "Give me a hand," she says tensely. "If Fiore or Yourdon turns up while we're here . . ."

"Check." The magazines are vaguely banana-shaped and don't fit very well, but I can get four or five in each file box before I put them back on the shelf. Janis has six machine pistols lined up before her on a chair, still in their synthesis gel capsules. "Did you get the letter?" I ask.

"Yes. So did Norm." Her husband—I don't know much about him. "They're pulling things forward. Once they institutionalize the police and stop relying on isolation to do their work for them, we're in trouble."

"Agreed." I pause. "Ladies' sewing club?" That was my idea, when I was Robin, but Janis fronted it, and after my one meeting with them while I was being Reeve, I guess she's going to have to sort them out.

"I invited them here for lunch. Hurry up!" She's very twitchy this morning.

"Okay, I'm hurrying." I get the last of the magazines stashed in box files on the shelves, for all the world looking like innocent hard copy files of Curious Yellow. "I invited Sam round. I think he's on message."

"Oh, good. I was hoping you two would sort things out." A brief smile. "Now let's go upstairs. We've got a library to open before we can overthrow the government."

19

Longjump

SUBTLETY isn't going to get us very far at this point, so Janis orders up a delivery of sandwiches from a catering outfit working from the back of a cafe, and when the ladies' sewing circle and revolutionary command committee shows up, we lock the front door, hang out the CLOSED sign, and pile downstairs.

"We've got one day to organize this," says Janis. "Reeve, you want to summarize the situation?"

Heads turn. From their expressions, I don't think they were expecting me to be here. I smile. "This place—this polity—was originally designed as a glasshouse, a military prison. It works too well; the YFH cabal figured that a prison doesn't just keep people *in*, it keeps other people *out*. So they set it up as a research lab, what we're now seeing." She gestures at the shelves of box files on the back wall. "They're working on developing a new type of cognitive dictatorship, one spread via Curious Yellow, and they're breeding up a population of carriers for it. When we get to the end of the 'experiment' time-scale they're planning on reintegrating everyone into general society—and using your children to spread it." I see Janis's hand move unconsciously to her stomach. "Do you want to help them?"

A mutter goes round the room, growing quickly: "No!"

"I'm glad to hear that," Janis says drily. "Now, this raises the question—what is to be done? Reeve and I have been working on an answer. Anyone want to guess?"

Sam sticks his hand up. "You're going to blow the longjump gate anchor frame," he says calmly, "stranding us teraklicks from the nearest other human polity. And then you're going to hunt the cabal down and shoot them, find their backup networks and offline them, then jump up and down on the smoking wreckage."

Janis smiles. "Not bad! Anyone else?"

El sticks her hand up. "Hold elections?"

Janis looks taken aback. "Something like that, I guess." She shrugs. "But that's getting a little ahead of ourselves, isn't it? What haven't I mentioned?"

I clear my throat. "We know where the longjump gate is. Which is good news and bad news."

"Why?" asks Helen. They're beginning to get involved, which is good, but could turn bad if Janis and I don't present them with a reasonable picture. They're not idiots, they must know that we wouldn't have brought them in on the cellar if the situation wasn't desperate.

"Reeve?" prompts Janis.

"Okay, here's the frame: We're on a MASucker that somehow got de-crewed during the censorship wars. At a guess, CY broke out during a scheduled crew shift change or something. Anyway, the polity we're in is actually a quilted patchwork of sectors spliced together by shortjump gates in all those road tunnels, but they're all in a single physical manifold aboard one ship rather than scattered across separate habs. That's why it was possible to turn it into a prison. There's only one longjump gate in or out of the MASucker, and it's stashed at one end of an armored pod on the outside of the hull with a shortjump gate at the other end of the tunnel—this is standard MASucker security, you understand. Someone outside could throw a nuke through at the ship and it would be expended outside the hull. Anyway, we first need to take and hold the shortjump gate leading to the longjump pod, then we need to trash the longjump pod.

"We need to sever communications between us and their base of operations in the surgeon-confessors' hall, then *make sure everybody knows*. Yourdon and Fiore have gotten away with running this existential dictatorship unopposed because they've got a sufficient proportion of us convinced that we're in line for a payback if we play along. Hanta gives them an ace in their hole. They don't need to worry about the payback; eventually she'll have time to just adjust everyone who drifts out of line. Once we're cut off from the outside, the cabal lose their backup and their social leverage, and we've got a straight fight. But if we don't succeed, they can just block the gates between parish sectors and mop us up in detail, one sector at a time."

I pause to lick my lips. "I spent some time on a MASucker before the war. The door to the longjump pod was stashed near the bridge, uh, the administrative block—which would correspond to either the cathedral or City Hall in the new structure Yourdon is assembling. I did some snooping around last week, and I found where Yourdon lives. He's got a suite up on the top floor of City Hall, with security up to the eyeballs—I didn't get in, but I poked around the lower levels—and it turns out that City Hall bears a remarkable resemblance to the Captain's Lodge on the MASucker I was aboard. In which case, the T-gate to the longjump pod will be on the top floor, in a secure suite adjacent to the captain's quarters."

I stop.

Janis stands up. "There you've got it, folks, so let's keep this simple. We all have invitations to the ceremony at City Hall the day after tomorrow. I propose that we go there. I've had the fab here"—she waves at the assembler—"turning out kits with shielded bags so you can carry them away without fear of surveillance. Reeve?"

I clear my throat. "Plan is, we take our kit along and cut loose as soon as Yourdon steps up to the front to address everyone. Team Green's job is to secure the hall, drop any armed support the bad guys have, and kill as many copies of Yourdon, Fiore, and Hanta as we can find. They'll have backups or multiples running live, but if we do everything *fast*, we can stop the instances in City Hall getting word out. Meanwhile, Team Yellow will go up to the captain's—the Bishop's—quarters and blow the longjump pod right off the side of the ship. Any questions?"

Hands go up.

"Okay, here's what we'll do. El, Bernice, Helen, Priss, Morgaine, Jill, you're all on Team Green with Janis, who's in overall charge. Sam, Greg, Martin, and Liz are Team Yellow with me. I'm in charge. Team Yellow, hang around, and I'll brief you. Team Green, eat your lunch, then go back to work—come back to the library individually this afternoon or tomorrow, and Janis will sort you out, back you up, and brief you."

There's more muttering from the back. Janis clears her throat. "One more thing. Operational security is paramount. If anyone says any-thing, we are all . . . not dead. Worse. Dr. Hanta has a full-capability brainfuck clinic running in the hospital. If you give any sign outside of this basement that you're involved in this plan, they'll shut down the shortjump gates, isolating you, and flood us with zombies until we run out of bullets and knives. Then they'll cart us away and turn us into happy, smiling slaves. Some of you may figure that's better than dying—all right, that's your personal choice. But if I think any of you is going to try to impose that choice on *me* by going to the priests, you will find that *my* personal choice is to shoot you dead first.

"If you don't want to be in on this, say so *right now*—or hang around upstairs and tell me when everyone else has gone. We've got an A-gate; we can just back you up and keep you on ice for the duration. There's no reason to be part of this if you're frightened. But if you don't explic-itly opt out, then you're accepting my command, and I *will* expect total obedience on pain of death, until we've secured the ship."

Janis looks round at everyone, and her expression is harsh. For a moment Sanni is back, shining through her skin like a bright lamp through camouflage netting, frightening and feral. "Do you all understand?"

There's a chorus of yesses from around the room. Then one of the pregnant women at the back pipes up. "What are we waiting for? Let's roll!"

TIME rushes by, counting down to a point of tension that lies ahead.

We've got logistic problems. Having the A-gate in the library base-ment is wonderful—it's almost indispensable to what we're attempting to do—but there are limits on what it can churn out. No rare isotopes, so we can't simply nuke the longjump pod. Nor do we have the design templates for a tankbody or combat drones or much of anything beyond personal sidearms. You can't manufacture T-gates in an A-gate, so we've got to work without wormhole tech—that rules out Vorpal blades. Given time or immunity from surveillance we could probably work around those restrictions, but Janis says we've got a maximum feedstock mass flow of a hundred kilograms per hour. I suspect Fiore, or whoever decided to plant this thing in the library basement, throttled it deliberately to stop someone like me from turning it into an invasion platform. Their operational security is patchy after the manner of many overhasty and understaffed projects, but it's far from nonexistent.

In the end Janis tells me, "I'm going to leave it on overnight, building a brick of plasticized RDX along with detonators and some extra gun cartridges. We can put together about ten kilos over a six-hour run. That much high explosive is probably about as much energy as we can risk sucking without triggering an alarm somewhere. Do you think you can do the job on the longjump gate frame with that much?"

"Ten kilos?" I shake my head. "That's disappointing. That's *really* not good."

She shrugs. "You want to risk going technical on Yourdon, be my guest."

She's got a point. There's a very good chance that the bad guys will have planted trojans in some of the design templates for more complex weapons—anything much more sophisticated than handguns and raw chemical explosive will have interlocks and sensor systems that might slip past our vetting. The machine pistols she's run up are crude things, iron sights and mechanical triggers and no heads-up capability. They don't even have biometric interlocks to stop someone taking your own gun and shooting you with it. They're a step up from my crossbow project, but not a very *high* step. On the other hand, they've got no telltale electronics that Yourdon or Fiore might subvert.

"Did you test the gun cartridges? Just in case?"

Janis nods. "Thunder stick go bang. No fear on that account."

"Well, at least *something's* going to work, then." I'd be happier if we could lay in a brace of stunguns, but since I'm not wearing Fiore anymore, that would be kind of difficult to arrange.

Janis looks at me. "Make or break time."

I breathe deeply. "When has it been any other way?"

"Ah, but. We had backups, didn't we?" Her shoulders are set defensively. "This time it's our last show. It isn't how I expected things to turn out."

"Me neither." I finish packing my bag and straighten up. "Do you think anyone will crack?"

"I hope not." She stares at the wall, eyes focused on some inner space. "I hope not." Her hand goes to her belly again. "There's a reason I recruited gravid females. It does things to your outlook. I've learned that much." Her eyes glisten. "It can go either way—peeps who're still role-playing their way through YFH in their head get angry and frightened, and those who've internalized it, who're getting ready to be mothers, get even angrier about what those brainfuckers are going to do to their children. Once you get through the fear and disbelief, you get to the anger. I don't think any of the pregnant females will crack, and you'll notice the males who were along all have partners who are involved."

"True." Janis—no, Sanni—is sharp as a knife. She knows what she's doing when it comes to organizing a covert operation cell. But if she's a knife, she's one with a brittle edge. "Sanni, can I ask you a question?"

"Sure." Her tone is relaxed but I see the little signs of tension, the wrinkles around her eyes. She knows why I used that name.

"What do you want to do after this?" I grasp for the right words: "We're about to lock ourselves down in this little bubble-polity like something out of the stone age, a *generation ship* . . . we're not going to be getting out of here for gigasecs, tens of gigs, at a minimum! I mean, not unless we go into suspension afterward. And I thought you, you'd be wanting to escape, to get out and warn everybody off. Break YFH from the outside. Instead, well, we've come up with a case for pulling down the escape tunnel on top of ourselves. What do *you* want to do afterward once we've cut ourselves off?"

Sanni looks at me as if I've sprouted a second head. "I want to retire." She glances round at the basement nervously. "This place is giving me the creeps; we ought to go home soon. Look, Reeve—Robin—this is where we belong. This is the glasshouse. It's where they sent the damaged ones after the war. The ones who need reprogramming, rehabilitation. Yourdon and Hanta and Fiore belong here—but don't you think maybe *we* belong here, too?" She looks haunted.

I think for a minute. "No, I don't think so." Then I force myself to add, "But I think I could grow to like it here if only we weren't under pressure from . . . them."

"That's what it was designed for. A rest home, a seductive retirement, balm for the tortured brow. Go on home to Sam." She walks toward the stairs without looking at me. "Think about what you've done, or what he did. I've got blood on my hands, and I know it." She's halfway up the stairs, and I have to move to keep up with her. "Don't you think that the world outside ought to be protected from people like us?"

At the top of the staircase I think of a reply. "Perhaps. And perhaps you're right, we did terrible things. But there was a war on, and it was necessary."

She takes a deep breath. "I wish I had your self-confidence."

I blink at her. *My* self-confidence? Until I found her frightened and alone here, I'd always thought *Sanni* was the confident one. But now the other conspirators have gone, she looks confused and a bit lost. "I can't afford doubts," I admit. "Because if I start doubting, I'll probably fall apart."

She produces a radiant smile, like first light over a test range. "Don't do that, Robin. I'm counting on you. You're all the army I need."

"Okay," I say. And then we go our separate ways.

I walk home, my mesh-lined bag slung over one shoulder. Today is not a day for a taxi ride, especially now that there's some risk of running into Ike. Everything seems particularly vivid for some reason, the grass greener and the sky bluer, and the scent of the flower beds outside the municipal buildings overwhelmingly sweet and strange. My skin feels as if I've picked up a massive electrostatic charge, hair follicles standing erect. I am *alive*, I realize. By this time tomorrow I might be dead, dead and gone forever because if we fail, the YFH cabal will still have the T-gate, and their coconspirators won't hesitate to delete whatever copies of us they have on file. I might be part of history, dry as dust, an object of study if there ever is another generation of historians.

And if *do* somehow manage to survive, I'll be a prisoner here for the next three unenhanced lifetimes.

I have mixed emotions. When I went into combat before—what I remember of it—I didn't worry about dying. But I wasn't human, then. I was a regiment of tanks. The only way I could die would be if our side lost the entire war.

But I've got Sam, now. The thought of Sam's being in danger makes me cringe. The thought of both of us being at the mercy of the YFH cabal makes me a different kind of uneasy. *Bend the neck, surrender, and it will be fine*: That's the echo of *her* personal choice coming back to haunt me. I rejected her, didn't I? But she's part of me. Indivisible, inescapable. I can never escape from the knowledge that I surrendered—

Sanni has surrendered, I realize. Not to Yourdon and Fiore, but to the end of the war. She doesn't want to fight anymore; she wants to settle down and raise a family and be a small-town librarian. Janis is the real Sanni now, as real as she gets. The glasshouse may have been subverted and perverted by the plotters, but it's still working its psychological alchemy on us. Maybe that's what Sanni was talking about. We're none of us who or what we used to be, although our history remains indelible. I try to imagine what I must have looked like to the civilians aboard the habs we conquered through coup de main, and I find a blind spot. I know I must have terrified them, but inside the armor and behind the guns I was just me, wasn't I? *But how were they to know?* No matter. It's over, now. I've got to live with it, just the way we had to do it. It seemed necessary at the time: If you didn't want your memories to be censored by feral software, or worse, by unscrupulous opportunists who'd trojaned the worm, you had to fight. And once you take the decision to fight, you have to live with the consequences. That's the difference between us and Yourdon, Fiore, and Hanta. We're willing to harbor doubts, to let go; but they're still fighting to bring the war back to their enemies. To us.

These aren't good thoughts to be thinking. They're downright morbid, and I can live without them—but they won't leave me alone, so as I walk I try to fight back by swinging my bag and whistling a jolly tune. And I try to look at myself from the outside as I go. Here's a jolly librarian, outwardly a young woman in a summer dress, shoulder bag in hand, whistling as she walks home from a day at work. Invert the picture, though, and you see a dream-haunted ex-soldier, clutching a kitbag containing a machine pistol, slinking back to her billet for a final time before the—

Look, just stop, why don't you?

That's better.

When I get home, I stash the bag in the kitchen. The TV is going in the living room, so I shed my shoes and pad through.

"Sam."

He's on the sofa, curled up opposite the flickering screen as usual. He's holding a metal canister of beer. He glances at me as I come in.

"Sam." I join him on the sofa. After a moment I realize that he's not really watching the TV. Instead, his eyes are on the patio outside the glass doors at the end of the room. He breathes slowly, evenly, his chest rising and falling steadily. "Sam."

His eyes flicker toward me, and a moment later the corners of his mouth edge upward. "Been working late?"

"I walked." I pull my feet up. The soft cushions of the sofa swallow them. I lean sideways against him, letting my head fall against his shoulder. "I wanted to feel . . ."

"Connected."

"Yes, that's it, exactly." I can feel his pulse, and his breathing is profound, a stirring in the roots of my world. "I missed you."

"I missed you, too." A hand touches my cheek, moves up to brush hair back from my forehead.

At moments like this I hate being an unreconstructed human—an island of thinking jelly trapped in a bony carapace, endless milliseconds away from its lovers, forced to squeeze every meaning through a low-bandwidth speech channel. All men *are* islands, surrounded by the bottomless oceans of unthinking night. If I were half of who I used to be, and had my resources to hand—and if Sam, if Kay, wanted to—we could multiplex, and know each other a thousand times as deeply as this awkward serial humanity permits. There's a poignancy to knowing what we've lost, what we might have had together, which only makes me want him more strongly. I move uneasily and clutch at his waist. "What took you so long?"

"I'm running away." He finally turns his head to look at me side-long. "From myself."

"Me too," Throwing caution to the wind: "Is that part of your problem? With being . . . this?"

"It's too close." He swallows. "To what they wanted me to be."

I don't ask who "they" were. "Do you want to escape? To leave the polity?"

He's silent for a long while. "I don't think so," he says eventually. "Because I'd have to go back to being what I want not to be, if that makes sense to you. Kay was a disguise, Reeve, a mask. A hollow woman. Not a real person."

I snuggle closer to him. "I know you wanted to grow into her."

"Do you?" He raises an eyebrow.

"Look, why do you think *I'm* here?"

"Point." He looks momentarily rueful. "Do *you* want to leave?"

We're not really talking about staying or leaving, this is understood, but what he really means by that— "I thought I did," I admit, toying with the buttons on the front of his shirt. "Then Dr. Hanta sorted me out, and I realized that what I *really* wanted was somewhere to heal, some-where to be me. Community. Peace." I get my hand inside his shirt, and his breath acquires a little hoarse edge that makes me squeeze my thighs together. "Love." I pause. "Not necessarily her way, mind you." His hand is stroking my hair. His other hand— "Do that some more."

"I'm afraid, Reeve."

"That makes two of us."

Later: "I want what you described."

I gasp. "Makes two. Of us. Oh."

"Love."

And we continue our conversation without words, using a language that no abhuman watcher AI can interpret—a language of touch and caress, as old as the human species. What we tell each other is simple. *Don't be afraid, I love you.* We say it urgently and emphatically, bodies shouting our mute encouragement. And in the dark of the night, when we reach for each other, I dare myself to admit that it might work out all right in the end.

We aren't bound to fail.

Are we?

BREAKFAST is an affair of quiet desperation. Over the coffee and toast I clear my throat and begin a carefully planned speech. "I need to go to the library before Church, Sam, I forgot my gloves."

"Really?" He looks up, worry lines crisscrossing his forehead.

I nod vigorously. "I can't go to Church without them, it wouldn't be decent." *Decent* is one of those keywords the watchers monitor. Gloves aren't actually a dress code infraction, but they're a good excuse.

"Okay, I suppose I'll have to come with you," he says, with all the enthusiasm of a condemned man facing the airlock. "We need to leave soon, don't we?"

"Yes, I'd better get my bag," I say.

"I have a new waistcoat to wear."

I raise an eyebrow. His clothing sense is even more artificial than my own. "It's upstairs," he explains. For a moment I think he's going to say something more, something compromising, but he manages to bottle it up in time. My stomach squirms queasily. "Take care, darling."

"Nothing can possibly go wrong," he says with studied irony. He rises and heads for the staircase to our bedroom. (*Our* bedroom. No more lonely nights.) My heart seems to catch an extra beat. Then it's time to clear up the detritus, put the plates in the dishwasher, and get my shoes on.

When Sam comes downstairs, he's dressed for Church—with a many-pocketed vest under his suit jacket, and, in his hand, the briefcase we packed yesterday. "Let's, uh, go," he says, and casts me a wan grin.

"Yup," I say, then check the clock and pick up my extra-large hand-bag. "Let's roll."

We arrive at the library around ten o'clock, and I let us in. The door to the cellar is already open. I reach into my bag as I go down the steps, conscious that if someone's blown the operation, then the bad guys could be waiting for me. But when I get to the bottom I find Janis.

"Hi, Janis," I say slightly nervously.

"Hi yourself." She lowers her gun. "Just checking."

"Indeed. Sam? Come on down." I turn back to Janis. "Still waiting for Greg, Martin, and Liz."

"Right." Janis gestures at a pile of grayish plastic bricks sitting on one of the chairs. "Sam? I think it'll work better if you carry these."

"Sure." Sam ambles over and picks up a brick. Squeezes it experimentally, then sniffs it. "Hmm, smells like success. Detonators?"

"On the sofa." I spot the stack of spare magazines and take a couple, then check they're loaded properly. "Where are the cogsets?" I ask.

"Coming." Janis waves at the A-gate. "We need to synchronize our watches, too."

"Okay." This isn't going to work too well without headsets and cognitive radio transceivers, but they're last on our list of items to assemble because they're too obvious. They're easier to sabotage than metal plumbing and chemical explosives, and a lot likelier to tripwire the alarms in the A-gate than a collection of antiques. If the radios don't work, our fallback is crude—mechanical wristwatches and a prearranged time to start shooting.

Sam stuffs bricks of Composition C into his vest pockets, squeezing them to fit. The vest bulges around his waist, as if he's suddenly put on weight, and when he pulls his jacket on it hangs open. What he's doing reminds me of something I once knew, something alarming, but I can't quite remember what. So I shake my head and go upstairs to wait behind the front desk.

A few minutes later Martin and Liz arrive together. I send them down to the basement. I'm getting worried when Greg appears. We're running short of time. It's 10:42 and the meeting is due to start in just a kilosec or so. "What kept you?" I ask.

"I feel rough," he admits. I think he's been drinking. "Couldn't sleep properly. Let's get this over with, huh?"

"Yeah." I point him at the cellar. "Gang's down there."

T minus ten minutes. The door opens, and Janis comes out. "Okay, I'm off to start the show in the auditorium," she tells me. A fey smile. "Good luck."

"You too." She leans forward, and I hug her briefly, then she's off, walking down the library path toward City Hall.

"Where's Sam?" I ask.

"Oh, he had something extra to do down there," Liz says, a trifle sniffily. "Last-minute nerves." A moment later he comes up the stairs. "Come on, Sam, want to miss the show?"

I open my mouth. "Time to move!"

Fragments of memory converge on a point in time:

Five of us, three males and two females, walking along the front of Main Street toward City Hall. All in our Church outfits, with subtle changes—Sam's vest, my shoes, Martin's bag. Discreet earbuds adding their hum to our left ears, flesh-toned pickups parallel to our jawlines. Businesslike.

"Merge with the crowd, then when they head for the auditorium doors, break left under the door labeled FIRE EXIT. Meet me on the other side."

Purpose. Tension. Beating heart, nervousness. A faint aroma of mineral oil on my fingertips. The usual heightened awareness.

Cohorts and parishes of regular citizens—inmates—are gathering on the front steps and in the open reception hall of the biggest building on Main Street. Some I recognize; most are anonymous.

Jen looms out of the crowd, smiling, converging on me. My guts freeze. "Reeve! Isn't it wonderful?"

"Yes, it is," I say, slightly too coldly because she stares at me, and her eyes narrow.

"Well, excuse *me*," she says, and turns on her heel as if to walk away, then pauses. "I'd have thought you'd be celebrating."

"I am." I raise an eyebrow at her. "Are you?"

"Hah!" And with a contemptuous smirk, she wheels away and latches on to Chris's arm.

A cold sweat prickles up and down my spine—sheer relief, mostly—

and I head toward the FIRE EXIT sign, which is conveniently close to the rest rooms. I pause for a second to glance around and check my watch (T minus three minutes) then lean on the emergency bar. The door scrapes open, and I step through into a concrete-lined stairwell.

Click. I glance round. Liz lowers her gun. *I'm too slow today*, I think hopelessly. I mute my mike. "Two minutes," I say, backing into the corner opposite her niche. She nods. I reach into my bag, pull out my gun, stuff the spare magazines into my pockets, and drop the bag. Click. That's me.

One minute. Sam and Greg and Martin, the latter looking slightly harried. I key my mike. "Follow me."

A couple of weeks ago, wearing Fiore's stolen flesh, I explored this complex—extremely cautiously, taking pains to be certain that Yourdon was occupied elsewhere at the time. The first floor contains the lobby and a big auditorium, plus a couple of things described on the building map as "courtrooms." The second floor, which we pass without stopping, is wall-to-wall office space. The third floor . . . well, I didn't spend much time there.

We reach the door and pause. "Zero," I say, tracking the sweep of my watch hand.

A second later there's a chime in my headset. *"Go!"* says Janis. "Now."

Greg opens the door fast, and Martin and Liz duck through, then pronounce the bare-floored corridor clear. I lead us along it, then there's another door, and Greg forces the exit bar from our side. *Carpet*. A short, narrow passage. *Yourdon must have left by now, surely?* I rush forward and find myself in a boringly mundane living room, furnished in dark age fashion except for the smooth white bulge of an A-gate in one corner. "Here," I say. "Spread out."

We're not experts at house searches. Doubtless if there was armed resistance waiting for us, we'd be easy prey. But the house is empty. Three bedrooms, a living room, an office—there's a desk and an ancient computer terminal, and books—and a kitchen and bathroom and another room full of boxes. It's *empty*. Empty of personality as well as anachronisms like a longjump gate.

"What now?" asks Sam.

"We check out front." I walk up to the front door of the apartment, then Greg squeezes past me and unlocks it. He pulls it open and steps out, then I follow to see where we are, and the ground leaps up and whacks me across the knees with a concussive jolt too deep to call a noise.

"*Panic one,*" Janis says in my ear, a prearranged code for Team Green. *That was a bomb*, I think dizzily.

There's a click behind me, then a scream of pain. I whip round and that saves my life because the short burst of gunfire hammers past me and catches Liz instead, bullets slapping into her body as she spins round. I keep turning and drop to one knee, then fire a continuous burst that empties the magazine and nearly sprains my wrists.

"* * *," says Janis, in my ringing ears.

"Repeat." I'm staring at Greg. What used to be Greg. Someone behind me is making horrible sounds. I think it's Liz. "We have a code red, two down."

"I said, Panic two," says Janis. "They've got a Vorpal—"

Pink noise fills my ears, and her voice breaks up: cognitive radios meet heuristic jamming. "Come on!" I yell at Sam, who's bending over Liz. "Follow me!"

We're on a landing at the top of the stairs. Yourdon's apartment covers one side of the building, but on the other side—there's a door. I dash toward it, reloading on the go. *Greg tried to kill me*, I realize. *Which means he warned them. So . . .*

I pause at one side of the door and wave Sam to the other. Then I brace myself and unload the entire clip through it at waist height.

While my ears are ringing, and I'm fumbling the next magazine into place, Sam kicks the door in and quickly shoots the police zombie slumped against the side of the corridor in the head. (That one was still moving, hand creeping toward the shotgun lying in the floor; the two bodies behind it aren't even twitching.) Seeing how efficiently Sam steps in gives me a momentary chill of recognition. *No hesitation.* Behind us, Liz is still moaning, and Martin won't be good for anything. "What is this place?" I ask aloud.

"More offices." Sam kicks a door open and duck-walks through it.

"Modern offices." I follow him. The next door is more substantial, opening onto a glass-fronted balcony above a room with open floor space, an office-sized assembler at one side, and a row of glassy doors . . . "Is that what I think it is?"

Bingo. "Gates," I say. "A switch hub. How do we get down—"

"Hello, Reeve," says my earpiece, in a voice that sets my teeth on edge. *"This isn't going to work, you know."*

Where did Fiore get a headset from? Greg? Or have they captured one of Team Green?

Sam looks as if someone's poleaxed him. His jaw is literally gaping. Too late I realize he's on the same chatline.

"You've lost, Reeve," Fiore adds conversationally. I can hear noises in the background. "We know about your plot. There are guards outside the switch chamber, and if you get past them and make it to the longjump pod, you'll die—there's an active laser fence in there. I'm most disappointed in you, but we can still work something out if you put down your popguns and surrender."

I touch my index finger to my lips and wait until Sam nods at me, to show he's got the message. Then I walk toward the door onto the staircase leading down into the switch chamber and its bank of short-jump gates.

I don't want Sam to see how sick I feel.

"You don't know shit, Fiore," I say lightly.

"Yes I do." He sounds smug. "Greg's unfortunate death makes further concealment irrelevant. Bluntly, you've failed. You can't—"

I rip my earbud out and throw it away, frantically miming at Sam to do likewise. He pulls it out of his ear and stares at it. As he's about to toss it there's a dual bang. He doubles over as a thin reddish mist sprays from his left finger and thumb, retching with pain.

"Sam!" I yell at him. He cradles his damaged hand, panting. "Sam! We've only got a few seconds! Fiore can't stop us, or he'd already be up here! Sanni's got him pinned down! We've got to blow the longjump pod before he gets away! Give me your jacket!"

"No choice—" He takes a shuddering breath and shakes his head. "Reeve."

I place my gun at my feet and take him by the shoulders. "What is it, love?"

A moment of awful tenderness, as I see the pain in his eyes. "I'm sorry," he says brokenly. "I couldn't be what you wanted."

"What—"

And his good fist, still wrapped around the butt of his gun, whacks me across the back of my head, propelling me straight into a pit of darkness from which I only emerge when it's far too late.

Epilogue

TO cut a long story short, we won.

IT feels very different when you watch a replay of a body tumbling off a cliff, in free fall toward the harsh ground so far below, and it's not your body, and there are no second chances.

In the years since Sanni and I—and the rest of our ragtag resistance network—kicked the door shut and overturned Yourdon's pocket dictatorship, I've watched the video take of Sam's death many times. How he sapped me, then gently laid me out on the floor, grunting with effort as he rolled me into the recovery position so I wouldn't choke on my own vomit. How he straightened up painfully afterward and put his gun down. How he walked along the row of shortjump doors, looking for the one opening on the short metal corridor with the handrail and the ring of support nodes halfway along it. How he paused, and went back to move me so that I wasn't lined up with it. And then how he stepped through.

What does it take to step into a corridor, knowing that your enemy said there's a laser fence halfway along it? And as if that isn't enough, to do so wearing a waistcoat with ten kilos of plastic explosives weighing down its pockets?

Sam gets halfway along the corridor. There's a momentary flash, then the door bulges and turns black as the T-gate does a scram shutdown and ejects its wormhole endpoint through the side of the pod. It's not very dramatic.

And that's how we reach the foot of the cliff.

While I was unconscious, Janis and her team did what was expected of them. I think that she was expecting betrayal all along, because she had a few surprises of her own. Yourdon, at the front of the hall, chopped her in half with his Vorpal blade: I can only imagine his shock when another Janis stepped out from behind the fire escape and blew a hole through his chest. *I should have realized she was playing a tricky game*—her excuse about taking all night to run off ten kilos of high explosives was far too convenient—but in hindsight, she didn't trust anyone by that point. Even me.

While I was unconscious, Fiore—desperate, trapped in the police station down the road by a squad of murderous Sannis—patched through his netlink and got onto our command circuit which was, as expected, compromised by design. But Sanni was one jump ahead of him all the way. Greg had told him what was going on that morning. Fiore thought that a laser fence and extra security guards would suffice. These psywar types, they don't think like a tank, or a fighting cat. Two of me—despite being seriously pissed at Sanni for making them live in the library attic and stay away from Sam—took him out with a rocket-propelled grenade, while three other squads fanned out and combed the parish churches for cowering revenants. As Janis later explained, "When the only soldier you can rely on is Reeve, you make the most of her." But I won't bear a grudge, even though two of me died.

Because when the dust stopped raining down on the cowering cohorts in the auditorium, while our other instances raced through the administration block and the hospital, frantically hunting down assemblers and deleting their pattern buffers before another Yourdon or Fiore could ooze out of them, it was Janis who stepped up to the lectern and fired a shot into the ceiling and called for silence.

"Friends," she said, a faint tremor in her voice. "*Friends.* The experiment is over. The prison is closed.

"Welcome back to the real world."

THAT all happened years ago. The river of history waits for nobody. We live our lives in the wake of vast events, accommodating ourselves to their shapes. Even those of us who contributed to the events in question.

Maybe the oddest thing is how little has changed since we overthrew the scorefile dictatorship. We still have regular town meetings. We still live in small family groups, as orthohumans. Many of us even stayed with the spousal units we were assigned by Fiore or Yourdon. We dress like it's still the dark ages, and we hold jobs just like before, and we even have babies the primitive way. Sometimes.

But . . .

We *vote* in the town meetings. There are no scorefile metrics with hidden point tables that some smug researcher can tweak in order to make the parishioners jump. We don't dance like puppets for anyone, even our elected mayor. We may live in families as orthohumans, but we've got an assembler in every home. Mostly we don't *want* to be neo-morphs. Many of us spent too much time as living weapons during the war. We *do* have—and enthusiastically use—modern medical technology, with A-gates everywhere. The costumery and lifestyle upholstery is harder to explain, but I put it down to social inertia. I saw a blue her-maphrodite centaur in a chain-mail hauberk and no pants in the shopping mall the other day, and guess what? Nobody raised an eyebrow. We're a tolerant town these days. We have to be: There's nowhere else to go until we arrive wherever the *Harvest Lore* is carrying us.

As for me, I don't have to fight anymore. I've got the best of my sur-rendered self's wishes, without any of the drawbacks. And I've been so lucky that thinking about it makes me want to cry.

I have a daughter. Her name's Andy—short for Andromeda. She swears she wants to be a boy when she grows up; she isn't going to hit puberty for another six years, and she may change her mind when her body starts changing. The important thing is we live in a society where she can be whatever she wants. She looks like a random phenotypic cross between Reeve and Sam, and sometimes when I see her in the right light, just catching her profile, my breath catches in my throat as I see him diving off that cliff. Did he know I was already pregnant when he carefully made sure I was out of harm's way, then jumped? It shouldn't be possible, but sometimes I wonder if he suspected.

Andromeda was delivered—surprise—in the hospital, by the nice Dr. Hanta. Who no longer needs a gun pointing at her head all day long, since Sanni gave her a choice between reprogramming herself to let her patients define their own best interests or joining Yourdon and Fiore. After going through with the birth, I went back to being Robin, or as close to the original Robin as our medical 'ware could come up with. Natural childbirth is an experience all fathers should go through at least once in their lives (as adults, I mean), but I needed to be Robin again: the only version of me that doesn't come with innocent blood on his hands.

It's late, now, and Andy is sleeping upstairs. I've been writing this account down longhand on paper, to help fix these events in my memory, like the letter someone wrote to me so long ago that I can barely remember what it was like to be him. Even without memory surgery, we are fragile beings, lights in the darkness that leave a trail fading out behind us as we forget who we have been. I don't actually want to remember much about what I was, before the war. I'm comfortable here, and I expect to live here for a long time to come, longer than my entire troubled life to this point. If all I remember of the first half of my life is a thick pile of paper and Sam's conflicted love for me, that will be enough. But there's a difference between not remembering and deliberately forgetting. Hence the stack of paper.

One last thought: My wife is dozing on the sofa across the room. I have a question for her, which I'll wake her up for. "What do you think Sam was thinking when he walked down that tunnel?"

Oh. *That's* useful. She yawns, and says, "I wouldn't know. I wasn't there."

"But if you had to guess?"

"I'd say he was hoping for a second chance."

"Is that all?"

She stands up. "Sometimes the truth is boring, Robin. Go on, put that in your memoir."

"Okay. Any other comments before I finish up here? I'm going to bed in a minute."

"Let me think . . ." Kay shrugs, an incredibly fluid gesture that involves four shoulder joints. "No. Don't be long." She smiles lazily and heads for the staircase, swinging her hips in a way that suggests she's got something other than sleep in mind. She's been a lot happier since she stopped being Sam, which she did very shortly after the panicky last-minute backup in the library basement. And so, you may be assured, am I.

Good night.